A Hint
of Mischief

Daryl Wood Gerber

Kensington Publishing Corp.
www.kensingtonbooks.com

Praise for the Fairy Garden Mystery series

"Enchanting series launch from Agatha Award winner Gerber. . . . Cozy fans will wish upon a star for more." —**Publishers Weekly**

"Likable characters . . . and an entertaining but not-too-intrusive fairy connection make this a winner. . . . Fans of Laura Childs's work will enjoy Gerber's new series." —**Booklist**

"Full of fun, whimsy, and a baffling whodunit. . . . After finishing the book fans might want to try their hand at making their own fairy garden, or test the delectable recipes in the back of the book." —**Mystery Scene magazine**

"A charming murder mystery. . . . The addition of real fairies adds a delightful twist. . . . Courtney is an engaging heroine backed by a fun, diverse cast." —**Criminal Element**

"*A Sprinkling of Murder* is an enchanting mystery that asks you to believe. Believe, not only in fairies, but in yourself and the intrinsic goodness of people." —**Cozy Up with Kathy**

"Lively characters and plenty of action keep the pages turning. Paranormal cozy fans will have a ball." —**Publishers Weekly**

"*A Glimmer of a Clue* is an enchanting and delightful combination of the whimsical and the cozy mystery genre itself." —**Fresh Fiction**

"I really enjoy this author's writing voice and the way she crafts a plot, and *A Glimmer of a Clue* is no exception."
—**Reading Is My SuperPower**

"Reading *A Glimmer of a Clue* in one sitting wasn't my plan for the day. However, a couple of chapters in, I knew I wouldn't put it down until the last page. It was a well-plotted mystery, within a magical tale." —**Lisa Ks Book Reviews**

"This book is exactly what I look for in a cozy mystery. Interesting and likable sleuths, plenty of suspects, a little humor to keep it from being too heavy, but still a great mystery."
—**The Book's the Thing**

Kensington books by Daryl Wood Gerber

The Fairy Garden Mystery series

A Sprinkling of Murder

A Glimmer of a Clue

A Hint of Mischief

To my PlotHatchers, with all my heart.
You have been instrumental in keeping me on track!

Acknowledgments

When we love, we always strive to become better than we are.
When we strive to become better than we are, everything
around us becomes better, too.
—Paulo Coelho

I have been truly blessed to have the support and input of so many as I pursue my creative journey.

Thank you to my family and friends for all your encouragement. Thank you to my talented author friends Krista Davis and Hannah Dennison for your words of wisdom. Thank you to my PlotHatcher pals: Janet (Ginger Bolton), Kaye George, Marilyn Levinson (Allison Brook), Peg Cochran (Margaret Loudon), Janet Koch (Laura Alden), and Krista Davis. You are a wonderful pool of talent and a terrific wealth of ideas, jokes, stories, and fun! I adore you. Thanks to my Delicious Mystery author pals Roberta Isleib (Lucy Burdette), Krista Davis, and Amanda Flower. I treasure your creative enthusiasm via social media.

Thank you to Facebook fan-based groups, Delicious Mysteries, Cozy Mystery Review Crew, Save Our Cozies, and so many more. I love how willing you are to read ARCs, post reviews, and help me as well as numerous other authors promote whenever possible. We need fans like you. Thank you to all the bloggers like Dru Ann Love and Lori Caswell, who enjoy reviewing cozies and sharing these titles with your readers.

Thanks to those who have helped make this third book in the Fairy Garden Mystery series come to fruition: my publisher, Kensington; my editor, Wendy McCurdy, as well as Elizabeth Trout; production editor Carly Sommerstein; and cover artist Elsa Kerls. Thank you to my biggest supporter, Kimberley Greene. Thanks to Madeira James for maintaining constant quality on my website. Thanks to my virtual assistant Christina Higgins for your creative ideas. Honestly, without all of you, I don't know what I would do. You keep me grounded.

Last but not least, thank you, librarians, teachers, bookstore owners, readers, family, and lifelong friends, for sharing the delicious world of a fairy garden designer in Carmel-by-the-Sea with your friends. I hope you enjoy the magical world I've created.

CAST OF CHARACTERS
(listed alphabetically by first name)

Humans

Arista Kenton, neighbor
Austin Pinter, historical fiction author
Brady Cash, owner of Hideaway Café
Christopher Cox, ex-fiancé of Courtney
Cliff Gill, owner of Carmel Collectibles, uncle to Glinda
Courtney Kelly, owner of Open Your Imagination
Dylan Summers, detective, Carmel Police Department
Eudora Cash, romance author and Brady's mother
Farrah Lawson, famous actress
Georgie Gill, niece of Glinda, tennis phenom
Glinda Gill, owner of Glitz Jewelers
Hattie Hopewell, Happy Diggers garden club chair
Hedda Hopewell, loan officer
Holly Hopewell, Courtney's landlord and neighbor
Jeremy Batcheller, owner of Batcheller Galleries
Joss Timberlake, assistant at Open Your Imagination
Kipling "Kip" Kelly, Courtney's father, landscaper
Leanne Cox, wife of Christopher
Lissa Reade, aka "Miss Reade," librarian
Meaghan Brownie, half owner of Flair Gallery
Misty Dawn, trust fund baby
Nova Pasha, jewelry designer
Odine Oates, owner of Fantasy Awaits
Phoebe and Perri, sorority sisters
Rafaela, housekeeper for Misty
Redcliff Reddick, police officer
Renee Rodriguez, owner of Seize the Clay
Tish Waterman, owner of A Peaceful Solution Spa

Twyla Waterman, daughter of Tish, works at spa
Violet Vickers, wealthy dowager
Wanda Brownie, art representative, Meaghan's mother
Yolanda Acebo, sister of Yvanna, part-time employee
Yvanna Acebo, employee at Sweet Treats, weekend baker for teas
Ziggy Foxx, half owner of Flair Gallery, Meaghan's partner
Zinnia Walker, a Happy Diggers member

Fairies and Pets

Callie, aka Calliope, intuitive fairy in Meaghan's garden
Cedric Winterbottom, nurturer fairy to Misty
Fiona, righteous fairy to Courtney
Merryweather Rose of Song, guardian fairy and library fairy
Phantom, Holly Hopewell's black cat
Pixie, Courtney's Ragdoll cat
Zephyr, nurturer fairy to Tish

Chapter 1

'Tis merry, 'tis merry in Fairy-land,
When fairy birds are singing,
When the court doth ride by their monarch's side,
With bit and bridle ringing.
—Walter Scott, "Alice Brand"

"Thief!" a woman cried outside of Open Your Imagination, my fairy garden and tea shop. I recognized the voice. Yvanna Acebo.

I hurried from the covered patio through our main show-room, grabbed an umbrella from the stand by the Dutch door, and headed outside, quickly opening the umbrella so it protected me from the rain. "Yvanna, what's going on?"

Yvanna, a baker at Sweet Treats, a neighboring shop in the courtyard, was dressed in her pink uniform and standing at the top of the stairs that led through the courtyard, hands on hips—no umbrella. She was getting drenched.

"Yvanna!" I shouted again. "Were you robbed? Are you okay?"

She pivoted. Rain streamed down her pretty face. She swiped a hair off her cheek that had come loose from her scrunchie. "I'm fine," she said with a sigh. "A customer set her bag down on one of the tables so she could fish in her purse for loose change. Before we knew it, someone in a brown hoodie slipped in, grabbed the bag, and darted out."

"Man? Woman? Teen?"

"I'm not sure." Her chest heaved. "That's the second theft in this area in the past twenty-four hours, Courtney."

"Second?" I gasped. Carmel-by-the-Sea was not known as a high-crime town. Well, that wasn't entirely true. We had suffered two murders in the past year. Flukes, the police had dubbed them. "Where did the other theft occur?"

"There." She pointed to the Village Shops, the courtyard across the street from ours. Carmel-by-the-Sea was known for its unique courtyards. "At Say Cheese."

"The thief must be hungry," I said. Say Cheese had a vast array of cheeses, crackers, and condiments. "Were you scared?"

"No. I'm miffed." A striking Latina, Yvanna was one of the most resilient women I knew. She rarely took a day off because she had a family of six to feed—two cousins, her grandparents, her sister, and herself.

"Call the police," I suggested.

"You can bet on it."

We didn't have CCTV in Cypress and Ivy's courtyard yet. Maybe I should mention it to our landlord. I returned to Open Your Imagination, stopped outside to flick the water off the umbrella, and then moved inside, slotted the umbrella into the stand, and weaved through the shop's display tables while saying hello to the handful of customers. Before heading to the patio, I signaled my stalwart assistant Joss Timberlake that all was under control.

"Do not argue with me!" Misty Dawn exclaimed. "Do you hear me? I want tea. Not coffee. Tea!" Misty, a customer, was standing by the verdigris baker's racks on the patio, wiggling two female fairy figurines. When she spotted me, she uttered a full-throated laugh. "You're back, Courtney. Is everything okay outside? Did I hear the word 'thief'?"

"You did."

"Hopefully nothing too dear was stolen."

In addition to my business, the courtyard boasted a high-end jewelry store, a collectibles shop, an art gallery, and a pet-grooming enterprise.

"Bakery goods," I said.

"And no one got hurt?"

"No one."

"Phew." Misty gazed at the figurines she was holding. "I swear, I can't get over how young I feel whenever I visit your shop. It takes me back to my childhood, when I used to play with dolls. I'd make up stories and put on plays. At one point, maybe seventh grade, I thought I was so clever and gifted with dialogue that I'd become a playwright, but that didn't come to pass."

Misty, a trust fund baby who had never worked a day in her life, even though she had graduated Phi Beta Kappa and had whizzed through business school, had blazed into the shop twenty minutes ago, hoping to hire me to throw a fairy garden birthday party for her sorority sister. In the less than two years that the shop had been open, I'd only thrown three such parties, each for children.

"Let's get serious." Misty returned the figurines to the verdigris baker's rack, strode across the covered slate patio to the wrought-iron table closest to the gnome-adorned fountain, and patted the tabletop. "Sit with me. Let's chat. I have lists upon lists of ideas." She opened her Prada tote and removed a floral notepad and pen.

Fiona, a fairy-in-training who, when not staying at my house, resided in the ficus trees fitted with twinkling lights that surrounded the patio, flew to my shoulder and whispered in my ear. "She sure is bossy."

I bit back a smile and said, "The customer's always right."

"How true," Misty said, oblivious to Fiona's presence.

To be fair, Misty was a force. She was tall and buxom with dark auburn hair, sturdy shoulders, a broad face, and bold features; I doubted she had ever been a wallflower. Every time I'd seen her at this or that event, always dressed in stunning jewel tones as she was now, her red silk blouse looking tailor-made, I'd been drawn to her like a moth to a flame.

Pixie, my adorable Ragdoll cat, abandoned the mother and child customers she'd been following for the past three minutes and leaped into Misty's lap. Misty instantly started stroking the cat's luscious fur. Pixie didn't hold back with her contented purring.

"Sweet kitty," Misty cooed.

"Pixie doesn't like just anyone," I said.

"Of course not. She knows a cat lover when she sees one, don't you, Pixie?" Misty tipped up the cat's chin. "Yes, you do. You know you do. I have three handsome friends for you to play with, Pixie. A calico, a tuxedo, and a domestic short-hair that I rescued. I love them all." She returned her gaze to me. "Now, Courtney, where were we?"

"You want to throw a party."

"For my good friend Odine." She stressed the O in her friend's name. I'd met Odine Oates a few times and was pretty certain she pronounced her name with the accent on the second syllable. "She's a descendant of one of the first families of Texas. She moved here when she was fourteen, and we became fast friends."

"Nice."

"And she's the first of us to turn forty," Misty continued. "I'm the last." That fact seemed to tickle her. "She has always loved fairies. She displays fairy art everywhere in Fantasy Awaits." Odine owned a jewelry and exotica art shop. "Have you visited it in the Doud Arcade?"

"I have."

Much of the shop's jewelry featured fairies, sorcerers, or mythical creatures. The art included distinctive pieces that she'd found around the world, including kimonos, vases, swords, statues, and so much more. For her wall décor, she had commissioned a local artist to re-create well-known fantasy artwork, including dragons and gnomes and the famous Cicely Mary Barker fairies, all depicted on four-by-six-foot canvases.

"I remember that place," Fiona whispered. "You bought that necklace for Joss."

A dragon pendant with an emerald eye. Joss adored dragon paraphernalia.

"It was scary there," Fiona added.

To a fairy Fiona's size, I imagined seeing giant-sized fairies, gnomes, and dragons would be frightening. She wasn't more than a few inches tall with two sets of beautiful green adult wings, one set of smaller junior wings, and shimmering blue hair. Her silver tutu and silver shoes sparkled in any light. By now, she should have grown three full sets of adult wings and lost her junior wings, but she'd messed up in fairy school, so the queen fairy had booted her from the fairy realm and subjected her to probation.

"I want to have the party in my backyard," Misty went on.

At one time Misty's family had owned a grand Spanish estate on the iconic 17-Mile Drive, the road popular because it led to Pebble Beach golf course, beaches, viewpoints, and more, but she had downsized recently, wishing to live in Carmel proper so she could walk to restaurants and art galleries at a moment's notice. She had purchased a two-story gray-and-white home on 4th Avenue with the charming name of Gardener's Delight—many homes in Carmel had names—and had hired my father's landscaping company to revamp both the front and rear yards. Her gardens were the envy of all her neighbors.

"Here we go." Joss placed a tray set with two Lenox Butterfly Meadow–pattern teacups, a plate of lemon bars, and the fixings for chamomile tea on the table. "May I pour?"

"Please," I said.

"Boss, we have a ton of things to do," she said, filling Misty's cup first. "A shipment is coming in and a busload of tourists is about to disembark. They'll be swarming the courtyard in less than an hour."

"She won't be long," Misty said on my behalf. "I'm very organized. This will only take a few minutes." She held up her notepad.

Joss pursed her lips, trying not to smile, which made her look even more elfin than normal.

"I like your shirt, by the way," Misty said to Joss.

"This old thing?" Joss plucked at the buttons of the parrot-themed shirt she'd bought in Tijuana. "It's fun. I like color."

"So do I." Misty opened her notepad, silently dismissing Joss.

Over fifty and seasoned in the picking-up-clues department, Joss winked at me and returned to the main showroom. Through the windows, I watched as she moved from display to display, straightening teacup handles, garden knickknacks, and strings of bells—fairies enjoyed the sound of bells.

Misty took a lemon bar, bit into it, set it on her saucer, and started reading the bullet-pointed list she'd created. "I want to have wind chimes everywhere."

Something breakable inside the shop went *clack . . . shatter.* Joss *eek*ed, and then Fiona shrieked, and my stomach lurched. Fairies hated breakage of any kind. Joss waved to me that she was all right and held up a multicolored wind chime. Was the accident a freak moment of timing, or was it fate?

Fiona zipped off to check on Joss. She couldn't help pick up the broken pieces, of course, but she could offer Joss a whisper of encouragement. Joss, like me, could see Fiona.

Misty hadn't seemed to notice the fracas, too intent on her list. "I want the guests to make fairy gardens. You'll instruct them, of course."

In addition to selling fairy gardens and items for fairy gardens, I taught a weekly class and gave private lessons about how to construct them. I experienced a childlike joy whenever I completed a project. So did my customers.

"I want party games and favors," Misty went on, "like you would for a children's fairy party, but more adult."

That would take a bit of thinking on my part. Children relished games like the lily pad relay and a fairy tale obstacle course. What would adults enjoy?

"And I'll want you to paint a mural on the wall facing the backyard."

"Me? Paint?" I snorted. My talent was purely in the gardening department. My mother had been the painter. A painting that she'd titled *Starry Night*, like the van Gogh painting, hung on the bedroom wall in my cottage. My father hadn't been able to part with any of the others.

"Hire someone." Misty flourished the pen. "I want the mural to feature lots of flowers and vines with fairies frolicking throughout. I saw one on the DIY Garden Channel and it was stunning. I'll download some pictures and email them to you."

Fiona circled Misty's head, waving an imaginary wand, I'd thought, until I realized she was mimicking Misty's gestures with the pen. I couldn't very well say *Cut it out,* so I frowned. Fiona stopped and soared to a ficus branch so she could hold her belly while laughing.

Later, I would have to have a chat with my sassy fairy. Because she was classified as a righteous fairy, which meant she needed to bring resolution to embattled souls, she could earn her way into the queen fairy's good graces by helping humans such as myself. But she had to toe the line. She couldn't act like an imp all the time.

Only last year did I learn that there were classifications of fairies. Four, to be exact. Intuitive, guardian, nurturer, and righteous. Up until then, I'd always thought fairies were merely types, like air fairies, water fairies, and woodland fairies—Fiona being the latter. Also, up until then, I'd forgotten about fairies. As a girl, I'd seen one, but I'd lost the ability when my mother passed away. That is, until Fiona came into my life.

"Alrighty then," Misty said, standing. "Come up with a plan."

"Would you mind leaving me your list?"

"I'll text it to you." She took a picture of her list, requested my cell phone number, and sent me a copy of it. "There you go. Oh, and I'd like to have the party Saturday."

"In three days?" I gulped.

"No, silly, next Saturday. Ample time. Eons before you get hit with Valentine's Day traffic."

Ten days! Ha! The last fairy party I'd thrown had taken me a month to prepare. On the other hand, because it had taken a month, the birthday girl's mother had thought she could make numerous changes to the menu, favors, and events. A tighter timeline might make this party, for adults, easier to manage.

"Can do?" Misty asked in shorthand. "There will be twelve of us."

"Can do," I chimed.

As Misty left the store, Fiona followed me to the modest kitchen behind my office. I set the tray fitted with tea goodies on the counter, filled the sink with soapy water, and started by washing the teacups.

"Something feels off to me," Fiona said, perching on the teapot's handle. "That's the right word, isn't it? *Off?*"

"Yes, that's the correct word. What feels off?"

"She's in too much of a hurry."

"Or she's not as organized as she claims," I countered. "I'm sure everything will go as steady as—"

A teacup slipped from my hand and plunged into the water. When I lifted it, I realized it had cracked in two.

"Oh my." Fiona clutched her head with her hands. "This is not good. Not good at all."

"What isn't good?"

"Misty. Her excitement for this party."

Suddenly, my insides felt jittery, probably because I'd recently grasped that I should trust my fairy's instincts. According to Fiona's mentor, Merryweather Rose of Song, the more mature Fiona became, the more her intuitive instincts would kick in. In addition, Merryweather had been teaching Fiona how to cast spells—good spells, not evil ones—making certain that whatever new ability she learned wouldn't go haywire.

"Go on," I urged.

"She's too eager." Fiona fluffed her wings.

"She seemed fine to me."

"What about the way she said her friend's name?"

"I'm not following."

"She said, 'O-dine.'" Fiona stressed the O as Misty had. "But that's not how you say her name. When we were at her shop, Odine told us how to pronounce it," Fiona went on. "She chanted, 'Odine. Odine. Odine.'"

My fairy was right. Odine had repeated her name, sounding much like a witch preparing for an incantation.

Fiona swatted my hair. "I'm telling you. Something's off."

And then lightning lit the sky, thunder rumbled overhead, and Fiona nearly swooned.

Chapter 2

How to tell if a fairy is nearby: a soft bell chimes.
—Anonymous

Inviting Fiona to accompany me, I strode to the office and placed a finger on the edge of the Zen garden positioned at the upper-right corner of the chalked chestnut desk. "Sit here."

Fiona did. She dug into the sand with her toe and drew concentric circles to calm herself.

I picked up the cordless phone and dialed my best friend, Meaghan Brownie. She and I had been friends since our sophomore year in college. "Hey, there," I said. "It's me. I have a side job for you if you're willing."

At one time, Meaghan had hoped to become an art professor at a college, but when she came to Carmel-by-the-Sea, she fell in love with the area and gave up her college plan. Six months later, she opened Flair Gallery, located at the other end of the Cypress and Ivy courtyard, just past Sweet Treats.

Meaghan enjoyed selling other artists' pieces, but she was an artist in her own right. She loved creating big, bold, abstract florals, Hawaiian in tone.

"What kind of side job? I'm kind of busy at the gallery."

"C'mon, Ziggy can take up the slack." Ziggy Foxx, an eccentric gay man in his forties with ice-white hair, was co-owner of the gallery. "And now that he-who-shall-remain-nameless is out of your life, you have more downtime."

"Him," she grumbled. She'd kicked Nameless out two months ago. I was glad she had. A frustrated artist and introvert, he'd always gotten jealous whenever Meaghan wanted to do something social with friends. "Did you know he moved to Arizona?"

"What's in Arizona?"

"Got me."

"Good riddance."

"Uh-huh," she said, but I wasn't certain her heart was in it. "So what's the side job?"

"Painting a fairy garden mural on the rear wall of Misty Dawn's house. She's hired me to put on an adult fairy garden party."

"Misty Dawn? Honestly? She's like one of my best customers. Or she was. Haven't seen her lately. But . . . wow! Misty. Will it be a big to-do?"

"It's a small soiree."

"Even so, how fun. I'm in."

"But you have to paint it fast because the party is in ten days."

Meaghan chuckled. "Yeah, right."

"Truth. Ten days or less. Think you can come up with something? She wants flowers and vines and lots of fairies having fun. She said she'll send pictures she's seen on the DIY channel."

"No need," Meaghan said. "I already have a vision."

"Woot! Thank you! I'll get you access and provide all the paint you need. And a ladder. You'll probably need a ladder." I'd forgotten to ask Misty how big the wall was.

"No worries. I've got all that. This will be fun."

When I ended the call, I joined Joss in the main show-room, and Fiona, who had recovered, coasted out to the patio to play with Pixie.

I quickly filled Joss in about the particulars of Misty's party, and then I gestured toward the trio of customers who were examining the teacups and saucers displayed on the antique white oak hutch. "Do they need our help?"

"Nah. They're fine."

"How about those two by the book carousel?" A short while ago, we'd decided to stock a few books that featured fairies. *Irish Legends for Children* told stories that were a rich part of Irish history. There was even a pronunciation guide to help read unusual Irish names, like Ailill and Mac Fiachr.

"Nope," Joss said. "They've selected some teacups. Their next stop is the patio. Also, add repainting the Dutch door to our to-do list. I think we've kicked it closed too many times to count."

The book carousel was right next to the door.

"On my list." I'd decorated the shop in white with stylish splashes of blue and slate gray for color, the theme inspired by the colors of our Cape Cod–style courtyard. "Speaking of lists, I'm already mentally detailing what we need to do for Misty's party. Buy eight-inch pots as well as order extra figurines and furniture and landscaping items."

"Renee's pottery would be perfect."

Renee Rodriguez owned Seize the Clay, a pottery store located in the Village Shops. A former police officer and fi-ancée of Detective Summers, she had been making pottery for years and had always deemed it a hobby until she'd left law enforcement. Turning forty, she had confided to me a while ago, could cause a person to make all sorts of life-changing decisions.

I dialed Renee and left her a message.

"I've got a few game ideas, boss," Joss said. "All of them outdoors."

"What if it rains?" I thrust a finger toward the ceiling. Rain continued to patter the roof.

"I already checked. The weather report looks good for a week from Saturday."

I hoped she was right. February was the rainiest month in Carmel, and in ten days, anything was possible. I strode through the French doors to the patio, thankful for the protection of the pyramid-shaped, tempered-glass roof. Pixie meowed. I petted her and then made my way to the learning-the-craft area at the far end. In addition to a long table for students, there was a smaller table where I'd demonstrate techniques, pots arranged on and around shelving, myriad miniature plants, and a cabinet that held bags of soil, a lectern, and tools.

Joss followed me. "First off, how about floating wuzzles? We did it for the Sayles's party." She grabbed a towel from the cabinet to wipe down the tables.

I moved to the ferns and pinched off dead leaves. "The Sayles's guests were six years old."

"I know, but it's still a fun game. As the music plays, Misty and her pals will do their best to keep their wuzzles in the air."

"Their balloons," I translated.

Joss tittered. "We make it even more fun by ordering them to spin and clap and yell 'I believe in fairies,' while keeping the balloons afloat."

"They're adults," I reminded her.

"Yep. When the music stops, all the women will grab a balloon and hold it in their hands." She waved the cleaning cloth overhead. "Then you, our illustrious party planner, will call out a color, and whoever is holding that color balloon will win a prize, like a fairy figurine, plant, or pot."

"Let's write these ideas down."

Joss hurried into the shop and returned with a pad and pen.

"We could give them all fairy wings," I went on. "I've seen those at the party store. And we could ask them to do a fairy obstacle course."

"Oh . . . oh . . ." Joss waved her hand. "We could paint plastic plates like mushroom caps and put them all over the yard. They can't step on the caps at all costs."

"At one turn, they'll have to blow bubbles through a hula hoop."

"Yes!" Joss snickered. "At another turn, they have to hop three times and make a funny face into a warped mirror; and at another, they have to jump on a pile of pillows."

"We could also play pass the treasure," I said. "That's where we pass around a special surprise wrapped in layers of fairy gauze."

"When the music stops, whoever is holding the treasure must unwrap another layer of fairy gauze and make a wish."

"Exactly. The one to unwrap the last layer discovers the treasure." I frowned. "Is all of this too silly?"

Joss spread her arms. "Misty wants a fairy party. We're going to give her a fairy party. I'm sure her friends will enjoy letting their hair down. There will be lots of laughs." She made a list of items we needed to purchase.

The two of us returned to the showroom.

For the next couple of hours, I attended to my customers.

At five minutes to closing, Joss said, "You should talk to Brady about catering the party."

"Brady. Of course. And I'll ask Yvanna to make the sweets."

Brady Cash and I had gone to high school together. He was a senior and I was a freshman when we met and bonded in photography club. After he graduated, however, we'd lost touch. Long story short, we'd become reacquainted last May, when Meaghan and I had entered the Hideaway Café in the Village Shops and learned that he was the new owner. Now our friendship was blossoming.

Joss eyed the telephone.

I shook my head. "I'll touch base with him tomorrow. I'm too tired tonight." I went home, ate a simple dinner while doodling with more party ideas, and flopped into bed at ten.

Thursday morning, I arrived at the shop fresh and ready to tackle the day. The rain had passed. I set Pixie on the patio. Fiona divebombed her, forcing Pixie to swipe at her with a paw. I warned them to play nice—they always did—then I dialed Brady, left a message about catering the fairy party, and fetched dusty boxes of wind chimes from the stockroom beyond the kitchen.

"Help me unpack these, would you?" I asked Joss when I returned to the showroom. "We'll use them for the party. Misty wants wind chimes everywhere."

"Of course she does."

"Glad we're not wearing clothes we need to dry clean," I said as I brushed dust off my nubby, tangerine-colored sweater and Joss brushed dust off her lime-green T-shirt. Both of us had donned jeans.

"Where'd you find these?"

"Behind the boxes of four-inch clay pots."

"I think we need to do a little cleaning," she teased.

The first set of wind chimes consisted of Corinthian-blue cylinders, which were beautiful, with a resonant sound. The second set was made of delicate seashells and featured a blue-and-gold mermaid at the top.

As we were hanging them on the preordered rack behind the sales counter, Misty sashayed in with a petite woman with caramel skin, inch-long dark hair, a nose ring, and at least four piercings in each ear. Her dark eyes were dramatically outlined in black. Possibly tattooed. I couldn't place her age.

Misty said, "Courtney, I want you to meet Nova Pasha, the jewelry designer I want to use for the party."

"Hi, Nova." I extended my hand.

When we shook, she attempted a smile, but it was tight, tentative. I noticed tattoos on the inside of her arm when she pulled her hand away. One was a sorceress holding an aqua-and-pink crystal ball. Another was a multicolored snake with a flower lei around its neck.

"She'll make party favors for all," Misty said. "She creates eccentric pieces, like the one she's wearing."

Nova fingered the exotic white-topaz pendant that complemented her white-silk V-neck jumpsuit.

"I've referred many of my friends to her. She has pieces featured at Odine's store, too. You might have seen some." Misty pronounced Odine's name correctly today, which made me giggle. Fiona had been right about her purposely mispronouncing it. *Why?* I wondered.

Misty gave Nova a nudge and guided her through the shop. "Isn't the shop as lovely as I told you? The wind chimes. The china. The good vibes."

Nova *ooh*ed.

"Nova is very spiritual," Misty added. "She always wears white."

"Not always," Nova whispered. She wasn't exactly mousy, but she wasn't dynamic, either. Maybe she was shy around Misty, given Misty's larger-than-life personality.

Fiona sailed to my side, fluttering in front of me to draw

my focus. "Some think the name Nova is Celtic and means cloud, while others think that the name derives from a princess named after the Nile River."

Where did she come up with that information? I wondered. *Is her mentor teaching her world history, too?*

I followed Misty and Nova to the patio. We settled at a wrought-iron table. "What kind of favors are you thinking about giving, Misty?"

"I don't know. Earrings? Necklaces? Show her what you brought, Nova." Misty pushed up the sleeves of her turquoise dress, ready to get down to business.

Nova opened her rhinestone-studded tote bag, pulled out a velvet jewelry holder, and unfurled it. On top of the velvet, attached by loops, was an assortment of items: enamel as well as bejeweled unicorn pins; gold dragonfly earrings; beaded necklaces with mermaid, fairy, or dragon lockets; silver bracelets featuring charms of all the fanciful creatures.

I whistled. "Pretty."

"Which one will Odine like best, Courtney?" Misty asked.

"How about the pins?" I suggested. Every time I'd visited Fantasy Awaits, Odine had been sporting a dazzling brooch. "Do you have styles other than the unicorn?"

"Do you mean like fairies?" Nova's voice was reedy, in keeping with her reticent demeanor. "I can do that."

"How did you two meet?" I asked Misty.

"In college. Nova was in a different sorority, but we're dear friends."

Looking more closely, I did see crow's-feet, indicating that Nova was older than she came across.

"Misty! Yoo-hoo!" a leggy redheaded woman sang as she sashayed through the French doors, the skirt of her off-the-shoulder gold dress swishing with each step, a matching winter shawl draped over her arms.

Farrah Lawson, as beautiful in person as she was on screen, reminded me of Rita Hayworth singing, "Put the Blame on Mame." Saucy, sexy, and confident. From all accounts in the movie magazines, Farrah was also as nice as she was pretty.

"Surprise!" Farrah opened her arms and rushed to Misty to envelop her. "I'm here early!"

"Farrah, I didn't expect you until tomorrow. Odine will be so happy. She implored me to make sure you'd come." Misty broke free and faced me. "Courtney, this is Farrah Lawson, another of my sorority sisters."

I knew already because Misty had texted me the guest list for the party.

Farrah put a coquettish hand on one hip and the other to the side of her head. "And star of the next Stefan Samaras movie *Startled*."

"No way. You're doing a movie with Stefan Samaras?" Misty's eyes widened. To me, she said, "Stefan Samaras is possibly the hottest director in the universe right now. He's made nine epic films." To Farrah, she said, "You go, girlfriend."

Farrah had gorgeous cheekbones, a wide luscious mouth, and riveting eyes. "Courtney, you are so sweet to put this party together for Odine." Her voice was sultry and oozing with charm. "We Delta Gammas stick together." She eyed Misty. "Did you tell Courtney our history?"

"I haven't had time."

Nova, who had been forgotten with Farrah's entrance, started to roll up the jewelry bag.

"We both dabbled in theater arts in college," Farrah began.

"Farrah starred in everything," Misty said.

"And Misty always played the rollickingly funny side-kick."

Misty blushed. "'Rollickingly funny' might be a stretch."

"You had such great timing." Farrah batted Misty's arm. "Remember how Professor Saunders said playing character roles would only enhance your own character in years to come?"

"I do." Misty buffed her fingertips on her dress. "And it has. I'm a real card."

The two of them laughed.

"Courtney, you might not know this," Misty said, "but I've always been a big supporter of the arts in Carmel. The Golden Bough Playhouse. The Academy of Performing Arts."

"Misty's connections are how I got my big break," Farrah added. "Misty—"

"Let me share the story. Thanks to—"

"A former lover."

Misty blushed. "A man I once knew who became a successful director-producer in Los Angeles—"

"She told him about me." Farrah clapped a hand to her chest. "*Me!*"

"I told him she was trying to break into movies and—"

"I'd done a few commercials and was auditioning for television like crazy," Farrah said, "but film roles weren't coming to me."

Hard to believe, given her gorgeous hair and looks. She had, as they say, the whole package.

"Misty chatted him up," Farrah went on. "So—"

"My story," Misty said, cutting her off. "I got in touch with him and referred him to her fabulous website, and *voila*, he was smitten. He had to meet her."

Farrah said, "My career skyrocketed when I costarred in his breakout movie, *The Lone Star Starlet.*" She bussed Misty on the cheek. "I will never be able to thank you enough."

Misty's eyelids fluttered.

Farrah peered past Misty. "Is that you, Nova? I'm so sorry I didn't notice you there, all in white. You sort of blend in."

Nova lowered her chin and remained as quiet as a dormouse.

"Still making jewelry?" Farrah asked.

"Mm-hm," Nova hummed.

"Good for you." Farrah said to me, "Back in college, Nova was a costume designer for the arts department and planned to work professionally as a clothing designer, but that dream fell through."

"Even so," Misty said, "she has made a decent living with her jewelry."

"True."

"The rest of us—Farrah, Odine, and I—were all over the map when it came to course of study," Misty went on. "At one point Odine and I had the overblown notion of becoming doctors, and Farrah was going to save the planet. Oh, the science courses we had to take!" She chortled. "Then I wanted to own a cruise line, and Farrah considered becoming a teacher. I loved to travel, and she enjoyed the way kids processed information. By our junior year, we changed our focus again. Odine and I majored in econ—money was a driving factor, I won't lie—and Farrah switched to theater, her true passion. Nova was the only one who basically stayed true to her original path: design."

Nova blushed at what seemed to be a compliment.

"About a year ago," Misty went on, "Farrah commissioned Nova to make an exclusive piece she could wear to an awards show."

Farrah said, "That's right. Nova came up with a corsage-like thing that was . . . you know . . ." She wove her hands together but didn't completely capture whatever it was she was trying to describe.

"It was a bracelet, Farrah," Misty said.

"Right. It was black velvet and gold and pearls and so . . ." She twirled a hand.

Nova blanched, looking for all intents and purposes as if she was afraid that if she opened her mouth, she might say the wrong thing.

"She's going to make each of us something special for the party," Misty said, mindless of Nova's discomfort.

"Hopefully not a bracelet," Farrah joked.

Misty patted the table. "Farrah, sit. Let's catch up. Courtney? Would it be possible to have some tea out here?"

"Of course." We served high tea on the weekends, but we always had tea or coffee available for our customers. We'd ascertained that they lingered longer when sipping a beverage and chatting amiably.

Nova rose.

"Nova, sit down," Misty said.

"I have to go."

"But—"

"I have . . . another appointment. Bye." Nova rushed from the patio and through the shop.

Fiona whispered, "Should I follow her and douse her with a happy potion?"

I nodded discreetly.

Fiona flitted away.

"So tell me, darling"—Farrah put her clutch on the table and settled into a chair—"are you dating anyone?"

Misty's laughter sounded liked bells. "No, not since the shopping-mall tycoon."

Farrah squinted. "The shopping-mall tycoon? The one with the curly hair?"

"The very same. Daddy liked him, but he turned out to be sort of kinky."

"I'm sorry." Farrah petted Misty's hand.

"And you?" Misty asked. "Your social media pages are rife with photos. I can't figure out which ones are for publicity and which are the real you."

If the most recent tabloids were to be trusted, Farrah had a current boyfriend, an actor who was doing a movie in Asia.

Pixie romped to Misty and bounded into her lap. Misty introduced my Ragdoll to Farrah, waving Pixie's paw as if she were a puppet, and the two women continued chatting.

Heading toward the doors to ask Joss to bring tea, I encountered a lean, handsome man in neon blue-and-yellow bicycle shorts and top, a bike helmet tucked under his arm. He stopped in the archway, blocking my ability to slip past.

We sidestepped left and right. Jokingly, I said, "We'll dance later."

He grinned. "Excuse me, I heard Farrah was here."

"Word travels fast."

"She sent a text. We know each other."

"Aren't you . . ." I tilted my head before aiming a finger at him. "You are. You're the author Austin Pinter. *Land Before Time, In the Age of the Dragons, Dragons and Damsels.*" I enjoyed reading historical fiction. "You look just like the picture on the book jacket, buzz cut and all."

"Thank you."

"You haven't written a new book in a while."

"No." His nose twitched. "My publisher is impatiently waiting. I keep telling her a writer can't force the story, but I haven't been inspired lately. I'm doing eons of research at Harrison Mem to stir my creative juices."

Harrison Memorial Library was located at Ocean Avenue and Lincoln Street. Though it wasn't huge, it had a terrific collection of books, including fiction and nonfiction as well as e-books and cookbooks.

"You're a local?" I asked, surprised. "I haven't seen you around town."

"I stick pretty much to myself. I live down the street from the library." He gestured to Farrah. "If you don't mind."

"Of course." I stepped aside and beckoned Joss, who was at the register. "Could you bring out tea for the four of us? Pretty please?"

"You got it." She gave me a thumbs-up.

I peeked quickly to the right. Nova had left the shop. I didn't see Fiona. Perhaps she'd followed her outside.

Austin hurried to Farrah and tweaked her ear lobe. She swiveled her head, and her lips broke into a wide grin. "Austin, darling." She rose and gave him a warm hug then cupped his cheek. "Still as gorgeous as ever. And clammy. Did you ride here?"

"I did."

"Is the writing going well?" Over her shoulder, she said to Misty, "You know Austin, don't you?"

Misty got to her feet. "Do I look like I've lost my marbles? Of course I remember Austin. Sigma Alpha Epsilon, right?"

"Good memory," he said.

"You and Farrah were lovers senior year."

Farrah's cheeks bloomed pink. Had the word *lovers* caught her off guard? Had she and Austin had a serious fling?

To me, Misty said, "Austin wasn't an actor like the rest of us at SCU. He was always a writer. You wrote a play in college, if I'm not mistaken, didn't you, Austin?" She tapped her chin with her finger. "What was the name? *The Day Before Last*?"

Austin said, "*The Day Before,* but close."

"And now you're writing historical fiction. So impressive. It's always fun to be able to play around with history," Misty said. "To be able to change the facts and so on."

Farrah studied her. "Was that a dig about my sweet Austin?" She slipped her hand around his elbow.

"No, of course not. I love fiction. It was a joke." Misty fanned the air. "Austin, I remember you having a sense of humor way back when."

"Still do."

"Nonfiction is for educators and reporters, don't you think?"

"Agreed." He had an easy smile. Nice teeth. He spun around and clasped Farrah by the shoulders. "Babe, I'm sorry. I can't stay. I have a business meeting. How about dinner?"

"Well . . ."

"You can't fly all the way from London and turn me down."

I gawped. She'd flown to town from London? She had to be exhausted due to the time change.

"Drinks for sure. I'll text you." Farrah kissed him gently on the lips. "Mm," she hummed. "You've always been a good kisser."

Austin bid us good-bye and strode out the way he'd entered, with a jaunty confidence.

Joss passed him carrying a tray set for tea. She put it on the table. I thanked her and said I'd pour. For a brief moment, she stared at Farrah. I whispered that, yes, we did have a famous movie star in our presence. Joss patted her chest in mock awe and returned to the showroom.

"Well, that was a surprise," Farrah said.

I frowned. Austin said she had texted him. How big a surprise could it have been? I offered her a cup of tea. She readily accepted it.

"He looked good, don't you think, Misty?" Farrah asked, removing the spoon from the honeypot and drizzling some into her tea.

"He did, but, Farrah, sweetie. Um . . ." Misty rolled her lip between her teeth. "You aren't leading him on, are you?"

"Whatever do you mean?"

"He's a nice guy. He has a good reputation. Don't make him fodder for the movie rags."

"Fodder?"

"All the men you date wind up shattered, heartbroken, or bewildered. How about you leave this one intact? He's nice."

"Ha!" Farrah jeered. "Nice guys finish last."

Chapter 3

As the clocks are striking twelve—oh, how extremely sly!—
All the blossoms open up, and out the fairies fly.
—Anonymous, "What the Toys Do at Night"

"I can't believe it!" Odine Oates exclaimed as she trotted past customers in the shop. I watched her through the window, trying to keep the tassels of her amethyst silk shawl from knocking china cups or knickknacks to the floor. "You're here!" She strode through the French doors, dramatically removing her shawl and draping it over one arm as she hurried to the table. Her stride strained the hem of her royal-purple jacquard dress. "Sugar, you look amazing!"

Farrah stood and drew Odine into a hug. "You, too."

"Liar."

Odine, who was about Misty's size, although thicker in the waist, didn't look a day over thirty, with her long blond-and-lavender, ombre-streaked hair swept off her oval face.

"I saw photos of you online," Odine said, fiddling with the glittery wildflowers brooch pinned to the bodice of her dress. "You were in London with some gorgeous-looking men. Shooting what?"

"Startled."

"Great title."

"Stefan Samaras is the director," Misty said. "Farrah's the star."

"This time," Farrah responded modestly.

"You've been a star for ten years straight," Odine countered. "That's not going to change. Who could resist you?" She held Farrah at arm's length, and I noticed that she, like Nova, had tattoos on the inside of her arms, including stars, moons, and an ethereal fairy holding a bouquet of purple flowers. "What's the role?"

"A temptress."

"Typecasting," Misty wisecracked.

Odine swatted Farrah's arm playfully. "Sit. Tell me everything." She drew Farrah to a chair and the two of them faced each other.

Fiona flew out of the ficus and hovered over Odine's head. She inhaled and wrapped her arms around her teensy body. "She smells good. Like honeysuckle. My mother loves honeysuckle."

My breath caught in my chest. It was the first time I'd heard her reveal a detail about her mother. Did she miss her? Was she alive? Could she leave the fairy kingdom?

"Tea?" I poured a cup for Odine and nudged the cup and saucer toward her.

She accepted it and said to Farrah, "I can't believe you made it to town, sugar. Thank you for coming. It means the world."

"I wouldn't have missed it. Darling"—Farrah patted Misty's forearm—"what would we all do without you? You were our party planner in college, and here you are again, the hostess with the most-est."

Misty frowned. "Perhaps not the most-est, but I do my best."

Farrah folded her arms on the table. "Odine, how is that gorgeous husband of yours?"

Odine's smile vanished. She blinked. Trying to keep tears at bay? "He's traveling."

"Traveling?" Farrah raised an eyebrow.

Misty thwacked Odine's arm.

"What?" Odine snapped.

"Tell her the truth."

Odine scrunched her nose. "He's on a worldwide sailing trip."

"Without you?" Farrah asked.

"Solo."

Misty thumped her again.

Odine gave her the evil eye. "Stop it!"

"Did he leave you?" Without waiting for a response, Farrah grabbed Odine's hands. "Darling, he was never right for you. Truth be known, he wasn't right for anyone. You are well rid of him."

"He's not gone forever." Tears leaked down Odine's cheeks. She wriggled from Farrah's grasp and irritably swiped the tears away.

"Sometimes a woman has to be single to be appreciated," Farrah said. "Isn't that right, Misty?"

"Sometimes," Misty murmured, clearly not convinced.

"You know what?" Farrah bolted to her feet. "We need a spa day. Courtney, what's the best spa in town?"

"A Peaceful Solution."

"I love that place," Misty said.

Odine sniffed. Didn't she like it, or was she still fighting tears?

"Perfect," Farrah said. "Let's book it for tomorrow. For all of us. You, too, Courtney. My treat."

I said, "I'm not positive the spa can accommodate four—"

Farrah said, "I'll make sure it does."

"Nova, too?" Misty asked.

"Of course. Do you have the telephone number on you, Courtney?" Farrah opened a keypad on her smartwatch, ready to type.

I pulled my cell phone from my pocket, opened Contacts, and rattled off the number to the spa.

Fiona wafted to me as Farrah blazed onward. "Something's wrong. I feel it. In here." She patted her solar plexus.

Not again. I motioned with my chin at Odine, who was using a tissue to wipe the tears off her face.

"No, it's not her," Fiona said. "Well, it might be." She settled on my arm and drummed her fingers. Her touch felt like raindrops.

A pair of customers crossed the threshold to the patio and made a beeline for the verdigris baker's racks.

I moved to the far side of the fountain so I could talk to Fiona out of earshot of the others. "Could your forebodings be related to Nova? She seemed pretty distraught. I'm not sure why. Farrah was nice enough to her. Hey, maybe she got an emergency text. I saw a glow on her cell phone."

Fiona shimmied. "Maybe."

We glanced at Farrah, Misty, and Odine. Farrah was nodding and smiling and chatting to her friends to confirm their spa appointments. When she ended the call, she whooped.

"Done. Spa day tomorrow. Ten a.m. I love it." Grinning, Farrah flipped her hair with her hands and shook her head like a model would do in a hair commercial. "Odine, this will be your best birthday ever." She clasped her friends' hands. "Say it with me . . ."

The three women crooned, "Best birthday ever!"

★   ★   ★

When Misty and her friends left, I decided I needed to get hopping on the party plans. Meaghan was on tap for the mural, but seeing as Misty wanted each of the attendees to make a fairy garden, I needed pots. "Off to see Renee," I said to Joss.

Fiona coasted to my side. "Renee wants to see a fairy. I should tag along."

"Do so at your peril," I teased.

Renee did not want her fiancé, Detective Dylan Summers, to know she harbored the hope to one day meet a fairy. He, like my father, was logical. Everything was black and white. There was no room for anything fanciful in his life.

The Village Shops' courtyard, which boasted a striking dark-red wood-and-stone façade, was tiered like our courtyard; however, it consisted of more units than ours because three of them were two stories.

I entered Seize the Clay and took in the white décor and drank in the pleasant aroma of wet clay. Instantly, I felt the calm Renee promised to all customers.

"It's so pretty in here," Fiona said. "Like our place but different."

"Mm-hm."

One of Renee's assistants was showing a man handmade plates. The other was showing a woman the choices of specialty dog-food bowls. Lots of people in Carmel-by-the-Sea owned pets. They were constantly on the lookout for new ways to pamper their furry friends. Three more customers were browsing vases.

"Look what the cat dragged in," a man said.

I spun around and spotted my father standing with none other than Detective Dylan Summers by the coffee mug display. My father and I looked nothing alike. He had cocoa-brown eyes and dark-brown hair while I had light eyes and blond hair. And he was tan, like a man who worked the land all day should be. I was diligent about lathering my fair skin with sunblock. Summers, although not nearly as rugged as my father, was equally handsome. Both were in their fifties and stood over six feet tall. Summers was clad in a white shirt, tan trousers, and loafers; my father was wearing jeans and a green golf shirt imprinted with his business logo.

"Hi, Dad. Hello, Detective. What are you two doing here?"

"Going to lunch," Dad said.

It didn't surprise me that they were meeting up. Before turning to landscaping, my father had been a cop. A freak accident while chasing a thief had ruined his knee and ended his career. He and Summers hadn't served on the force at the same time; they'd met through mutual friends and occasionally played golf.

"I wanted to pick out something for Wanda first," Dad added. "Dylan suggested a mug."

Meaghan's mother Wanda was dating my father, a big surprise to Meaghan and me when we'd found out. My father hadn't dated in over twenty years. Wanda, after kicking out her abusive husband—Meaghan had been five at the time—had vowed never to need a man again, but she and my father had met and fallen for each other. I loved seeing him happy.

"Ugh, ix-nay on the mug." I grunted. "Get her a flower vase or a pretty cake plate."

"That's what I said." Renee pushed through the white curtain from the stockroom where she also housed the kiln and gave classes. Dressed in skinny jeans and a fashionable oversized sweater, her dark hair cascading in loose curls over her shoulders, she seemed relaxed and in her element. If I hadn't first met her as a cop, I'd never have believed she'd been one. "Mugs are too impersonal."

Fiona swooped to Renee and orbited her head. Renee petted her hair as if feeling a breeze. Fiona tittered.

Dad picked up a mug that read *She believed she could, so she did.* "Don't you think this will inspire her to paint more?"

"Wanda loves all shades of purple," Fiona declared.

"This"—Renee crossed to a white plate adorned with dainty purple flowers—"would suit her better. Promise."

I studied my fairy. Had she somehow influenced Renee's decision?

My father returned the mug to its shelf and accepted the plate. "Wrap it up. So, Daughter"—he folded his arms—"did I hear right? You're throwing a fairy party for adults?"

Before branching out with Open Your Imagination at the tender age of twenty-nine, I'd worked for my father's landscaping company. He hadn't been pleased when I'd quit to make fairy gardens. He didn't believe in fairies and wished I wouldn't, either.

Summers sniggered.

"Cut it out, Dylan." Renee slipped past him to the cash register. "Courtney, I have your pot designs picked out. I'll show them to you after I ring your father up. They're really cute."

"*Cute,*" my father echoed.

"Honestly, Kip," Renee chided. She took his money and then swathed the plate in tissue paper and slotted it into a white tote bag. "If I didn't know better, I'd think you and my fiancé were in high school. A fairy party sounds divine. Fun. Different."

"It'll be unusual for sure," Summers cracked.

"Out of my way, rogue," Renee said.

"Milady," Dylan said, and gallantly brandished an arm to let her pass.

Renee whacked his chest with a hand and retreated into the stockroom.

"Detective," I said, leaning an arm on the sales counter, "have you had any success finding the thief that robbed that woman in Sweet Treats and Say Cheese?" Asking the question made me wonder whether the two incidents might have been why Fiona had sensed bad vibes.

"No."

"Anything to go on?"

"All we've come up with from the two witnesses is someone in a brown hoodie, no hair color or length, and no distinguishing facial marks because the culprit was in and out so fast." He slipped a hand into his trousers pocket. "Teen-sized," he added. "Slim."

"Ergo, not a grown man."

"Doubtful. Why the creased forehead?" he asked.

"I'm worried about Carmel," I murmured. "We don't get crime like this. If I can help—"

"Don't you worry," he assured me. "CPD will solve it without you."

I huffed. "Forgive me if I care, but one of the robberies happened in my courtyard. At my friend's place."

My father chortled.

I whirled on him. "What is so darned funny?"

"Pay up," Dad said to Summers.

"Did you have a bet on me?" My jaw dropped open.

"I told him you'd want answers," he replied. "You wouldn't be able to help yourself."

"Da-ad," I droned. "C'mon."

"No, sweetheart, you c'mon. This is police business. You have a shop and a fairy to look out for."

I threw him a nasty look. I wasn't the only one he taunted. He had chided my mother for believing in fairies, too. It was a bone of contention between us. I jammed a fist onto one hip. "Be forewarned, you two. If the thief crosses my doorstep, I will not hesitate to respond. Are we clear?"

Summers handed my father a five-dollar bill. "Crystal clear."

"Here we are," Renee said, emerging from the stockroom carrying a stack of white glazed pots, similar to the ones she'd done for me a few months ago, each featuring a flower fairy. "I came up with another choice, just in case. Don't go anywhere." She retreated to the stockroom again.

I found my father studying the pot with the yellow fairy on it.

"Your mother," he said over his shoulder, "told me about a fairy that looked like this."

"Aurora," I whispered. She was the first and only fairy I'd seen until I met Fiona. She was as pretty as the sunrise with a cheery disposition. How she had adored the color yellow, like the yellow of buttercups and daisies and daylilies.

Summers nudged my father. "Don't drink the Kool-Aid, bro."

Renee returned with another set of pots. "*Men*. Go to lunch, you two."

When they departed, she turned to me. "What do you think of these, Courtney?"

Each pot was a different pastel color with a border of flowers.

"They're beautiful. You are so talented."

"I'm feeling inspired."

"I'll order six of each."

"Perfect. I can have them for you early next week." Renee gazed toward the ceiling. "So, um, is she here? Your fairy? I thought I felt something earlier. Overhead."

"She is."

Renee peered hard. After a long minute, she gave up. "This is my favorite pot." She held up one of the white pots, which featured a blue fairy, similar in style to Fiona.

"It should be," Fiona sang and leaped onto Renee's shoulder. With finesse, she pirouetted down Renee's bare arm.

Renee brushed her forearm, missing Fiona. Delighted, my intrepid fairy glided to Renee's shoulder and tiptoed to Renee's ear. She whispered into it.

Renee's eyes opened wide. Had she heard Fiona? She gazed at me in amazement. "Was that . . . Is that . . . ?"

Fiona flew away and Renee swiveled in that direction. I didn't think she could see her yet, but she was darned close.

Chapter 4

The flickering fairy-circle wheeled and broke
Flying, for all the land was full of life.
—Alfred Lord Tennyson, "A Fairy Revel, Before the
Coming of Guinevere"

"Courtney!" Eudora Cash, a well-known historical fiction author in her mid-fifties, sauntered into the shop looking as if she'd recently posed for the photograph on her book jacket, her strawberry-blond hair in a twist, her makeup flawless, her ecru linen suit stylish.

In my nubby sweater and jeans and cuddling Pixie in my arms, I felt way underdressed. I set the cat on the floor of the showroom and gave her backside a nudge. She scampered to the patio.

"Dory, hello." I'd been reading Eudora's books for years but had never known she was the author because, growing up, I'd called her Dory. She was Brady's mother.

"I'd like you to meet a friend of mine. This is Violet Vickers." Eudora extended an arm toward a regal woman in a silver two-piece suit. "Violet, this is Courtney."

Violet fingered her tight white curls and smoothed the

shawl collar of her elegant jacket. "Lovely to meet you finally." Violet was a dowager who donated to numerous worthy causes. "I've heard such lovely things about you. Your place is lovely."

"Lovely," Eudora echoed, then chuckled. A dimple appeared in her right cheek every time she smiled, just like one did for Brady. "Violet, there's no need to be nervous here—unless, of course, you're afraid to meet a fairy."

"Afraid? Bother!" Violet exclaimed. "I'm not afraid of anything."

On cue, Fiona, the imp, soared toward Violet and tried to catch her attention.

The woman glanced right and left, muttering under her breath while flapping a hand as if she were being attacked by wasps. Apparently, she could sense Fiona, but I was certain she couldn't see her. Not yet, anyway.

Overwhelmed by giggles, Fiona floated to the patio and settled on the top of the fountain.

"Courtney, show Violet all the figurines." Eudora gestured toward the French doors.

I guided them outside.

"Wait until you see," Eudora gushed. A month ago Brady had brought her to the shop for the first time, and she'd fallen in love with the place. Within minutes, she'd thrown herself into making a fairy garden dedicated to Carmel's history.

Pixie followed us, her tail swishing my ankles.

"Violet would like to commission a pot." Eudora poked her friend. "Tell her what you'd like, Vi."

"Eudora Cash!" Violet fisted her hands on her hips. "If you don't stop bossing me around, I won't let you go anywhere with me again. Ever."

"I'm sorry. Usually, you're able to speak for yourself, but you clammed up the moment we entered Open Your Imagination."

"What if I did?" Violet relaxed her arms and lifted her chin. "Courtney, I want a garden like the one you made for the Beauty of Art Spectacular a few months ago."

I swallowed hard. Her reference drew me to the night a woman was killed with a dragon-style letter opener that I'd installed in one of the fairy gardens I'd designed for the event. I shook free of the memory. "What color would you like the pot to be?"

"Cobalt-blue."

The same as I'd used for the Spectacular. Swell. *Smile, Courtney.* I could push painful memories aside as well as the next person. "How large?"

"At least three feet tall."

I stored a few of those at the cottage. I made large, commissioned items in the polycarbonate greenhouse in my backyard. That way I could immerse myself in creating the story.

"I have the perfect spot in my garden," Violet continued. "If I like what you design, I would like to commission another dozen. I have quite an expansive yard."

"Violet bought Misty Dawn's estate on 17-Mile Drive," Eudora said. "Show her pictures, Vi."

Violet removed her cell phone from her purse and scrolled through her photo app. She displayed photos to me. I'd seen similar ones in *Carmel Estates*, a real estate magazine that featured elegant local homes. I kept past issues of the magazines in my file drawer because I liked to browse them for gardening ideas.

"Misty sold me the Miró that was hanging in the foyer."

"Le Vent Parmi les Roseaux?" I asked.

"Yes. *The Wind Among the Reeds.* It's so fresh and fun."

"I've always liked that one, too."

Violet beamed. "My husband would have appreciated the way I've decorated the house, rest his soul." She blinked back a tear.

Eudora patted her friend's arm. "I know how much you miss him."

"Ten years and yet I think of him every day." Violet sniffed. "Courtney, if possible, I'd like the garden by Wednesday. I have dinner guests coming Thursday. They're influential in the San Francisco theater scene. Is that possible?"

"Of course." I'd make it happen. "Do you have a theme in mind for this garden?"

"I'd like it to be about love. Love is the essence of life itself, don't you think?" Not waiting for a response, she said, "Shakespeare wrote, 'If thou rememb'rest not the slightest folly that ever love did make thee run into, thou has not loved.' *As You Like It,* act two, scene four."

Eudora grinned. "Courtney, if you haven't guessed, Violet is a huge patron of the arts and loves to wax dramatic. She's seen every one of Shakespeare's plays."

Violet preened. "In cities around the world."

"I've been to Ashland, Oregon," I said.

"Ah, yes," Violet hummed. "The Oregon Shakespeare Festival is fine indeed."

"Violet donates to our local theaters as well as many museums."

"And our fine library," Violet added.

"Lissa Reade and Violet are like this." Eudora crossed her fingers—*best buddies.*

For the next hour, Eudora, Violet, and I talked about our favorite books while gathering figurines and other items for her love-themed fairy garden. While shopping, Violet must have said *I love this* or *lovely* a dozen times. She selected an oversized red-and-white toadstool, a thatched-roof house, a crossing bridge, a fairy on a swing, a fairy kissing a bird, a turquoise bubbling river. In less than an hour, she'd selected enough items to make two fairy gardens. Every time I told her she'd chosen plenty, she saw another item that she adored.

Joss checked on us occasionally. She didn't need my help with customers; she was concerned that I might need a breather. I told her I was fine and searched for Fiona. She seemed to have disappeared. Had she sprinkled fairy dust on Violet, causing her to buy more than she should? If she had, she could suffer consequences. Coercion was not allowed.

"There. Done." Violet clapped her hands.

Eudora said, "About time."

"Don't make fun."

Moving toward the register, Violet stopped short and viewed her basket of goodies.

"What now?" Eudora sighed.

"You know what? I've changed my mind."

Eudora gasped.

"I want Courtney to decide what to put in the garden. Use your imagination. Surprise me. Except you must keep these two lovely fairies in white. Here you go." She pulled them from the basket. "Money is no object."

At closing time, I said to Pixie, "Let's go, girl."

She leaped into my arms and nuzzled my neck.

"Love you, too." I bent to pick up the bags I'd filled with possible items for Violet Vickers's fairy garden and startled when Fiona alit on my shoulder. "Where have you been?"

"Napping."

"Did you coerce Mrs. Vickers to approve an unlimited budget?"

"Absolutely not." She huffed, causing her adult wings to spread. "Fairies aren't allowed to do that. We can calm. We can inspire. But we cannot coerce. Ever. I know the *Dos* and *Don'ts* of my abilities."

"Hmm. Is there a list I could refer to?" I teased.

"A list? Ha!" She blew a raspberry and pointed to her head. "We just know."

"Got it. Silly me. Shall we take the long route and do a little window shopping?"

"Yes, please."

I didn't live far from Open Your Imagination, so I often changed up my route in order to take in the display windows of other stores in Carmel. One of my favorite courtyards to wander through was Su Vecino on Dolores Street, which grew up around the Mexican restaurant that opened in the 1950s. According to lore, the serape worn by Clint Eastwood in the film *The Good, the Bad, and the Ugly* hung in the restaurant. Eastwood, at one time, had been mayor of Carmel.

As we neared the courtyard's entrance, Fiona tapped my neck. "Look. Is that Farrah Lawson?"

"Mm-hm."

Farrah was walking with Austin Pinter, who was no longer in biking clothes but clad in jeans and a body-hugging burgundy sweater. Farrah, dressed warmly for the cool weather, had looped her arm through his and was leaning into him, grinning from ear to ear, oblivious to people passing them.

"They look pretty cozy, don't they?" I murmured.

"Yes, but as Shakespeare would say"—Fiona held up a finger—"'The course of true love never did run smooth.' *As You Like It,* act one, scene two."

I gawked at her. Months ago, she and Joss had read all the Sherlock Holmes short stories. Subsequently, she'd become an adorable know-it-all, readily telling me something was *afoot*. Lately, however, Joss had been introducing her to Shakespeare's comedies. I'd had no idea she could quote from them.

"They can't be in love," I said. "They haven't seen each other in years."

"You and Brady fell in love the moment you re-met."

I *tsk*ed. "We're not in love. We're seeing each other. We haven't—"

" 'The lady doth protest too much, methinks.' " Fiona thrust a confident finger into the air. "That's from *Hamlet,* spoken by Queen Gertrude in response to his overacting within the play he put on."

I gawped at her. "You're reading Shakespeare's dramas, too?"

"Joss wants me to be fully educated. She says my mind is like a sponge. That's a good thing, right?"

"Yes. A mind like a sponge is a good thing." I tickled her tummy and returned my attention to Farrah and Austin as they rounded the corner.

Had they fallen in love instantly after reuniting earlier, or had they been having an affair all these years and no one had picked up on it? Not even the movie magazines? None of my business, I told myself, and continued on.

When we arrived at Dream-by-the-Sea, the name of the cottage I rented from my neighbor Holly Hopewell, I set the bags of items for Violet Vickers's love-themed fairy garden in the foyer and then went to the kitchen and made us all something to eat. Tuna for Pixie, pomegranate seeds for Fiona, and a crab-and-avocado salad on bibb lettuce for me. I poured a glass of sauvignon blanc and, rather than eat at the table in the nook, I threw on my peacoat, switched on the fairy lights in the backyard, and took our meals to the wicker table outside. I'd placed it at the center of the rays of paths leading to the four corners of the yard.

The feng shui of what I'd created pleased me. I treasured spending time here. I'd landscaped to my liking, with wisteria, impatiens, and herbs growing naturally beneath the towering cypress trees. I'd completed all the fairy gardens I'd envisioned, including the antique Amish wagon that I'd bid on at the Beauty of Art Spectacular. It held a tribute garden, honoring my friendships with Meaghan, Brady, Joss, and even my father, with whom I'd clashed for a full year after leaving his landscaping business. I'd also finally splurged and purchased the copper fountain I'd had my eye on, which featured a fairy pouring water into a shell. The sound of burbling water soothed my soul.

I finished my meal and pushed my plate away.

Gaily, Fiona leaped around the edge of the table. "I have ideas for the love pots."

"For Mrs. Vickers?"

"Mm-hm. She donates to libraries and museums, and she seems to have a lust for life. How about you make one for the love of books and another for the love of art and another for the love of her fellow man—"

"She only hired me to make one so far."

"She'll order more. What do you think? Brilliant?" She stopped jumping and smugly stared at me, arms folded, one foot propped to the right.

"Brilliant."

She yawned and stretched her arms. "I'm very tired. My brain is, too." Without saying goodnight, she retired to my bedroom.

I retreated to the desk in my living room and for an hour interacted online with friends in the *Fairy Garden Girls Dig It* chat room. We batted ideas around for love-themed fairy gardens, and by the time I signed off, I knew I'd landed on some good ideas.

Climbing into bed, I saw a text message from Brady: *Sorry I dropped the ball. I'm in. Can't wait to cater a fairy garden party. Let's talk tomorrow.*

"It's Friday," Joss announced as she breezed into the shop, the flaps of her green floral camp shirt fluttering open; beneath it she was wearing a pale-green T-shirt. "My slogan-T-shirt day." She stopped by the sales counter where I was setting cash in the register and propped a hand on one hip. "What do you think?" She drew a finger across the words on her T-shirt: *Leave a little sparkle wherever you go.*

"I love it. I want one."

"Found it at Tee Shop on Ocean Avenue." She skirted around me to start a pot of coffee.

"You're in a good mood. Did you go on a date last night?" She'd been seeing a guy she'd met at speed dating named Danny. She had yet to introduce us.

"Nope. I visited my mom." Her mother lived in a nursing home and suffered from dementia. "She was in good spirits. Lucid. I read to her."

"Something by Shakespeare?"

Joss grinned. "Has Fiona been quoting to you?"

"She can't seem to help herself." The shop's telephone rang. I answered. "Open Your Imagination."

"Today's the day!" a woman trilled. "Spa day. Ten a.m." It was Farrah Lawson, sounding as buoyant as ever. "You're on for a mani-pedi."

"Can't wait," I replied half-heartedly. I had so much to do.

Joss spanked my arm. "Stop that. You deserve it. Don't worry about this place. I've got it covered. No classes today. Only prep for tomorrow's tea and receivables for the fairy party."

"And this afternoon's visit to Misty's house. Meaghan. The mural. You and I"—I gestured between the two of us—"checking out the backyard for where we'll set up the games."

"Right." She snapped her fingers. "We'll close the shop for two hours and get it all done." She prodded me to respond to Farrah.

"See you at ten," I said into the phone, and ended the call.

"Don't go anywhere yet," Glinda Gill said as she sashayed into the shop with her niece Georgie, a pretty, preteen tennis phenom. Georgie was the younger spitting image of her aunt—bobbed blond hair, full lips, and alert eyes. The two were wearing matching chocolate brown leggings, zipper hoodies, and fawn-brown flats, and they were carrying shopping bags. "It's Georgie's birthday next week, so we're having a girls' day. She wants to make another garden."

Fiona winged to Georgie, stopped midair in front of her face, and sang "Happy Birthday." Fairies loved to sing. Georgie smiled but didn't let on to her aunt that she could see and hear Fiona.

"Let's pick out what you need," Glinda said. "My treat." Glinda, in her early fifties, wasn't married and didn't have children, but she had a relationship with her niece that I envied. "Courtney, would you help us?"

"Sure." I followed them to the patio.

Pixie hopped off the chair she'd been napping on and trotted to Georgie. She batted her with her tail. Georgie knelt to pet her, and then rose and tentatively fingered the figurines. Seeing her standing in profile, I recollected Dylan Summers's description of the thief that was at large in Carmel. Brown hoodie. Teen-sized. Slim.

No, Courtney. It's not Georgie. She is as good as gold. Not to mention, I was certain she wouldn't jeopardize her future in tennis by doing anything illegal.

I made a mental note to touch base with Summers again and see how his investigation was going, whether he wanted me to show interest or not.

Over the course of the next fifteen minutes, I deduced that Georgie wanted to make a teacup garden, so I steered her to the miniature fairies, where she chose a fairy that was reading and the most endearing white cat with huge eyes.

We retreated to the showroom to find the perfect teacup. Beaming with excitement, she selected a Royal Albert Rose Confetti–pattern cup and saucer.

I packaged up the other items she'd need to make the garden and warned her about the hazards of using a glue gun. Teacup gardens needed a base, like Styrofoam, and glue was the only way to make it stay in place.

Before she left, Glinda said, "My Uncle Cliff is coming to tea tomorrow."

"Your Uncle Cliff?" I shook my head, not following.

"Carmel Collectibles." The shop was located at the far end of our courtyard, next to Glinda's jewelry store, Glitz.

"No way. You and Cliff are related?"

She cocked a hip and in her best Mae West imitation drawled, "Don't tell me you don't see the resemblance?"

"Um, sure I do. *Not,*" I joked. Cliff was a cherry-cheeked seventy-year-old with a paunch.

She whacked my arm playfully. "Keep an eye on him for us, will you? That Hattie Hopewell has him wrapped around her finger."

"He could do worse."

When they left, I had five minutes to make it to the spa.

"Welcome to A Peaceful Solution, ladies," Tish Waterman said as Farrah welcomed Misty, Odine, and me into the reception area. Tish was in her sixties, and despite the scar that abraded her cheek—a mark that was a reminder of the life she'd led before—she exuded confidence. "Please have a glass of cucumber water before we get started." She indicated the glasses on a tray to our right. "I hope you'll enjoy your treatments." She finger-combed her short, carbon-black hair and returned to the reception desk. In her white A-line uniform, she appeared even thinner than usual.

The spa was decorated in what I considered resort chic. Its walls were a soft gray with a cloudlike texture. The furniture was light teak with chartreuse cushions. Displays of the various cucumber-lily creams and lotions the spa sold filled the teak shelves behind the check-in counter.

"I'm sorry Nova couldn't join us," Farrah said to Misty.

"She's suffering a horrible headache."

Farrah frowned. "Too bad."

I wondered if Nova was truly ailing or whether she'd turned down the invitation because she felt anxious in Farrah's presence.

"Let me show you to your various rooms." Tish started down the hall. "This way."

The hall was decorated with images of lilies in silver frames.

Tish stopped at a room. "Miss Lawson, this is my daughter Twyla. She will be doing your facial."

When I'd first met Twyla, a broken woman in her late thirties, her shoulders had been hunched and her demeanor cautious, as if her experience of living with a cult had drained all the confidence from her. But now she was poised. Her dark hair graced her shoulders, her skin radiated health, and her gaze was direct.

"Please follow me," Twyla said, without showing any indication of being in awe of Farrah.

Farrah threw us all a broad smile. "See you on the other side. Have fun."

Next, Tish introduced Misty and Odine to their masseuses, after which she guided me into the mani-pedi room.

I couldn't remember the last time I'd been to a spa. Not only did I not have the time, but the expense was way out of my budget. I had a laundry list of furniture pieces I wanted for the house, plus I wanted an additional lens for my Nikon digital camera.

My nail technician, as she introduced herself, was a beautiful Asian woman. Like Tish and Twyla, she was wearing a pristine white uniform. She handed me a fluffy white robe. "So your pants don't get wet."

I stepped into the dressing room, removed my jeans and cranberry-colored cardigan, and threw the robe over my pink tank top, and for the next hour, I allowed myself to be pampered. There was nothing like a good foot massage.

And then, as my manicurist was buffing my short, unpolished nails—nail polish was a waste on a gardener—a woman screamed.

Chapter 5

She told them of the fairy-haunted land
Away the other side of Brittany,
Beyond the heaths, edged by the lonely sea.
—Matthew Arnold, "Merlin and the Fay Vivian"

Barefoot, I hurried into the hallway. Odine and Misty, clad in robes like the one I was wearing, were facing Farrah. She was weeping hysterically. Twyla was standing in the doorway of her treatment room, hands locked, head bowed.

"They'll never be the same again," Farrah wailed.

"What happened?" I asked.

Farrah glared at me. "Look!" She pointed to her eyebrows. "They're . . . *Ooh*. She . . . She waxed them and made a mess. What am I . . . I have to return to filming in London the day after Odine's party. These won't match previous shots."

Honestly, Farrah was being overly dramatic. I'd never read a news article complaining that she was a diva, but right now, she was acting like a prima donna. A deft hand with an eyebrow pencil would make the contours of her brows the same.

"You!" Farrah aimed a finger at Twyla.

Tish pushed through the door from the reception area, a concerned look on her face. "What's going on?"

"Your daughter ruined my eyebrows. Ruined them. I requested a simple wax."

Tish hurried to her daughter and wrapped an arm around her. "Sweetheart, what happened?"

Twyla said, "She flinched when I applied the wax. I warned her it would be warm."

"I've never had a waxing," Farrah said. "I've always had my eyebrows tweezed or threaded. I had no idea."

"I'm sorry," Tish said.

"I want a full refund," Farrah demanded. "For me and all my friends."

"That won't be possible." Tish raised her pointy chin. "You set an appointment for a treatment. You received that treatment."

"She shouldn't be an aesthetician," Farrah stated. "She should have her license revoked."

"C'mon, Farrah," Misty said, "calm down."

"I could microblade them for you," Tish said. "For free."

"No way will I let anyone in this establishment near my face again."

Odine slung an arm around Farrah. "Sugar, I know a woman who does microblading a couple of blocks away. We'll get this worked out."

Farrah shrugged her off. To Twyla, she said, "You'd better watch your back, lady. I am ticked off, and when I'm ticked off, no one should get in my way."

Tish inhaled sharply. "Miss Lawson, I have enjoyed seeing you in the movies, and I have enjoyed reading about your life, but I had no idea that you could be so . . . so . . . demanding."

That made two of us.

"Demanding? Me? Never!" Farrah turned on her heel, entered the treatment room, and slammed the door.

Tish whispered to Twyla and gave her a nudge. Twyla dashed down the hall and disappeared into what I imagined was the employees' lounge. To Odine, Misty, and me, Tish said, "I am truly sorry. Did you all enjoy your sessions?"

The three of us nodded.

"I will refund Miss Lawson's treatment. That's only fair." Tish strode to the reception area and let the door swing shut.

"Well, that was something," Odine said. "I've never seen Farrah so upset."

"This movie really matters to her," Misty said. "Her career has been waning. Turning forty in Hollywood is like turning fifty in any other profession."

"So much for a relaxing spa day," I kidded, trying to ease the tension.

"A cosmo by my favorite mixologist should smooth her feathers." Misty gazed toward Farrah's room. "Will you all join me at Carolina's?"

"I can't," I said. "I have to return to work. I'll see you this afternoon at your house."

"I'll go with you, Misty," Odine said. "In the meantime, I'll schedule the microblade appointment."

I slipped into my treatment room, put on my clothes, gave my technician a hefty tip, and headed to Open Your Imagination.

Gardener's Delight—Misty's house—was a two-story, gray-and-white home and a far cry from the expansive Spanish estate she'd once owned. I'd passed by it many times to inspect my father's handiwork, which was elegant, with plenty of native plants and potted ferns lining the slate walkway to the front door. A tall pine loomed at the front of the property to the right of the path. To the left stood a simple stone fountain surrounded by annuals.

Misty, looking spiffed up for a business meeting in an

emerald-green blouse, straight-legged black slacks, and heels, met Joss, Meaghan, and me at the front door and offered us a tour.

"There are three bedrooms and two and a half baths upstairs," she said, guiding the three of us and Fiona, unbeknownst to Misty.

"I love the vaulted ceilings," I said, peeking into the living room. Deep-gray furniture faced a light-gray-tiled fireplace. Picasso's *Tête de femme* hung on one wall and Joan Miró's *The Tilled Field* adorned another.

Passing the study, Misty murmured, "I'm afraid this room is pretty empty. I'm still unpacking the furniture I stored, and a bookbinder is touching up all my leather-bound books."

Empty? The bookshelves were barren. The only furniture was a simple rosewood desk and matching chair, plus an ornate hand-carved wooden chair that reminded me of a piece I'd seen in a movie set in medieval times. The three pieces stood atop a round Persian rug. From what I remembered from the *Carmel Estates* spread, Misty's previous study had been handsomely adorned with a variety of antique tables and chairs, lovely cabinets, and Tiffany lamps.

"I miss my old house," Misty continued, as if sensing my dismay, "but honestly, it was so lonely and isolating. Without my parents . . ." They'd passed away two years ago. "I love being here. Now I'm walking to all the cafés and art galleries. I see my friends more often."

"I totally get it," I said. Living near downtown made it so much easier to have a life without driving everywhere.

"Iced tea?" Misty asked, opening the door of the sunroom leading to the backyard.

"Yes, please," I said for all of us. "Thanks."

"Don't mind my snobs," Misty joked, pointing to three cats—a calico, tuxedo, and domestic shorthair—nestled on pillows arranged in the corner. Not one deigned to peek at us.

"They're pretty," I said.

"Shh. Keep that to yourself. They already have swelled heads." She wiggled a finger. "Take a peek at the rear wall and yard. I'll be right back."

Meaghan, who had dressed like an artist in a paint splatter-print smock top over leggings, pushed through the screen door first. Then Fiona shot past her and disappeared into the cypress tree on the left.

"Where—" I started, and stopped. She loved to explore. She would return.

Meaghan whistled. "Your father did an amazing job with the garden."

Dad believed in bilateral symmetry. The backyard boasted two cypress trees at the far corners like mine, which he'd left in place, but he'd removed everything else and had planted a border of white iceberg roses along all three sides of the fence. A crushed stone path abutted the roses. Moving inward, he had created four beds of green-and-white perennials. At the center of those, he'd laid a lawn, and in the center of the lawn was a bronze fountain featuring two swans, their necks inter-twined.

Joss pulled out her cell phone to take photographs of the yard so we'd have a record of every nook and cranny. I hadn't brought my Nikon. We didn't need professional documenta-tion. I pointed out the small patio to the left of the sunroom. Joss snapped a photograph. To the right were two floral chaise longues in need of a good scrubbing. Joss recorded a voice memo on her cell phone and continued snapping pictures.

Meaghan strolled to the grass and spun around to view the wall that Misty wanted painted. "Courtney, Joss, c'mere. Yipes!"

We joined her.

Lush green vines were growing up the corners of the house and over the eaves of the sunroom.

"The jasmine is pretty," Joss said.

"Yes, but, um, the wall is much larger than I imagined," Meaghan whispered.

"You don't have to paint the sunroom," I said, "and the kitchen window takes up a lot of space, too, so it's about the equivalent of one wall."

"The paint's chipped, but I suppose I can work around that." Meaghan held up both hands, thumbs crossed, and peered through the V-shape to envision her idea. "I'll need help. Is it okay if I ask Mom to assist me?"

"No problem. It's going to look amazing," I assured her.

"Yoo-hoo, look who's here." Misty pushed through the screen door carrying a tray set with a pitcher of iced tea; tall, etched glasses filled with ice; a sugar bowl; and long-handled spoons. She'd draped a kitchen towel over one arm.

Yvanna Acebo, clad in her Sweet Treats pink apron over her white uniform dress, trailed her. She had jumped at the chance to provide desserts for the party. "Hello, everyone. I've got goodies to taste." She hoisted a wicker picnic basket.

"By the way, Misty," I said, "I've secured Brady Cash and the Hideaway Café to do the catering."

"I love the food at Hideaway. Excellent choice. Now, Yvanna, let's set up on the patio table." Misty placed the tray on a chair, wiped the table with the towel, and moved the tray to the center. "Sit, everyone."

Yvanna removed plastic to-go boxes from her basket. "I have fairy cookies, an apricot-preserves tea cake, and chocolate-cinnamon snails."

"Snails?" I asked.

Yvanna giggled. "I've heard fairies love snails, and I'm thinking I'll include strawberries dipped in white chocolate to look like toadstools."

"I love it." Misty helped herself to a fairy cookie decorated with colorful sprinkles and hummed her approval. "Yum. They're so light. Did you use almond extract, Yvanna?"

"I did . . . and cream of tartar," Yvanna said. "Courtney's nana's secret ingredient."

I'd shared the recipe with her knowing the cookies would be a perfect addition to our teas.

"Meaghan"—Misty pointed with half a cookie—"I heard you say through the kitchen window that the exterior paint is peeling. I'll have someone sand that down tomorrow morning, first thing. I've had a never-ending to-do list since I moved. The place needs a major face-lift. I bought it based on location, location, location."

The word *face-lift* made me think of Farrah and her mishap at the spa. "Misty, how was Farrah after you went for cosmos?"

"Much better. Laughing about the whole thing, actually. She's already meeting with the microblader." Misty polished off her cookie and added a teaspoon of sugar to her iced tea. She stirred it with a long spoon. "A few mini tattoos and she'll be right as rain."

"Great. Hey, did I tell you? I met the woman who bought your 17-Mile Drive home. Violet Vickers."

Misty lost hold of the spoon. It clattered to the table. "Sheesh. What a dolt I am." She mopped up the splatter with a napkin. "So you met Violet. Isn't she *lovely*?"

I tittered.

Meaghan threw me a questioning look. "Are you making fun of Violet? She's a client of mine."

"No, no." I made a *pfft* sound. "It's just that Violet says *lovely* a lot."

"A lot," Misty echoed.

We taste tested the remainder of Yvanna's goodies. Then Yvanna provided Misty with a menu of other possibilities, from which Misty selected three additional cookies and lavender scones.

When Yvanna left, I rose to my feet. "Joss, after I help Misty with these dishes, let's have a look-see at the yard for the games."

Misty fanned her hand. "My housekeeper will be here later on. She'll see to the dishes. You all focus on what you need to do." She set the glasses, used napkins, and spoons on the tray and carried the tray into the kitchen.

"Follow me," Joss said, traipsing to the leftmost cypress. "I was thinking we could stage the obstacle course along the crushed-rock path, putting the challenges at each corner—"

"*Psst,*" Fiona whispered from a branch. She was waving furiously. "Courtney!"

Misty was in the kitchen, her back to the yard. Meaghan was making a sketch at the patio table.

Joss nabbed my elbow and steered me toward the tree.

"What?" I peered up at Fiona.

"Do you see him?" she asked.

"Him?" I glanced around. No one was lurking in the yard. "Him, who?"

Out of nowhere, a drift of deep-green sparkling particles surrounded Fiona, and she laughed gaily. "Him!"

When the dust settled, a fairy appeared. A *he* fairy with wizened cheeks, messy, brown, silken hair, pointy ears, and green wings with long tendrils. He wore green leggings, and his short-cropped jacket barely covered his paunch. "Cedric Winterbottom," the fairy said with a distinctly British accent, and bowed with extreme grace. "At your service."

"No, he's not," Fiona said. "He's at Misty's service. He's her fairy. And I wasn't socializing, in case you were wondering," she said, defensively. "He appeared as I was resting."

"I must keep an eye out for intruders," Cedric said.

"Intruders?" Joss repeated.

I gawped at her. "Joss, you can see him? And hear him?"

Joss grinned from ear to ear. I was happy for her. Up until now, the only fairy she'd been able to see was Fiona. We weren't clear why. She'd traveled to Ireland. She'd kissed the Blarney Stone.

I refocused on Fiona and Cedric. "Which intruders?"

"Anyone who might harm my mistress," Cedric explained. "I have been by her side for more than thirty years." That would explain his mature look. "She is rather vulnerable, trusting everyone when she should trust no one."

"Can Misty . . ." I hesitated.

"Can she see me? No, alas." Cedric frowned. "When she was young, we chatted and played for hours on end, but when she turned twelve, she forsook me. Fairies were for children, not budding teens, she said. Ever since that time, I have tried with all my might to make myself known to her, but it is not to be. No matter." He waved a hand. "I am hers forevermore. When the queen fairy gives the word, we fairies must comply."

I glanced at Fiona. Was she mine forevermore? If that was true, why hadn't Aurora, the first fairy I'd ever seen, remained in my life? Perhaps she had been my mother's fairy. I'd never considered that.

"How have you communicated with Misty—your mistress—since then?" I studied his face. Thirty-plus years was a long time to stay with anyone if there wasn't some way to connect.

"I sing lullabies to her while she sleeps."

Fiona enjoyed singing to me, too.

"Cedric is a nurturer fairy," Fiona said. A nurturer fairy could ease hearts and minds. "Like Zephyr," she added.

Zephyr was Tish Waterman's fairy. Not everyone in

Carmel had a fairy, but there were a number who did. Not everyone could see their fairy, either, Misty being a prime example.

"Tell Courtney the rest, Cedric," Fiona said.

Apparently, Cedric had confided a lot to Fiona during the time that we'd been tasting Yvanna's treats.

"I am concerned about my mistress's housekeeper."

I said, "Why?"

"I believe she might have light fingers."

"Why would you say that?"

"Things have gone missing. My mistress has not said a word, so she might not have noticed, but how could she not?" Cedric threw his arms wide, the tendrils of his wings flicking with the force. He jammed his fists on his hips. "What am I to do?"

"Tell me about the housekeeper," I suggested.

"She's a bitty thing, not much bigger than her." He pointed at Joss, who was barely five feet tall. "It's not like she could run off with any of the larger antiques in her arms, but my mistress has many collectibles."

Fiona said, "Courtney, maybe you could talk to Misty about this."

I wondered momentarily whether the housekeeper might be the town thief but pushed the notion from my mind. It was wrong to judge someone before meeting them. "Hasn't the housekeeper been with Misty for years?"

Cedric shook his head forcefully. "No. She's new. The previous housekeeper wanted to stay on at the estate."

"I'll do what I can."

"Bless you." Cedric spiraled into the air and zoomed into the cypress tree. Gone in the blink of an eye.

"Well, he was something else," Joss said.

I glanced at the kitchen. Misty wasn't visible.

Seconds later, she pushed through the screen door. "More visitors," she announced, striding to the patio table and laying out a white tablecloth. "Nova, this way."

Nova Pasha, in a long-sleeved black midi dress and black glove boots, followed Misty. So much for only wearing white. Over her shoulder she carried her rhinestone-studded tote bag.

"Nova has brought jewelry to show us," Misty said. "Gather round."

Nova unpacked her tote and unfurled the jewelry holder. She displayed an array of silver-and-blue and silver-and-red brooches. One featured a fairy holding a flower. Another, a butterfly with a ladybug passenger. A third, a spray of purple flowers being visited by a bee. Each was embellished with exactly the right amount of glitz or bling.

"They're beautiful," I said. "I'm partial to the butterfly."

Joss picked one up and *ooh*ed. Meaghan did the same.

"You're really talented," I said.

Nova's reticent demeanor blossomed with the praise. "Thank you."

Fiona sailed to my shoulder and whispered, "Ask her about yesterday. Ask her if she's okay."

I didn't have a clue how to raise the subject.

Impatient with my hesitancy, Fiona hovered above Nova and wiggled her fingers. Silver dust appeared. I didn't know if her wings created it or her fingertips. It was magical and awesome. The dust landed on Nova's hair and vanished.

"I'm sorry for running out yesterday," Nova said. "You probably think I'm rude, but I had an appointment I had forgotten about."

It sounded like a fib, but I didn't press. Fiona wasn't allowed to douse anyone with a truth potion, but she could help them find calm, confidence, and inspiration.

"I heard about your adventure at the spa, though," Nova continued. "Odine phoned me."

Misty snorted. "I'm sure she gave you an earful."

"Farrah." Nova clicked her tongue. "What was she thinking? She can be so—" She covered her mouth with one hand.

Fiona elbowed me. "Tell her to go on."

"We're all friends here," I said to Nova. "Farrah can be what?"

"Critical."

Misty gave Nova a squeeze. "And you, my friend, can be overly sensitive."

Nova threw Misty a blistering look. "She hated that bracelet I made for her, Misty. You know she did. She panned it all over social media."

Meaghan gasped. "She didn't."

Nova bobbed her head. "I lost ten sales because of her rant. She said my jewelry was amateurish. But it wasn't. It was—"

"Striking, mysterious, glamorous." Misty painted the air with her hand. "Farrah didn't get it. She likes sleek chic, you know what I mean? And didn't you tell me three other actresses in Los Angeles ordered nearly the same bracelet?"

"I said *almost* ordered," Nova replied. "They passed on them."

Misty snapped her fingers. "Hey, maybe you should make the same kind of bracelet for the party favors. Wouldn't that fluff Farrah's feathers?"

Nova grumbled under her breath.

Misty chortled. "You said you wanted to do the jewelry to impress her."

"Not true," Nova said with a bite. "I'm only doing the favors because the party is for Odine. If Farrah requested them, I wouldn't—"

"I think someone needs a glass of wine," Misty said. "Any other takers?"

"I can't," Nova murmured. "I—"

Misty put a finger to her friend's lips. "Courtney, Joss, Meaghan?"

I shook my head. "I have a lot to tackle at the shop."

Joss and Meaghan both passed, too.

"This way, girlfriend." Misty curled her hand around Nova's elbow and ushered her away.

Walking toward the sunroom, Nova muttered, "Farrah. I still can't believe you think she'll help you get that role in the movie."

"She said she would."

"Has she yet? No, she has not. She never will. Why are you still friends with her?"

"It's not that big a deal." Misty glanced over her shoulder at me.

I pretended not to be listening.

"That's not what you said last week," Nova said, opening the screen door and stepping into the house.

Misty let the screen door close with a *clack*.

Seeing them in the kitchen chatting by the sink, I had an idea. "*Psst*, Fiona." I beckoned her with a finger. She was tip-toeing around the jewelry on the table, studiously eyeing each piece. "Would you tell Cedric that his mistress seems a bit stressed? Maybe he could give her a nurturing potion."

She saluted. "On it." She zoomed to the cypress.

Within moments, a flurry of sparkling green particles materialized. Cedric emerged from them and whooshed into the house.

"Does he always make such an entrance?" I asked Fiona.

"I believe he does. He comes from a very dramatic line of fairies."

How did she know so much about him this soon? I stored the question for another time.

Moments later, Nova strode to the patio, retrieved her brooches and tote, bid us a nearly inaudible farewell, and left.

"Courtney, my friend and current employer," Meaghan said, "I've got what I need. I'll be back here tomorrow at nine sharp."

"Charge anything you need on my credit line at the hardware store."

"You can bet on it." She bussed my cheek and exited through the house. "Bye, Misty! See you soon."

Joss checked her watch and said she needed to get back to the shop. I reminded her to order the balloons and other items we might need for the party games and told her I'd return shortly.

Moments after Joss left, Misty sauntered from the house, stopped on the top step, and rubbed her shoulder with the opposite hand. "Perhaps ten days wasn't enough time to coordinate all of this."

"If we don't make it, Farrah won't be able to attend." *Not that Nova will be upset about that,* I mused.

"True. We want everyone here. Our other sorority sisters are so excited to see her."

I drew near. "Hey, I didn't mean to listen in on your conversation with Nova, but it sounded like you're hoping to become an actress."

"Become?"

"Not become. You have acted. But I mean as a professional. Is that true?"

"One can dream." She glanced upward wistfully. "There are only so many luncheons and benefits someone with my name and stature can do before one gets bored out of her gourd."

"And Farrah said she'd help you?"

Misty pursed her lips. "Why shouldn't she? After all, I was the one who introduced her to Berto Bagnoli."

"Nova didn't seem to think—"

"Nova." A long stream of air seeped through Misty's lips.

"Nova has issues. She wants to be loved by everybody. Why? Because she's had her heart broken by more men than I care to count. Have you ever had your heart broken?"

"Once."

"Then you know it hurts. When someone like Farrah poops on Nova's parade, she takes it personally. She'll get over it."

"Back to you and the acting . . ."

"In college, I had aspirations of becoming an actress."

"I thought you said you'd wanted to become a doctor and then a cruise ship owner."

Misty sighed. "Yes, well, all my goals were pipe dreams. My parents had other ideas for my future, which is why I settled for an MBA. I'm confident you understand my reasoning, having read the article about you leaving your father's business. Now that my folks have passed on, rest their souls"—she placed a hand over her heart—"perhaps it's time for me to do something that I truly want to do. Even if I am too old at forty."

"You don't look a day over twenty-nine."

"Bless you."

I clutched her upper arm. "I hope whatever you choose to do makes you happy."

"That's the intent." Her winning smile was mixed with a sly glint.

Chapter 6

Fairies, awake!
Light on the hills!
Blossom and grass
Tremble with dew.
—William Allingham, Songs from "Prince Brightkin"

The moment we returned to the shop, Fiona claimed she was exhausted and disappeared. If only I could do the same, but a shop owner's work is never done.

The remainder of the afternoon zipped by, with Joss and me both working furiously on pre-party planning without falling behind on our regular chores. Pixie, the slugabed, left us alone, preferring to snooze in the rays of sunshine filtering through the patio's pyramid-shaped roof.

Around three, we had a walk-in private lesson. The man, fastidious and in his forties, wanted to make a fairy garden for his grandmother, who was in a nursing home. He spent an hour picking out the figurines, flowers, and the perfect pot before he was ready to sit at the craft table to put it together. As we worked side by side, I told him how sweet it was that he would take such a thoughtful gift to his grandmother. He shared that she had raised him and had kept him on the straight and narrow. He owed his life to her.

Within seconds of his departure, another walk-in lesson showed up. She was a slender blond woman in jogging clothes. Pulling on her pigtails, she explained that she wanted to make a garden lickety-split for her six-year-old daughter, an imp if there ever was one, she confided. In record speed, she picked two girl fairy figurines—one playing leapfrog with a huge green toad; the second dancing with her arms spread wide. Then she chose a swing set, red bicycle, three red-and-white toadstools, and a rustic bench. She allowed me to select the succulents, saying she didn't know much about *things like that*. Twenty-five minutes later, she walked out the front door with her purchase and a smug smile on her face.

At five, Fiona zipped through the French doors. She soared to me at the sales counter and landed on my shoulder.

"Did you have a good nap?" I asked.

"I couldn't sleep, so I went to do some research with Merryweather."

"About?"

"The fairy doors that have been cropping up all over Carmel."

I tilted my head.

"Haven't you seen them?" she asked breathlessly.

"You can show me after work."

"Can we leave now? Before it gets too dark?"

I consulted with Joss, who had no problem holding down the fort by herself. She had no plans for the evening. Buttoning my cardigan, I grabbed Pixie and off we went. The sun was at its lowest point, but it wasn't pitch black yet. The flashlight on my cell phone would provide extra illumination if necessary.

Fiona hightailed it to Ocean Avenue and veered left, motioning with an arm, her wings flapping double-time to make haste. "There's one," she said, pointing to a coast redwood.

A fairy door, for the uninitiated, is a miniature door, usually set at the base of a tree, behind which might be a small space where people left notes or wishes for fairies. Fairy doors could also be installed into a fairy garden pot. We had numerous choices at the shop, but some of the best I'd ever seen were made by do-it-yourselfers using Popsicle sticks, slats of wood, bamboo, and more.

I bent beside the redwood and inspected the arched resin door, which was painted light green with dark green branches weaving across it. "Artistic," I said.

"Next . . ." She cruised ahead and hovered beside a Monterey pine.

The door at the base resembled the front of a cottage carved into a hill—*Lord of the Rings* hobbit-style, to be succinct—with a round entry, etched-glass windows, and an octagonal lamp.

"Charming," I said.

"There are more."

She guided me from street to street, pointing out the various sightings. She'd dubbed one the butterfly door because butterflies and flowers decorated its arch.

"I think someone wants to travel to the fairy realm," Fiona stated. "Which is not allowed without an invitation."

"Really?" I asked. "Says who?"

"Says the queen fairy."

"That goes against all fairy tales I've ever read. Fairies use the doors all the time to enter the real world."

"Yes, but not the other way around. Merryweather is extremely concerned."

I fanned the air. "I think these are harmless. They're probably a parent and child sharing a love of crafting."

Turning down 8th Avenue, I drew to a stop.

Fiona said, "What's wrong?"

I hitched my chin. Austin and Farrah were strolling arm in arm. *Are they getting serious?* I wondered.

"Ooh," Fiona crooned. "Austin lo-oves Farrah."

"Stop. It's not our business."

Austin steered Farrah to the right at Lincoln, and the two of them disappeared.

When we pushed through the gate at Dream-by-the-Sea, I realized I was starving. Beyond starving. All I'd eaten was a modest breakfast and the sweet treats Yvanna had brought to Misty's. "Must eat," I whispered.

Before I could put the key in the doorknob, however, my sixty-something neighbor and landlord called to me from the white picket fence separating our yards. "Courtney, I did it!"

"Did what, Mrs. Hopewell?"

"Dear, it's not missus."

"I meant to say, Holly."

"No, I mean, I'm not a missus. Hopewell is my maiden name. How else did you think I could have two sisters with the same last name? We certainly didn't marry three brothers from the same family." She chortled.

I reddened. "But I've always called you Mrs. Hopewell."

"Because that's how your mother introduced me. I didn't correct her. Or you." She clasped my arm and had a good laugh. "It's neither here nor there. You call me Holly now."

"And your sister, Hattie?"

"Also uses her maiden name. She can't stand her ex-husband. And Hedda, as you know, hasn't ever married."

"Got it."

"Now let me tell you what I did. I came up with a name for my cottage." She primped her curly, gray-streaked brown hair and pushed up the sleeves of her graphic sweatshirt. "What do you think of Black Cat Cottage?"

On cue, Holly's black cat leaped to the top of the fence and roamed from one end to the other and back to Holly.

"I've always owned black cats," she stated. "With names like Inky, Ebony, and Shadow." She swooped her cat into her arms. "Phantom is my favorite, of course."

So that was its name. I'd never heard her say it aloud. She had two adorable Pomeranians, as well, which had to be inside her house, or I'd have heard them yapping.

"Black Cat Cottage. I like it," I said, though it didn't exactly suit her white gem of a house, with its peaked roofs and dormer windows.

"My grandson came up with it while we were playing video games."

I bit back a smile. Holly was averse to the computer and the internet, yet she didn't mind playing video games and texting with her grandson. It was what kept her so young. That, and her art. She was a fabulous artist. She'd taught my mother how to paint.

"I have to tell you, dear, my garden is coming along, thanks to you. It's probably time for me to try my hand at making a large fairy garden, don't you think? I mean, I've made a teacup one and some modest-sized ones." She'd become hooked after learning how to prune a bonsai. "But a large one for the backyard would be nice, to go with the one you gave me." I'd made her a thank-you fairy garden that was a play on Monet's famous water lilies paintings. She worshipped Monet.

"That's a great idea."

"It should have the same palette as my now-tamed yard."

When I'd first moved in, not only was my garden overrun, but Holly's was as well. She had an artist's eye but not a green thumb. After putting my yard in order, I'd offered to help her with hers. She'd soaked up the information about the steady climate of the area and what grew in sandy soil, and now her garden sparkled with eye-catching lilac dahlias, lush lavender, brilliant purple swords of Madeira, and white roses.

Phantom wriggled in her arms. She set him down. "I'm also considering putting a fairy door at the base of the cypress. What do you think?"

Fiona whooshed to me. "Ask her what you're thinking."

"What do you think I'm thinking?" I whispered.

"You're wondering if she and her grandson put the doors around town."

Sometimes Fiona's extrasensory ability astonished me. She swore she never intruded in my thoughts but claimed she could pick up things because I mulled things over loudly. How one *mulled loudly*, I wasn't exactly sure.

"Say, Holly, are you the one putting fairy doors around town?"

"No. Are there really a few? I'd love to see them."

I told her where we'd seen a couple, and she promised to keep a lookout for others.

Walking into the house, I continued to question who had set doors around town and why. It had to be one person, right? No, not necessarily. A Girl Scout troop could have decided its members could fulfill a merit badge requirement by crafting them.

While I was preparing stir-fried vegetables and salmon—I really was hungry—my cell phone rang. *Brady.* I answered, tucking the phone between my ear and shoulder. I didn't want my dinner to burn or overcook. "Hi," I said. "Busy at the café?"

"Not too. Tell me about the fairy party. Misty Dawn will be the talk of the town."

"Get out of here." I laughed. "Could you meet tomorrow afternoon at the shop to go over a menu?"

"I'll make the time. I don't have to serve fairy-sized portions, do I?"

"Now you're joshing me." I switched off the gas burner and moved the skillet to one side. "We want human food for real humans, but with a fanciful twist."

"Fanciful." He hummed. I imagined him scratching his chin as he often did when thinking. "This could keep me up all night."

"Have a shot of brandy before bed," I suggested.

"Ah, a woman after my own heart." He blew me a kiss and hung up.

Fiona fluttered in front of my face. "You like him."

I flapped a hand. "What do you want to eat?"

"Mallow," she said matter-of-factly. "Crisp, raw mallow."

"I happen to have some." I went to the garden, plucked some seeds off a mallow plant, returned to the kitchen, and rinsed them thoroughly.

Fiona nestled on the rim of the plate I'd set for her and nibbled. Next, I prepared a bowl of tuna for Pixie, who always waited patiently for Fiona to be fed first. When she approached her bowl, I plated my food and set it on the kitchen table. While I ate, I hunkered down with a field guide about ferns.

An hour later, as I was unpacking the fairy figurines for Violet Vickers's fairy garden in my backyard greenhouse, my cell phone jangled. I scanned the readout and didn't recognize the number. Even so, I answered. "Courtney Kelly."

"Hey, babe," a familiar voice said. Christopher Cox. My ex-fiancé.

My whole being quavered. I'd erased his contact info from

my digital address book. Apparently, he hadn't erased mine. In the past, the tenor of his voice had warmed me to my toes. No longer. "What do you want?"

"Is that any way to greet an old friend?"

"Chris, I'm busy. Can you get to the point?"

"I'm in town with my family. My wife has never visited here. I thought I'd show her the sights, and I was hoping you and she and I could have dinner Sunday. I'd love for you to meet her. I've arranged for the children to go to a kids' camp at the hotel."

My jaw dropped. I couldn't in my wildest dreams have imagined this request. Socialize with him? After all these years? After all the hurt? "Uh . . ."

"Say yes. Please. If you're seeing someone, let's double-date."

"Uh . . ." I repeated dully.

"My treat. I owe you that much."

Yeah, you do.

"Aubergine," he suggested, a well-known upscale restaurant in the famous L'Auberge hotel. "You used to love going there."

"No," I replied quickly. I did not want to take a walk down memory lane. Aubergine was where he'd proposed. However, if he was willing to foot the bill for such a pricey place, I suggested another restaurant on par with Aubergine. "How about Saison? It's fairly new, but people rave about it. On Dolores. It's casual but elegant and has a great fish menu."

"Done. Seven thirty. See you then. Looking forward to it."

I wasn't.

Saturday was typically one of our busiest days. I hadn't determined why. Possibly because tourists had the weekends off from their jobs, or it was the fact that we hosted specialty teas on the patio. Either way, I appreciated the extra business.

Throughout the morning, Joss and I kept busy ringing up purchases, wrapping them in tissue, and setting them into our pretty white bags. Other than fairy figurines, the most popular item seemed to be wind chimes. We sold out of all but one set. Luckily, I'd put aside a half dozen for Misty's party.

Fiona might have had something to do with the uptick in sales. I saw her flitting from one chime to the next, dashing them with glittery dust while whispering in her fairy tongue, "*By dee shunned le lun mahaw.*" I figured she was bringing good luck to each of the wind chimes, thereby bestowing good luck on the purchaser, but I wanted to ask her later to translate. I understood a few of her words. *By dee* meant *May God* and *mahaw* meant *upon you.* Beyond that, I was stymied.

In the early afternoon, when it was time to prepare for the tea, I was relieved to have a moment to step onto the patio and catch my breath. I drank in the sunshine spilling through the tempered-glass roof. Pixie scurried to me and batted me with her tail.

I bent to scratch her under the chin. "Don't worry, little one," I assured her. "I'm fine. I just have a lot on my plate."

Luckily, today's tea would be simple, with no theme, only tasteful music and delicious goodies. Customers would be able to chat and enjoy themselves in our relaxing environment.

"I'm here," Meaghan warbled, as she wheeled her Celtic lever harp in its bag onto the patio. "I've added a new song to my repertoire, 'First Snow.'" She continued to the learning-the-craft corner at the far end of the patio. "Wait until you hear it. It's so beautiful. Callie suggested it."

Five months ago, Meaghan had become aware of the ethereal green fairy in her garden. Callie, or Caliope as she was more formally known, was the intuitive fairy that had helped Fiona and Tish Waterman's fairy locate Twyla after her escape from the cult.

"Terrific. Can't wait to hear it."

Yvanna appeared next. "Courtney, I've brought raspberry lemon zest scones and carrot Bundt cake. Also, I thought lemon sugar cubes might be nice for customers to add to their teas."

"That all sounds delicious."

"Did you try making the brookie recipe I gave you?" Meaghan's eyes twinkled with anticipation.

Yvanna fisted a hand on her hip. "If you'd have let me finish, I've also brought brookies."

"What's a brookie?" I asked.

"A brownie-cookie," Meaghan said. "I've been working on perfecting the recipe. Once I nailed it, I shared it with Yvanna." Meaghan adored making brownies. All her life, given her surname, Brownie, she'd been concocting recipes.

"Sounds incredible."

As Yvanna and her younger sister Yolanda, who looked like Yvanna with dark hair, caramel brown eyes, and an easy smile, started setting out teacups and tea caddies, women and men meandered to the patio. By the look of how many were entering with our gift bags, I figured our cash register was still going *cha-ching*.

And they weren't done shopping. Many continued to browse the figurines on the verdigris baker's racks. A few selected pots for their new gardens. I adored the smiles our merchandise brought to so many buyers' faces.

"Co-ourtney," my landlord's sister Hattie warbled in her throaty alto voice as she stepped onto the patio, her red hair a new shade of red—almost auburn—her rustic outfit like something out of an L.L. Bean catalogue. She was on the arm of Cliff Gill, Glinda's uncle and owner of Carmel Collectibles.

"The Happy Diggers would like another group lesson." The Happy Diggers was a gardening group chaired by Hattie. Thanks to her, they were regulars at Open Your Imagination. "Do you think we could arrange that?"

"Sure," I said. "Joss has the schedule inside. I'll always make time for you." How I appreciated repeat customers.

Right behind Hattie came Hedda, her younger sister. With her was the handsome sixty-something owner of Batcheller Galleries, Jeremy Batcheller, and his elegant Dalmatian. Hedda and Jeremy had started dating a month ago. They'd met when she and I had been enjoying lunch at Devendorf Park.

Hedda clutched my elbow. "We have to get together soon. It's been too long."

"It has."

Hedda, a loan officer at Carmel Bank, was much more conservative than both of her sisters, even though she was younger than Holly by a dozen years and Hattie by fourteen. She preferred understated clothing, like the herringbone jacket and navy slacks she was wearing. Yet she wasn't too buttoned-down. She adored flashy eyewear, and she had the heart of a philosopher.

She twirled a finger in front of my eyes. "I can see there's a lot going on in that brain of yours. Have you taken my advice?"

Not long ago, she'd urged me to find inner peace. I was pretty certain I was close, but not all my dreams had been realized yet. "I'm meditating," I said.

"That's a start."

Brady appeared in the arch of the French doors and waved. "Should I wait in your office?"

I held up a finger, signaling *Just a sec,* and strode to a spot near Meaghan, where I announced to the crowd to have a good time relaxing on such a beautiful winter's day. When Meaghan began to play, Yvanna and her sister wheeled a double-shelved cart down the ramp to start tea service.

I caught up to Brady and said to Joss, "We'll be in the office."

Brady followed me down the hall. "You look good. I like you in purple."

I'd thrown on a purple sweater with a scalloped collar and a pair of black capris. I liked to look somewhat nice at our teas. No jeans or bib overalls.

"You look nice, too."

Brady was handsome and tan and, like his mother, had an engaging dimple in his right cheek. A hank of hair often fell rakishly on his forehead. We'd been dating—if one could call it that—for the past two months. We were taking it slowly. He, because he'd gone through a messy divorce. Me, because of the way Christopher had dumped me the day after our engagement party.

I motioned for him to sit in the Queen Anne armchair, and I settled into the chair behind the desk. Fiona whirled in behind us and alit on the rim of the Zen garden. Pixie loped in next and pounced into Brady's lap.

"Well, hello," he said warmly, tickling her under the chin. "Didn't you like the music on the patio?" She purred loudly enough that even I could hear.

"Pixie much prefers individual attention," I said. "So . . ." I picked up a pen and pulled a sheet of paper off the pad on the blotter. "Menu."

"First, what kind of events are you planning for this party?"

I told him Joss's and my ideas. "The fairy wish station will be a lot of fun. We'll give each guest a teensy jar of magic dust. They have to close their eyes and make a wish. When they open their eyes, they turn three times and then open the jar of magic dust and throw it—the wish—into the air so fairies can grant it."

"Real fairies?" He wasn't making fun of me, like my father would. He wanted to believe.

Fiona floated to him and paused in front of his face. He didn't blink. She frowned and returned to the Zen garden. "Stubborn," she muttered.

"Real fairies," I replied. "But wishes don't always come true instantaneously. Some might take years."

"Uh-huh." He grinned. "Will it only be women in attendance?"

"Sorority sisters. Twelve of them. One is Farrah Lawson."

He whistled. "Wow. A celebrity. Her career has been on the rise for a number of years. I wonder if she knows—" He shook his head. "Probably not."

Brady's ex had left him for a wealthy older actor in Los Angeles whose most recent screen performance, much to Brady's delight, had been a bomb.

"I would imagine she socializes with a younger set," I said.

"You're probably right." He clapped his hands once. "Okay, back to the menu. I was thinking fairy wands made of fruit and devilled eggs made to look like bumble bees."

I screwed up my mouth. "Get real. What do you really want to serve?"

"Well, I read online that fairies like savory foods and small portions, so I was thinking appetizers. Avocado and bacon on toast with a spicy green onion salsa, tahini chicken wings, artichoke hearts with lemon-butter dip . . ."

My mouth started to water. "Go on."

"Stuffed potato skins, buffalo cauliflower poppers, and shrimp salad bites."

"I'm all in. This sounds great." I'd eaten at Brady's restaurant often enough to know I could trust him to put together an amazing array. "And you're right. Sitting down to a hefty meal won't suit these women. They'll want to roam and chat."

"I'll send you a printed menu later this afternoon." He rose to leave.

I saw him to the door.

He paused, gazing at me with those delicious eyes. "Hey, I've been seeing fairy doors all around town."

"Me, too. Fiona showed me—" I winced and pressed my lips together.

"Don't worry about saying your fairy's name. I may not be able to see her, but I believe she exists." He placed a warm hand on my arm. A shiver of desire coursed through me. "What did she show you?"

"A few fairy doors. Two on Ocean Avenue and another around the corner. She's concerned. She wants me to figure out who's putting them around."

"Is it a bad omen to see them?" His forehead creased.

"I don't have a clue." I glanced at Fiona. She raised both hands in a *Who knows?* gesture.

"I've got an idea." Brady brushed a stray hair off my face. "Why don't we take photographs of them on your day off? Maybe we can figure out the mystery together."

I would never forget our many photography club outings. We'd bonded while talking shop and honing our craft.

"Sounds like a great idea if I can find the time. With the fairy party coming up . . ."

"Let me know." He kissed me gently on the mouth. We hadn't gone further yet. He hadn't pressed.

"Brady," I said, my heart pounding in my chest. "I . . ." I hesitated.

"You're nervous about something. I see it in your face. Talk to me."

"Christopher is in town with his wife. He wants to have dinner. Would you . . ." I lowered my eyes.

"Be your date?" He tilted my chin upward with his fingertip. "I'd be honored." He leaned in for another kiss, but something went *bang*.

The door to the shop. I jolted. So did Brady.

"Fiona!" a youthful female cried. Not a human voice. A fairy's. A second later, Zephyr, a gorgeous fairy with lavender eyes, lavender wings, and silver hair, came into view. "It's horrible. Farrah Lawson is dead!"

Chapter 7

*How to tell if a fairy is nearby: you might be
followed by a crow or raven.*
—Anonymous

I gripped Brady's elbow to keep him from leaving my office.

"What's wrong?" he asked. Clearly, he hadn't heard Zephyr.

"Farrah Lawson is dead."

"How do you—" He swiveled his head, looking for a fairy. "Is she . . . Did Fiona . . ."

"Her friend is here." I focused on Zephyr. "What happened?"

She threw her arms wide. "She was poisoned."

Fiona covered her mouth with a hand.

"Poisoned?" I repeated. "Are you positive?"

"Yes," Zephyr replied. "At the place she was renting. The police think it happened last night."

"The police?" I squawked. "How did they find out? I mean—"

"The housekeeper found her. The door was open. She entered and . . ."

I moaned.

"What?" Brady asked. "Tell me."

I recapped.

"Wait!" Zephyr held up a hand. "There's more. Twyla was seen in the vicinity. You know how angry Farrah was that Twyla messed up her eyebrows. She warned Twyla to watch her back. The police think Twyla might have—"

"Twyla? They think she killed her? No way."

"Tish is beside herself." Wings flapping steadily, Zephyr wrapped her arms around her slender body, her unease palpable. "She's at the spa. Could you . . . Would you . . . comfort her? My magic isn't working on her right now. She needs a human."

I pecked Brady on the cheek and said, "I've got to help Tish. At her spa. Her daughter—" I didn't finish. "I'll call you later and fill you in." I jogged-walked through the shop, saying to Joss as I passed, "I'm heading to A Peaceful Solution. Brady will tell you the rest."

Minutes later, I pressed through the door to the spa. The reception area was empty, but I heard voices down the hall. Detective Summers's voice was distinctive. With no one to stop my progress, I hurried to Tish's office and strode inside. Like the rest of the establishment, the spa's office was decorated in resort chic. Twyla, her face tearstained, was standing with her back pressed against the gray wall, her gaze fixed on the floor. Tish, who was sitting at her teak desk, glanced at me, chin quivering.

"Courtney, thank you for coming," Tish said, choking back tears.

Summers whipped around. Officer Redcliff Reddick, a

lanky redheaded man who was a good six inches taller than Summers, turned and took me in, too.

I said, "You can't possibly think Twyla, who wouldn't hurt a fly, had something to do with Farrah Lawson's death."

"Miss Kelly," Summers said dismissively, "you may leave."

"No, please stay!" Tish exclaimed. "I mean, please, Detective, would you please allow her to stay?"

Had Tish contacted a lawyer to represent Twyla yet? Did she need to?

Fiona and Zephyr winged into the office and settled on the file cabinet to the right of the desk. Zephyr fidgeted. Fiona clasped her friend's hand to calm her. Seeing as she was there in the capacity of righteous fairy, I didn't think the queen fairy would regard Fiona's presence a sociable visit.

Summers tamped down his annoyance. "As I was saying, Mrs. Waterman—"

"The housekeeper found the body," I said.

"How did you—" Summers cut me a harsh look.

"Yes, the housekeeper," Tish confirmed.

"And Farrah was poisoned?" I asked.

Summers's nostrils flared. "Hold on. How did you hear about the murder? How did you know Officer Reddick and I were here? We just arrived." He narrowed his gaze.

"The barista at Percolate clued me in. She knows Tish and I are friends." A white lie was harmless. Percolate, a coffeehouse I frequented, was next door. "The walls between the spa and the café are thin," I explained. "So was Farrah poisoned?"

"We aren't sure," Reddick answered. "The coroner is at the crime scene with the techs."

"What's your first instinct?"

"The coroner believes—"

"Officer!" Summers warned.

"Sir, Miss Kelly has helped us solve two murders. Don't you think—"

"Yes, I do think. In fact, I do all the thinking around here, got it? Zip it."

"But, sir"—Reddick splayed his hands—"she's bound to find out. You know how she is."

"Yeah, I know." Summers growled under his breath. "Miss Kelly, please leave."

"I'm staying to support Mrs. Waterman and her daughter." I squared my shoulders. If my father couldn't cow me, then neither could Summers. "Tish, would you like me to stay?"

"Yes."

Summers cleared his throat and rotated his neck to remove the tension. "Fine. Move over there. To that chair. Sit. Don't say another word." He drilled his gaze into Twyla, who had been watching the two of us like a tennis match. She was clutching her hands together so tightly the blood had drained from them. "Now, Miss Waterman, you were seen walking in the vicinity of Miss Lawson's rental."

By whom? I wondered.

"I walk," she said, her voice breathy and tight.

"For how long?"

"An hour. Sometimes two. I leave around six thirty and get home before nine."

Summers eyed Tish. "Is this true?"

"Yes, sir. Being held captive in that cult did things to her. It's hard for her to settle down at night. She's worried that someone might snatch her or—"

"I understand." Summers drew his worn leather notebook from the pocket of his chinos, took off the rubber band that held it together, and slid the pen marred with teeth marks from its loop. "Do you walk the same route, Miss Waterman?"

"Sort of. I walk up 8th Avenue to Mission and turn right." Twyla signaled with her fingers. "And I go down 12th Avenue to Scenic Road." Scenic was the street nearest the ocean. "Then I weave around and head up 13th Avenue, where I take Mission again, and go back down 8th or 9th Avenue, and—"

"Got it."

"Sometimes I cut across Lincoln or Dolores and then go up or down."

"You just tour that section of town, 8th to 13th, Mission to the beach?"

"Yes."

Tish said, "She doesn't want to stray too far from home."

"Where's Farrah's Airbnb?" I asked.

"On Lincoln near 12th," Reddick said. "It's a stone cottage with lots of charm." His face reddened with mortification. "Not so charming now."

"I sat and stared at the ocean for a bit, around seven," Twyla said.

"Hold on," Summers cut in. "You said you stop at Scenic Road."

"Sometimes I cross it and go to the sand and sit and listen to the waves."

"Did anyone see you?"

"Not that I remember, sir, but I wasn't paying attention. I was . . ." She inhaled sharply and exhaled slowly, blowing the air through tight lips, as if trying to calm her heart. "I get hypnotized by the ebb and flow of the surf."

"Did you see anyone when you were walking, Miss Waterman?" Summers pressed.

"Sometimes I see a woman on Camino Real. She has really red hair and likes to water her plants at night."

"Did you see her last night?"

"She wasn't there." Twyla began gnawing on her index finger.

"Did you see anyone else?" Summers wrote another note in his notebook.

"There was a man walking his dog. A chocolate Lab. I'm not sure the man saw me. He was talking on his cell phone. He was wearing a baseball cap."

"Okay," Summers said. "Good. Anyone else?"

"Someone in a dark jacket with a hood, like a rain jacket, was bent by a tree on 13th near Lincoln. He was digging near the base."

"It was a he?" Summers asked. "Are you certain?"

"Well, no. The hood was up so I couldn't tell if it was a he or even whether he . . . she . . . was young or old."

I flashed on the thief in the brown hoodie. Of course, he or she might not have been the same person Twyla saw, but if a person wanted to remain anonymous, wearing something with a hood seemed the way to go.

"The tree was on the street by that storybook cottage with the red door," Twyla added.

"That would be Dolores near 13th," I said. "It's white with red framing around the windows and heart-shaped cutouts in the stucco. Like a Comstock, but not an original."

"You're an architecture maven now?" Summers chided.

"On occasion." I cherished knowing the history of Carmel. Hugh Comstock had arrived in Carmel a number of years after the town had incorporated in 1916. A farmer's son, he'd loved to draw and design. When he fell in love with Mayotta Brown, who made dolls, he stayed, they wed, and he designed the famous Hansel House, with its flared eaves and irregular chimneys—like nothing the town had seen before, as steeped in Spanish-Mediterranean architecture as it had been. "Detective," I said, "is it possible someone is framing Miss Waterman, setting her up to take the fall?"

Summers stared at me. "Why would you think that?"

"Because of the incident earlier in the day. Miss Lawson was very upset. Any number of customers at the spa could have heard her fly off the handle." I didn't want to believe any of Farrah's friends had killed her, but maybe there had been another customer with an axe to grind.

Summers considered my theory and rotated a hand. "Continue."

"If someone had it in for Miss Lawson and knew Twyla's routine, they could have plotted Miss Lawson's demise within that time frame."

Summers closed his notebook. "Miss Kelly, Farrah Lawson came into town for a birthday party. The only people who could have known she would be here were the hostess and guests for this party, and of course, Miss Waterman and her mother."

"And business associates," I added.

He scowled. "From what I understand, everyone adored Farrah Lawson. She was well loved in the movie industry. She didn't have enemies. Yesterday's outburst was one of the few times that she'd ever shown a dark underbelly of dissatisfaction."

I pressed my lips together. *A dark underbelly of dissatisfaction?* If I didn't know better, I'd guess the detective had read Eudora Cash's novels. "If it would help," I said, "I could give you a general timeline for Miss Lawson's whereabouts yesterday. Perhaps following her trail will steer you toward her real killer."

"Yes," Tish said under her breath. "Yes, tell him."

Summers folded his arms. "I'm all ears."

"In the morning, we all met here at the spa for what Farrah had dubbed a *spa day*—her treat. In actuality, we all received one session. It didn't go well for her, and—"

"Understatement," Reddick muttered, then snorted.

Summers lasered him with a dismissive look. Reddick swallowed hard.

"What I mean is," I continued, "she was upset at the end because she'd allowed Twyla to wax her eyebrows, but—"

"It was Twyla's first time!" Tish blurted in her daughter's defense. "Her first time on a *customer*," she revised. "She'd done many waxings on the staff without issue. But Farrah flinched, saying the wax was too hot."

"Mo-om," Twyla warned. "TMI."

I grasped the shorthand: *Too much information.*

"She warned Twyla to watch her back," Tish added, "but I promise you my daughter did not and would not retaliate."

Taking up where Tish left off, I said, "Misty Dawn—she's the person throwing the fairy party—offered to introduce Farrah to a microblader—"

"What's that?" Reddick asked.

"An aesthetician who tattoos eyebrows." I demonstrated with a fingertip. "But before Farrah agreed to that, Misty treated everyone to a cosmo at Carolina's. I"—I placed a hand on my chest—"abstained and went back to work, but I met up with Misty later, and she said Farrah was fine. Calm. Over it. She went to the microblader and her upset vanished. And then, on my way home last night, I saw Farrah walking with Austin Pinter down 8th. I'd seen them together Thursday night, as well."

"I know Mr. Pinter," Summers said. "I've heard him speak at the library."

Knock me over with a feather. Summers went to the library?

He attended lectures? *Stop, Courtney*. I chastised myself for judging him out of hand. It wasn't as if he was a cop 24-7. In fact, I'd discovered a few months ago that he sketched.

"Farrah and Austin were lovers years ago," I went on. "In college. Both nights they were walking arm in arm, all cozy, and it seemed to me that they had picked up where they'd left off, which was interesting, considering she has . . . *had* a boyfriend. He's an actor."

"Doing a film in Asia," Reddick added.

Summers arched an eyebrow. "How do you know that?"

"I read stuff online." Reddick pulled out a well-used leather notepad that resembled the one Summers used and made a note, probably to inform the boyfriend of Farrah's demise. "Actors date actors all the time. It's part of the business."

Acid crawled up my esophagus. Who would call Farrah's people? And her director and agent or manager, and her family, if she had any? The list was endless.

Summers lasered me with his gaze. "Miss Kelly, are you suggesting Mr. Pinter might have killed her?"

"No, sir. I'm not willing to throw anyone under the bus, but he might have been the last person to have seen her alive." *Other than the killer.*

"What time was this?"

"Around six fifteen," I said. Fiona and I had been looking for fairy doors for at least an hour.

Summers scribbled a memo and redirected his attention to Tish and Twyla. "Who else had appointments at the spa yesterday?"

"I could get you a list," Tish replied, eager to help.

"You know," I interrupted, "there might be others that Farrah knew in town. She's not from here, but bigwigs from Hollywood come to Carmel-by-the-Sea all the time. Producers, directors, actors."

"Bigwigs who would want her dead?" Summers scoffed. "Get real."

I hated when he dismissed me like my father would, but I quashed the urge to glower at him. It wouldn't win me brownie points.

When Fiona and I returned to the shop, Joss had already closed up. Pixie, who was nestled on the sales counter, scowled at me. "I did not forget you," I assured her, scooping her into my arms.

The moment I got home, I phoned Brady. I wanted to fill him in. Fiona, who had worried nonstop since we'd met with the police, flew to the kitchen to search for her meal. I couldn't douse her with silver fairy dust, and eating calmed her. Pixie, sensing my dismay, stayed by my side. Brady, the hostess informed me, was working the kitchen. A sous chef had called in sick, and he couldn't break free. I left a message to stop by the shop tomorrow and take some photos for my website, as he'd promised over a month ago, and I would fill him in.

Next I reached out to Misty.

She answered the phone sounding as if she'd been crying for hours. "Courtney," she sniffed.

"You heard."

"Yes. It's so sad." More sniffles. "Who would do this to her? She had her whole life ahead of her and a huge future in movies. I heard Twyla Waterman is a suspect."

"A person of interest," I corrected.

"Can you imagine? That mousy thing a killer? Have you spoken to the police?"

"I have."

"They left me a message. They want me to come to the precinct tomorrow to chat. I've been away at a board meeting all day." She blew her nose. "Meaghan and her mother were at the house today. I had the painter come over super early, as promised, to clean off the chipped paint. Meaghan got a real jump on the mural. It's looking wonderful."

"Misty . . ." I hesitated, my stomach wrenching with concern. "Are you positive you want the party for Odine to continue, given the circumstances?"

"Yes, of course," she said, her voice high-pitched and tense. "Farrah would want us to celebrate."

I wasn't so sure about that. Wouldn't she prefer her friends mourn her? "Will there be a funeral for her?"

"Geez, I haven't a clue."

I posed the questions I'd wondered at the spa. Who would call her director, her agent or manager, and her family?

"I suppose I should," she said. "It's my fault Farrah came to town. Odine insisted that she take part in the fun. O—" Her voice cracked. "Odine. I have to tell her what happened. And Nova, too. Yes," she said, her voice growing stronger. "It's up to me. As hostess. I'll call them. Oh, dear, and Austin and—"

"Odine might know already," I said. "I mentioned your name and hers to the police because we were at the spa when the to-do between Farrah and Twyla took place."

"Of course. That's how they knew to contact me."

"Also, I told them about seeing Austin around dusk, walking with Farrah."

"Austin? A killer? Not a chance. That man was besotted with her." Misty drew in a deep breath and exhaled. "But, Courtney, to your question, I'll contact her people, and yes, I still want to have the party. Don't you worry about a thing. I'll make certain we honor Farrah as she would want us to. *Ciao*."

"Yoo-hoo!" a woman called from my front door. "Your father and I are here. May we come in?"

I hurried to the foyer, cell phone in hand. Wanda

Brownie had pushed open the door. My father was a step behind her. Wanda kissed me on the cheek and handed me a bouquet of daisies and a bottle of Scheid pinot noir, my favorite.

"Kip?" She motioned to him.

My father gave me a decorative bag with a Say Cheese label on it. "We thought we might have cocktail hour and sit in your garden, if you have time."

"That sounds like a great idea."

"I love what you've done in front," Wanda said. She resembled Meaghan right down to her towering height and curly brown tresses, though she preferred more form-fitting clothing, like the tie-waist burgundy jumpsuit she was wearing. "All the wind chimes and such. So inviting."

I headed into the kitchen, saying, "Wanda, I heard you and Meaghan made a dent on the mural at Misty Dawn's house."

"We did. It'll be sublime. Who knew a mother and daughter could work in sync?"

I poured wine into three Baccarat goblets and plated the cheese and crackers on a Royal Doulton Pacific Splash–pattern china serving platter. "Manchego," I cooed. "My favorite."

Dad put his hand on my back. "I heard a rumor that you met with the police today."

"A rumor?" I asked. "Or did you speak with Dylan?"

"He might have touched base. To set up a round of golf."

"Uh-huh."

My father passed a glass of wine to Wanda and picked up the other two. They strode to the backyard. I followed, carrying the cheese platter.

Over his shoulder, he said, "Dylan worries about you."

"Liar," I said, and winked at him as I set the cheese platter on the wicker table. The temperature was mild, somewhere around sixty-five, and the heady scent of cypress and pine filled the air.

Wanda set cocktail napkins next to the platter and took a seat. "Why did you meet with the police, dear?"

I filled them both in.

"Oh, my," Wanda said, her voice quavering. She had been the subject of a murder inquiry a few months ago.

Fiona wafted to her and petted her hair. Sadly, Wanda was mindless of Fiona's presence. How she wanted to see a fairy. She was jealous that Meaghan could.

Pixie scampered down the walkway to the Amish-wagon fairy garden. She stood on her hind legs and propped her forepaws on one of the wagon's wheels. Fiona bolted to her and did loop the loops above the wagon.

"What's going on, girl?" I asked.

Pixie meowed.

Was Fiona scouting the garden for a fairy sighting? I hadn't seen additional fairies about.

"Probably a rodent," my father said.

"I don't have rats, Dad."

He downed a cheese and cracker and followed it with a sip of wine. "If you do, my suggestion is peppermint oil. Three drops of peppermint oil—"

"To one gallon of water," I said. "Put it in a sprayer and spray around the corners of everything. Yes, Dad, I used to work for you, remember? I know all your tips."

He chortled. "Yes, you do. If it's not rats . . ."

"It might be a fairy, Kip," Wanda said.

Dad hooted. "Not you, too!" He shook his head and focused on me. "So tell me about Twyla Waterman. What do the police have on her?"

"Not much. She was sighted in the area." I filled them in.

"I'm worried someone might be framing her, by knowing her routine as well as having heard about the fracas between her and Farrah."

"You should make a list of everyone in town who might have known Miss Lawson," Dad said. "Give that to the police. It's the best way you can help."

"I already have."

"Then steer clear."

"But, Dad—"

"No buts. Dylan's the detective, not you."

Fiona swooped in front of my father.

He must have felt the movement because he swatted the air and said, "For bees out here, you might want to consider planting bee balm, echinacea, and hostas."

"As if we could grow echinacea here," I teased. Coneflowers—echinacea was a purple variety—grew in prairies and open wooded areas in central and eastern America. "I did install hostas in the shade." I pointed. "And you'll note I've planted lots of blue, purple, and white flowers." Bees flocked to those colors. "I am definitely contributing to the pollination of bees. Even so, they do fly around where no flowers abound, as do fairies."

My father threw me a withering look. "That was no fairy that whizzed past me. It was a bee. Or a wasp."

Wanda tittered and excused herself to the ladies' room.

The moment she entered the house, my father leaned toward me. "I need suggestions for gifts. Wanda liked the plate I bought at Seize the Clay, but I'd like a grander gesture for, you know, Valentine's Day. Ideas? I'm new at this and nervous about buying the wrong thing."

"Jewelry is always good," I said. "But nothing too extravagant. A pretty bracelet or a brooch."

"A brooch." He mulled that over.

"Fantasy Awaits in the Doud Arcade has a good selection," I said. "I know an artist who sells her pieces there."

Thinking of Nova made me recall how upset she'd been that Farrah had panned the bracelet she'd made. Would a social media snub drive a person to commit murder?

Chapter 8

When she vanished through the orchard
Fairies airy, shy, and wary,
Peeped like mice at set of sun; stealthy, creeping one by one.
—Florence Harrison, "Pixy Work"

Sunday morning, I rose, took a run on the beach to drink in the sunshine and good vibes, then showered, dressed in loden-green capris and a long-sleeved floral T-shirt, and made a tasty breakfast of poached eggs with Hollandaise sauce. Nana, my father's mother, had taught me how to make the recipe. *It takes a delicate touch with sauces,* I recalled her saying. *One mustn't drench the eggs.* As I stirred the sauce, I tried to think of something Grandma Bea, my mother's mother, had taught me, but I couldn't come up with anything. After my mother's death, she and Pops couldn't look at me without crying, and my father had told them, in no uncertain terms, that if they couldn't find a smile around their only granddaughter, they shouldn't come over. Within weeks, they moved to Arizona. They'd come to my high school graduation, and they sent annual Christmas cards, but other than that, I didn't have much contact with them.

I pushed the sad memory aside and dished up my meal. While I ate, Fiona abandoned her plate of pomegranate seeds and marched on the table, one end to the other, her little feet making quite a *thump-thump*.

"What's got you upset?" I asked. She rarely marched. She'd been restless last night, flying to and fro instead of sleeping.

"I believe Twyla saw the fairy-door person."

"You mean the man or person in the hooded rain jacket that was digging at the base of a tree by the storybook house?"

"Yes."

I'd thought the same thing but hadn't mentioned it at the time.

"I visited the spot this morning and, indeed, there is a new door. Beneath a pine. It's handmade. Carved wood, but the edges are uneven. It's painted blue, like our front door, and the door swings open, but there wasn't a note behind it."

"You are quite the sleuth."

"*Ta,*" she said, meaning *thanks*, and then she reddened. Fairies were not good at accepting compliments. Pride was frowned upon. "I hung around a while longer thinking the creator might return, but he did not."

"We aren't certain it was a *he.* We'll have to be patient with this."

"*Gepyid,*" she whispered, "*befinde ēad.*"

"Translate," I requested.

"It takes patience to find happiness."

I reached for her. She hopped onto my hand. "Yes, it does. It also takes patience to find the truth."

"*Rīht,*" she said, then added, "which means truth."

"And figuring out who's placing fairy doors around is not high up on our list for learning the truth. Clearing Twyla of murder takes precedence."

She let out a stream of air that made her gossamer hair flutter.

"By the way," I said, "what did you say yesterday? In the shop. It sounded like *By dee shunned lun mahaw*."

"*By dee shunned le lun mahaw*," she said, stressing the additional *le*. "May God shine his light upon you."

"*Lun*. Light. That makes sense." I studied her face. "Were you blessing the wind chimes?"

"Yes."

"*Ta*," I said.

She curtsied. "*Wilcuma*. Translation: *You're welcome*. But back to Twyla. If she saw the man in the hood, maybe she could describe him."

"Don't you remember? She couldn't. She didn't even know if the person was a *he*." Discussing Twyla made me want to reach out to Tish. I rang her but hung up when I heard the bells chime at the congregational church across the street. Ever since Twyla's return, Tish had been devout about attending church. She wouldn't answer her phone during a service.

An hour later, I arrived at the shop ready to greet customers and solve puzzles. Pixie was more than happy to take a snooze on the patio. Fiona disappeared into the ficus, most likely to nap.

A class with five thirteen-year-olds was on the morning's schedule. Georgie Gill had booked it. Around ten, she and her girlfriends tramped in, in single file, each *ooh*ing and *aah*ing as she passed the rack of books and displays of china. One with red braids, who wasn't watching where she was going because she was looking upward as if searching for a fairy, bumped into a display of wind chimes. The melodious clatter startled her. Georgie and the others laughed.

"Hi, Courtney, we're here," Georgie said. As pretty as ever in a pink hoodie and leggings, she nearly skipped out to the patio, beckoning her friends to follow her.

I trailed them. "You know what to do, Georgie. Go to the learning-the-craft table and have everyone look for items for their gardens. Tell them about creating a conversation. You've made enough to know the spiel. Remember to choose some sand and pebbles to create a base for your figurines."

She gave me a thumbs-up and steered the others to the verdigris racks.

Fifteen minutes later, Georgie poked her head into the showroom. "We're ready when you are."

Joss, who was using a feather duster to spruce up the displays, whistled softly to me. "You know, with all the business we've had lately, we should consider hiring a part-time employee so you can focus on the parties and teas and private lessons. I was thinking a teen like Georgie might be a good fit. She could come in a couple of afternoons a week—"

"You mean when she's not practicing tennis or doing schoolwork?" I asked, with a smirk. "If I'm not mistaken, she has no free time other than Sunday morning. She is on the court at six a.m. and back out there the moment school is over, until six p.m. Plus she has a full practice schedule on Saturday. And she doesn't drive."

"You're right." Joss plucked a feather off her stylized-pineapples shirt. "How are you doing, by the way? You didn't see the body or the crime scene, but you did meet Farrah. You knew her, even if it was only for a short time."

"I'm okay, but I'm sad for her friends, and I'm worried about Twyla."

"Has she been arrested?"

"I can't imagine. Simply being seen in the neighborhood is not enough for police to convict. I wonder if they've searched her mother's house for poisons."

Joss's mouth fell open. "Farrah was poisoned? With what?"

"The police wouldn't reveal that. I don't even know if Farrah drank it or if the killer injected it."

"Poison." Joss shook her head. "No, no, no. Twyla definitely didn't do it. She wouldn't poison anybody. Not after her experience with the cult, where they force-fed her drugs to keep her in line."

"Exactly!" I smacked the sales counter. "The police have to expand their search, that's all there is to it."

"And you'll make certain they do."

"Me? Ha! Detective Summers would like me to take a long walk off a—"

"Co-ourtney!" Georgie crooned.

I smiled at Joss. "Yes, we need backup. Put together an ad for the perfect person. I'll approve it later. And I'll reach out to Tish to see how everything is going. At least the police are questioning Farrah's friends. Maybe they'll solve it that way."

As the teens fashioned their fairy gardens, Fiona appeared and glided above them, enjoying their energy. All had chosen eight-inch pots, at Georgie's suggestion, and they were talkative to the max. The one with red braids was madly in love with a boy in high school. The girl who was wearing way too much makeup said she was in love with the same boy.

Uh-oh.

The teen with multicolored braces, who was pouring blue sand on top of packed soil, splashed the two of them with a pinch of sand.

Fiona giggled and applauded.

Then Braces said that friendship was more important than boys any day. Georgie concurred.

"Hey, did you hear"—Red Braids brushed sand off her cheeks—"there was another shoplifting thing?"

Makeup Girl bobbed her head. "And it wasn't food this time. Whoever it was swiped a pair of hair clips from Birgitte's."

Georgie squealed. "No way! My aunt didn't tell me."

Glinda hadn't told me, either. Birgitte's was the high-end dress shop next to Glitz.

"When did this happen?" I asked.

"Last night. After the shop closed," Braces said. "I can't believe you didn't know, Georgie. But then, you were, like, sort of AWOL last night."

"Yeah," Red Braids said. "Where were you? We were supposed to hang out and get burgers."

"Um . . ." Georgie's cheeks tinged pink.

"Are those new hair clips you're wearing?" Braces pointed accusingly. "Are you the shoplifter? Girl, say it ain't so!"

"What? No!" Georgie caressed the barrettes in her hair. "I've had these since I was six. You've seen them before."

"No, I haven't," Braces said.

I gulped and glanced at Georgie's cute hoodie. Was she the thief, a theory I'd quickly dismissed the other day? Had her friends just blown a hole in whatever alibi she had prepared?

"I was . . ." Georgie picked up the boy fairy figurine she'd chosen for her garden, a mischievous imp holding a pea shooter in hand, and she blinked back tears. "I . . ."

"Spit it out," Braces said.

"I was with Nick."

"Nick!" Red Braids shrieked. "My Nick?"

"You mean *my* Nick?" Makeup Girl whined.

Braces jumped to her feet and pointed at all three. "You, you, and you, quiet. I'm excited to learn that Georgie is not a shoplifter. Aren't you? And if you think about it, if hunky old Nick is willing to date all three of you, don't you think, like, he might not be good enough for any of you?"

"Hooray!" Fiona cheered. "I love when wisdom prevails. Ladies, may I have your attention?"

Only two of the four looked directly at her.

Fiona whistled using her fingers. Pixie came running and pounced into the lap of Red Braids, who had no idea Fiona was addressing her and her friends. Pixie stood on her hind legs and tried to bat Fiona, who spiraled out of reach.

"Ladies, the two of you who *can* see me," Fiona continued, "you must convince your friends that friendship is the most important thing in the world. I miss my friends in the fairy kingdom, and I would do anything to get back to them. Do not jeopardize friendship. Do you hear me? Do it. Tell them!" Blowing through a fisted hand, she produced a sound like a royal trumpet. *Parum, parum!*

Whewie! What a speech. And the trumpet blare? That was new. I applauded her.

Georgie grabbed Red Braids's and Makeup Girl's hands. "I'm so sorry. Bethann is right. We've been friends for at least ten years, and we'll be friends forever. Along the way we're bound to like the same guys, but we have to be true to each other. Agreed?"

"Agreed," the friends chimed.

Braces—Bethann—grabbed hands to close the circle. "Friends forever. That's what I want my fairy garden to represent. That means I need more fairy figurines."

"And no boy ones," Georgie piped, leaping out of her seat with the impish boy fairy and swapping him for a pink fairy holding a bird. "This is you, Bethann," she said, brandishing the new fairy. "You love bird-watching."

"And hiking and running," Red Braids said.

"Courtney," Georgie said, "will you help us put the gardens together?"

How could I say no? The positive energy emanating from the girls was infectious.

An hour later, as they were leaving the shop with their finished gardens, Fiona's mentor, Merryweather Rose of Song, sailed in. "Courtney, hello-o!"

The mature fairy had iridescent gossamer hair like Fiona, but unlike Fiona who was a wisp of a girl, Merryweather was mature and slightly plump. Her loose-fitting dress was a regal crimson and her three sets of adult wings sported matching polka dots, which always made me smile. I'd inquired about them once. She'd said the queen fairy had allowed her to magically embellish her wings any way she'd wanted, once she'd earned her final set. That could explain why Cedric, an older fairy, had such an unusual look to him, as well.

"I believe Fiona is on the patio," I whispered.

"I'm here to see you. Miss Reade wanted me to impart some news."

Lissa Reade was the librarian at Harrison Memorial Library. Merryweather spent most of her hours at the library inspiring readers.

"Do tell, Merryweather," I said, guiding her behind the sales counter, out of earshot of customers checking out the Spode china. Someone might think me a *wee bit daft* if they saw me talking to the air.

"For the past week, Lissa has been very excited because Austin Pinter has been doing research again. In the library garden, of all places. She adores that young man."

One of my favorite aspects of the library was its drought-resistant garden, revamped over a decade ago, thanks to the Carmel-by-the-Sea Garden Club, which had raised the funds for the makeover. My father's company had put in a bid, but he hadn't won the contract. He'd promised me a hand in the design if he did. I treasured the library. After my third birthday, my mother had taken me to it every weekend to check out books.

"I'm happy to hear that," I said, "given what Austin told me the other day about not being inspired to write." How had he taken the news of Farrah's death? The police or Misty should have contacted him by now.

"He's been uninspired for so long, Miss Reade said." Merryweather *tsk*ed. "She could see it in his stature and hear it in the timbre of his voice. He'd grown lackluster. She was heartened to learn he'd joined a writing critique group, except he missed the meeting Saturday morning, so she's worried."

Fiona drew near and hovered next to Merryweather. "This is horrible. Austin missed a meeting?"

"How did you know I was here?" Merryweather asked.

"I heard you."

"Don't lie. We were whispering."

"I intuited you," she admitted.

I shuddered. To be honest, the fact that she could intuit things was a little freaky. "Why are you upset by the news about Austin?" I glanced between the two.

Fiona wrung her hands. "There is a darkness that surrounds him, as if a lie is consuming him."

Whoa! Was Fiona developing a heightened sense of awareness about everyone in town? Would the queen fairy be pleased or irritated?

"Perhaps we should seek him out," Merryweather suggested. "Would you like to accompany me, Fiona?"

"Absolutely."

Joss yodeled, "Hello-o, Brady! She's back here."

I spotted Brady sauntering carefully through the displays, mindful that the camera bag he'd slung over his shoulder did not knock any of the china or crystal bells we'd recently added to the displays.

I met him near the French doors and pecked him on the cheek. "Thanks for helping out."

"Admit it," he grinned. "This is just your way of seeing more of me. I know very well that you can take your own photos."

"Wrong. I'm a macro photographer. You, on the other hand, see the whole picture." Macro photography, which my mother had taught me when I was nine, was an art form, but not a form everyone enjoyed. Whereas most people enjoyed a big, grand, beautiful sunrise or blazing sunset, macro photographers paid attention to the smallest detail. I remembered Mom guiding my gaze to a ladybug on a leaf or a fly creating a ripple in a puddle of water or a grasshopper balancing on the lip of a rose. She'd wanted me to take pleasure in the simple or the hidden, and yes, even the magical. When she died and I lost my ability to see fairies, I'd been distraught. When Fiona appeared to me the day I opened the shop, my heart had leaped at the possibility that once again I would be able to unlock my heart and see the *little picture*.

"Follow me." I guided Brady to the patio where a half-dozen customers were browsing the baker's racks. "I'd probably need their approval if you took pictures of them, so for now, avoid customers in your photographs, if you can, and focus on the fountain or trees, if you dare to be artistic."

"I dare." He grinned that devil-may-care grin that made me woozy.

When would I admit to myself that I was falling for him?

I moved to the customers to see if there was anything I could help them with. Only one wanted help. As I posed questions about the garden she wanted to create—fun, fanciful, serious?—I glanced over my shoulder at Brady. He wasn't snapping photos. He was peeking between the leaves of the ficus. I bit back a smile. He was as eager as Meaghan had been to see a fairy.

"Is that her?" a young girl squealed. "Mommy, is that the lady who can see fairies?"

I pivoted to see a gap-toothed girl running toward me, arms wide. Behind her trailed twin freckle-faced boys.

Following the two of them were Christopher Cox, looking as good as he had when we'd been engaged—tawny hair, long limbs, winning smile—and the slender pigtailed blond woman who had bustled in to make a purchase Friday afternoon before closing. Today her hair was loose and wavy. Both she and Chris were wearing cargo shorts and matching blue *I Love Carmel* T-shirts.

"It's you," I said to the woman, who was obviously Christopher's wife.

He gazed at her. "Do you know each other?"

His wife licked her lips timidly. "No, I . . . Yes, sort of. I came here Friday and bought things to make a fairy garden."

"For me?" their daughter squealed.

"Yes, sweetheart," the woman said. "It's a surprise. Go look at the pretty things on the shelves." She pointed to the verdigris racks and returned her focus to me. "I'm Leanne."

"Nice to meet you." I extended my arm. When she didn't shake, I slipped my hand into my pocket. "Why didn't you introduce yourself Friday?"

"I was, um . . ."

"She's shy with adults," Christopher said, on her behalf. "Get her in front of a room full of children who want to learn how to play piano, however, and you'd think she'd swapped personalities."

Leanne smiled, seemingly grateful that her husband was filling in the blanks. One of the freckle-faced boys tucked against her leg. She petted his hair.

"I play piano." The daughter skipped to us. "Mommy says I'm good."

"You're getting good," Christopher corrected, and gave her a nudge. She trotted back to view the figurines. He winked at me. "We don't want her to develop a swelled head."

Brady moseyed over. "Chris, remember me? Brady Cash. We went to high school together."

Christopher acknowledged him with a nod. "Yeah, you

were a senior. A photographer, if I recall." He tapped Brady's camera. "You worked on the school yearbook and won all the awards."

"Not all," Brady said. "Courtney put me to shame in one competition."

"I was lucky." I laughed, but it sounded forced because I was still focused on Leanne. She'd barely put any thought into the items she'd purchased the other day. Why had she really come in? To check me out?

Christopher slung his thumbs in the belt loops of his shorts. "We just wanted to stop by and show the kids the shop."

I didn't ask how he'd known about it. I supposed his parents could have filled him in on my career change, or Leanne might have searched my online profile. Or Christopher had.

"It's a great-looking place," he said. "Are you glad you're out of that boring old landscaping gig?"

I bridled. "Landscaping was never boring, Christopher. It just wasn't a good fit for the rest of my life."

"Right, right."

"Mommy, look!" the daughter cried, holding up a ballerina fairy figurine.

"C'mere, Mommy," her brother said, pointing.

Leanne and her bashful son shuffled to them.

Brady hooked a thumb over his shoulder. "I'm heading back to take photos of the showroom."

"Sounds good," Christopher said. "Nice to catch up with you."

Over his shoulder Brady added, "See you at dinner."

My ex's jaw dropped. "You're joining us?"

"Yeah. Courtney and I are an item now." As he sauntered away, I saw Brady's shoulders shaking. He was laughing, elated that he'd caught Christopher off guard.

"Daddy!" the children beckoned.

Like a doting father, Christopher excused himself from me to join them.

Fiona whooshed to me, a worried expression on her face.

"Why are you back so soon?" I asked.

"I got a feeling you needed me."

"And Merryweather?"

"She'll report back if she learns anything about Austin." She pointed an arm. "Who are they?"

"An old friend and his family."

She gasped. "Not *him.*"

"Yes, *him.* Don't worry. They'll be out of our lives in—"

Crash! A figurine fell to the floor. Then another. The girl backed up, crying. One of the twins threw up his hands, meaning it wasn't his fault. Christopher cut a woeful look at me. Leanne paled with mortification.

Fiona went rigid.

Chapter 9

They have faces like flowers
And their breath is wind
That blows over grass
Filled with dewy clover.
—Fiona Macleod "Mider's Song"

Needless to say, Fiona was so upset with the breakage that I had to take her to the office and coax her to draw circles in the Zen garden until she calmed down.

"Twice," she murmured over and over. "Twice. In one week. This does not bode well. Plus the thefts? And the murder? Is it me? Is it my fault?"

I gaped at her. "Don't be silly. How could any of this be your fault?"

"Because I'm gaining knowledge. Because I'm intuiting things. Because I'm learning spells and potions and—"

"For the good."

"Yes, but . . ." She stopped making circles. "I'll ask Merryweather to visit the queen fairy. She'll have answers."

I petted her lovely wings. "That's a great idea. For now, stay here and rest."

Christopher offered to pay for the broken figurines, and

Leanne apologized profusely. I told them it was no problem—accidents happen—and I put together a token gift package for the children. They left beaming.

Minutes later, Brady finished photographing and said he'd see me at six thirty. On his way out, he winked.

When I checked on Fiona later, she was curled into a ball in the center of the sand, fast asleep.

The remainder of the day went smoothly. No upsets. Plenty of sales. At five, as I was on the patio taking a tally of plant supplies I needed to order, Joss wandered out. She requested to leave early, to visit her mother again.

My insides snagged. "Is everything all right?"

"She's fine."

"You'd tell me if it wasn't?"

"Of course." But something flickered in her eyes. She was worried.

I laid a hand on her shoulder. "If you need a day off . . ."

"No!" She planted her hands on her hips. "If you must know, I'm going more often because lately Mom has been telling me stories about my father. I want to hear all of them before she fades again." Joss's father died when she was in her early twenties. "The head nurse thinks it might be because they've put up Valentine's Day decorations. Many patients are recalling the loves of their lives." Her eyes misted over. "I've been recording what Mom says."

"How lovely. Go. Take a day or two off if you need to."

"I don't, but that reminds me—I created an ad for part-time help. It's by the register."

"Super. I'll look it over. Go." I blew her a kiss.

At five thirty, with no customers in the shop and all the china cups returned to their proper location, I decided to close early. I could use the extra time to dress for dinner—a dinner that I was not looking forward to. Before gathering Pixie, I reviewed the ad. As always, it was perfect; Joss was a godsend.

I opened the Dutch door and Fiona winged to me looking much better, her eyes bright. Rather than accompany me to dinner, she elected to go to a class with Merryweather at the library. She wanted to learn more about photo kinesis, a power all fairies could master. She assured me that she didn't want to blow anything up, which a fairy could do using such a powerful skill. She was simply going to learn how to direct her energy toward restoring plants and natural things that were injured. I didn't see how a course like that could upset the queen fairy and told her to have fun.

Dressing for dinner was a challenge. Brady liked me in my black sheath, but it felt too upscale, as if it might send off the wrong signal to my ex. Ultimately, feeling confident in red, I landed on my thigh-length red sweater over black leggings and boots. Checking myself in the mirror, I adjusted the cowl neck of the sweater, centered my mother's silver fairy locket—the one holding her picture—and applied a dab more eye shadow. When the doorbell rang, I told Pixie I'd be home soon.

Brady smiled when he caught sight of me. "Hello, beautiful." He pecked me on the cheek. "Red suits you."

"Blue suits you," I said. He'd worn a light-blue button-down shirt tucked into chinos and had draped a dark-blue cashmere sweater over his shoulders.

He offered me his arm, and we walked to Doud Arcade, home to the iconic Carmel Hat Company, Kris Kringle Christmas shop, Saison, and Fantasy Awaits.

I said, "After dinner, I'd like to peek in the Fantasy Awaits window if you don't mind. Odine creates some wonderful displays."

"Sure thing."

Saison's décor was simple yet elegant, with deep-blue walls, palms in giant blue pots, and cherrywood tables—no tablecloths. Its intimate bar area was jam-packed with customers.

The sushi-style counter facing the open kitchen and lobster tank was also filled with diners. A staff of twelve or more moved rapidly in the kitchen, some tearing snippets of dried herbs from the bouquets hanging alongside the copper pots overhead, while others chopped vegetables. Their banter was congenial.

A hostess in a blue dress with a mandarin collar and sexy side slit led us to a table where Christopher and Leanne were seated. Christopher rose as we approached. In a retro beige jacket over white polo shirt and chinos, he looked like he could be cast in the classic TV show, *Miami Vice*.

"Super restaurant choice, Courtney," he said. "We've ordered cocktails." He motioned to two martini glasses filled with a red concoction. "What'll it be?"

"A glass of pinot for me," Brady said, pulling out my chair. "Courtney?"

"I'll take a glass of chardonnay."

Brady drew a finger along the nape of my neck before he sat. A shiver of delight swizzled down my spine, making me realize I couldn't imagine wanting to be with anyone other than Brady if I had to endure a dinner with my ex and his spouse.

Christopher snapped his fingers at a waitress. Leanne, whose skin tone nearly matched the color of her pale-pink sheath, didn't seem pleased by the snap but let it pass. The waitress, who was clad like the hostess in a blue cheongsam, took our drink orders and left.

"The menu selections look good," Christopher said. "I love Wagyu beef, but the lobster with grilled pineapple wedges is calling my name. Honey?"

Leanne said so softly that I could barely hear her, "Buffalo-milk cheese on field greens."

"That's all?" I asked as I studied the entrees.

"She's such a bitty thing, she doesn't eat much," Christopher said. "You're like a bird, aren't you, hon?" He tucked a wave of curls behind her ear. "My little sparrow."

At any other time, I might think his words were endearing, but Leanne flinched. Had she taken his affections wrong? Was there trouble in paradise? I glanced at Brady, whose chin was quivering. Was he fighting the urge to laugh?

He closed his menu and folded his hands on the tabletop. "So, Chris, you're a judge now?"

"I am. Living the dream in the City."

The City was a nickname for San Francisco.

"Leanne," Brady said, drumming up conversation like the charmer I knew him to be, "it must be difficult raising three kids in San Francisco."

"We visit the parks and museums."

I said, "So you teach piano. How many students—"

"Bunches," Christopher cut in. "In the condo, we set up a private studio for her. With a baby grand."

"Wow," I said, impressed.

"At one time, she was on the path to be a professional pianist. The Los Angeles Philharmonic made her an offer—"

"But I got pregnant," she said.

"There went that dream." Christopher patted her hand. "But she hasn't regretted the decision, have you, hon? She adores our kids. And her students love her."

Our waitress brought our drinks and we ordered dinner. Brady decided on the black cod with roasted chestnuts, and I chose the scallops with sunchokes, a thin-skinned root vegetable of the sunflower plant, our waitress explained. Throughout dinner, the conversation continued with the same rhythm: Brady or me asking a question, and Leanne getting out half answers or no answers before Christopher took over. Not once did he ask Brady or me about our respective work.

I spotted a waitress with a tray of cocktails leading Misty,

Odine, two other women I didn't recognize, and Austin to a table across the room. Austin, decidedly sloppy with his plaid shirt half untucked and hair mussed, seemed unsteady on his feet. Misty gripped his elbow and guided him into his chair.

"Excuse me," I said to my dinner companions. "I'll be right back."

I strode to Misty and the others. "Hi," I murmured, as the waitress placed their cocktails on the table. "I'm so sorry for your loss."

Misty raised a flute of something bubbly. "Courtney. Perfect timing. We're mourning dear Farrah. We were just getting ready to toast her. Everyone, raise a glass. To Farrah. May she be a star in heaven."

Each repeated the toast.

Misty sipped her drink and then introduced the other two women—sorority sisters who were Odine's friends because they'd graduated before Misty and Farrah had joined the sorority. "They'll be at the party Saturday."

"Nice to meet you," I said, feeling awkward. What else could I say? I focused on Odine. "How are you?"

Her mascara was smudged as if she'd been crying but had dabbed the tears. "Hanging tough," she said. "It's all such a shock."

Misty took hold of my hand and said, sotto voce, "I contacted Farrah's parents and left a message. I'm waiting for a return phone call."

"Good." I glanced over my shoulder at Brady. He threw me an amused look. "Um, I'm sorry, Misty. I have to go back to my dinner guests."

"Of course. How selfish of me. You're not here alone. You're—" Misty gazed in the direction I had. "You're with Brady Cash? Well, how nice for you. He is a doll. Go. We'll talk." She gave me a nudge. "Actually, wait!" She pulled me back. "I was hoping I could arrange a private fairy garden lesson for all of us girls tomorrow." She gestured to her tablemates. "Please say yes. I know it's spur of the moment."

"You're making fairy gardens at the party."

"I know, but we could all use something light and fun to focus our attention on now, not days from now." She squeezed my hand. "Please?"

"Is eleven good?"

"Perfect."

I hitched my chin in Austin's direction. He was slumped in his chair, chin lowered, eyes at half-mast. "Will he be okay?"

"He's overwhelmed. I invited him to join us, and he was up for it until he started drinking. After two Chivas on the rocks, he started to mutter, 'If only . . .'" Her eyelids fluttered. "If only what? I asked, but he wouldn't go on. If only Farrah hadn't come to town? If only he'd been there to defend her? I can't get the rest out of him, but I haven't the heart to put him in a cab and send him packing. Besides, I'm too curious how he'll complete the sentence. Coffee should sober him up." She released me. "Go on. Finish dinner. I'll see you tomorrow."

For a mourning friend, Misty certainly seemed in control of her emotions, but I reminded myself that she sat on numerous boards. Given that kind of governance, she'd probably learned how to compartmentalize them.

I resumed my seat only to discover that Christopher had ordered desserts for everyone. The specialty of the house. Caramel ice cream topped with brandy sauce and crushed macadamia nuts. I rolled my eyes at Brady. All I'd wanted was for the evening to end.

Brady chuckled. "The judge makes the rules."

"You learn fast. Eat up." Christopher tattooed the table

with his fingertips. "Hey, did I tell you, my ultimate goal is the Supreme Court?"

"In California," Leanne added.

"Right."

Wow! Christopher in the Supreme Court, I thought. He always had dreamed big.

Leanne said, "Chris loves the Earl Warren Building. The court is—"

"All done in oak and has a coffered ceiling, and the skylight is thirty feet high." Christopher sounded like an ebullient boy. "It's gorgeous. And the mural of California above the bench is so cool. Isn't it, hon?"

Leanne nodded.

The waitress brought the check on a tray and asked if we needed anything else. Chris told her no and reached into his jacket pocket for his wallet. He withdrew a credit card.

Brady made a move for his wallet. "Let me cover this."

"No way, man. You're our guests."

The waitress took the tray with payment and moved on.

"Just the other day, Leanne was saying how much she wanted to meet you, Courtney. I can't deny her anything." Christopher beamed at his wife. "Right, hon?"

I gritted my teeth. If he said *right, hon?* one more time, I thought I'd lose it.

"Yes." Leanne smiled tightly. "I'm glad you could join us."

I said, "Thank you. I'm happy I got the chance to meet your kids. They're very sweet." Even if they had broken two fairy figurines and had freaked out my fairy. "How long are you in town?"

"We're here until the end of the week," Christopher said. "Doing the works, including the aquarium and a trail ride and other fun things, like taking the history walking tour, a nature hike, and a whale-watching trip. Maybe we'll run into you."

"Maybe you will."

The waitress returned with the processed bill on the tray and didn't hover. Christopher signed it and pulled a valet ticket from his jacket pocket. Then he and Leanne rose. So did Brady and I.

Brady excused himself to the men's room, adding, "In case they bring your car around fast, thanks for the evening, Chris. Good luck with your career, and Leanne with your teaching."

"Thanks, buddy," Christopher said. "I appreciate the good vibes."

Christopher and Leanne exited the restaurant first.

I said to Brady, "I'll wait for you in front."

As he crossed the dining room to the far side of the restaurant, I stepped outside and drank in the refreshing air. After the tense dinner, I was feeling cooped up and eager to get moving.

Christopher and Leanne were standing near the valet stand. She had her back to me.

"What were you thinking, Chris?" Leanne said, under her breath. "The least you could have done was split the check. It's not like we're rolling in dough. If you'd ask your sister for help like I'd suggested—"

He tapped her shoulder to hush her and turned to me. "Great seeing you, Courtney."

Leanne whirled around and forced a smile. "Yes, I really enjoyed spending time with you and Brady. You two look very much in love."

"We're . . ." I let the sentence hang. I didn't need to say that we weren't in love and give Christopher any notion that I was still pining for him. "We're a really good match." It was the truth. How we acted on that connection going forward was up to us.

A valet pulled a Lexus SUV in front of the restaurant and

hopped out. He opened the passenger door for Leanne. She climbed in.

"Here you are, sir," the valet said, offering Christopher the keys.

"Thanks." Christopher handed the young man some bills, then refocused on me. Softly, he said, "You're something special, Courtney Kelly. I never should have let you get away."

"I'm glad you did."

He winced at my response but quickly recovered. "Touché." He slipped into the driver's seat.

The screech of his tires added a punctuation mark to his last comment.

Chapter 10

Fairies, black, grey, green and white,
You moon-shine revellers, and shades of night,
You orphan heirs of fixed destiny,
Attend your office, and your quality.
—Shakespeare, "Fairy Orders for the Night"

A minute later, Brady exited the restaurant and took my elbow. "Fantasy Awaits," he said.

"Indeed."

He steered me along San Carlos and through the court-yard to Odine's store. In the display window stood a pair of large, bejeweled dragon statues. They were guarding a gold-and-blue Egyptian-beaded collar necklace.

"Geez," Brady said. "Who wears jewelry that bulky?"

"Lots of women."

"Would you wear it?"

"It's a tad bold for my taste."

Brady peered past the display into the shop. "Wow, those posters of dragons and fairies are huge."

"Yep." I leaned in to look. Our shoulders touched. "She's added photos of flowers now, too."

"Gigantic purple flowers," he said, and took a step backward. "How do you know about this place?"

"When I first considered opening the shop, I took a lot of walks around town, touring all the courtyards to get ideas. I saw this one, noticed the fairy-themed items, and entered. I was blown away by the exotica. Knives, statues, glassware, kimonos."

"A lot of it looks Asian."

"Yep. Odine, the owner, is a world traveler. She's picked up pieces everywhere and has clientele across the nation. Another reason I like to stop in"—I leaned in conspiratorially— "is she seems to know something about everyone in town. She's a good little talker."

"Ah, the truth comes out."

He turned toward me, his gaze drinking in my face. He moved in to kiss me, when out of nowhere a cat darted between us. A short-haired silver cat.

I backed up. "Whoa! What the—"

Brady chuckled. "Did your fairy put the cat up to that?"

"My fairy is nowhere around."

"Was it an omen?"

"Omen? You don't believe in omens. Don't go all woo-woo on me." I swatted his arm then clasped his elbow, and we strolled out of the courtyard. "Thanks for coming to dinner. It helped ease the tension."

"Speaking of tension, how did you ever fall for that guy?"

I had been wondering the same thing.

"He's full of himself," Brady said.

"He is. I see that now. He's changed."

"The way he gloated about his wife giving up her career for him was . . . I don't know what it was." He shook his head.

"Sometimes couples make sacrifices."

"I'm not certain she's happy with the one she made," he said as we veered down Ocean Avenue.

"Way back when, he was charismatic and sweet."

"And not cocksure?"

"He was very confident. And very smart."

"Did he dominate the conversation?"

"No. Well, sort of. He had a lot to say."

Brady snickered. "About himself."

I cackled, sharing in the dig.

"I remember him as a freshman," Brady said, "swaggering into my dad's diner with his folks. BMOC. Star swimmer. Straight As. The day he won a scholarship to Stanford, I thought his head might explode, his ego was so swollen."

I raised an eyebrow. "Why would his swagger have bothered you? At one time, you were BMOC."

"Never."

"You were a starter on the basketball team."

"Not until my senior year. I had to work hard to earn that honor."

"Did throwing hoops with me help?" I bumped his hip with my own.

"It didn't hurt."

Before Christopher came into the picture, in addition to Brady's and my time together in photography club, we'd spent a lot of hours on the basketball court. My father had taught me how to nail free throws. It had been one of the ways for us to connect after my mother died.

"Back in high school, why didn't you tell me that you didn't like him?" I asked.

"It wasn't my business then."

"But it is now?"

His cheeks tinged pink. "Me cave man." He pounded his chest once with his fist. "Me want to protect pretty lady from ogre."

I elbowed him. "FYI, I'm fully capable of protecting myself."

"Yes, you are." He uttered a full-throated laugh, then sobered. "Leanne certainly is edgy."

"She has reason to be. I overheard her chastising Christopher when they were waiting for their car. I think they might be having financial trouble."

"With three kids, that's easy to understand. On the other hand, they're taking this pricey vacation. Can't be all bad."

"Maybe he's maxing out their credit card."

"True."

When we reached my house and I opened the front door, he stopped me and gently rotated me toward him. "I'd like to give you a proper kiss, if that's okay."

I lifted my chin and smiled. "I was hoping you would."

He drew me into his arms, one hand cupping the back of my head. The kiss was electric, not fraternal, and everything I'd dreamed it would be. For a moment, I thought my knees might give way. A long minute later, he ended the kiss and whispered goodnight.

I went to sleep wondering if our relationship might have taken a sharp turn to the right.

The next morning Joss arrived minutes after I did. She looked rested and cheery in a yellow T-shirt emblazoned with a magnificent blue-winged fairy sitting atop a white unicorn, its neck adorned with a wreath of roses.

"Where did you find that?" I inquired.

"Online. Isn't she gorgeous?" Joss outlined the fairy with her fingertip. "Doesn't she remind you of a Schleich fairy?"

"She does." Schleich fairies were larger than typical fairy figurines, more in scale with action toys. We carried a few. "How's your mom?" I fluffed the sleeves of my fuchsia-striped popover top.

"Great. I collected a good fifteen minutes of memories. I had no idea my dad played in a band in his twenties. He was a saxophonist. Mom thinks she has some recordings of his, but she doesn't know where they might be, so I'll have to go through the storage container I rented for all her things when I moved her. And he collected butterflies." Her eyes grew teary. "I do remember some framed specimens. Again, all in storage. Guess it's time to dust it all off, take a look, and then . . . pass it along."

I caressed her shoulder. "I'm glad you're getting some nice memories. Sorry to cut this short"—I hooked my thumb over my shoulder—"but the plant guy is on the patio. I've got to approve what he brought today."

"Have at it. I see Pixie. What's she doing?"

"What do you think?" My sweet Ragdoll was racing around the fountain on the patio. "Chasing Fiona."

"Did you talk to Tish?" Joss asked, while starting a pot of coffee.

"No, dang it. She didn't call me back, and yesterday got away from me." Before heading to the plant guy, I picked up the shop's cordless phone and dialed A Peaceful Solution. The receptionist told me Tish wasn't available. I inquired whether she had an update on Twyla. She said she'd let Tish tell me the news. My stomach twisted in knots. What news?

For the next hour, I ordered more plants and soil with our rep and then busied myself with chores like dusting the wind chimes and sweeping the patio. Anything to keep my mind off Twyla's fate.

At eleven on the dot, Misty, Odine, and the two sorority sisters showed up. All were casually dressed in T-shirts or tanks and distressed jeans. Odine introduced the two blond women as Phoebe and Perri, both from San Diego. They were a couple and owned an apple orchard. I asked them if they knew a friend of mine, a garden-to-table farmer near La Costa. They didn't but said they would look her up.

Misty handed me a pink tissue-paper flower. "For you. Isn't it fun? I've made over fifty for the party so far. In my senior year, my decorating committee and I made a hundred for the prom."

"Very cute."

Chatting about what I'd planned for their private lesson, I led them to the workstation in the learning-the-craft area on the patio. I'd preset the table with shears, garden gloves, and trowels. Setting the flower down, I eyed a pair of elderly women who were browsing the goods on the baker's racks. One was inspecting a unicorn figurine. I heard her confide to her friend that she hoped her granddaughter would love what she planned to make. I ambled to them and told them to feel free to ask me for help. They promised they would.

"Courtney, I invited Nova to join us if she has time," Misty said, setting her purse on the rectangular table. "She couldn't make last night's dinner, and I'm not positive she'll make it today. She's incredibly busy crafting the jewelry I requested and filling other orders. Wait until you see what she's come up with. Odine, you should consign more items for your inventory."

"I would, but I have to admit her pieces aren't selling— not for my lack of trying."

A shadow loomed over the table. I took in Austin, who didn't look worse for wear having overindulged last night. In fact, in his red-and-yellow bicycle shorts and top, he appeared as handsome as he had when I'd first met him.

"Am I invited to the party? I want to make a fairy garden." He cracked a cockeyed grin and placed his bicycle helmet on the bench.

"Absolutely," Misty said. "The more the merrier." She

glanced at me, swallowing hard. "*Merrier* wasn't what I meant. We're not merry. In fact, we're heartbroken. I hope you won't judge us for doing our best to keep our spirits up, Courtney."

"I don't," I said. "I understand."

"Farrah would hate it if we moped around. She was always so upbeat. So positive. So . . ."

Odine petted Misty's shoulder. "So Farrah."

"Yes. There's no other word to describe her. She was exceptional. Everyone"—Misty clapped her hands—"let's choose our fairy figurines. Whatever you like. This is on me today. Money is no object."

I spread my arms. "First, choose a pot. We have a wide selection." I pointed to the array. "There's no right or wrong. Shallow, deep, wide-mouthed, or teensy. Got it? Once you've done that, bring it to the table. Then consider adding an environment piece, like a slide or pond or waterwheel. I'll talk to you about the plants that will complement your choices after we've reassembled."

Misty invited her friends to follow her to the pots. Phoebe and Perri obeyed.

Austin held back and gripped Odine's arm. "Did the police contact you?"

"Yes. They questioned what happened at the spa. I told them how upset Farrah was."

"Forgive me for listening in"—I cleared my throat—"but did you tell them that Twyla was rattled but not angry by Farrah's outburst?"

"Of course I did," Odine said. "That girl wouldn't hurt a flea." She regarded Austin. "Did they question you?"

He rubbed the back of his neck. "Yeah, Saturday morning."

Aha. That must have been why he'd missed his critique group.

"I can't believe she's g-gone." His voice cracked.

"Me either," Odine commiserated.

"She canceled our date Friday night."

No she didn't. I'd seen them together.

"I thought you went out for drinks on Thursday night," Odine said, looking baffled.

"We did, and then we set a dinner date for Friday. We met up, but halfway through cocktails, she said she had someone else to meet."

Odine said, "You don't know who?"

"Probably some guy." He shrugged a shoulder. "There I was, believing we were hitting it off. She was all lovey-dovey and then, whammo, around half past six, she was like, 'Sayonara, baby.' I should have remembered she was fickle that way, but I'd hoped she'd grown out of it, you know, and—" He stopped himself, eyes wide. "Man, you must think I'm a pig. I didn't mean to disparage her."

"You have a lot of history with her, sugar," Odine said. "I get it. Dump you once, shame on her. Dump you twice?" She shook her head.

I was confused. Didn't Austin know about the actor boyfriend? Had he truly hoped to win Farrah's heart when she'd only planned to be in town for a few days? On the other hand, if they'd been an item before, maybe he'd hoped to rekindle what they'd had.

Odine took hold of Austin's elbow and steered him toward the pots. "What did you do after that?"

I trailed them, eager to hear the rest of his story.

"I went home." He selected a simple clay pot.

Odine opted for one of Renee's glazed ones and, tucking it under her arm, nudged Austin toward the racks of figurines. "I wish I'd known. We could have gone out. I went back to the shop to do boring books."

"I tried to write, but it was difficult with the party going on at my neighbor's. The rock band was so loud. Isn't there an ordinance in Carmel for that kind of thing? I barely got one page written."

Inserting myself into the conversation, I pointed out a fairy duo that Odine might like, a fairy and dragon perched on a seesaw. She found the item amusing but settled on a trio of dragon fairies with loveable faces. Austin picked a pair of boy and girl fairies sitting on a bench fishing.

"I want a fairy door," Odine said. She skirted around Misty and the sorority sisters. Austin followed.

"Misty," Phoebe said, "Odine told us you want to start acting. Is it true?"

"I wouldn't be starting," Misty said, stressing the last word. "I acted in college, and I've done a couple of plays since then. *Cat on a Hot Tin Roof* at a small theater in Los Gatos. That was a long drive. And *Plaza Suite* at Pacific Rep. All gratis, but tons of fun."

"But getting into films now?" Phoebe pressed. "At your age?"

Misty blanched, then raised her chin defiantly. "Steve Carell didn't get his big break until he was forty-three."

"But he's a guy," Perri said.

Misty mumbled, "Double standard," and selected a violet fairy that was sitting on a toadstool.

"Did Farrah know you wanted to launch your career?" Phoebe asked.

"Yes, she did," Perri said, elbowing her partner. "Don't you remember what Odine told us? She was worried Farrah would see Misty as competition."

"Bah." Misty blew air through her lips.

"That's not exactly what I said," Odine protested.

Misty fanned her hand. "Farrah had a booming career. She knew she had nothing to worry about from a peon like me."

"A *peon*." Phoebe snuffled. "As if. You're gorgeous and have a va-va-voom figure."

"I . . . Thank you, but . . ." Misty's eyes grew teary. She pressed her lips together as if that would stem her emotions. "I really miss her," she whispered.

Phoebe patted her back. "We know."

Regrouping, Misty chose two more fairies and said, "I've got what I need. Do you?" She didn't wait for their responses. She took her items to the table.

I gathered a number of plants for the group and organized them by height at the far end of the workstation.

Austin took a seat on the bench beside Odine and placed his figurines and a blue resin pond surrounded by cobblestones in front of him. "Odine, do you know who Farrah met after she left me?"

"Sugar, I have no idea." Odine clapped a hand to her chest. "Farrah didn't confide in me."

I studied Austin, noting how much he was acting like a jealous lover, and I recalled the words Misty said he'd mumbled repeatedly last night when drunk. *If only*. Had he followed Farrah to the rental house and killed her before she could go on her other date? *If only*. Did he wish he could change what he'd done?

"You and she were close," Austin said.

"*Were*," Odine stated, "before she became famous. Distance in our friendship was to be expected, of course. We traveled in different circles and lived so far apart."

"I thought you two were like this." Austin crossed his fingers. "She came back from London to celebrate your birthday. She told me it was because she adored you."

"Don't get me wrong. We treasured each other. We'd just lost touch." Odine's lower lip started to quiver. "Having our friendship wane saddened me in the same way it saddened me when I lost touch with my business partner after she married and moved to Oregon. She has kids now and not a spare moment to breathe." Continuing to fight her emotions, she toyed with the trio of dragons figurine, running her finger along the blue one's spine. "Distance between friends happens, but now with Farrah gone . . . murdered . . . I guess we are all feeling . . . adrift. How I hope the police find who did this."

"Me, too."

"You know, if Farrah confided in anyone, it would have been Misty."

"Confided in me?" Misty sat taller. "About what?"

"About meeting someone Friday night," Odine said. "Austin thinks Farrah hooked up with another guy. Do you know who?"

Misty shook her head. Fresh tears sprang to her eyes. "She didn't tell me a thing."

Chapter 11

Why, by her smallness, you may find that
she is of the Fairy kind,
And therefore apt to choose her make whence
she did her beginning take.
—Michael Drayton, "The Eighth Nimphall"

Close to noon, Misty paid with a credit card, thanked me for being so flexible, and left with her friends, each happy with her garden and vowing to recommend the shop. I told them how much I'd appreciate that. Word of mouth mattered to a small business.

When the last exited through the Dutch door, Joss said, "Guess who I saw walking toward Sweet Treats? Tish and Twyla."

"Good. She's not in jail. Phew."

Joss prodded me. "Go talk to them. Find out what's what."

She was right. I needed a clue as to what the police might be investigating. If only Summers would confide in me. *Yeah, right. If only.*

The day had grown chilly, so I threw on a cardigan over my striped top and trotted up the courtyard stairs to the bakery. A half dozen customers were peering into the glass display case, which was packed with dozens of croissants as well as two chocolate cakes, one pink cake, a unicorn-themed cake, and myriad cookies. The three retro pink stools were occupied at the counter. Yvanna was behind the counter, filling an order.

Tish and Twyla, both dressed in blue puff jackets and jeans, were sitting at one of the café-style tables. I strode to them and noticed their mugs of hot cocoa sat untouched on the table. They had not ordered Twyla's favorite sugar cookies, either.

"Hello," I said.

"Courtney, hi." Tish gestured to the extra chair. Her eyes were lackluster, her mouth grim. "I've been meaning to return your call."

Twyla's face was tearstained.

I perched on the edge of the chair, nervous to hear the *news* the spa receptionist had said Tish would convey. "Where does the police investigation stand?"

Tish said, "We thought it was going well, but now . . ."

"Th-they—" Twyla stammered. "They want to . . ."

"They want to question her again!" Tish cried. "Someone saw her knocking on the door of the Airbnb."

Heavens. That was incriminating if it was true. "Did you knock?"

Twyla pressed her lips together.

Tish said, "She did."

"I wanted to apologize to Miss Lawson," Twyla mewled. "She'd told me she was staying at a place on Lincoln and described it. I was familiar with the house, since it was on my route, so I walked up the path and knocked on the door. Lights were on but she didn't answer."

"What time was it?"

"About seven thirty or quarter to eight." Twyla chewed on her thumb.

"Did you hear anything inside? Any movement?"

"A footstep," Tish said.

"But only one," Twyla added.

I tried to do the mental math. When was Farrah killed? Before or after Twyla's knock on the door? Had the coroner established a time of death? I'd seen Farrah and Austin turn onto Lincoln around six fifteen, and Austin told Odine that Farrah was, like, *Sayonara, baby* around half past six. "Maybe Farrah saw you approach but was avoiding you."

"Maybe." Twyla's voice quavered. "I wondered if I'd imagined the footstep."

"You didn't see anyone peek through the drapes?" I glanced from her to her mother.

"I wasn't looking in that direction." Twyla folded her arms across her narrow chest, looking more like a waif than a grown woman. "I waited. When she didn't answer, I left and continued on my walk."

"Do you know who witnessed you knocking?"

She shook her head. "The police didn't say. We're going to the precinct—" She sucked in a sob.

"After our cocoa," Tish said.

No wonder they hadn't drunk any. The sooner they finished their drinks, the sooner they'd have to face Detective Summers.

Tish patted her daughter's arm. "We'll sort this out, sweetheart. Promise. You didn't kill her." She focused on me. "Courtney, if you hear anything or learn anything or figure out who did this, because you of all people with your link to, you know . . ." She twirled a finger.

Did she mean my link to the fairy world? Fairies couldn't divine the truth without good old-fashioned sleuthing.

"You have to tell us." Tish clasped my right hand between both of hers.

"I will."

I returned to the shop. Joss, who was on the telephone, beckoned me with a furious wave. I weaved through the display tables to the sales counter. "Is something wrong?"

"It's Misty." She thrust the phone toward me. "It sounds urgent. She *had* to speak with you ASAP."

Heart pounding, I took the cordless phone. "Hi, Misty, what's up?" *Please don't tell me there's another dead body.*

"The moment I arrived home, Brady Cash called me and invited me to come to Hideaway Café for a tasting of appetizers."

I let out the breath I'd been holding, covered the mouthpiece, and said to Joss, "No emergency."

"Phew."

"I told him I wanted you there," Misty said in a chipper voice. "Are you free?"

"I could eat."

The Hideaway Café, like the other buildings in the Village Shops, boasted a striking dark red wood-and-stone façade. The entry patio that held six small, white, iron tables included bowers of flowers and the fairy garden I'd made for Brady. It was one of my favorites and featured a miniature café, a bonsai tree lit with fairy lights, and three cherry-cheeked fairy figurines, each carrying a different food item.

A waitress showed me to a table set for two on the rear patio. Misty was already there sipping a glass of white wine.

"I love this place," she said as I took my seat. "The ambience is so scrumptious."

Strands of twinkling lights arced across the expanse of the patio, and triangles of draped tent-like material served as the roof.

"I absolutely adore the jazzy music," she added.

The strains of a guitar filtered through a speaker system.

"Brady will bring things out in a bit. Want some wine?" she asked.

"I'd better not. I need a clear head if I hope to make it through the afternoon."

Misty had changed clothes since making the fairy garden earlier. She checked the cuffs of her sapphire-blue silk blouse and crossed her arms on the table. "I have to tell you, I'm worried sick about Twyla Waterman. I just heard the police want to question her again."

"Who told you that?"

"The facialist I see every few weeks at the spa texted me. Tish must be worried to death." Misty's face drained of color. "That was the wrong word. I can't believe it slipped out of my mouth."

"Twyla didn't do it. Dylan Summers will discover the truth." At least I hoped he would.

Misty agreed. "I meant to tell you earlier that I contacted Farrah's mother. She's overseas and can't return until Sunday. She begged me to manage things, and I said I would, but I swear, there's so much to do. Contact the funeral parlor, apply for death certificates, and such." She ticked off a list on her fingertips. "I've touched base with Farrah's business manager and her agent. They're notifying the film crew. Needless to say, everyone is devastated."

"Shouldn't her business manager take care of the certificates?" I asked.

"Yes, but he requested that I—" She exhaled sharply. "He sensed that I'm a get-it-done person, and I am. I will do everything I can for my friend. I still can't believe that she's gone. Like that!" She snapped her fingers. "Her mother said Farrah wanted an understated funeral, like cremation and burial at sea." She took a sip of wine. "She said Farrah's father's burial—I got the feeling she and her husband were estranged at the time—was much too showy. She suggested I help Farrah's friends put together a memorial for her in Los Angeles in a month or so, once her boyfriend has wrapped his movie and is back in town."

"So the boyfriend is real and not a tabloid rumor?"

"Uh-huh. That seems appropriate, doesn't it? A month?"

"I suppose so."

"Her business manager will handle distribution of the will. Farrah had no husband and no children, so I imagine everything she owned reverts to her parents. That's what would have happened if I'd died before my folks." Misty took another sip of wine. "When they passed on, it was horrific for nearly six months. Do this, sign that. I felt like an automaton most of the time. With so much paperwork, there's barely time to grieve."

"Here we are, ladies," Brady said, placing a platter of appetizers—two of each choice—on the table, followed by a folded paper menu. He looked as handsome as ever in a white shirt and black trousers, hair slightly tousled. "Courtney, I'm glad you could make it." He winked at me and then picked up on the tension at the table. "Am I interrupting something?"

Misty said, "No, sweetie, we were simply talking about how death can be such a blow, not just to family members, but also to friends and business acquaintances and, well, everyone."

"Oka-ay," he said, dragging out the word.

I offered a supportive smile indicating that I, too, hadn't expected to chat about the topic.

"No more of that convo." Misty shimmied off the bad vibes. "Tell me what we're looking at. That avocado thing looks yummy."

Using his forefinger as a pointer, Brady said, "That's avocado and bacon on toast with a spicy green onion salsa."

Misty didn't hesitate. She took one and bit into it. "Heaven. It's a keeper."

Pleased, Brady continued. "Next are tahini chicken wings, then artichoke hearts with lemon-butter sauce."

I took an artichoke heart and popped it into my mouth. Butter dripped down my fingers. I blotted them with a napkin. "These are tasty but messy."

"Gotcha." Brady recited the remainder of the appetizers. "Stuffed potato skins, buffalo cauliflower poppers, and shrimp salad bites. Plus stuffed endive with herbed goat cheese, sweet potato chorizo sausage bites, and blue cheese crostini with balsamic-roasted grapes."

"Wow. I need a list," Misty said, "or I won't remember a thing."

"That's what those are for." Brady pointed to the folded menus, and then pulled two golf pencils from his chest pocket and placed one in front of each of us. "Courtney, would you like a glass of wine?"

"I'll stick with water." I dipped a cauliflower popper into the ranch dressing. "Yum! Love this one. Nice and spicy."

Misty said, "How many appetizers do you think we should have per person?"

I referred to Brady. "Six to eight choices?"

"Is Sweet Treats providing dessert?" he asked.

I nodded.

"Six to eight should be ample," he said.

"But eight to ten will look better," Misty said. "Not to mention what if someone, like me, absolutely loves the avocado and bacon and eats them all before the others spot them?" She shooed Brady away. "Go. Do your thing. Come back in a half hour and we'll have the menu set."

Misty was, indeed, a get-it-done person. In less than thirty minutes, she'd chosen her favorite appetizers, but she'd doubled the amount for four of them, just in case. She patted her stomach. "I'll be putting on pounds this week, I fear, but what the hey? I'm not an actress. I don't have to starve myself to death." She realized that she'd made another faux pas and blanched. "I swear, my mouth has no brain, and my brain has no heart. Forgive me."

"Gallows humor comes with the territory," I said warmly. "Been there, done that."

When I returned to the shop, two customers were inside the showroom checking out the china cups. Two more were flipping through books from the top of the book carousel. I found Joss sitting on the patio with Pixie in her lap. Fiona was dancing on water as it spilled from the top of the fountain into the base. Two customers were checking out glazed pots.

Fiona zipped to me. "Is everything okay?"

"Just fine. The menu for the party is set. Misty is holding herself together extremely well."

"I'm talking about with Twyla. She's been on my mind." Fiona made a gesture like she wanted to pull out her gossamer hair. "Zephyr and I spoke to Merryweather about her. We're considering doing a calming spell."

"A calming spell," Joss repeated. "That won't keep her out of jail if the police find enough evidence to book her."

"She knocked on a door." Fiona mimed the action. "That's not enough evidence. And would a murderer knock?"

That gave me pause. Who was the witness, and had he or she stuck around long enough to have seen Twyla walk away from the house?

"Courtney, dear," a woman trilled.

I startled and clapped a hand on my chest.

"Did I frighten you?" Holly Hopewell strolled through the French doors. "Little old scary me?"

"I didn't see you walking through the showroom," I admitted.

"Maybe it's because my outfit is so monotone." Her curly

hair was secured in a rainbow-colored hair claw that matched her colorful jacket.

"Ha! You'll never be monotone. What do you need?"

"I want to buy something for my adorable daughter-in-law. Perhaps a china set or a fairy garden do-it-yourself kit. Could you help me?"

"Of course. Tell me about your DIL. What are her hobbies?" I'd seen the woman a couple of times when she and her husband had brought their son, one of Holly's many grandchildren, to visit Holly at the house. She was pretty but didn't spend much time on makeup, and she didn't dress in fussy clothes. She wore plain T-shirts and jeans and tennis shoes. I doubted a china cup and saucer would be something she'd appreciate.

"She's in her thirties, and she's a property manager for my properties as well as Hattie's enterprises."

Although explorers were the first to discover Carmel, the town hadn't boomed until after the 1906 earthquake hit San Francisco and authors and painters migrated south, looking for a community that would foster the arts. The first to establish themselves in the area had been lucky enough to build up great wealth. The Hopewells fell into that group.

"She's a real people person," Holly went on, "but she doesn't miss a thing when it comes to noticing what needs attention in a building." She raised a fist. "'Action now!' That's her motto."

"Is she creative?"

"She can sew like a dream, and she loves to do crafts."

"DIY kit it is," I said.

On the verdigris baker's racks, at the bottom, sat do-it-yourself kits I'd assembled in wicker baskets. Each included a clay pot, a package of dirt, a nice selection of environmental pieces like benches, stumps, and toadstools, plus two figurines—usually a fairy boy or girl and an animal—and a sign-post, which was how I'd labeled each package.

"All we need, after you choose the theme, are some suc-culents. We'll make it easy for her to create her first garden."

"Perfect." Holly stooped to study the kits. Over her shoulder, she said, "I almost forgot to tell you, dear, I found another fairy door. It's in front of the green cottage with three gables on Monte Verde."

"I know that house. With the gigantic Monterey pine."

"That's the one." She chose the Secret Garden package that included a fence and swing set, a squirrel carrying books, and a beautiful pink fairy. "This will be perfect."

I asked her to follow me into the shop to ring her up. "Did you see who put the door there?"

"No. It must have shown up last night. It's so arty. Home-made, I think, given the gobs of hot glue I spotted. Moss and stones surround a door made of Popsicle sticks, and there are lovely silver hinges." She set her purse on the sales counter and handed me a credit card. "I looked for a message but didn't find one. Perhaps someone got there before I did and swiped it."

"You're not supposed to take the notes."

"Of course not. Even I know that. But not everyone fol-lows the rules."

I wrapped the basket in cellophane, tied it with a big blue bow, and slipped it into one of our gift bags. I put the plants into a separate bag.

As Holly left, I reviewed our conversation about her find-ing another fairy door—no note, if there had been one; had someone taken it?—and my thoughts returned to Farrah Law-son's murder as well as Joss's conversation with Fiona. How had the killer entered and fled the Airbnb without being seen? Had whoever it was come and gone before Twyla's arrival, or had he or she been inside when Twyla had knocked on the door?

To keep my promise to Tish and her daughter, I wanted to scope it out. I wouldn't be able to go inside, of course, nor did I want to, but I intended to look for ingresses and egresses. Maybe the police had overlooked something.

Chapter 12

At the end of the day, I closed up shop and, with Pixie in tow and Fiona riding on my shoulder, walked the extra blocks to the Airbnb on Lincoln Street. The stone cottage was dark. No lights were on inside. Small lantern-style footlights lit the path to the front door, which was flanked by a statuesque cypress in the center of sparse grass to the right and a small perennial garden bordered by a short, white picket fence to the left.

Seeing Twyla approaching the front door would have been easy from a number of angles. Because it was a corner house, I moved to the right and peered along the side of the house. "Three windows, easily accessible, and no door," I whispered.

Fiona darted off my shoulder and soared to the left side of the house. She returned in a flash. "Two windows and no door on that side. A very tall gate leads to the rear." She flew off to the right.

Pixie mewed.

I said, "Yes, I know. A righteous fairy can get into places that would be legally off limits to me."

Waiting for Fiona's return, I studied the neighbors' houses. The one to the left, on the same side of the street, had been remodeled recently with a room over the garage. The new stone façade would need some aging to match the façade of the main house. The smoky-gray cottage directly across the street was overrun with flowerless vines. There was a light on inside, and if I wasn't mistaken, a woman was peering at me through a break in the drapes. Was she the witness?

I waved and headed toward the woman's path. The drapes snapped closed. Moments later, the front door opened.

The woman, who was barely five feet tall with wispy white hair and a wrinkled neck, didn't step outside. She tightened her pink robe and jutted a bony finger in my direction. "I know you," she said. "I heard you speak at the city council meeting."

I, along with my fellow business owners, often attended meetings. It was the best way to stay on top of new ordinances and grievances. It was where Tish Waterman and I had first locked horns. How glad I was that we'd become friends.

"You own that fairy shop," she said.

"Fairy *garden* shop," I replied, moving closer.

"Nice cat."

"Thank you . . ." I noticed the name *Smith* on the doormat. "Mrs. Smith."

"Is there a fairy about?" She searched the sky.

"Possibly." I smiled. "Were you the person who saw Twyla Waterman knock on the stone cottage door last Friday night?"

"I was." Her voice was husky, as if she'd smoked all her life.

"Did you see her leave?"

"No. I'd been told if there were ever suspicious characters to call the owner."

"You didn't call the police?"

"Are you deaf?" she squawked. "I said I contacted the owner."

"Yes, ma'am, I heard you. So the owner must have reported her to the police."

"I suppose. Miss Oates is very good about keeping the neighborhood clean and safe. Many of these Airbnb owners don't." She clicked her tongue. "She won't rent to riffraff."

"Miss Oates?" I asked. "Would that be Odine Oates?"

"Yes. Lovely woman. She owns a jewelry and exotica store as well as three houses in town. She's rather well-to-do."

I recalled Misty telling me Odine was a descendant of one of the first families of Texas.

"Thank you, ma'am," I said to the woman, and made my way toward the stone cottage while mulling over the news. Odine owned the rental. It made sense that Farrah would have rented from her friend—or Odine might have given it to her gratis—but I found it surprising that I hadn't picked up on that tidbit. On the other hand, when would I have? When Odine had rushed to greet Farrah at Open Your Imagination, they'd talked nonstop. When I'd seen her at Saison and at the shop earlier today with her sorority sisters and Austin, she'd been thoroughly engaged. Even so, you'd think that the topic would have cropped up. I mean, her friend had been murdered in her rental home.

"What are you doing here?" a man asked gruffly.

I turned toward the voice and gasped. Dylan Summers faced me, arms folded across his sturdy chest. In a leather jacket, dark shirt, and black jeans—not his typical garb; was he trying to blend into the night?—he looked menacing.

"Detective," I said. "I was taking a walk with my cat. What are you doing here?"

He glowered at me.

"Did you know there are fairy doors popping up all over town?" I improvised. "We were looking to see if there were new ones, and what do you know? Our search took us down this street."

He hitched his chin toward the neighbor's house. "Why were you talking to Mrs. Smith?"

"Because . . ." *Think fast, Courtney.* "She wanted to admire my cat. You've met Pixie, haven't you?" I wiggled the cat's forepaw.

Summers's gaze narrowed. "Nice try. Look, there's nothing you can learn here."

"Did the coroner determine a time of death?"

"He did. Between six thirty, when Miss Lawson left Mr. Pinter, and seven fifty-two, when Miss Lawson's Fitbit stopped working."

"That's not a very big window." I tilted my head.

"No, it's not, and it doesn't help us rule out Miss Waterman."

"You talked to her earlier, didn't you? At the precinct?"

He shifted his feet.

I said, "I met her and her mother at Sweet Treats. They told me everything. Did she mention that she might have heard a footstep after she knocked?"

"Hearing a footstep does not prove Miss Lawson was alive, Miss Kelly."

"Exactly, but what if she was already dead, and the killer was trying to hide the fact that he or she was inside?"

"Let's not speculate, okay? I like to work with facts." He unfolded his arms and shoved his hands into his pockets.

"Do you honestly think Twyla Waterman is capable of poisoning someone?"

"The girl . . . young woman . . . was held in a cult for all those years. She had been drugged to keep her in line. They could have taught her how to drug newbies."

"I thought you only worked with facts."

He frowned.

"Was Farrah Lawson drugged?" I asked. "I mean, was the poison in something she drank or injected?"

He didn't answer.

"Did you find Twyla's fingerprints inside the house? Did you find poison on her person? I presume you searched her place of residence."

"Miss Kelly, stop." He sighed.

"C'mon, Detective. You and my dad are friends, and I'm friends with your intended. Call me Courtney. Please."

He sighed. "Courtney, look, I get that you are loyal to friends. But this is my case. My jurisdiction. Please do what you do best. Make fairy gardens and keep your nose out of this."

Fiona flew to me and whispered in my ear. "There's an entry to the house in the back. It requires a key, and it doesn't look jimmied."

I tamped down a laugh, enjoying when she used investigator-style talk, much of it gleaned from reading Sherlock Holmes stories.

"Good night," Summers said.

"Wait. Did you know Odine Oates owns the rental?" I asked.

"Yes. Needless to say, she's distraught that a friend of hers was murdered here."

"Do you consider her a suspect?"

"Simply because of ownership?" Summers checked his watch. "Doubtful."

"She would have had easy access."

"Lots of folks have keys to the place. The cleaning crew. The food delivery service. A neighbor."

"Why didn't Farrah stay at one of the upscale inns or hotels?" I asked. "She had the means."

"Because Miss Oates assured her that she would have a better chance of keeping out of the public eye if she stayed in a home."

Also a better chance of being murdered without anyone seeing the killer, I noted.

"Actresses can be hounded by paparazzi and locals," Summers went on.

"I've heard you interviewed Austin Pinter. Did his alibi sound weak to you?"

"When did you ask him—"

"I didn't. He and Odine Oates shared their respective alibis when they came to my shop to make fairy gardens."

"They came—"

"Misty wanted a few of Odine's birthday guests to have a fairy garden experience in addition to the one they'll have at the party this coming Saturday. To ease their sorrow."

Summers sucked in his cheeks, no doubt to keep himself from mocking me.

"Did you verify their alibis?" I asked.

"Mrs. Oates was at her shop doing the books. The deli that provided her dinner confirmed that. As for Mr. Pinter, we're following up."

"One last question," I said. "Is Twyla Waterman in custody?"

"She remains a person of interest. Good night, Courtney."

"Good night, Dylan." He growled, and I quickly revised, "Detective."

After a light meal of julienned zucchini and sautéed cod drizzled with a lemon-wine sauce, I threw my peacoat over my cardigan and blouse and schlepped to the greenhouse carrying the bags of items I'd brought home to use in Violet Vickers's fairy garden. Fiona accompanied me. Pixie remained inside, having retired to her favorite pillow.

The moment I stepped into my private haven, I breathed easier. How I enjoyed the scent of wood shelving and the aroma of herbs growing in the array of pots. How I treasured the exclusive collection of fairy figurines and environmental pieces and pots, including oversized containers that I didn't sell at the shop so that my creations would look like no other.

"Hello, everyone," I joked, waving to the array of figurines.

"What are you thinking of creating?" Fiona asked, tiptoeing around the rim of the glazed blue pot.

"'What the world needs now, is love, sweet love,'" I crooned.

Fiona tittered. "It's a good thing you didn't want to become a rock star."

I stuck my tongue out at her. "I happened to be in the choir in high school. Even Dad thought I had a lovely voice."

"My father—" She jammed her lips together.

I leaned toward her, on tenterhooks. Would she tell me something personal about her life in the fairy kingdom? When she didn't continue, I said, "Is he the fairy king?"

She kept mum.

"Is there a fairy king, or is it more like a beehive? One queen and a lot of drone fairies?"

The notion made her giggle, but she still didn't comment. She flitted overhead and hummed a ditty that I didn't know the words to. Had her father sung it to her? Did she miss him?

She stopped midair. "Courtney, has anyone written a love song using the words from a Shakespeare sonnet?" She threw her arms wide. "'So long as men can breathe or eyes can see, so long lives this, and this gives life to thee.'"

"Brilliant!" I cried.

She curtsied.

"Yes, you were brilliant, but the idea was brilliant. Violet loves the arts. She's seen every Shakespeare play. This creation will be about Shakespeare's stories of love."

Inspired, I pulled out the pair of white fairies Violet had selected from the bags, and then fetched another boy and girl figurine, each in blue clothing, from the shelves. The boy was on bended knee. The girl held a bouquet of flowers. I stretched to grab a three-piece medieval castle, complete with ivy climbing the walls and flags waving from the turrets, off the top shelf. Of course the castle would need to be surrounded by a moat. I would make that using blue stones and hot glue, and I'd add a resin footpath to represent the drawbridge. A miniature pennant banner at the foot of the bridge would finish the entrance.

I filled the pot with my homemade mixture of soil, topped the center with some brown sand, and then placed the castle on the sand. Next I positioned the two girl fairies directly in front. The boys would be positioned on the other side of the drawbridge. The one on bended knee would be pledging his troth.

Fiona inspected the castle from all angles.

"What are you doing?" I asked.

"I keep thinking about the back door to the rental house."

I nodded. "I suppose the killer could have come and gone that way without being seen. The street entrance was . . ." I paused. "Hold on. The housekeeper said the door was ajar. Do you think she meant the back door?"

"That's not what's bothering me." Fiona flapped a hand. "Like I said, the lock didn't look like it had been jimmied, so whoever entered must have used a key, but I didn't see one anywhere."

"It could be hidden."

"Or whoever used it stole it."

Had Summers thought to ask Odine about that when he'd questioned her?

I told Fiona what Mrs. Smith had revealed to me. "I wish I could have asked her more questions. She might have been able to tell me whether anyone, other than Twyla, had approached the house. On the other hand, she would have contacted Odine if someone had."

Fiona soared to the top of the castle and posed like a ballerina on one of the flagpoles, both arms and one leg extended.

I admired her form. I'd taken ballet as a girl but gave it up after my mother died.

"Do you think Austin followed Farrah to the house?" she asked.

Austin had been miffed that Farrah had ditched him. Maybe he'd tailed her to see if she'd been lying about having a date.

"He could have seen Twyla approach," Fiona continued, "and then waited until she'd moved on before slipping around the back to knock on the door. Farrah recognized him and answered—"

"Ergo, no need for a key." I recollected my encounter with Dylan Summers moments ago. In his dark jacket and shirt, he could have blended in to the scenery. I supposed the killer could have done the same. "Did Merryweather learn anything more about—"

My cell phone rang. *Brady*. I answered. "What's up?"

"It was good seeing you today."

"You, too. Your food was amazing. Misty was over the moon."

"Thanks. So tomorrow . . ."

"Tomorrow?" I repeated, my voice rising.

"It's your day off. Do you want to take the morning and go fairy door hunting?"

A smile spread across my face. I wasn't due at Misty's until noon. "You bet I do. I'll bring sweets and coffee and meet you at Ocean and Lincoln at nine."

"I'll be there." He blew me a kiss and ended the call.

Fiona cruised to the blue pot, balanced on the rim, and sang, "Courtney lo-oves Brady."

I swatted her with a finger. Laughing, she held her belly and did somersaults midair. Oh, to be a fairy.

At the crack of dawn Tuesday, Fiona whooshed off to meet Merryweather at the library. I rolled over, pulled the comforter to my neck, and went back to sleep. At seven a.m., as sunlight peeked through the window, I awoke feeling bright, chipper, and eager to solve a mystery. I downed a glass of fresh-squeezed orange juice and dressed in a pair of camouflage leggings, a white Henley shirt, and my photographer's jacket with its multiple pockets. Then, with my Nikon slung around my neck, I leisurely strolled to Percolate to pick up two tall Americanos and two maple bars. I remembered going on an outing with Brady and the rest of the photography club back in high school. He'd brought a box of maple bars—his favorite, he'd explained to us. Ever since, they'd been a favorite of mine, too. I'd tried to get Christopher to try one, but he'd always pooh-poohed them. That should have been a red flag for me.

I pushed the thought of him from my mind and concentrated on carrying the coffees without spilling them.

"Hi-ho!" Brady said, waving from the corner as I drew near. His jeans had fashionable rips in them. His white T-shirt looked new. Like me, he'd worn a photographer's jacket, and his camera hung on a strap around his neck. He motioned to a bench in the library's garden. "Shall we sit and sup before we take our tour?"

"Sounds perfect." I kissed his cheek. "You smell good."

"Irish tweed soap." He scrubbed the soft stubble on his chin and, like an actor in a commercial, added, "A manly soap."

Overhead, a seagull cawed on its way to the ocean. Even though the beach was several blocks away, we could hear the surf crashing on the sand. The rhythmic sound made me feel more relaxed than I had in days. It didn't hurt that I was sitting beside a man of whom I was growing fonder by the day.

"Here." I withdrew a maple bar wrapped in wax paper from the bag and handed it to him. "And an Americano for each of us." I pulled them from the holder. "So how many fairy doors have you seen?"

"About six."

"Me, too. Wonder if they're the same six."

"We'll find out."

We sat in companionable silence, listening to the breeze whisper through the pines, sipping our coffees and enjoying our snack. When we finished, we tossed our garbage into one of the town's trash cans and off we went.

"There are two on Ocean Avenue," I said.

"Two? I've only seen one."

For the next hour, I showed him my discoveries and he showed me his.

I bent to photograph the fairy door he'd found on Monte Verde.

"Come on, macro ace," he teased. "Do your thing with

the wee photos." He'd taken dozens with a wide-angle lens to get the scope of the doors to the trees.

I leaned closer to capture the rough-hewn texture of the wood door. It was painted in bold red, yellow, and blue. Miniature roses surrounded the door's plaque, which read *Welcome to Fairy Land*. Next I took pictures of the miniature mailbox and RV trailer.

Over my shoulder I said, "This is a lot different than the others we've seen. More paint. More depth. Do you think the same artist made all of them?"

"Got me. This is your bailiwick." He offered a hand to help me to a stand.

I brushed off my knees.

"So tell me why fairy doors are important," Brady said. "And are they different from fairy rings?"

"That discussion might require a moment to recuperate on the beach."

"You're on."

We walked the few blocks and took the stairs down to the sand. Kicking off our shoes, we strolled barefoot until we found a spot far from other beachgoers—not that there were a lot of folks out on a Tuesday morning. We sat. Warmth radiated through my leggings.

"Okay, here goes." I began. "A fairy door is a way to communicate with the fairy world. Often one will leave a note or a wish or a gift behind the fairy door for fairies to find."

"And a fairy ring?"

"They're also known as fairy circles or elf rings. They're often made of arcs of mushrooms in a field or a forest. Some people, thanks to folklore, are afraid of them, thinking they're linked to the devil."

"Are they?"

"No. Now fairy portals, which are my favorite"—I tapped my chest—"can occur in a variety of places."

"Portals."

"Mm-hm. You can find them in forests and hills as well as caves and wells."

"Like the ones I've seen on your blogs."

"Yes."

The week I'd opened the shop, I had started writing a blog to entertain as well as enlighten customers. Two blog posts included photographs of fairy portals I'd found in nature.

"Can mere mortals cross through these portals?" Brady asked.

"Mere mortals can," I said in an Irish brogue, "but if they darest, they might not make it back to this world . . . ever." I let the sentiment hang in the air.

Brady chucked my shoulder. "I still want to see one. You've promised to take me."

"A promise I shall keep," I said, continuing with a brogue, "but thou must heed my warning." I screwed my fingertip into his cheek.

He grabbed my finger, pulled me close, and planted a kiss on my lips. We stayed like that for a long moment until he broke the spell.

"Up!" he ordered, and popped to his feet. "Onward. You only have an hour before you have to be at Misty's. We have more fairy doors to view."

All in all, we photographed a dozen fairy doors of varying sizes, shapes, and colors. No two were alike, although most seemed lighter in tone than the rough-hewn one. Did that say something about whoever had made them? Were two or more artists at play?

Before saying goodbye, we agreed to compare photos after we processed them. Maybe studying the artwork would help us determine the crafters.

★ ★ ★

On the way to Misty's house, my cell phone pinged. I scanned the readout. *Christopher.* I groaned. What did he want? Reluctantly, I answered. "Hey."

"Hey, yourself. The kids and the wife are at the beach. I was wondering if we could meet for coffee. As a foursome Sunday night, it was hard to get the lowdown on you. I'd like to catch up."

"Sorry. I can't. I have a meeting. All afternoon."

"Busy lady."

"I am."

"How about a drink later, then?" he asked, in a come-hither tone.

"Chris, no. Thank you. Dinner was nice. It was lovely meeting your wife. Now we need to say—"

"Hold it. Can I be frank? Honestly, I can't believe you buy into this crap about seeing fairies, Courtney."

My heart jolted. "That was rude."

"C'mon. You're a bright woman."

"And bright women can see fairies."

"Get real."

With all the jeers I'd endured in recent months, nothing compared to his scorn. Tersely, I said, "Goodbye, Chris. Have a good life. Don't contact me again." I ended the call.

Breathing high in my chest, not sorry in the least for my response, I trekked up Misty's pretty path and paused by the door before entering. I needed to put on my game face.

Meaghan had arrived minutes before me, Misty advised me as she led me along the hall. Joss had already come and gone. Passing through the sunroom, I saw that my organized assistant, bless her heart, had transported the balloon inflator, the multicolored wind chimes, shepherd's hooks to hold them, and some prep items for the party games.

Misty's tuxedo cat, sleeping in a bundle with the other two, raised its chin and scrutinized me. I whispered, "Hello. Sorry to disturb you." It yawned and went back to sleep.

Stepping outside, I yelled, "Hello!"

"Up here!"

I spun around to take in Meaghan's progress with the wall. She was teetering at the top of a super-tall ladder, which made me a tad woozy.

"How's the air up there?" I kidded.

"Ethereal."

"In your floral shirt, I thought you were doing performance art. You nearly blend in."

She stuck out her tongue.

I retreated a couple of steps to get the full picture. She and her mother had painted a huge garden with dainty pink-and-white fuchsias, bright yellow yarrow, lavender foxglove, and rosemary.

"Wow! It really is amazing."

"Thanks. Mom and I will be adding the fairies tomorrow. I'm planning on stealing images from the Cicely Mary Barker fairies. Hope that doesn't offend your sensibilities."

"Works for me," I said. "Where is your mom?"

"She had a client who needed hand-holding. A sale didn't go through. The client is almost broke and floundering."

"Oh, my. Good luck."

"Beverages, ladies?" Misty exited the sunroom carrying a tray filled with glasses and a pitcher of water as well as tea. "Rafaela will bring out some snacks and sandwiches in a bit. I have to change for a meeting."

She returned inside and veered toward the kitchen. Through the kitchen window, I saw her greet a petite older Hispanic woman in a white uniform.

Fiona materialized out of nowhere and cried, "Follow me, quick!"

I trailed her to the cypress.

"As you know, I met with Merryweather earlier," she said, her words running together. "We studied photo kinesis again."

Aha. I'd been wondering what lesson had been in store.

"But toward the end of our session, she confided that she had seen a person in a hooded rain jacket planting yet another fairy door. In front of Misty's house. I had no idea. Knock me over with a feather!" Fiona smacked her forehead. "So I hurried here to inspect it. Did you see it? At the base of the pine in front? It's small and easy to miss."

"I didn't." Why, of all places, would the fairy door person put one in front of Misty's house? Was Misty the mysterious crafter? Was she setting out doors all over town, hoping a fairy might grant a wish?

"I came here to speak with Cedric about it. He didn't know a thing, but he has something else to impart." Fiona whistled into the tree, her whistle sounding more like a breath of wind.

Cedric Winterbottom appeared and hovered in front of me while tugging on the hem of his short, cropped jacket. His messy silken hair wafted in the breeze. "Milady, lovely to see you. At your service." He bowed graciously.

"Tell her what you told me," Fiona urged. "About Misty's housekeeper."

Cedric hesitated.

"Go on." Fiona wiggled her fingers.

"Fiddle-faddle. All right then. I heard Rafaela on the telephone talking to a friend, and she said she heard Misty squabbling with—"

"Farrah Lawson," Fiona inserted.

"Yes. Her. She said Misty was yelling at Farrah about a roll, but Farrah hadn't tasted any of the food for the party, so what would she care?" Cedric lifted his chin dramatically.

"Housekeepers can be gossips, and . . ." He clapped a hand to his chest. "Who's the gossip now? Me. I should be quiet."

"No. Tell Courtney everything. You also said you don't trust Rafaela because . . ." Fiona rotated her hand. Why was she insistent he tell the story, seeing as she seemed to know all the details?

"Because"—Cedric primped the tendrils on his wings—"things have disappeared from the house."

Like an entire set of furniture from the study? I mused.

"Can you be more specific?" I asked.

"Two pieces of art and some silver."

I gasped. "Are you positive?"

"Certain."

"Have you seen Rafaela take these things?"

"No. They vanish in the night."

"Rafaela doesn't sleep here, does she?"

He shook his head. "But she has the keys and code, and Misty is often out at night. She's very social."

"We shouldn't judge Rafaela out of turn," I said. "There might be a perfectly good explanation for the disappearances. Perhaps Misty sent the paintings and silver out for cleaning."

"Perhaps," Cedric admitted reluctantly. "I shall take heed." In a flurry of energy, he spiraled into the air and retreated into the cypress.

I made my way back to the others while wondering about the missing items. Was Misty aware? Should I mention it to her? She'd want to know where I'd gotten my info. I could say her fairy told me, but would she believe me?

Replaying the argument Cedric had overheard, the word *roll* pealed in my mind. Could Misty and Farrah have been arguing about a *role,* as in the part Farrah had promised to help Misty get? The part Nova said Farrah would never deliver? Had that made Misty mad enough to lash out and kill Farrah?

No, poisoning someone and getting in and out of the rental home without being seen required planning and stealth. Misty's anger would have taken a different form. A slap. A confrontation. Unbridled indignation.

"Courtney!" Meaghan beckoned me. "I need your approval."

Chapter 13

❧

I have kiss'd the cheek of the rose,
I have watch'd the lily unclose,
My silver mine is the almond tree,
Who will come dwell with flower and me?
—L. E. Landon, "Fairies on the Sea Shore"

As I headed to my pal, Misty hurried from the sunroom, cutting me off. "Courtney, I have to leave." She'd changed from jeans and a T-shirt into a tailored red suit, white silk blouse, and red pumps. "Ask Rafaela for anything you need: snacks, beverages."

"Misty . . ." I began.

"What is it?" She checked her Rolex watch.

Knowing she was in a hurry, I said, "It'll wait. But we need to talk."

"If it's about payment, I'll be using a credit card."

"It's not."

"Good. Gotta go." She mimed a telephone in her hand. "Call me. *Ciao.*"

Over the course of the next hour, Meaghan tweaked the wall, touching up some of the fuchsias, and I walked the yard, visualizing the party games. Then we sat on the patio and ate the sandwiches Rafaela had prepared. My favorite was a turkey, ham, and Swiss on rye. The mustard–mayo combination that she'd added to it was divine.

At four, I told Meaghan to wrap it up, and I went to the front of the property to inspect the fairy door at the base of Misty's pine tree. Fiona wasn't kidding about the size. It couldn't have been two inches tall and an inch wide. For miniature fairies, I decided. A teensy red bistro table set for two stood to the left, a bouquet of daisies resting on one of the chairs.

I glanced around to see if one of Misty's neighbors was watching—maybe a secret admirer—but I saw no one.

Minutes later, Meaghan tapped me on the shoulder. "Don't forget you and Yvanna and I are having dinner at my place. I invited Nova to join us, too. She called your cell phone." She handed it to me. "You left it on the patio table."

"Oops."

"Nova wants to show you the jewelry she made, but she couldn't make it over this afternoon. Hope that's all right."

"Of course. I'm bringing wine."

Exhausted, I slogged home but urged myself to perk up. I had to finalize Violet Vickers's pot before dressing for dinner. I'd promised to deliver it the next day. Over the years, my father had stressed the value of meeting deadlines. Repeat business came from satisfied customers.

Walking to the greenhouse with Pixie sticking to me like a shadow, I murmured, "We'll just be out here for a bit, kitty cat, okay?"

She meowed.

Fiona, the tease, flitted above Pixie's head. The cat craned her neck to see her and stumbled into a plant. She hissed.

Holly Hopewell yelled to me. "Courtney, dear!" She

waved from beyond the fence, her face bathed in the glow of fairy lights that she had added to her yard after seeing mine. "Come closer. Look who's visiting me."

Violet Vickers rose and raised a glass of white wine in a toast. "Cheers."

"I didn't know you two were friends," I said.

"Violet and I go way back. Wa-ay back," Holly quipped. "She bought my first painting."

"I've been a fan ever since."

Dressed in a silver sweater dress, Violet seemed ready to attend a theater event. Holly, in contrast, was wearing a white smock splattered with paint. Recently she'd added an art studio with big windows in her yard. A local artist-slash-carpenter had constructed it for her. I was pretty certain she was sweet on him.

"Can I see your creation for me?" Violet's eyes sparkled with eagerness.

"It's not quite done. That's what I'm finalizing right now."

"Are you loving it?" she asked.

"Absolutely. I think it's inspired." I winked. "You'll see."

"Would you like some wine to arouse your creative juices?" Holly held up a bottle.

"No. I'd better keep a clear head."

Fiona glided to Holly and orbited her, waving frantically, trying to get her attention. Holly didn't blink. Violet didn't see her, either. Fiona returned to me, giggling.

"Courtney, before you go," Holly said, "you won't believe what Violet just told me. Eudora Cash is missing her latest manuscript."

"No! Missing how? As in she misplaced it?"

"She believes it's been stolen."

"Oh, no." My heart wrenched. Had the hooded thief upped his or her game? First cheese and sweets, then hair clips, and now a manuscript? "Did she contact the police?"

"She did. Sadly, they're not convinced they can do anything. She doesn't have a security system, and there are no closed-circuit TV cameras in her neighborhood."

Carmel-by-the-Sea had installed twelve cameras in six locations at the main entrances and exits of town to deter wrongdoing, but sadly, visitors were not the only ones who committed crimes.

I sighed. I didn't want Carmel to become suspicious and wary and resort to using CCTV, but with the spate of robberies, should the city council consider it? "I hope she had a backup on her computer."

Violet frowned. "Not a chance. She writes everything in longhand. She's old school."

"I'm certain the police will recover it. It's not like whoever took it could publish it."

"Let's hope so." Violet shook her head glumly. "It's not easy doing what she does. Nearly six months of research goes into every novel."

"Research!" I thrust a finger into the air. "Her research notes will protect her from anyone being able to publish the book. She has her notes, right?"

"She does."

"That's a relief. Please give her my best."

Pixie nudged my ankle. *Time to create.* "Yes, kitty, I've got to get cracking." I waved to the women. "Have a nice night."

I headed toward the greenhouse, frustrated by how much bad karma was cropping up in Carmel. A murder and a number of thefts. What was next? Maybe that was why the fairy doors had begun to appear. Someone had felt the negative vibes creeping in and wanted to balance the bad with the hopeful. Was the crafter tuned in? Was it a fortune teller, or could it be Lissa Reade, the librarian, taking a cue from Merry-weather Rose of Song?

"Hello-o!" Hattie Hopewell, followed by her sister

Hedda, pushed through Holly's rear gate. "You didn't answer the door when we rang. Hope we're not intruding. Hi, Violet. Hello, Courtney!"

I pivoted and waved.

"We're on our way to dinner with our sweet beaus and thought we'd stop in for a quick hello," Hattie announced.

"He's not my beau." Hedda poked her sister. She liked to keep her personal life private.

"You've been on three dates. That's a beau. Don't argue." Hattie fluffed her red bob.

Seeing Hattie gave me pause. Was it possible that she was the redheaded woman Twyla claimed to have seen on her walk? Hattie lived around the block on Camino Real, not far from the rental house. "Hattie, do you water your plants nightly?"

"I do. Moisture is best applied at night, as you very well know."

"Last Friday, a young woman was walking in the neighborhood—Twyla Waterman, Tish Waterman's daughter. She works at A Peaceful Solution spa. Do you know her?"

"I've never been in."

"Twyla is slim and has black hair. She said she's seen you out on other occasions, but you weren't out that night when she passed by."

"I did water that evening, but I was delayed. I needed to chat with my lawyer. Why? Does it matter?"

"No. If you didn't see her, you didn't. However, did you happen to notice a man walking a chocolate Lab?"

"Yup. Pat Humphrey. Ooh, that man." She huffed. "He sits at his computer from dawn to dusk day trading, then gets up, hooks the leash on the dog, and with cell phone in hand, continues to day trade. He pays zero attention to the dog. Zero!"

Hedda clucked disapprovingly.

"He goes out about the same time I do," Hattie added.

"Thanks." I retreated to the greenhouse and dialed the precinct on my cell phone. The clerk that answered said Detective Summers wasn't in. I left a message detailing what I'd gathered from the Hopewells. I hoped he wouldn't chastise me for sharing helpful clues.

I spent an hour finalizing the details of Violet's garden, pleased with the way the bonsai tree and ferns that I'd installed to create a forest beyond the castle suited the scale of the piece and how, at the last minute, I'd decided to add three small huts to represent the nearby village and villagers peddling their wares. Bringing a fairy garden to life requires a fertile imagination.

After setting up an appointment with the deliveryman to take Violet's garden to her house in the morning, I fed Pixie and Fiona and dressed for dinner. I opted for a pair of black slacks, my scoop-necked red sweater, and a puffy black jacket. The temperature had grown cool, and I was walking. I hated whenever I allowed myself to get chilled to the bone. My fingers never forgave me.

Meaghan lived in an attractive Craftsman, its exterior decorated in Laguna stacked stone and fenced with scrolled ironwork. The garden was primarily daylilies of all colors, which were gorgeous when in bloom.

Fiona had requested to come along. I warned her that she was not to socialize with Callie, the intuitive fairy that lived in Meaghan's garden. She promised she wouldn't, but she did want to ask Callie if she was sensing who might be setting out the fairy doors. I gave her my blessing. The queen fairy wouldn't mind proper sleuthing.

"Welcome," Meaghan said, letting me in. "What did you bring?"

"Scheid chardonnay. You said you were serving seafood salad."

"Perfection. Go into the living room. I've already un-corked a bottle of wine, and there's sparkling water, as well. We'll save this deliciousness for the meal."

Meaghan waltzed into the kitchen, the folds of her cro-cheted ecru dress undulating with each step. "Yvanna is al-ready here. She brought homemade coffee and chocolate ice cream for dessert."

"Yum!"

The interior of Meaghan's home boasted Old World charm, with hand-laid walnut floors and intricate Italian tiles. I adored the blue-and-white décor, probably because that was what I'd chosen for my place. Many pieces by artists featured in Flair Gallery decorated the walls and built-in shelves.

Yvanna was sitting in a Regent armchair. I chose the sofa. Blue floral napkins sat on the coffee table alongside a Wedg-wood Hibiscus–pattern platter filled with cheese and crudités.

"There's been another robbery in the courtyard," Yvanna said matter-of-factly as she adjusted the collar of her crisp, white, button-down shirt.

"No way!"

"Mm-hm. At Carmel Collectibles. The thief stole two Valentine-heart wands that were in a bin by the front door. Cliff didn't see the sneak until he was on his way out the door. He had three customers, so he didn't pursue."

"Well, get this: I just heard that Eudora Cash's manuscript was stolen from her house."

Yvanna's lips trembled. "*Dios mio*. This is scary. What is going on? I mean, no one has been hurt, but even still . . ." She murmured a prayer in Spanish.

Was my theory at Misty's correct? Had she been robbed not by the housekeeper, but by whoever was pulling off these other thefts? Was the thief getting bolder? Had he or she sneaked into Odine's Airbnb? Had Farrah caught the thief in the act? Was her death a result of a robbery? No. Not possible. Poisoning her after robbing her didn't seem reasonable. Hitting her, knocking her out cold, or shooting her made more sense. The incidents were unrelated.

Yvanna picked up her glass of sparkling water and took a sip.

"You're right," I said. "The good news is no one has been hurt during these robberies. I think teenage boys"—or girls, I reflected, seeing as the thief was described as slight; not Georgie or her pals—"are daring each other to steal something. To feel the rush."

The front door opened. "Knock, knock." Nova poked her head into the living room.

Fiona followed her inside and gave me a thumbs-up. She must have discovered something from Callie. I couldn't wait to hear.

"Meaghan's in the kitchen, Nova," I said, "but I wouldn't go in if I were you. She can be territorial. She doesn't like intrusions."

"Gotcha." Nova, clad in a white shawl slung over a white three-quarter-sleeve tunic and white leggings, was plainly feeling more spiritual.

"Beverages are right here," I said. "Wine or sparkling soda?"

"Wine, thanks." She settled on the sofa next to me and set her rhinestone-studded tote on the floor.

"Did you bring the jewelry for the party?" I asked.

"I did." She patted her tote.

From the kitchen, Meaghan yelled, "Don't show them anything until I'm there, Nova! Almost ready."

Nova said to Yvanna, "My friend loved the kaiser rolls I brought her." To me she said, "Sweet Treats makes the best kaisers. Have you had one?"

"I haven't, although I have had their biscuits." I poured

wine into two Waterford crystal glasses, one for me and one for her.

"Nova never buys sweets," Yvanna said. "Only a savory roll will pass her lips."

The word *roll* made me think of the conversation that Misty's housekeeper had overheard between Misty and Farrah. Had she meant *roll* or *role*?

"Sugar isn't good for the body." Nova helped herself to a piece of Cheddar cheese, the move exposing the ink work on her arms.

"Is tattooing?" I asked, instantly regretting how quickly the question had popped out of my mouth. "I'm sorry, that was insensitive."

"No, it's fine," she said. "People ask me all the time. It's not unhealthy, if done properly. Needles breach the skin, of course, which means one could get an infection or have an allergic reaction, and some dyes, especially standards like red, yellow, green, and blue are more allergy-reactive than others, but it's all a matter of who is doing the art, you know?" She displayed her forearm to us. "I haven't had one bad experience."

I said, "The snake with the lei around its neck is exotic. Does it represent something?"

"Snakes are symbols of fertility or creative life force," Nova said. "I like to think of it as the latter for me. I have no desire to get pregnant. The lei was my doing. I got it on a trip to Hawaii."

"Which island did you go to?" Yvanna asked. "I've always wanted to visit Hawaii."

"I went with my parents to Maui a year ago," Nova replied.

"You're friendly with your parents?" I asked. "How nice."

"Friendly doesn't tell the whole story. Without them, I

couldn't stay in business. I live and design in the unit above their garage. Up on Santa Rita." She pointed.

"Tell me about Maui," Yvanna said.

"It's beautiful. The trip to Hana is ridiculously long, but seeing the volcano at sunrise is awesome. And snorkeling in Lahaina is the best. The water is so clear. We stayed at the Kea Lani in Wailea-Makena. Every room has a view."

"Wow." Yvanna blinked.

I pointed to the sorceress tattoo. "Does that one have significance?"

"Yes," Nova replied. "Its owner possesses a superior knowledge and wisdom. I wasn't feeling very powerful before I got it, but I have to say, when I look at her, I feel like I'm the most powerful being on earth."

Fiona blew a raspberry. "She is not the most powerful being."

Of course she wasn't, but sometimes focusing on a picture, whether it was a tattoo on one's body or a Post-it note on a mirror, could change one's attitude. Heck, even toying with a Zen garden could boost one's confidence.

"I'd never get a tattoo," Yvanna said. "I'm afraid of needles. Piping icing is much more my speed."

We all laughed.

"Dinner's on," Meaghan announced.

We convened in her dining room, which was also done in blue-and-white tones. She'd set four places with her blue-themed china on white tablemats. On each plate sat a seafood salad, consisting of plump shrimp, flaky crab, baby scallops, grape tomatoes, and chopped green onions on top of butter lettuce.

"You all replied that you have no allergy to shellfish," Meaghan reminded us.

"It's beautiful!" I exclaimed. "Where are we sitting?"

As casual as my pal could be, when dining, she had rules.

"Courtney, you sit at the far end. I'll take this end, and Nova, you face the window. Yvanna, opposite Nova." Meaghan handed me the bottle of wine. "Why don't you pour?"

I did the honors.

"Nova, I'm dying to see the brooches," Meaghan said, lowering herself into her chair.

"Why don't we wait until after dessert?" Nova suggested.

"Good idea."

For the next while we chatted about how flavorful the salad dressing was—Meaghan had added serrano peppers to the recipe—and then we turned our conversation to the fairy party event. I told them the menu Brady was planning. Each hummed her approval. Meaghan, Nova, and Yvanna said they didn't know the attendees other than Odine and Misty; I admitted to having met two of Odine's older sorority sisters when they'd come to make fairy gardens.

When conversation waned, Meaghan made coffee and Yvanna served up her coffee and chocolate ice cream with a side of incredible caramel sauce. Nova abstained. I didn't have the willpower. The ice cream was so good that if I'd been home alone, I would have licked the bowl.

"It's time, Nova," Meaghan said, clearing the dishes. "Show us your wares."

Nova poured herself another glass of wine. Then she fetched her rhinestone-studded tote bag and pulled out a different jewelry holder. This one was red brocade. She unfurled it on one end of the table. Three of her business cards spilled out.

"May I take one?" I asked.

"Please do."

Unlike the velvet jewelry holder, this one consisted of multiple zippered pockets. She slipped a half dozen items out of the pockets. Like a display model, she swept a hand across her goods. "Rather than a brooch, I made shawl holders or shawl pins, some might call them." She placed one in her palm and rounded the table to show it to each of us.

"Pretty," I said.

The holder was two pieces. One was circular and featured a fairy's head with flowing hair in tooled silver. The other piece was a long silver pin, similar to a hatpin. At one end of the pin hung a lovely colored flower. At the other end was a twist cap.

"So practical," Meaghan said. "Yet elegant."

Meaghan stood to inspect the others. Yvanna and I rose, too. The features of each shawl holder's fairy's face or hair were different, as were the colors of the flowers.

"Show us how they work," Meaghan said.

"Will do." Nova left the room and returned with the shawl that she'd left on the sofa. She looped it around her shoulders, crossing two pieces close to her neck, then unscrewed the cap end of the hatpin, set the cap on the table, placed the fairy head on top of the fabric, and laced the pin through it. She capped off the sharp end of the pin and threw her arms wide. The shawl remained in place. "Voila."

Yvanna clapped. "Every guest will love it."

"I made one for each of you, too," Nova said. "If only Farrah . . ." She let the sentiment hang.

My insides tensed. "If only Farrah what?"

Chapter 14

❦

Dipping flowers in her cup, so the merry fairies sup;
Sip and laugh, and laugh and tip, loving cups from lip to lip.
—Florence Harrison, "Pixy Work"

"If only she had lived to have seen these," Nova said.

I let out the breath I'd been holding. *If only.*

"I wish she'd trusted me to grow as an artist. The whole reason I offered to make these for Misty was to prove to Farrah I had the artistic ability." She motioned to us. "You three, of all people, know that one piece of art does not define an artist."

I definitely did; I'd made some disastrous fairy gardens. "It's so hard as we start out," I said, to reassure her. "We put things on our social media, and it reflects who we are. The brand is the brand. We'll earn reviews that we don't like, but we get over them. It's just one opinion."

"That's what I told Farrah last year when she came to town for a week," Nova said. "I told her even though one bad review wouldn't destroy my overall standing, it hurt, but I added that I forgave her. She said she—" Nova's voice caught. "She said she understood. As an actress, she was careful about which projects she chose to do. She didn't want to make a fool of herself, which was why . . ." She blinked, a moment of panic in her eyes.

"Which was why . . . what?" I asked.

"No, I can't. I shouldn't."

"C'mon, you're among friends. What happened?"

"There was this project she wasn't certain she wanted to do because there was nudity involved. Berto Bagnoli was helming the project. She really wanted to work with him again. She wasn't a prude—she had an incredible body—but she was hesitant because it was a horror film, so . . ." She rotated a hand. "So she asked Misty to read the script and give her opinion." Nova took a sip of wine and then another. "Misty adored the script and said Farrah should do it, but Farrah, being in a snippy mood, said, 'If you like it all that much, you do it. I'll make sure Berto reads you.'"

I gasped. "For a leading role?"

"Yep. Misty took her at her word. However, flash forward, Farrah wound up doing the part—the film hasn't been released yet—and the director didn't bring Misty in for a reading."

"Ouch," Meaghan said.

Nova nodded. "Misty, who was hurt by Farrah's disregard, told her so. Chastened, Farrah promised to find another opportunity for Misty, but . . ."

"But she died," Meaghan murmured.

Tears leaked down Nova's cheeks. Were they real? Was she raising the issue between Farrah and Misty to throw suspicion off herself? After all, she'd told Misty how Farrah had panned her work all over social media. Was that enough motive to want her dead?

Leaning toward Meaghan, I whispered, "Would you ask Nova where she was on the night of the murder?"

Meaghan gawped at me. "Why? You can't think—"

"She had a bone to pick with Farrah."

"No. I won't." Lifting the coffee pot from the warmer on the side table, she said, "More coffee anyone?"

"I'll take more wine." Nova held up her glass. "Just a smidge."

Yvanna said, "I'll pass on the coffee. I have an early morning tomorrow, but let me help with the dishes before I go."

"Nope. I'm doing the dishes," Meaghan said. "Thanks for bringing dessert."

Yvanna blew kisses to everyone and headed out.

Fiona whooshed to my side. "I could ask Callie if she's allowed to coerce Meaghan into asking the question."

"Yes, great idea."

Fiona followed Yvanna out the front door and returned before the door had time to shut. Fairy speed astounded me, but I didn't question it. Callie, Meaghan's green fairy that many might mistake for a grasshopper or praying mantis if they spotted her in a garden filled with green, strappy plants, sailed in behind Fiona and hovered over Meaghan's head. Being an intuitive, she didn't need potions like Fiona. She could merely use her brain power to affect change. She did, however, like to hum. The tune was lilting and peaceful.

In a matter of seconds, Meaghan's forehead softened, and her eyes glistened. Lifting her chin, she smoothed her hair and approached Nova. "Earlier today, while we were setting up the party in Misty's backyard, we were discussing where we were on the night Farrah died. Courtney told me she'd heard Odine was at her shop doing bills, and Austin said he'd gone home to work on his book. Misty chimed in next. She was doing crafts for the party at home. I'd gone home to crash because I'd painted all day. And Courtney was—"

"Looking for fairy doors around town," I said.

"Fairy doors?" Nova tilted her head. "I haven't seen any."

"I'll tell you where to look. They're truly whimsical."

"And you, Nova?" Meaghan opened her hand, palm up. "Where were you that night?"

Nova's eyes widened. "Me?"

"It's just a game we were playing."

Fiona circled Nova's head and splashed her with green dust.

"I went stargazing," Nova said.

I glanced at Fiona. She raised both arms in an *I didn't do it* gesture. Green dust was designed to help someone trust another person.

"I drove south along the coast toward Big Sur and stopped in one of the turnouts," Nova continued, as if spurred on. "It was amazing. There was Orion, of course. That's so easy to see. And there was Dorado."

"Dolphinfish," I stated. I was up on which constellations graced the sky. On many occasions, my father had taken my mother and me stargazing. How I cherished those memories.

"That's right, and there was Caelum—that's the sculptor's chisel," Nova added. "I know that one because my uncle pointed it out once. He's the person who taught me how to be a metalsmith."

"Did anyone see you?" I asked.

"I doubt it. I mean, I don't know. I was the only car in the turnout." She started to tremble. "Why are you asking me? I didn't kill Farrah." She wrapped her arms around herself and heaved a sigh. "I wish I knew who did. It's putting a pall over Odine's birthday party."

In truth, Farrah's murder was casting a pall over all of Carmel.

★   ★   ★

Before I fell into bed, I noticed a text message from Brady. He wrote: *I enjoyed this morning. Sleep tight.* I peeked at the picture that accompanied the text. It focused on a new fairy door, not one we'd seen on our morning tour. When had it cropped up? I sent him a picture of the one at Misty's and paused. Did I dare ask about his mother's missing manuscript? No, that wasn't a topic to dig into this late at night.

When my alarm rang at six a.m. the next morning, I hopped out of bed bursting with energy. There was so much to do at the shop today. Meet with the book salesman, talk to our china suppliers, and figure out if Joss had posted the ad for a part-time helper. I'd approved it.

To focus my energy, I ran two miles on the beach even though it was drizzling. I hoped it wouldn't be raining Saturday. I hadn't arranged for a tent and doubted I could find one at this late date. Joss had promised it wouldn't be. But when I returned to the cottage, I checked the weather report, just in case. Clear skies for the weekend. Phew. I showered and dressed in a yellow, long-sleeved T-shirt and my favorite denim overalls with floral appliqués, fed Pixie and Fiona, and downed a protein-rich hibiscus berry smoothie.

At seven fifteen, after arranging for the delivery of Violet Vickers's garden to her home, I donned my yellow slicker—Fiona tucked herself beneath the hood—grabbed the cat, and hurried to work.

Joss waltzed in five minutes after me.

"What are you doing here so early?" I blew on my mug of freshly brewed coffee.

"Couldn't sleep. Mom took a turn for the worse last night." Her face was haggard, her eyes tired. She shrugged out of her fisherman's rain jacket and hung it on a peg beyond the coffee and tea station. "It was my fault. I pressed her too hard for information about Dad. She needed sedation."

I placed a hand on her shoulder. "Don't blame yourself. Give her a couple of days to recoup and then visit her again. She'll have forgotten all about it."

Fiona whooshed away and returned in seconds. She alit on Joss's shoulder and blew something from her opened hand into Joss's face.

"What . . . What was that?" Joss sputtered.

"A forgiveness potion," Fiona trilled. "I learned how to make it a few weeks ago. It's made with dried lavender and spiderwort."

Joss wriggled her displeasure. "I hate spiders."

Fiona cackled. "Don't be silly. Spiderwort is a pretty purple plant. We don't grow it here. My supply came from Virginia. It's good for many things, but we fairies have discovered that it helps one with forgiveness as well as with mending a broken heart." She kissed Joss on her cheek, then breezed to the patio and into the ficus.

"Her supply?" Joss asked, a hint of humor in her tone.

"A turn of phrase. I think her mentor gets the supply." I wasn't clear how that worked. Did fairies have their own postal system?

Joss smiled. "You know what? I feel better already. Say, have you spoken to Misty?"

I hadn't and I needed to. I really wanted to ask her about her missing items. Her fairy seemed convinced the housekeeper was stealing from her. I wanted to make certain the town thief wasn't the culprit. I set my coffee aside and dialed her number, but she didn't answer. I left a message.

Midmorning, it was still drizzling. Even so, customers and passersby might want to sit a spell, so I went to the wrought-iron tables on the sidewalk that fronted the shop and wiped them with a dry cloth. Right before I headed inside, I spotted Detective Summers entering Seize the Clay.

"Joss!" I yelled into the shop. I stowed the moist cloth behind the Dutch door. "I'm running across the street for a bit."

"Your coat."

"I can handle a spritz of water. I won't melt," I quipped. Summers would loathe my interference, but I had more to impart.

Entering the pottery shop, I brushed the moisture off my face and hair and drank in the aroma of sage incense. Instantly, I felt infused with confidence. Renee was standing at the sales counter with her betrothed. A number of customers roamed the shop. I strode to Summers. "Good morning, you two."

Summers grinned. "Aren't you too old for overalls?"

"I'm teaching a class of teenagers this afternoon who happen to think they're rather chic."

Renee stifled a snort. "Help you, Courtney?"

"I came to talk to your other half."

"Swell," Summers muttered. "Yes, I got your message about Pat Humphrey, and yes, I contacted him. He doesn't remember seeing anyone in the neighborhood Friday night. Not Twyla Waterman. Not anyone. The guy is going to develop a sore neck, given how often he's reading his cell phone."

"You know about that?"

"He's a menace in a crosswalk."

"No one else has come forward to help Twyla?"

"Nope."

"I saw that Tish put out flyers." I'd seen one on the lamppost in front of the shop.

"Which I've requested she remove. It's against the city's policy."

The city council of Carmel-by-the-Sea had enacted a lot of quirky rules. Not marring the beauty of the town by affixing ads and the like to lampposts was one of them.

"Anything else?" Summers threw an amused glance at Renee, who was doing her best to listen in on our conversation while ringing up a customer.

"Might I ask if you've taken a long look at Nova Pasha?"

"Courtney," Renee chided as she skirted the sales counter, "you're pushing your luck with Dylan. And why, for heaven's sake, are you throwing shade on Nova?"

"Look, I don't want anyone to be guilty, but someone is," I stated. "Nova had a beef with Farrah. A big beef." I explained her motive. "I have to admit that I had no idea Farrah Lawson could be a spiteful person. She has a good reputation amongst her peers, according to what I read in magazines and on social media, but deliberately hurting Nova's business—"

Summers held up a hand. "Got it."

I cocked a hip. "I know you won't let me in on what poison was used to kill Farrah, but can you at least tell me whether it was imbibed or injected? Someone who gets a lot of tattoos probably knows her way around needles."

"So do those with medical backgrounds," he countered.

I threw him the stink eye and headed for the exit. Before reaching the door, I spun around. "On a totally different matter, did you find out who stole Eudora Cash's manuscript?"

Renee gawked. "Someone filched her work?"

I nodded. "Plus she does it all in longhand. She doesn't have a backup, although she does have her research notes."

"The department is looking into it," Summers said.

On my way out the door, I heard Renee telling him how worried she was with all the bad juju going on in town. Summers tried to assuage her fears, but I could hear in his voice that he was concerned, too.

When I returned to the shop, I mopped the moisture off my hair, face, and shoulders, snatched my cleaning cloth from behind the Dutch door, and headed toward the stockroom.

By the register, Joss was chatting with Yvanna's younger sister Yolanda.

Joss caught sight of me and motioned for me to join them. "Courtney, two things. First, Violet Vickers phoned and said she loved, loved, loved the garden. Isn't that *lovely*?" She winked.

"Lovely." I winked back.

"Second, I think we've found our part-timer. Yolanda's hours at Savvy Diner were cut, and she would like to work for us on the weekends and perhaps Wednesdays. How does that sound?"

I took Yolanda's hands in mine. "Perfect!" We wouldn't have to do a background check or anything, seeing as she'd already been helping us for the Saturday teas.

"I've even convinced her to take on managing this weekend's tea by herself so I can help you at Misty's soiree," Joss added.

"Lifesaver." Until now, I hadn't figured out how I'd run all the party games on my own. I could manage children's parties by myself, where there were plenty of mothers willing to help, but an adult party? Meaghan had offered to assist, but having Joss there would make it go that much more smoothly.

"Just so you know," Yolanda said, "I'd prefer if you call me Yoly from now on. It's much easier for everyone to remember."

"Yoly it is," I said. "It suits you." Out of the corner of my eye, I spied Christopher's wife, Leanne, slipping into the shop. "Joss, do the paperwork, and Yoly, if you'd like to start today, you can spend the afternoon getting to know all the product and protocol."

"Excellent. I'm very excited."

"I'm going to take care of our new customer." I set the

dirty cloth behind the counter and strode to Leanne, who was admiring a petite wind chime fitted with a blue-winged fairy on its handle. "Leanne, nice to see you." I wondered if Christopher had mentioned our contentious conversation. Doubtful. "Are you alone?" I glanced out to the courtyard but didn't see any of her family.

"I am. Chris and the kids are hiking. I was"—she hooked her thumb over her shoulder—"across the street at the pottery shop when you came in."

"I didn't see you."

"You were occupied. I overheard you talking to that detective." She tugged on the tie strings of her oversized sweatshirt. "I, um, saw the flyers you referred to about Twyla Waterman, and well, I . . ." She gnawed on her chapped upper lip. "I saw her on Friday night."

"Where? What time?"

"On the beach. Sitting on a bench. She was staring straight ahead. She didn't see me. I'd gone out for air. The kids were driving me crazy at the hotel. Our dinner reservation wasn't until eight, so Christopher won the job of taking them to Kids Camp while I cleared my head."

I clutched her slim shoulders. "This is great news. You have to tell the police."

"Will they believe me?"

"You have no reason to lie. If Detective Summers is no longer at the pottery shop, the precinct is just a few blocks away." I gave her directions. "Please talk to him. For Twyla's sake."

She looked nervous but said, "Okay."

I didn't want to jump the gun and call Tish. I would let Summers do the honors. But I was over the moon. Twyla Waterman would be exonerated.

I lifted the petite wind chimes Leanne had been admiring and said, "Would you like this as a thank you? Free of charge."

She beamed. "That's so generous."

"Let's wrap it up."

While handing her the gift bag, my cell phone buzzed. Meaghan had texted: *Misty's house! Now!!!*

Chapter 15

When on the plains the fairies made a ring;
Then a field-cricket, with a note full clean,
Sweet and unforced and softly sung the mean.
—William Browne, "The Fairy Musicians"

I told Joss where I was headed, threw on my slicker, and hurried to Misty's house. Meaghan was alone in the gray-and-white kitchen, standing near the sink, filling a glass with water. The white tile counters glistened in the illumination coming from the recessed lighting in the vaulted ceilings. The soft gray walls radiated calm. My friend looked anything but.

Clandestinely, she beckoned me with a finger.

I tiptoed to her. "What's up?"

"Misty's in the back." She led me to the big plate-glass window in the living room. "I need to tell you something. You'll never guess what I heard. Before Misty got here, Mom and I were chatting with Rafaela—"

"The housekeeper."

"Yep. She and Mom just left. Rafaela confirmed what Nova said about Farrah promising to help Misty get a role in a movie. Rafaela was dusting in here when Misty was in the study, talking on the phone with Farrah. She heard their conversation because the speaker was switched on. She said Misty was very unhappy—*muy triste*—when Farrah told her she wouldn't get the role. Not ever."

"Not ever?"

"Uh-huh. Farrah said that Berto had his heart set on Farrah for that part, so she caved and said she'd do it. Misty yelled at Farrah that she'd promised, and Farrah tried to assuage her by saying she'd try to get Berto to consider Misty for the role of the farmer's wife. Misty screeched, 'The farmer's wife? She's sixty. No way can I play sixty!' And Farrah said, 'If you go without makeup.'"

I gagged. "She didn't."

"She did. Needless to say, when Misty stopped ranting, Farrah cackled and brushed it off by saying, 'Aren't you happy in Carmel, hobnobbing with the elite? Why try to start an acting career this late in the game?'"

Oof. That was the same sentiment Phoebe and Peri had expressed.

"As if that wasn't enough to pour salt on the wound, Farrah added, 'Working on a movie is not for the faint of heart, darling. I've developed a spine. I'm not convinced you could. One bad movie and suddenly you're poison. Nobody will hire you.'"

"Farrah said the word *poison*?"

"Yep."

"When did this happen?" I asked.

"Friday afternoon. After we left."

My stomach plummeted.

"There's more. Misty screamed at Farrah and called her names. She said she'd been counting on her with Berto. She said one role could lead to many, and with money being tight—"

"Money's tight?" The other day at the shop, Misty had

said *Money's no object,* but if it was an issue, then that might explain why she intended to pay for the party with a credit card.

"When Misty ended the call, Rafaela quickly put her earbuds in her ears so she could pretend not to have heard."

Fiona whizzed into the room. "There you are." She was out of breath. Her gossamer hair was windblown. "Joss told me you came here in a flurry. Merryweather found out something about Austin Pinter. He—" She tilted her head. "What's going on?"

I filled her in, and she zoomed away. To speak to Cedric.

Misty appeared in the arch of the hallway, cell phone pressed to her chest. "I thought I heard voices. How nice to see you, Courtney." She was dressed in a brilliant blue dress and matching pumps. "I got your message, and I can talk in a couple of minutes, but first I have to finish this call." She wiggled her cell phone. "Why don't you wait for me in the study?"

Meaghan squeezed my arm and said, "I've got to clean up my mess."

"The wall looks gorgeous, Meaghan," Misty crooned. "I'm so happy you and your mother took on the project. The fairies are beautiful. Just like I imagined."

Meaghan winked at me and hurried toward the backyard.

"Courtney, you'll add her fee to yours, okay?"

Silently, I calculated how much I'd have to cover and wondered, after hearing Meaghan's news about Misty's iffy finances, whether I'd get fully reimbursed.

I moved into the study while Misty remained in the living room talking on the cell phone. I skirted the desk, heading for the ornate hand-carved wooden chair to sit and collect my thoughts. I paused, however, when I noticed a receipt on top of the desk blotter from Aunt Teek's, an antique shop down the coast, for two Tiffany lamps and two antique cabinets. Misty hadn't bought them; she'd sold them. Another receipt was peeking from below. From Batcheller Galleries. Jeremy had paid Misty for one of Joan Miró's *Constellations* series paintings. I glanced at the walls and pictured the spread in *Carmel Estates*. It had included that particular painting, which had hung beyond the desk on a paneled wall. I recalled Violet Vickers saying Misty had sold her the Miró that Misty had displayed in the foyer. Was Cedric Winterbottom mistaken? Had other items, like silver, gone missing from the house not because the housekeeper or a random thief was stealing them, but because Misty was selling them? Was that why she'd sold her parents' estate? To make ends meet?

If she'd truly believed working as an actress would keep her afloat, was it possible that Farrah's refusal to help her had driven her over the edge, making her crazy enough to poison her friend?

"Courtney," Misty said, stepping into the study.

I jerked back a step, hoping she hadn't seen me snooping at the receipts, and studied her face. She didn't look like a killer, but then neither had the other two murderers I'd had the pleasure of meeting.

"I'm so sorry, but I can't talk right now." Misty held up her cell phone again, as if that explained all. "I have another business meeting."

With a bankruptcy attorney or a defense attorney? I thought flippantly.

"There are refreshments in the yard if you're hungry. I'll call you and set an appointment to chat. Bye." She turned to leave but spun back around. "Can't wait for the party. Odine will love it!"

When I stepped outside moments later, Fiona and Cedric flew to me. I wandered to the right, away from where Meaghan was packing up her painting supplies.

"Cedric is quite concerned," Fiona said.

"Quite," Cedric said in his British accent. "After our meeting the other day, I decided to keep my eye on Rafaela. When I couldn't catch her stealing an item, not even a spoon, I confronted her."

I gasped.

Fiona twirled a hand. "Tell her how you did it."

Cedric's green cheeks tinged greener. "I granted her a momentary reprieve."

"A what?" I glanced between them.

"A reprieve," he said, "is something we fairies can do to grant a nonbeliever the ability to see us. We can then erase the memory the moment the conversation is over."

"No way," I said, astounded.

"I can't do it," Fiona said. "I need all my adult wings. But Merryweather taught Cedric how to do it."

"When you confronted Rafaela, what did she say, Cedric?"

His wings billowed and settled. "She swore she would never steal because she is an honest, churchgoing lady. She feels sorry for Misty because she knows she has been struggling, and she prays for her often."

"Struggling," I said, "is an understatement if Misty is selling off her prized possessions."

Cedric worried his hands. "My, my."

"I saw documentation in the study. Your mistress is proud and probably won't want to admit it, but that might be why she sold the estate. I'm not clear as to what happened to make her struggle, and she ought to know how to manage finances given her degree in economics and her MBA, but it's possible that whatever happened pushed her over the edge, making her angry enough to kill."

"No!" Cedric shook his head. "I won't believe it."

"She told Meaghan she was here making tissue-paper flowers for the party on Friday night," I stated. "Can you corroborate her whereabouts?"

"I'd like to, but no-o," Cedric stammered. "I can't. I was out."

"Out?" Fiona asked.

He puffed his chest. "We're allowed to socialize."

"You can. I'm not allowed to until . . ." She let the rest hang.

"This is worrisome," Cedric said. "I can't believe my mistress is a killer."

"I don't want to believe it, either." I petted his wing. "But somebody did kill Farrah Lawson, and I'd like to help the police find out who."

"Odine knows all of my mistress's secrets," Cedric confided. "Talk to her."

Chapter 16

How to tell if a fairy is nearby: Strange jovial music.
—Anonymous

On the way back to work, I slipped into the Doud Arcade. Odine hadn't changed the display window for Fantasy Awaits. It still held the guardian dragons and the bulky jewelry Brady and I had seen Sunday night.

I pushed the door open, and a bell jingled. Fiona, given her fear of the oversized fairy and dragon posters on the shop's walls, huddled against my neck. "Relax," I whispered to her. "Take a deep breath. Smell the honeysuckle?"

On the sales counter, Odine had lit candles of varying sizes. Honeysuckle, in the language of flowers, happened to be the symbol of love and fidelity. Its heady fragrance was meant to induce dreams of passion. I remembered as a girl sitting on my best friend's fence. She and I would drink the juice from the trumpet-shaped flowers of the honeysuckle vines that had grown rampant over the fence, chatting about who we would marry. We had to fend off bees, but we welcomed the butter-flies.

"Hi, sugar," Odine said as I entered. She was at the sales counter ringing up a customer. "What a nice surprise. Be right with you."

An assortment of silk kimonos and colorful shawls hung on a rack to the right of the entrance. In addition to the gigantic art on the walls, the décor featured three display cases organized in a U-shape. On top of the cases were T-bar jewelry stands filled with necklaces and bracelets. The display case on the right held distinctive glass pieces, like wave-art sculptures, Tiffany bowls, and colorful crystal vases. The centermost case stored an array of charms and high-end jewelry.

The left case, in which I'd discovered the dragon necklace for Joss, contained all things dragon-related: Samurai swords with dragon hilts, blade-folding pocketknives with dragon enameling, copper Chinese dragon statues, and more.

Odine finished with the customer and approached me. "What a fun color for a slicker," she said. "You look like a school crossing guard."

I chuckled.

"Can I interest you in another dragon pendant?"

"No, I've come for—" *Think, Courtney.* I didn't want to admit that I'd dropped in to gather info on Misty. "A gift for my friend's niece. It's her birthday." I could give Georgie a trinket; she was a steady customer. "What music are we listening to?" I didn't recognize the orchestral tune piping through speakers.

"Mozart's sonata number seventeen in C."

"It's lively."

I strolled to the centermost counter. A Zen garden like mine sat next to the antique register. Odine had told me on my first visit that she'd set it there so she could meditate when business was slow. I leaned forward to view the contents of the display case: multi-gemstone earrings, cuff bracelets, and elaborate rings. "Ooh. I see you have a new set of silver charms, and they're not all mythical creatures." The charms were nestled in a velvet-lined box fitted with sixteen slots.

"I'm branching out," Odine said. "Birds and flowers hold a special appeal for tourists."

"Is that why you've added the gigantic photographs of purple flowers?"

"Mm-hm. Took them myself."

"I see you've added smaller photographs, too." I motioned to an array of boxed photographs of honeysuckle behind the register. "They're very pretty."

"Anything to attract new customers. Not everyone wants something *exotic.*" She mimed quotation marks with her fingers. "I had them all processed at Posey's Prints in Monterey."

"What lens did you use?"

"A One-oh-five millimeter, F-two. I've got a Nikon and *love* what I can do with it."

"I've got the same lens."

We smiled, bonding over our shared creative outlet.

I tapped the display case glass. "May I see the charms?"

"Sure thing." She fetched the tray and set it on the counter. "What does your friend's niece like?"

"As it so happens, she loves hummingbirds and flowers and—"

"How about this hummingbird sniffing some honeysuckle?" Odine dangled a charm on its small hoop.

Fiona pulled a strand of my hair. I got the message. *Get on with it.*

"It's lovely. Would you wrap it for me?"

"I'd be happy to." Odine returned the tray to its case and locked the cabinet.

"I was just over at Misty's," I said, hoping the segue sounded natural. "The party décor is coming along. Misty is pleased."

"Great."

"Although I heard she wasn't pleased with Farrah a few days ago."

"Farrah." Odine pressed a hand to her heart. "What a shame. I can't imagine—" Her voice caught. "I can't imagine what her family as well as her friends must be going through. I've been crying off and on for days. Misty, too."

"Misty contacted Farrah's family. She's going to help them arrange a memorial for her in about a month."

"That's sweet. I hope I can attend." Odine removed a tiny purple box from a drawer and placed it on the counter. "Why was Misty upset with Farrah?"

Perfect. She'd opened the conversation.

"Supposedly," I said, "Farrah offered to introduce her to a director for a role in a movie, but then Farrah reneged, and Misty got upset. Apparently, money's tight and she needed the job."

"Ridiculous!" Odine batted the air. "Misty doesn't need money. Who told you that?"

"My friend Meaghan said the housekeeper—Meaghan's painting the mural on Misty's wall—"

"I know Meaghan. I love Flair Gallery. She reps some extremely talented artists. Go on."

"Well, Meaghan said Rafaela heard Misty talking with Farrah. Yelling, in fact. The speaker for the telephone was on."

"*Pfft.* Number one, never listen to housekeepers. They're gossips." Odine set the charm on the synthetic cotton pad inside the purple box. She topped it with another layer of synthetic cotton, then donned the lid. "Number two, Misty wants to get into the acting business to have something to do. She's bored with a capital *B*. Being a trust fund baby isn't all it's cracked up to be. Yes, she donates time to this and that charity and sits on the boards of foundations, but that kind of life is not fulfilling. For her, anyway."

"She sold her estate." I handed Odine my credit card.

"To simplify."

"And a valuable piece of art."

"One can only have so many *things*." She emphasized the word. "At some point, they become a burden. When Misty's folks died, she was bereft and was simply getting bogged down. Tending to an estate requires constant attention." Odine tied the box with glittery purple ribbon, taking her time to make the loops equal in size. "Now she feels lighter and eager to do what makes her happy. For your information, I happen to know she's flush because, up until my husband left town, he did her books. He would have mentioned any financial issues."

Would he have? I wouldn't want Joss revealing my financial situation to my friends.

"You can't possibly think Misty had anything to do with Farrah's death," Odine added. "There are plenty of other suspects, Courtney. I saw two guys in town that Farrah dumped back in college. Let's just say neither was a happy dude. She broke hearts right and left. I've mentioned them to the police."

Behind Odine I spied Fiona hopping from pushpin to pushpin while checking out a series of oversized postcards pinned to a corkboard, including destinations like Panama, the Canary Islands, and Mozambique.

"Are those postcards from your husband's trip?" I pointed.

Odine glanced over her shoulder. "Yes. They're my visual map. I keep them as a reminder that he'll return soon. When he does, we'll resume where we left off."

Farrah had said Odine was better off without him, but Odine plainly didn't believe that. The dreamy look in her eyes gave her away.

"Back to Misty," I said, still craving more information. "If you say she's flush, I believe you, but I have to say, she spends money like water. The new house. The party. Treating friends right and left."

Odine chuckled. "That's her, sugar. It's who she's always been. She spoils many of us, perhaps because she never married or had children. We're her family. We're sisters. You should see some of her lavish dinner parties. Steak tartare, caviar on toast points. She is a foodie through and through."

"Why didn't she marry?" Immediately, I felt my cheeks warm. "That was rude. It's none of my business."

A woman in a navy-blue raincoat over jeans entered and veered right to inspect the kimonos.

"Need any help?" Odine asked.

The woman waved. "Just browsing."

"*Just browsing*," Odine whispered to me, conspiratorially. "Do you hear that a lot?"

"All the time. We can't push customers, or they get resentful."

"Exactly." Odine set the jewelry box into a glossy purple bag and tied the handles with ribbon. "As for why Misty never married, it's a sad story. A guy she met during a college summer fling broke her heart. He was a promising film director-producer and told her he had no room for distractions in his life if he intended to become a success." She aimed a finger at me. "Come to think of it, he was the guy who gave Farrah her big break." She tapped her chin with a finger. "What was his name? Berto? That's it. Berto something."

"Bagnoli," I said.

"Yes."

Interesting. Misty had requested a favor from him for a friend but not for herself, even now, umpteen years later? How bad had their breakup been? "Did Misty begrudge Farrah her success?"

"Heavens no. Misty knew Farrah had stars in her eyes and talent oozing from her pores."

"Did Misty ever consider moving to Hollywood to win Berto over?"

"She couldn't. Not with her folks calling the shots. They wanted her to marry this guy and that guy, but she hated all of them." Odine *tsk*ed. "According to her, they had rods up their wazoos. Around the age of thirty, she resigned herself to being an old maid."

I ached for Misty. What a tragedy to give up on life that young. Perhaps that was why she'd thrown herself whole-heartedly into causes.

Odine glanced to her right. The customer had moved to the display holding the swords and knives. "Those are all one of a kind," Odine said to the woman, and refocused on me. "Cash or credit?"

"Cash." I pulled my wallet from my purse and took out two twenties.

Odine pushed a button on the register. The machine *clang*ed.

"Uh-oh!" my fairy cried. "Oh, no!" She faltered and slipped. The noise must have scared her. Her wings fluttered but they couldn't expand. "Eeps!" She groped for a pushpin, caught hold, and then, as deftly as a gymnast on parallel bars, swung up and around, landing on a lower pushpin. But the pin wobbled and, like a domino chain reaction, one pushpin after another lost its hold and postcard after postcard spilled onto the floor.

"Yipes!" I croaked.

Odine whirled around and muttered about the darned heating system blowing out too much air. She bent to retrieve the cards. I cut around the counter to help. A few had landed writing side up, and I gaped. There were no words on any of them, and no postmark cancellations, either.

She caught me studying the blank cards and blanched. "I . . . I wanted to follow my husband's route. That way I could keep him close in my heart. You understand, don't you?"

"Absolutely. I kept track of my ex-fiancé and his career for a while before letting him go."

"You think I need to let my husband go?"

"No. I didn't say . . . I don't know . . ." I sputtered. "It's between you two."

Odine nodded.

I spied Fiona perched atop the cash register. She splayed her tiny arms, wings fluttering, miming that it wasn't her fault.

The door to the shop opened, the chime pealed, and Nova Pasha hurried in, her hooded black raincoat beaded with moisture, the tails of her black lace scarf wafting behind her. I considered Twyla's description of the fairy door craftsperson. Could it be Nova, using her creative talents in another way? Maybe she was attempting to interact with the fairy world in the hope that fairies might boost her business.

"Hi, Courtney. Hi, Odine." Nova shimmied the water off her raincoat. "I hate drizzly days. Hope it doesn't rain."

"Heavy rain isn't in the forecast," I said.

"Good to hear. Forgive me, Courtney, I'm sorry to intrude." She sidled next to me. "Odine . . ."

Odine set the postcards on top of the display case. "How can I help you?"

"I wanted to show you the shawl pins Misty commissioned for party favors. I might have made too many, but I'd like her guests to have a choice." She pulled her jewelry holder from her rhinestone-studded tote and set it on the countertop. She withdrew samples of the shawl pins. "What do you think? Misty hasn't been answering my calls. Courtney already saw them at dinner last night at Meaghan's."

"They're nice," Odine said. "Perhaps you'd like to vary the charms on the ends? They don't all have to be flowers, do they?"

Nova shook her head.

"I have something you might like. I'll be right back." Odine ducked through the purple curtain leading to her stockroom.

The customer who'd been admiring the dragon statues yelled, "I'll be back with my sister!" and exited.

The dragon statues were rather large, I noted. Nothing a shoplifter could pocket. No need to worry about the customer's speedy departure. I returned my attention to Nova. "I hope you had a good time last night."

"What are you doing here, Courtney?" she asked, a real non sequitur.

"Buying a charm for a friend."

"Which one?"

"A hummingbird."

"That's nice . . . and you're nice . . . usually."

I raised an eyebrow. "What do you mean *usually*?"

"The police questioned me a bit ago about Farrah's murder." Her mouth drew into a thin line. "Did you put them up to it?"

Alarm bells rang out in my mind. Nova looked peeved. No, more than peeved. Incensed. Had she killed Farrah? Was she contemplating how she'd get rid of me next?

I said, "I think they're questioning anyone who knew her."

"Don't lie. I know you did it after we played the *Where were you?* game last night." She fingered the postcards from foreign lands and shuffled through them. "I know I come across quirky, given the tattoos and, well, the *spiritual* thing." She mimed quotation marks as Odine had when saying the word *exotic*.

"I appreciate people who are spiritual," I murmured.

"Sure, but not woo-woo."

"As if I'm one to talk." I laughed. "I can see fairies."

Nova sucked in her cheeks. "About that. Can you really?"

"Mm-hm."

"Right." She twirled a finger beside her head.

Nonbelievers could be insensitive, but I didn't mind. If I could handle my father's ridicule, I could handle anyone's.

"For your information, I answered every question the police asked," Nova said. "I don't know if they believed me—stargazing is pretty hard to prove—but I didn't kill Farrah." She cocked a hip. "Yeah, yeah, I know she talked trash about my bracelet and said other junk about me on social media. Heck, she published mean stuff about other people she knew, too. She considered herself an influencer." She spread her hands. "And look, I'm fully aware that harming someone's reputation is a great motive for murder, but I didn't do it." Something flickered in her eyes.

"What aren't you saying?" I asked.

She didn't respond.

"Did you see Farrah that night?"

She blinked.

"Did you run into her as she was heading back to the Airbnb?"

She blinked, more rapidly.

"Did you follow her? Did things get out of control?"

"Stop. I did *not* do it. I didn't." Tears pooled in Nova's eyes. "You're cruel."

Whoa, Courtney, cool your heels. Who made you Columbo? I swallowed hard. What had come over me? I searched for Fiona, wondering if she'd dusted me with a potion, but saw her perched on the edge of the Zen garden, lost in thought. I had no one but myself to blame.

"I'm sorry, Nova," I murmured. "I didn't mean . . . I'm sorry."

She shrugged a shoulder with attitude and resumed fingering the postcards.

Trying to make nice, I said, "Those are from the places Odine's husband is visiting. She wants to have a visual map so when he comes home—"

"Bullpuckey!" Nova hissed.

I startled.

"He's not coming back." Nova cut a look at the stockroom. "Not after the fling with Farrah—"

"What fling?"

"Last year. When Farrah came to visit between gigs. She and Odine's hubby were all over one another. When Farrah found out he was married . . . to Odine . . . she swore she had no idea. . . . She ended it like *that*"—Nova snapped—"and pleaded for Odine's forgiveness. Delta Gammas stick together, she said. Odine bought that malarkey. And hubby?" She snorted. "Hubby took the breakup hard. I guess he'd really fallen for Farrah. Within weeks, he grew cold and heartless toward Odine, and off he went to sail around the world. Who does that?"

My heart ached for Odine. "Did she blame Farrah?"

"No. Odine blamed him. But a nanosecond later, she forgave him. That's the kind of person she is."

"With that kind of history, why would Farrah agree to come to Odine's party?"

"Because Misty begged her to. Misty wants us to be one big happy family, warts and all." Nova shuffled through the postcards and held up the postcard for Panama. "This was hubby's first stop."

Given the man's rocky history with Farrah, was it possible he'd slipped back into town and killed her? It was certainly a theory to pose to Detective Summers.

"Here we are, Nova." Odine, carrying a plastic baggie with an assortment of charms in it, pushed through the drapes. "Variety is the spice of life, don't you think?"

"Yes. They're swell. Thanks."

Odine passed her the bag and removed the postcard from her hand. "No charge."

"You're the best. See you Saturday." Nova didn't linger. She made a beeline for the door.

When she left, a slew of theories zinged through my mind. Stealing a man's husband or making a husband so forlorn that he would abandon his wife to sail around the world was plenty of motive to want someone dead. On the other hand, Nova swore that Odine had forgiven Farrah, and Odine had been kind enough to set up Farrah in her rental house.

"Courtney," Odine said, "you're staring at me. Is something wrong?"

"What? Um, no." I sounded less than convincing.

"Did Nova say something to upset you?"

I glanced over my shoulder at the door. *Nova.* Had she been following me? Had she come into Fantasy Awaits to seed my mind with doubts about Odine? She was adamant that she hadn't killed Farrah, but I'd seen something flicker in her eyes. She was hiding something.

Fiona landed on my shoulder and whispered, "We should leave."

"I was just thinking about Misty," I lied to Odine. "I'm concerned."

Odine flapped a hand. "I wouldn't worry about her. Misty always rallies. Always."

Chapter 17

Is a fairy a demoted angel,
or is an angel a fairy reunited with its Maker?
—Daryl Wood Gerber

Brushing droplets of rain off my slicker as I entered Open Your Imagination, I caught sight of a cluster of women peering at something on the sales counter. "What's going on?"

No one answered.

I skirted them and took in the view. A jewelry tray, similar to the one at Odine's, held silver, half-inch to one-inch charms, except these were all fairy charms. Joss was holding one up for examination.

"Where did you find these?" I asked.

"I made them. I've been meaning to tell you for weeks, and this morning when I came in, we got so busy . . ." Joss jiggled the charm that, other than being silver, was the spitting image of Fiona.

"You made them?" I gawked. Would wonders never cease? The woman was a marvel. Not only was she a wizard with numbers, a reliable employee, a dedicated daughter to her aging mother, and one of the best friends a person could have, but she could also fashion jewelry?

"I didn't *make them* make them." She guffawed. "I designed them and sent the designs to a silversmith. He shipped them back. I added the loops and chains."

Suddenly my insides roiled with worry. I placed a hand on her arm. "Are you planning a new career? Are you going to quit?"

"No. Don't be silly. Making these is a pastime to keep me from going crazy worrying about my mom."

"Aren't you dating that sweet guy?"

"Well, yeah, but not seven days a week. I like my *me* time." She returned to selling the charms. "By the way, we're splitting the profits fifty-fifty."

"No way, José," I said. "Seventy-thirty. You take the seventy. You're the one paying the silversmith and doing the heavy lifting."

"They are so-o-o heavy," she clowned, dangling an earring from one finger.

Fiona floated above the tray. "I like them all," she said. "Did I inspire you?"

Joss nodded.

"Excellent," Fiona said. "Fairies love to inspire. You know, these charms make me think of the one you bought at Fantasy Awaits, Courtney. Did you know that honeysuckle is not only the symbol for love but for lost love?"

"I did not."

"Merryweather told me."

Perhaps that was why Odine had lit so many candles and had hung the boxed photos of the flowers on the walls. I couldn't imagine how she felt having lost her husband to Farrah and then to the sea.

Fiona yawned. "Courtney, even though this afternoon has been stressful . . ."

Joss glanced at me and mouthed: *Stressful?*

I whispered, "I'll explain."

"I think we should go to the office," Fiona continued, "and kick around some ideas."

I squelched a smile. I couldn't imagine fairies kicking around anything. Did fairies play soccer? With fairy soccer balls? I peeked at the activity on the patio. Customers seemed content and not in need of assistance. Pixie was napping at the foot of the fountain.

"Let's go." I motioned to Fiona and strode to the office. After closing the door, I said, "What's up?"

Fiona landed on the rim of the Zen garden, did a twirl, and plopped to a sit. "Nova," she said, "is a conundrum. That is what Sherlock Holmes would call her. She is sweetness and sunshine and also darkness and misery."

"That could explain why she likes to wear white one day and black the next. She dresses to suit her mood."

"Today, she wore black. Do you think she's at war with you?"

"No. She was upset because I'd mentioned her name to Detective Summers and he'd questioned her. I didn't enjoy it when he questioned me, either. He can be . . . intimidating."

Fiona stirred the sand with her toe. "What do you think he has discovered so far?"

"Regarding Nova? Probably no more than I did. She claims she was stargazing the night Farrah died. Unless someone saw or *didn't* see her car at the turnout, it's pretty unprovable. Not much the police can refute at this juncture. I'm sure they are sorting through whatever evidence they have, like fingerprints or trace fibers." Were they looking to see who might have purchased whatever poison had been used? I wondered. Was it even an over-the-counter poison or a specialized concoction?

"Motive." Fiona kicked the sand. It *poof*ed in the air and fell. "It always comes down to motive."

"True. Nova was angry with Farrah because of her post on social media and the damage that might do to her reputation."

"We should look at it."

"Good idea." I rounded the desk, sat in the chair, and brought the sleeping computer to life. I accessed the internet and searched for Nova Pasha's social media profile. She had a website, Facebook page, Instagram, and more. Facebook seemed like the one Farrah would have accessed and posted comments on regularly, so I pulled up Nova's page. Her banner featured pieces of jewelry lying on a blanket of silver velvet. She'd included a headshot, her black-outlined eyes bright and her attitude sassy, which made her look much bolder than she typically came across.

The best way to find comments about something she'd created, I decided, was to scroll through her photos. She'd posted a lot of them: drinking wine with Misty; getting tattoos with Odine; hiking and gathering flowers with a bunch of other friends. There were pictures of the ocean and stars. Dozens of her holding a Ragdoll cat like Pixie. A single photo of her with a bookish-looking man—*Nathan Livingston,* the caption said. None of the photographs included Farrah.

I found a photograph of the corsage-style bracelet that she'd designed for Farrah and double-clicked on it. As described, it featured black velvet, gold, and pearls. It was too retro for my taste, but it was lovely, nonetheless. All comments showed up along the right-hand side of the screen. I scrolled through them—most were positive—until I caught sight of a comment from Farrah. It was scathing. More than scathing; it was brutal, with the words *tasteless, gaudy, amateurish,* and *garbage* weaved into the tirade.

"Poor Nova," I murmured.

I pressed the back arrow and found a photo of Nova kissing the nose of the cat, which she'd named Scooter. There were lots of positive comments about him.

I returned to the main set of photos, and out of curiosity, selected the photo of Nova with Nathan. The post that accompanied the photo read: *With much regret, I must share with you today about my good friend Nathan. He was my heart and soul, but he was sick, and now he's gone. I will miss him forever.*

"Wow, he died?" I whispered, tears pooling in my eyes.

"Oh, no." Fiona alit on my shoulder. "That's so sad."

I couldn't imagine posting something so personal on the shop's social media pages. That was what private messages, chat rooms, and emails were for. Fans of Open Your Imagination wanted to read about happy, positive events.

"Odine commented." Fiona pointed at the screen. "Misty, too."

Both had written: *I'm sorry for your loss.*

Farrah had responded with: *Good riddance.*

I yelped. "Honestly? What kind of nasty comment is that?" I'd been thinking Farrah was all fun and lightness, but she certainly had a dark side.

Curious to learn more, I typed Farrah's name into the search bar. A professional page emerged. She had over one hundred thousand followers. The photos she'd published, like other Hollywood stars' pages I'd visited, were of Farrah mugging with her famous friends; Farrah pitching books she liked to read; Farrah dressing for award shows; Farrah cooking in her kitchen. She looked happy. Normal. Not cutthroat and ruthless. But then I spied a picture of the bracelet Nova had made among Farrah's photos and clicked on it. The post, like Farrah's review on Nova's page, was caustic, questioning Nova's talent and her style, recommending that no one—*no one*—buy anything from her. She even lashed out at Misty, livid that she had recommended Nova in the first place.

My face grew hot. My fingers clenched. How could she? And if I felt this angry, I could only imagine how Nova had felt.

I closed the search engine and settled back in the chair. Why had Farrah felt the need to lash out at Nova? Had they vied for the same man at some point? Not Nathan. He wasn't Farrah's type. Perhaps someone back in college? Austin? No, he was devoted to Farrah now and probably had been then. Why had she taken on Nova with such ferocity?

"Everyone is guilty," Fiona said.

"What?" I lifted her with my finger and held her closer to my face. "What do you mean?"

"Sherlock Holmes says, 'When you have eliminated the impossible, whatever remains, however improbable, must be the truth.' That's from *The Sign of the Four.*"

"You never cease to amaze me."

"Fairies have good memories." She fluffed her wings with pride. "Therefore, everyone is guilty until we eliminate suspects. Do it."

"Do what?"

"The list. Like you do for your ideas."

When I planned fairy gardens, I often used a marker board to sketch the concept. When Meaghan's mother was a suspect in a murder, I'd used the same board to imagine who the suspects were. My intent hadn't been to compete with the police. I'd simply wanted to clarify in my mind what I'd discovered, and if necessary, could share with Detective Summers.

To free my mind of clutter, I queued up an instrumental violin playlist on my iPhone and propped the marker board on an easel that I stored in the closet. First, I added Nova's name on the board.

Nova Pasha: not in the sorority but part of the theater group; angry at Farrah for dissing her work on social media; swore at Odine's shop that she was innocent. Knows about needles and tattoos. Does she know about poisons? Was poison injected or imbibed? Motive: fury at Farrah's blatant disdain of her. Alibi: stargazing by herself. Hard to prove.

Misty Dawn: sorority sister; upset with Farrah, who did not help her get a role in a movie; might have money issues, though Odine swears she doesn't. Can't imagine she knows about poisons, but Misty is cagey. Why is she really selling her worldly goods? Motive: betrayed. Alibi: at home making tissue paper flowers for party. Witnesses?

Odine Oates: also sorority sister; Farrah had an affair with her husband, and then the husband left her to go on a worldwide sailing trip. Odine forgave Farrah and believes husband will return. Will he? Does she know about poisons? Like Nova, has tattoos. Might know how to wield a hypodermic needle. Owner of Airbnb where Farrah stayed. Must have keys. Motive: retribution for ruining her marriage. Alibi: at her shop doing the books and verified by Summers who questioned the deli that provided Odine's dinner. What about her husband? Where is he?

Twyla Waterman: no relationship to Farrah; Farrah warned her to watch out after facial treatment. Did Twyla kill her before Farrah could retaliate? Was she drugged during her time in the cult? Does she know how to drug someone? Motive: survival, reputation. Alibi: on her regular walk; stopped to look at ocean. Leanne Cox confirmed seeing Twyla sitting on bench by ocean. Does this truly exonerate her?

Austin Pinter: former lover; Farrah led him on Friday night and ditched him; he called her fickle and suggested she might have been meeting another man. He's a writer. Loves research. He might know about poisons. Strong, muscular, capable of overpowering Farrah. Motive: humiliation and/or jealousy. Alibi: at home writing and heard neighbor's loud rock music.

"Fiona," I said, "tell me about Austin Pinter."

"What about him?" She stopped stirring her feet in the sand.

"I know the police questioned him on Saturday morning, which could have been the reason he missed his critique group at the library. However, when you came to Misty's, you started to tell me what Merryweather had learned, but didn't, because you flew off to speak with Cedric."

"Austin." She sighed. "It's so sad. Merryweather found his diary. He is giving up his career and looking for a job. He typed up a new resume. That's why I sensed it was dire."

"It's not dire to give up a career if it's not the one that fulfills you," I said, having gone through that myself.

"No, it was the diary. In it, he wrote that he is despondent."

"Okay, that could be serious. He might need therapy." But it didn't make him a murderer.

I stepped away from the board and reviewed what I'd written. The office telephone jangled once and stopped. Joss must have answered.

Seconds later, she appeared in the doorway. "Problem, boss." She pointed to the phone. The hold button was blinking. "The tables for the party can't be delivered. The truck broke down in Sacramento."

"Sacramento?"

"Seems that's where their headquarters are, and the guy on the phone says they're committed to providing items for other parties in San Francisco this weekend, so they're fresh out. Any ideas?"

I shook my head and picked up the telephone. I thanked

the scheduling guy for alerting me. He promised to refund my deposit, and I ended the call.

Joss was peering at the marker board. "Cross Twyla off the list."

"Yes, of course." Unless Leanne Cox was lying, there really wasn't time for Twyla to get from the beach to the rental house before Farrah's Fitbit went silent.

"As for the others?" Joss folded her arms. "I really don't want Misty to be guilty."

I filled her in on the conversation the housekeeper had heard.

"Lordy, that's not good." She pointed toward the door. "I'd better get back. We have a lot of customers."

She left, and I dialed Brady.

He answered warmly. "Hey, beautiful. What's up?"

"I have a big favor to ask. Do you happen to know a company that supplies rental tables and chairs? My guy canceled for Saturday."

"For Misty's party?"

"Yes. I'll need to seat twelve . . . No, eleven." My throat grew tight, but I pressed on. "It's the chairs I'm most worried about. I want them to be nice. We can cover the tables with tablecloths. And two buffet tables," I added hastily. I'd almost forgotten about those. One for food and another for the fairy garden items. "And a bar setup."

He chuckled. "As it so happens, I know a guy who runs a café in town, and he has all of those items on hand."

"You're a saint." I glanced at the marker board. Rereading the motives brought something to mind. "Say, I've been meaning to ask you. I heard your mother's manuscript was stolen. Any luck finding it?"

"Not yet."

"Do you think the petty thief might be the culprit?"

"The police think it's a totally separate deal. Mom's . . ." He let the word hang.

"Upset."

"Very. It's not like she can re-create eighty thousand words in a month, when the book is due." He sighed. "I've been trying to move her into the twenty-first century. She has to learn how to scan everything into a computer, or at the very least, pay someone to type it into a document for her. She's so old school."

"I'm sorry. Please give her my condolences."

"Will do."

Fiona soared ahead of me as I strode into the showroom. I surveyed the crowd. Glinda and her niece were consulting with Joss at the sales counter. Three women were huddled by the Royal Doulton display that I'd rearranged earlier. A woman and young girl were sorting through the garden tools for kids. On the patio, Pixie was chasing a toddler, who was running from his mother and squealing with glee.

"Courtney, get over here." Glinda beckoned me. "I heard the buzz about Joss's jewelry and had to come see my competition."

Joss chuckled. "As if."

"Georgie has already picked out two sets of earrings she wants to buy for friends." Glinda pushed the hood of her raincoat off her head and primped her hair. "Will you guys be stealing all the teen business from me?" She winked.

"Ha! It's just a side gig, Glinda," I assured her and winked back. "Glitz will always be the premier jewelry store in this courtyard. Georgie, I have something for you."

"For me?" Her eyes widened. "Why?"

"Because it's your birthday week. Wait here." I fetched the charm I'd purchased at Fantasy Awaits from the office and handed it to her. "I hope you like it."

She opened the box quickly and let out an *eek*. "I love it. It's so cute. I have a charm bracelet that my mother gave me when I was five. Mostly I have tennis charms, but I see lots of hummingbirds and flowers when we go hiking, so this is perfect. Thank you." She threw her arms around me.

I hugged her back. "Enjoy."

"Courtney!" Holly Hopewell entered the shop, towing her sister Hedda by the hand. They couldn't have looked more opposite, Holly in a floral rain slicker over leggings, and Hedda in a tailored, tied-at-the-waist, mid-length raincoat.

"He is not," Hedda said to her sister as they approached.

"He is."

"He is what?" I asked.

"Jeremy Batcheller is her boyfriend," Holly said.

Not again. Poor Hedda. Her sisters were ganging up on her.

"Tell her what you heard Friday." Holly poked her sister's arm.

"Cut it out."

Holly prodded her again. Hedda huffed and shimmied her shoulders.

Fiona circled Hedda's head and dusted her with a glittery silver potion to calm her.

"Fine," Hedda conceded, and brushed raindrops off the shoulders of her coat. "I was leaving the library—"

"She heard Austin Pinter arguing with the dead woman," Holly cut in.

I gasped. "Farrah Lawson?"

Fiona stopped midair and gaped at me.

"When was this?" I asked.

"Around six thirty," Hedda said. "After the library closed. I'd lingered outside talking to a girlfriend. When she left for home, I heard them. They were sitting on a bench in the library garden."

That must have been where they'd headed after Fiona and

I had seen them turn onto Lincoln Street. According to Austin, he'd been upset that Farrah was ending their date early. He must have asked her to sit and explain why.

"Miss Lawson said something like, 'If you steal it, I will tell the world.'"

"I doubt she was warning him not to steal a library book. What if she"—Holly leaned closer to impart a secret—"was talking about Eudora's missing manuscript?"

Hedda blinked. "Now, Sis, stop. We don't spread rumors."

"Austin's an author," Holly argued. "An historical novelist, like Eudora. But he hasn't had a book come out in ages. And then Tuesday, the manuscript vanishes. What do you think, Courtney?"

The two of them stared at me. I worked through a theory in my head. Austin was despondent and was considering giving up his career. Why would he steal the manuscript? He couldn't publish it and expect to get away with it. More likely, he'd planned to rob a bank or a private citizen in order to fund his passion.

"Did you hear anything else?" I asked Hedda.

She shook her head. "Austin said something, and Miss Lawson sprang to her feet. She started to leave. He grabbed her arm. She wrested free, hissed that she had somewhere to be, and stormed off. He hurried after her but stopped at the corner and scratched his head. After a long moment—I was holding my breath—he pivoted, shoulders sagging, and slogged up Ocean Avenue. I didn't think any more about it. It didn't concern me."

Had Farrah's warning and subsequent dismissal enraged Austin and driven him to murder?

I regarded each of them. "Have you told the police?"

Hedda's cheeks reddened. "I didn't think it was my business, and maybe I misheard."

Holly tilted her head. "Courtney, what should we do?"

Fiona flew to my shoulder. "He could have veered right toward the Airbnb after Hedda moved on."

Honestly, I couldn't picture Austin killing Farrah. He'd been in love with her and had been bereft on Sunday when I'd seen him at Saison, as well as on Monday when he'd come to the shop.

"Courtney," Holly said, "we'd appreciate your two cents, dear."

"I think he's innocent. He claims he went home Friday night to write after he and Farrah parted ways, but he found it hard to do so because of the noisy rock band playing next door. I don't know if the police have followed up on that, but—"

"Excuse me! Sorry to listen in." Glinda edged between me and Holly. "It's a bad habit and one I'm trying to break—"

"No kidding," her niece quipped, eyes rolling.

Glinda ignored her. "There wasn't rock music playing that night in our neighborhood."

"You live near Austin Pinter?" I asked.

"Uh-huh. A couple doors down, but we were the only ones having a party. My boyfriend likes rock. I prefer jazz. I'll bet Austin heard Jimmy and me debating about it. Jimmy argued his case well. At the top of his lungs, I might add"—her boyfriend was a prominent attorney in town—"but I won." She blew on her fingertips and polished them on her raincoat. "Our guests were extremely pleased. It might have been loud, but it was jazz. Coltrane, mostly."

I exchanged a look with Fiona. Austin had lied about his alibi.

Chapter 18

The cowslips tall her pensioners be;
In their gold coats spots you see;
Those be rubies, fairy favours,
In those freckles live their savours.
—Shakespeare, "A Midsummer Night's Dream"

Glinda agreed to go with Hedda and Holly to inform Detective Summers, but only if I would give him a heads-up first. What was it about the guy that made so many of us tremble in our boots? His size? His curt I've-got-this-handled attitude?

Halfheartedly, I retreated to the office and dialed the precinct. Summers wasn't in. The clerk transferred me to Officer Reddick.

"Good day, Miss Kelly," he said in an official tone. "How might I help you?"

"I have a bit of news to impart." I proceeded to tell him about Austin Pinter's bogus alibi and his public set-to with Farrah Lawson. I added that Hedda, Holly, and Glinda were on their way to give their statements. "Apparently, he planned to steal something." I recapped Holly's theory that perhaps he was the one who had stolen Eudora Cash's manuscript. "I'm not on board with that, but they do write the same genre. On the other hand, I heard a rumor that he might give up writing and seek a new career."

Reddick listened attentively. I even heard him scribbling notes.

"You do realize it's all hearsay," he said.

"It's not hearsay that Austin lied about the music genre, meaning he was trying to give himself an alibi for the night of the murder." I told him about the way Austin had grilled Odine about what she did or didn't know about Farrah's date on Monday. "He sounded like a jealous lover."

"Thank you."

"One more thing before you hang up. You might want to look into Odine Oates's husband. Supposedly, he's on a solo sailing trip around the world, but if he sneaked into town, he could have, you know . . ." I paused for effect. "He had an affair with Farrah Lawson last year. When Farrah found out he was married, she ended the affair, and then he, angry with Farrah for dumping him, left his wife."

Reddick whistled. "Interesting. We did not know about the affair. That gives Mrs. Oates motive, as well."

"And lastly, Odine Oates said she alerted you to the fact that there were two guys in town that Farrah dumped during college. Odine thought they might hold grudges."

"She did, indeed." I heard more scribbling. "For your information, Miss Kelly, we have told Twyla Waterman that she is no longer a person of interest, due to Leanne Cox's testimony. So if I were you, I'd let this go. We'll handle it."

I sighed. "Really? You're taking Detective Summers's tack with me?"

"Yep." He hooted. "Do you want to know how to get on Detective Summers's good side?"

Did I ever.

"Facts only. He doesn't like to theorize. Like Sherlock

Holmes said in *A Scandal in Bohemia,* 'It is a capital mistake to theorize before one has data.' "

"Not you, too," I moaned. "My assistant has read every story about the great detective. Even his memoirs."

"We should hope to be half as smart as him. Have a good—"

"Hold on."

"What?" He tattooed his desk with such impatience that the sound resonated through the phone.

"For my edification, Officer, have you located Eudora Cash's manuscript?"

"No we haven't. Yet."

"Covering up a plot to steal something seems like a good motive for murder."

"You just said you didn't believe Mr. Pinter had done it."

"I've been known to be wrong," I said wryly.

Reddick sighed.

"Can you tell me who else might be on your radar?" I wondered whether the police were considering Nova or, sadly, even Misty.

"No."

"But—"

"Good day, Miss Kelly. I'll give your information to Detective—"

"Wait! One more thing. Did you find out what kind of poison was used to kill Miss Lawson?"

He remained silent.

"C'mon. What could it hurt to tell me?" I caught myself batting my eyelashes, and I winced. *Honestly, Courtney?* I hadn't used feminine wiles since I was in high school, and it wasn't like they would work, anyway. He couldn't see me. "Please? I won't share the information with anyone."

Fiona circled my head. If only she could douse him with her green potion to make him trust me.

"Starts with an *A*," Reddick murmured, and hung up.

I gaped at Fiona.

"I didn't make him talk." She mimed marking an *X* on her dainty chest. "Cross my heart."

I returned to the main showroom, wondering how many poisons started with the letter *A*. Why had Reddick revealed that to me? As a joke? Yeah, probably. *A* was, after all, the first letter in the alphabet. *Ha-ha. Forget it, Courtney.*

I headed for the patio. I needed to organize everything before leaving for the evening.

Joss was closing out the register. "We had bountiful sales today, boss."

"Good to hear."

I stepped through the French doors to the patio. Pixie scurried to me and nudged my ankle. I scooped her up and caressed her head. "Sorry, girl. It's been a busy day filled with distractions." I carried her to the workstation and set her on a bench. "Snooze while I straighten up." Customers had long gone. The sky had grown dark. Light rain splattered the tempered glass overhead. The sound comforted me.

Fiona whizzed past me and settled on Pixie's head. The cat batted her off. Giggling, Fiona soared to the top of the cabinet and crossed her legs. "Up here, kitty. Try to get me."

Often young customers came in and reoriented the figurines in the gardens I'd created. I understood and didn't blame them, but each night before leaving, I returned them to their proper places. The *Mary Poppins* and *Alice in Wonderland* designs seemed to draw the most attention, for obvious reasons. Mary's garden featured Mary at the forefront of a London rooftop, dancing with sooty chimney sweep fairies. Mary wasn't a typical garden fairy. In fact, she wasn't a fairy at all; she was a garden stake. Some prankster had moved her to the rear of the garden. Alice, who ought to have been running down a path of grass trying to escape the Queen of Hearts in a tiered, three-pot garden, was now located at the top and chasing the queen.

I lifted Mary and reinserted her at the forefront and reset Alice near the bottom of her garden, and then I stepped back, arms akimbo, and assessed both. "Good," I murmured.

"Courtney, dear," Violet Vickers said, striding across the patio. "So glad I caught you before you closed. I love, love, love the garden. It's lovely."

I bit back a smile.

"The castle and the boy fairies wooing the girl fairies was inspired. So Shakespearean and dramatic. I called earlier."

"Joss told me."

"I've been meaning to thank you in person, but life has been hectic."

Tell me about it, I mused.

"One foundation meeting after another."

"You and Misty Dawn," I said.

"Speaking of Misty, I'm a bit worried about her. I told you she offered me the Miró, which I snapped up. Well, this morning, she contacted me and asked if I'd like to purchase the Renoir. *The Reader*, I think, or *Girl Reading a Book*." Her forehead creased. "Do you think she's all right? I mean, I understood selling me the Miró, but the Renoir? It's such a personal piece. She said her mother purchased it for her when she was a girl." Violet placed a hand on her chest. "Do you think she's in financial trouble?"

"I'm positive she's fine," I said, pushing my own concern aside. "Her new place is lovely, and there's art everywhere."

"Wonderful. Good to know." Violet beamed. "Now, like I mentioned, I want a total garden redo."

"Total?" I flicked a piece of dirt off my overalls. "You said you wanted me to make a dozen fairy gardens, not redo the entire thing."

"Mercy!" She laughed heartily. "You won't be in charge of the redo. I've hired Kelly Landscaping for that."

"My father?"

"The very same. He has the best reputation around. You'll work together so the fairy gardens will be set at prime locations."

"Um, does my father know you're including fairy gardens?"

She frowned. "No. Should I have told him? Don't you two get—"

"We get along fine," I assured her, "but he doesn't believe in fairies and thinks my business is frivolous and a waste of time."

"Nonsense. We'll make it work. You'll see. I am a master of negotiation." Strolling toward the French doors, she said over her shoulder, "I want to start the overhaul in May when the weather is nice and flowers are blooming, so we'll discuss more over the coming months. Of course, we'll have to fix a price. I'll have my business manager contact you—"

A whistle rang out. Shrill. Harsh.

A woman in the courtyard yelled, "Thief!"

Not again.

I cut past Violet, through the showroom, and out the front door. Fiona trailed me.

The courtyard sparkled with twinkling lights. The rain was merely a drizzle. Even so, I heard the *splat, splat* of someone running. A slim person in a hoodie and tennis shoes was dashing down the stairs toward me. Meaghan followed while blowing a whistle, one arm raised overhead. I was no football linesman, but I had played soccer in junior high. As a goalie. I leaped forward in a crouch.

Unable to dodge me completely, the thief rammed into me and tumbled to the right, toward Wizard of Paws. I clambered to my feet and lunged. So did Meaghan. The two of us pinned the culprit to the cement.

I pushed off the lawbreaker's hood and gasped. Leanne stared up at me, her eyes flooded with tears.

"Oh, my!" Fiona bleated.

"Leanne," I whispered.

"You know her?" Meaghan looked aghast.

"She's my ex-fiancé's wife."

"Holy moly."

Joss came running out. "What the heck?"

Violet Vickers was on her heels. "Heavens!"

"Call the precinct," I ordered.

"Ziggy is already on it," Meaghan said. "Man, am I glad I have a business partner."

"Leanne." I lasered her with a look. "Did you rob Carmel Collectibles, Sweet Treats, and Birgitte's, too?"

She shuddered but kept mute, making me wonder whether she'd stolen something from Open Your Imagination when she'd come in alone. I pushed the thought from my mind.

"She was going bigger today," Meaghan said. "She pocketed that four-inch pen-and-ink by Hock."

I was familiar with it. Every time I visited Flair Gallery, I admired the artist's work. He did beautiful renderings of sea creatures and coral. None of them were cheap.

Leanne struggled to pull free. "Let me go."

"Not on a bet," Meaghan snarled.

A siren pierced the night air. Footsteps smacked the cement. I pivoted and saw Detective Summers hoofing it across the street. He must have been visiting his fiancée at Seize the Clay. At the same time, a patrol car pulled to a stop in the red zone in front of the courtyard. Officer Reddick leaped out. Both men drew to a halt beside me.

"What have we here?" Summers arched an eyebrow.

"The thief." I told him her name and added that she was on vacation with her family. "She just robbed Flair Gallery. I think she also stole from—"

"Got it." Summers regarded Leanne then Meaghan. "What did she take?"

Meaghan said, "A small, framed pen-and-ink. It's inside her jacket."

Summers pulled a zip tie from his pocket. "On your feet, Mrs. Cox."

Meaghan and I scrambled off her and helped her up.

"I didn't do it!" Leanne cried.

Summers said, "Open your jacket."

"No. I want to phone my husband." Leanne's voice quavered with fear.

"Open it, ma'am."

Reluctantly, she did, quickly catching the Hock drawing in its box frame before it fell to the ground. Her cheeks flamed pink. "Here." She offered it to Meaghan. "Please, may I call my husband? My cell phone is in my pocket." She wasn't carrying a purse, which was why no one had assumed the thief was female.

Summers allowed her to contact Christopher. She pleaded with him to come to the courtyard.

As luck would have it, he and their children were at a toy store a block away. They arrived within minutes.

Christopher's face grew dark. "What's going on?" he demanded.

"I . . ." Leanne began, tears flowing down her cheeks. "I'm sorry. I've been stealing things." She enumerated the places she'd robbed. "Inexpensive things."

Fiona *tsk*ed. "The hair clips from Birgitte's weren't cheap."

"I can't stop myself. I need help. I . . ." Leanne faced her children. "My sweethearts, Mommy has done something bad. I'm very sorry to disappoint you and Daddy."

"Don't be sad, Mommy," her daughter said, the words lisping through the gap between her front teeth.

"Detective"—Leanne focused on Summers, her lower lip trembling—"for the record, just in case you were wondering, I wasn't lying when I said I saw Miss Waterman last Friday night because I was . . ." She cut a look at Christopher, who was blistering with embarrassment. "I was casing a store to rob it. To talk myself out of it, I went to the beach to meditate. I was aware I needed treatment for my addiction. I also realized it was time to confess to my husband. I was working up the courage when I saw Miss Waterman on the bench and . . . and—" Leanne burst into tears.

Christopher's shoulders sagged. "That was the night I took the kids to dinner because you weren't feeling well?"

I gulped. She'd lied about having a late dinner reservation. Would Summers think she'd lied about seeing Twyla?

"Mm-hm." She hurled herself into his arms.

To his credit, Christopher comforted her. "Detective, is there any way we can fix this? Make reparations?"

Leanne twisted in his arms and submissively folded her hands in front of herself. "Detective, I never broke into any of the stores—they were all open for business—so I'm not guilty of breaking and entering. I don't know if that makes any difference."

I doubted it did.

Summers said, "Let's see how the judge will rule. For now, I'll need you to come to the precinct."

Leanne extended her arms.

Summers shook his head. "I think we can forgo the zip tie. Officer, if you would escort Mrs. Cox to your vehicle."

"Yes, sir." Reddick clasped Leanne's elbow. "Ma'am." He ushered her to the patrol vehicle.

Leanne glanced over her shoulder. The children started to cry. One of the boys reached for her. Christopher clasped both of his boys' hands and told his daughter to stay put.

Summers said to Christopher, "Mr. Cox—"

"Judge," Christopher said reflexively.

"Sir, I suggest you take your children to your hotel and arrange for someone to watch them, then come to the precinct. This could take a while." Summers provided the address before turning his attention to me. "Look at you and your pal, like regular Girl Scouts." He winked. "I'll give you both merit badges tomorrow."

Chapter 19

Out the little fairies fly and flutter in the air:
Oh, how lovely is the world, with moonlight everywhere!
—Anonymous, "What the Toys Do at Night"

Summers escorted Meaghan to one side to get more of her testimony, and Violet Vickers said she'd touch base with me soon.

"Courtney." Christopher hitched his chin, signaling for me to move with him to the sidewalk.

Joss said, "I'll finalize everything inside, boss. Good job! Do you need any first aid?"

"No, I'm fine." My hands were scraped, but thanks to the pavement being rain-soaked, the skin hadn't broken.

I followed Christopher and his children to the wrought-iron tables in front of the shop. He told them to sit. Fiona drifted above them sprinkling a yellow potion—to lighten their moods and make them hopeful, she explained to me.

"Courtney"—Christopher's voice cracked; he swallowed hard—"what am I going to do?"

"Do what you do best. Make a deal."

He frowned. His eyes moistened. "I had no clue."

I put a reassuring hand on his forearm. "How did she arrange so much time alone?"

"Headaches, upset stomach. I told her we should find a doctor." He worked his tongue inside his mouth. "She's been feeling pent up. Teaching isn't . . ." He hung his head. "It isn't fulfilling her."

I couldn't fix his or her problem. The best thing I could say was, "Get her treatment and then encourage her to pursue her dream."

Christopher blinked as realization dawned on him. "I've been a jerk. To her . . ." He lowered his voice. "And to you."

I removed my hand. "Past history. I'm happy with my life. Go and fix your future." I squatted to meet his children at eye level. "Your mommy will be fine. Promise."

"We know!" they chimed, proving Fiona's potion had taken effect.

Christopher clapped his hands. "Let's go, children. Back to the hotel and Kids Camp."

He shepherded them away and didn't look back.

I had my hand on the doorknob of the shop when I heard my father cry, "Courtney!"

He and Wanda were hurrying down the stairs. Dad was bundled in a raincoat. Wanda had dressed for a summer's day, with only a lilac shawl for warmth. I shivered. She had to be cold.

Wanda said, "Ziggy told us Meaghan pursued a thief. Where is—" She spied her daughter talking with Summers and drew her shawl more tightly around her shoulders. "Is she okay?"

"Fine."

"Did she catch the thief?" Dad asked.

"We both did. Meaghan and I were like—" I thought of

Summers's Girl Scout taunt. "Like Cagney and Lacey." I told them about the culprit turning out to be my ex-fiancé's wife.

My father didn't make a crack, which was nice, seeing as he despised Christopher for what he'd done to me. Instead he said, "What were you thinking?"

"At the time, I wasn't, but you know I can't sit idly by when—"

My father pulled me into his arms. "You've got to be more careful. I can't lose you, too. Please."

Emotion clogged my throat. Fiona drew near. I shooed her away with a flick of a finger.

When my father released me, he said, "We're taking Meaghan to dinner. Care to join us?"

"Can't. I have a ton of online work to do tonight, but thanks."

On my way home with Pixie tucked in my arms, I took time to breathe in the night air and listen to birds calling it a night. How I wished I could turn back the clock and erase the events of the past week. A murder. A thief. My ex coming to town.

"Do-over," I muttered.

"What's a do-over?" Fiona twirled mid-flight to stare me in the eyes.

"When a person can erase a piece of history, no matter how small, and tackle it with a finer understanding of the outcome."

She raised a hand. "I want a do-over. Except if I got one, then I might never have met you." She blew me a kiss.

Yes, I thought. *Sometimes a do-over might erase good things that happened.* If Christopher hadn't ended our engagement, I might not have invested in the store of my dreams and reignited a friendship with Brady.

I pushed through the gate to my cottage and strode up the

path. The light over the porch was out. I made a mental note to check the timer and opened the front door.

From out of nowhere, a hulking figure leaped at me. He grabbed my shoulders. I shrieked and dropped Pixie. She yowled and darted into the house. My rain slicker was slippery, making it hard for my attacker to keep hold. I ducked and eluded his grasp. Adrenaline pumping, I reached inside the door, grabbed the shovel I kept there for defense, and jabbed it into my attacker's foot. He wailed.

I whirled around and raised the shovel. "Back off!"

Austin Pinter's eyes were smoldering with anger. "You!" he snarled. "You told the police—"

"Don't come any closer."

"You sicced the police on me."

"No, I didn't," I lied, knowing I had. I'd given them reason to suspect him of murder.

Fiona dive-bombed Austin, but because of his buzz cut, he didn't have enough hair for her to tug. She jumped on his head but to no effect.

"They questioned me. They asked if I killed Farrah. I didn't!" he cried.

"A witness heard her warning that if you stole something, she would turn you in. Less than an hour later, she was dead."

"I didn't do it!" He spread his arms. "I am a peace-loving man."

"Attacking me is not the way to prove that," I sniped.

"Courtney!" Holly called from beyond the fence. "Is everything all right? I have mace."

Austin dropped his arms by his side and slid his hands into the pockets of his waterproof black cycling jacket. He heaved a sigh, looking chastened.

"I'm fine, Holly!" I yelled.

"I loved her," Austin whispered. "I always have. From the

moment we met. She was the essence of every woman I've written in my novels."

Wow. Talk about putting someone on a pedestal.

"All these years, I wrote her love letters," he went on. "She never responded, but I thought maybe, being here in town, we could talk. She didn't want to."

"You went for drinks."

"Oh, yeah, she agreed to do that, but that was it. I was a pawn. A toy."

Poor handsome, lovelorn sap.

"You lied about your alibi for that night," I said.

He met my gaze.

"Your neighbor wasn't playing rock music. Where were you?"

He drew in a deep breath and let it out. "I can't say."

"You were heard arguing with Farrah an hour before she died. She warned you that if you stole something, she would turn you in. Did you steal something that night?"

"No!"

"Courtney, is everything okay?" a man called from the street.

I recognized Brady's voice, but I didn't dare take my eyes off Austin.

"I'm fine. My guest is just leaving." I glowered at Austin. "If I were you, Mr. Pinter, I'd have a heart-to-heart chat with the police. You are a person of interest and will remain so until you come clean about whatever it was you were doing between six thirty and eight p.m. Friday night."

Looking like he wanted to crawl under a rock and hide, Austin slogged down the path, passing Brady on his way out.

Brady, a backpack slung over his rain jacket, gestured to the shovel in my hands. "Getting ready to dig something?" His eyes glinted with humor.

"Ha-ha. I keep a baseball bat by the back door, and I've got a pretty decent swing, but I am an ace with a shovel." I stowed my *weapon* inside the house and, feeling the weight of fatigue wash over me, slumped into the mission slat rocking chair on the porch.

Brady lowered his backpack with a *clunk* to the ground, crouched in front of me, and propped his arms across my thighs, peering up at my face. "Are you really okay?"

"Let's just say Austin wasn't happy that I disproved his alibi."

Brady whistled.

"What are you doing in this neck of the woods?" I asked.

"Taking a long walk to clear my head. We served over one hundred lunches today and held a retirement cocktail party for twenty at four o'clock." He scrubbed his hair. "All inside due to the rain. The noise was deafening."

"What's in that thing?" I pointed to the backpack. "It went *clunk*."

"A shovel," he joked. "Not as big as yours."

"You're a riot." I knuckled his arm. "C'mon, tell the truth."

"A pair of canteen cups," he admitted. "I had them shipped to the café. If we're taking hikes on your days off to search for fairy portals, like you promised, I thought we could use them."

I offered him a glass of wine, but he declined. He really did want to go home and crash.

"Will you be okay once I leave?" Giving my knees a tender caress, he rose to a stand and helped me out of the chair.

I brushed hair off my face. "I'll be fine. Holly has mace."

"Of course she does." He smirked.

"I don't think Austin will be back," I said. "He has a secret and is probably mulling over his options as to his next step. But I don't think he killed Farrah Lawson."

Brady smoothed my hair with his palm and kissed me gently on the lips. "Trust your gut but lock your doors anyway."

"I always do. Hey, any word on locating your mother's manuscript yet?"

"Nope, but she's okay. She's seen her therapist and says she's taking it in stride, claiming the universe might not have wanted her to publish it. It wasn't her best work." He started along the path. "Now my father, on the other hand, thinks the universe can go . . ."

He waved good-night, leaving me to fill in the blank.

Chapter 20

A light meal of plain broiled salmon and buttered stringed beans was all I could muster. I spent the hour or so online looking up poisons that might start with the letter *A*, just in case Reddick had accidentally revealed something he shouldn't have. As a gardener, I knew a lot about which sprays and plant additives might harm bees and butterflies, and having taken a couple of chemistry courses in college to fulfill requirements for my earth sciences degree, I'd learned a lot about which mixtures explode—I'd particularly enjoyed the basic vinegar and baking soda combo—but in truth, I hadn't studied poisons. In my search, I found arsenic, antifreeze, acrolein, Agent Orange, and more. I recognized arsenic, Agent Orange, and antifreeze of course, but none of the others. I started to look up acrolein and yawned.

Fiona, who'd been sitting at the top of the computer

screen, humming and kicking her legs, gazed at me and said, "Sleep."

Agreeing, I switched off the computer, traipsed to the bathroom, did my ablutions, and stumbled to bed. Pixie was already there, snoring her loveable cat snore.

Thursday morning, I woke late, passed on a run, and rushed through my normal routine in order to get to the shop on time.

When I entered, Joss aimed a finger at me. "Not your best look."

I'd thrown on a long-sleeved, loose-knit sweater that I hadn't realized, until I was halfway to work, had a gaping hole at the hem. My mother would have been able to patch it; I didn't know the first thing about knitting. I threw on an apron I often wore when making fairy gardens and twirled. "Better?"

"It's a start."

I told her about my search for poisons, to which she replied, "Are you positive Officer Reddick wasn't toying with you?"

"No I'm not, and you're right. Poisons are not my area of expertise. Let's get cracking. We have a lot to do for Odine's birthday party."

The day whizzed by with preparations for the party, two private fairy garden classes, and a surprise taste testing with Yvanna. At four in the afternoon, she'd dropped in, hoping we'd help her out. She wanted to add two more sweets for the event. How could Joss and I say no? Our favorite, hands down, were the chocolate crinkles. They were so moist and chocolaty.

The night came and went in a flash. By the time Friday rolled around, I was on pins and needles, praying the party would go well. My reputation didn't rely on its success, but I never wanted the shop to suffer any bad publicity if I could help it.

At noon, I went to Seize the Clay to pick up the pots Renee had completed, hoping secretly that Detective Summers would be there and give me an update. He wasn't. I asked Renee whether he'd solved Farrah Lawson's murder. Had he questioned Odine about her husband? Had he followed up on her husband's whereabouts? What about the old college boyfriends she'd told the police about? Renee, like Officer Reddick, made it clear that Summers didn't intend to loop me in. Ever.

"Stick with fairy gardening," she sang as I exited. "It's what you do best." Halfway across the street, I could still hear her laughing.

At two in the afternoon, I met Meaghan at Misty's house to finalize all the décor. Misty wasn't there; her housekeeper let us in. Rafaela told us that Misty had left the tissue paper flowers in a box in the sunroom along with the goodies Joss had delivered midmorning, including the warped mirror, pile of pillows, and more. I was glad we'd changed our minds about having everyone wear fairy wings. That would have been over the top.

My gaze returned to the pillows, and I frowned. Joss was dead set on including that challenge in the obstacle course, but I wasn't so certain I wanted adults jumping and falling. Would my liability insurance cover injuries at an off-site location? Probably not. And if any of the women were wearing heels? Yipes! I stowed the pillows in a closet. Out of sight, out of mind.

Meaghan picked up one of the tissue paper flowers. "We can't put these in the yard today or ever. Moisture will ruin them. The mirror should wait, as well."

"What if we adorn the indoor archways with the flowers?" I suggested. "They can set the whimsical tone as guests file out into the garden."

"Great idea."

"We can put out everything for the obstacle course tomorrow morning."

One by one I handed Meaghan the pushpins, and she attached the flowers near the archways' moldings.

"This is fun," she said. "I needed a break from the gallery."

"Ziggy's got it covered?"

"Now that the thief has been apprehended." She clicked her tongue. "I still can't believe it was Christopher's wife—"

"Don't," I said. "Let's not discuss that any further."

"Did Brady weigh in?"

It dawned on me that I hadn't told Brady about Leanne, and I hadn't told Meaghan about Austin Pinter's appearance at my house. I'd informed Joss, who'd suggested I alert the police, but I hadn't followed her advice. Austin had left and hadn't returned.

"Brady has been as busy as I've been," I said.

"Not so busy that he hasn't had time to roam my neighborhood with a flashlight."

"Huh?"

"Last night I caught him bent over a fairy door by the huge redwood at the corner."

"Was he taking photographs?"

"I don't know. I was hustling to get home to binge-read that mystery series by Hannah Dennison. Oh, how I'd love to visit England." She thrust out a hand. "Pushpin, please."

I gave her one. "What did the fairy door look like? Did you check it out this morning?" Brady and I hadn't toured Meaghan's neighborhood.

"I did. It was light brown and sort of wavy with a green

roof and pretty brass hinges. There were at least a dozen red-and-white toadstools, too. And a mailbox. Very whimsical."

"Did you open the mailbox? Was there a message inside?"

She playfully smacked her forehead. "It didn't even occur to me."

I sent Brady a text requesting he forward a photograph for my collection. Once the party was behind me, I wanted to do a blog post about all our discoveries.

The doorbell rang. Rafaela answered and announced, "Miss Courtney, a man is here."

I strode through the hall and saw Brady standing there. "Speak of the devil."

"Should my ears be burning?" He offered a rakish smile.

"Nah. Meaghan and I were talking fairy doors. In fact, I just texted you about one."

"Okay, I'll respond. In the meantime, your tables and chairs, ma'am, just like you ordered."

Beyond him stood two sturdy men whom I recognized from his kitchen staff. The café delivery van was parked at the curb.

"You are a gem." I motioned for the three of them to go through the side gate. "I think that'll be easier. I'll meet you in the back."

After his guys had positioned the tables and chairs where I'd directed them to, Brady told them to drive the van back to the café. He'd walk.

I studied the arrangement of tables and chairs.

"What's wrong?" Brady asked. "You're frowning."

"We'll have to wipe all of them down in the morning before draping the tablecloths." I sighed. One more item to add to my to-do list. I made a mental note that in the future, if we intended to put on more fairy garden parties, we needed to hire more assistants. "Would you like some lemonade before you leave?"

"I'm good. So why did you text me about fairy doors?" He scrolled through texts on his cell phone.

"Meaghan ratted you out." I escorted him through the house to the front door. "How dare you go fairy door hunting in her neighborhood without me."

He splayed his hands. "Sorry. I was restless after a bigger-than-expected dinner seating. I needed fresh air."

"More fresh air? How much can one man inhale?" I poked his chest. "I expect you to send me a photograph."

"Done." He opened his photo app, forwarded a photograph, and beamed.

"No moss grows under your feet."

"Never." He kissed my cheek. "How about a hike Tuesday? We can catch up."

"You're on."

When Saturday morning rolled around, I was as keyed up as a jack-in-the-box. Energy *boing*ed inside me. I stretched, showered, and dressed in a pretty pink blouse and aqua trousers. Pixie weaved around my ankles as I donned dangly silver earrings and a sparkly necklace. She knew something was up. I rarely wore jewelry, other than my mother's locket. I lifted her, thumbs braced beneath her forelegs, brushed my nose against hers, and explained that she would not be accompanying me to the party. She would be hanging out at the shop for the tea, where everyone would fawn over her. That seemed to appease her.

In the kitchen, I drank a glass of fresh-squeezed orange juice and ate two eggs, scrambled—I wouldn't need caffeine to keep me going, but protein was a must—and then I hopped into my Mini Cooper with the cat, pulled down the visor—bright sunshine was glaring through the windshield—and drove to the shop.

The night before, Fiona had elected to meet Merryweather for a mentoring session, after which she would return to the shop to sleep; a year ago she'd found a way in through a vent. She met me as I breezed into the store and set Pixie on the floor.

"I had the most wonderful class," she crowed. "I learned a new spell. Guess what it was? How to make myself disappear."

I guffawed. "No one can see you anyway."

"You and other fairies can, but just like this, *By dee déan dom non sealad*"—she intoned, then snapped her fingers and vanished.

"Where'd you go? Fiona?" My heart did a jig. I hoped she hadn't *spelled* herself into nonexistence. "Fiona!"

Poof. She reappeared and giggled. "Isn't it magical?"

"Magical indeed, but aren't you worried that the queen fairy will disapprove?"

"Merryweather taught me the incantation. It means *May God make me not seen.* I'm positive she got the okay first. At least I hope so." Fiona frowned. "I hope it wasn't a test. I . . . I . . ." Her wings shuddered. She emitted a fretful sob and soared into a ficus tree.

I trotted after her. "Fiona, don't worry." I heard her weeping and felt awful for putting doubt in her head. "I'm sure it's okay. Merryweather wouldn't steer you wrong." When she didn't respond, I said, "Rest up. I want you to go to Misty's party with me."

"I'm here!" Yoly Acebo made her way through the main showroom.

"You're early," I said.

She shrugged out of her quilted jacket, brushed her silky curls over her shoulders, and tugged the hem of her red crop-top sweater over the waistband of her jeans. "Joss wanted me to come in early. I've already got the lay of the land, but it never hurts to walk through something one more time." She disappeared down the hall to stow her purse and jacket in the office and returned. "Twyla will be here in a few minutes," she said.

Twyla Waterman, as it so happened, was a talented flute player. Tish had pleaded with Joss and me to let her play for this particular tea. Ever since the murder, Twyla had been restless at the spa and had needed an outlet, Tish said. When Joss raised the idea of hiring Twyla to tend the store on any of our party days, Tish couldn't have been more grateful.

"I'll go over the register and basic store info with her," Yoly said. "She'll pick the register up in a snap. The spa uses the same kind. When she's not performing, she'll tend the showroom while I set out the tea and cookies. Joss said it was okay."

"Terrific."

"Yvanna is bringing over some treats in an hour," Yoly added. "Good?"

"Good," I said. "The poet should arrive a half hour before the tea begins."

"Got it."

I moved to the book carousel to rearrange books. For some reason *How to Catch a Leprechaun,* part of the *How to Catch* series, always found its way to the lowest slot on the rack, probably because children were fascinated by the wonderful pictures, and parents let them sit and read as they browsed the showroom. If a couple ended up with sticky fingerprints, so be it. I would discount them. In addition, someone had turned a copy of *Fairy Gardening* by Julia Bawden-Davis and Beverly Turner—one of my favorite fairy garden design references—upside down. I rotated it and brushed off my hands.

The door swung open, and Twyla entered, her head lowered, a soft leather flute case slung over one shoulder. She was fiddling with a button on the bodice of her honey-colored smock dress.

"Hi, Twyla," I said.

Startled, she looked up, and I could see she'd been crying. "Oh. Hi."

I hurried to her. "What's wrong?"

She bit her lip. "Nothing."

I clasped her elbow. "Come with me." I guided her past a pair of customers intent on selecting just the right macramé plant hanger and around the sales counter. "Tea?"

"Um, okay."

I pulled a tissue from a box beneath the counter and handed it to her. While she dabbed her tears and nose, I poured hot water into a mug, added a bag of chamomile tea, and set the mug on the tray.

"Now what's going on?" I asked. "Can I help?"

She gazed at me through moist lashes. "You can't tell my mother."

I hated any conversation that started that way but agreed. "Go on."

"I'm getting all sorts of hate messages. Mostly on social media." She gasped for breath. "They're saying I killed Farrah Lawson and I should confess."

"But you've been cleared."

"That doesn't matter. I was in a cult. I'm an outcast."

"Your mother doesn't know?"

"Mom stays away from social media. She thinks it's awful, and I agree, but you know . . ." She picked up the mug of tea and blew on it.

I did know. When it first came out that I could see a fairy, haters and nonbelievers had come to the fore. Most of that nastiness had dissipated. "You have to let it go."

"But what if the police think . . ." She took a sip of tea and heaved a sigh. "What if they think that Mrs. Cox's statement can't be trusted since she, you know . . ."

Since she was a thief.

"There are a lot of mean women in town," Twyla whispered.

I hated to think there were cruel people in Carmel-by-the-Sea, but they existed everywhere. I petted Twyla's arm. "Let me take a look at your platforms and see if there's any way I, or others I know who tackle this kind of problem, might help. Lissa Reade, at the library, is a great warrior for this cause, too."

"I know Lissa."

"She'll be here today. Talk to her. She'll respect your privacy. But for now, I want you to be strong. Hold your head up high. Show everyone your smile and your talent." I nudged her. "Go to the restroom and touch up your face. I'll let Yoly know you're here."

An hour later, having touched base with Lissa by text and given her a heads-up about Twyla's plight, I grabbed Joss, who was pleased with how well Yoly was working out, and we hopped into my Mini Cooper and drove to Misty's house. Fiona, who had recovered from her pity party, hitched a ride on my shoulder. Meaghan was walking up the path as we arrived. All of us humans had been smart enough to wear flats, given we would be on our feet a lot, managing the food and events. Fiona had donned a pair of sparkly party shoes.

I rang the doorbell.

Misty, who had dressed to the nines in a blue-floral, V-neck dress that must have cost a pretty penny, greeted us at the door. "Welcome. I'm so excited." She grabbed my hand and pulled me inside. Joss trailed us. "Yvanna is already setting up the desserts, and Brady sent his best sous chef to arrange the appetizers."

"Good to hear," I said, and inhaled. "Yum! What's baking?" The aroma of brewed coffee wafted to me as did the scent of chocolate and cinnamon.

"Rafaela thought throwing a sheet of cookies in the oven would make the house smell homey. It's her grandmother's recipe. She left an hour ago and put Yvanna in charge of them."

"I'll be back." Fiona leaped off my shoulder and coursed through the house and out through the opened door of the sunroom, probably in search of Cedric Winterbottom.

"Pretty flowers," Joss said.

An elegant vase filled with lilacs stood on the entry table. In the living room, a vase filled with lavender graced the coffee table.

"Yes, they're a nice touch," I said.

"Aren't they?" Misty beamed. "Nova suggested them. She reminded me how much Odine loves the color purple."

Had Nova paid for those, or had Misty footed the bill for those, too? *Cha-ching.*

For the next three hours, we finalized every aspect of the party. Joss took charge of the party favors and games, and Meaghan, Yvanna, and I tended to the floral décor and tables. We hung a plum-colored table skirt around the buffet table and bordered the top with pink, lilac, and white flowers tucked into masses of green ivy. We draped mauve tablecloths over white bases for each of the dining tables and set centerpieces that complemented the buffet's flowers.

"Bowers of Flowers outdid itself," Meaghan said.

"They certainly did."

The owner of the fledgling flower shop had recently be-

come a steady customer at Open Your Imagination. Hiring
her for this gig had earned us a huge thank you.

"She set out business cards," Meaghan said. "That's okay,
isn't it?"

"Absolutely." I put a hand above my eyes to block the
glare. "Joss, do you need help?"

"All done." She had blown up balloons, wrapped treasures
in tissue and tied them with ribbon at both ends, placed the
flat plastic *toadstools* in strategic positions, and propped the
warped mirror by one of the cypress trees. "Except"—she spun
in a circle—"where are the pillows?"

Rats. I'd hoped she'd forgotten about them. I spilled the
beans.

She planted her fists on her hips. "You're the boss, but it
would have been funny seeing them all jumping in their
pretty frocks."

"Funny but dangerous."

"Look at what else I did." She'd printed instructions for
each game on fairy-adorned parchment paper. "Do you approve?"

"Absolutely." I appreciated her attention to detail.

A bartender who worked nights at Hideaway Café showed
up to handle the simple bar consisting of iced tea, spiked and
regular lemonade, champagne, and wine. He was a charmer
with a brilliant set of teeth and dimples that birds could nest
in. Yvanna had drifted to him, and the two were chatting.
They seemed to have instant chemistry.

At a quarter to one, Odine stepped through the sunroom
door wearing a slimming, purple-striped sheath and open-toe
pumps. Nova arrived minutes later looking chic and not at all
mousy in a black-and-white checkered blouse and black pants
tucked into boots, although the outfit had me baffled. Had she
missed the memo from Misty asking everyone to *dress for the*

occasion, meaning wear something suitable for a garden party, not a chess match? She gave me the side eye as she passed. I flashed on our heated tête-à-tête at Fantasy Awaits on Wednesday and forced a smile.

"Does Misty need help?" Odine asked me.

"Nope. You're the guest of honor. Grab a glass of champagne." I motioned to the bar.

Instead, Odine hurried after Nova. "Hey, girlfriend, hold up."

Nova crossed to the fairy garden table, which held Renee's pots, fairy figurines, succulents, and more. We'd adorned it in the same style as the other tables.

Odine gripped Nova's arm and said something. I picked up one word: *police*.

Wresting free, Nova strode along the path toward the leftmost cypress. Odine pursued her. I could only imagine that the police had questioned Odine, and she presumed Nova had put them up to it.

"Hello!" Phoebe and Perri said as they crossed the sunroom's threshold. Phoebe had on the prettiest blue chiffon blouse featuring fairies flying around a fountain. Perri, not to be outdone, was wearing a red-and-yellow number with large fairies frolicking with gnomes and elves, the larger kinds one would expect to read about in fairy tales.

"The flowers in the foyer are so pretty!" Phoebe exclaimed.

"*Tres, tres,*" Perri agreed. "Which reminds me, we should include flowers at the next apple harvest." She steered her partner toward a party table.

Ten minutes later, six other sorority sisters arrived en masse, having rented a limo. They all lived in San Jose and, judging by their liveliness, had already cracked open a bottle of champagne. "Odine!" they bellowed in unison the moment they saw her. "O-O-O, we're here!" they crooned.

Meaghan slinked next to me. "This could be a rowdy party."

I laughed. "As long as no one gets behind the wheel of a car afterward, no harm, no foul."

My humor fell flat, however, when I spied Odine still talking to—no, not *talking* to, but *haranguing*—Nova at the far end of the yard.

Chapter 21

Children, children, don't forget
There are elves and fairies yet.
Where the knotty hawthorn grows
Look for prints of fairy toes.
—Dora Owen, "Children, Children, Don't Forget"

"Wow!" One of the sorority sisters turned in a circle, drinking in every aspect of the backyard. "The wind chimes, the décor. What are those flat things in the garden, toadstools? Adorable."

Another said, "Enchanting."

Without taking my eyes off Odine and Nova—I didn't want them coming to blows—I pointed out the tables and bar to the newcomers. They thanked me and moved away. When Odine backhanded Nova's arm, I wondered whether I should intervene, but Nova threw up both palms to fend off any more attacks and, chin raised, strode regally in the direction of the party tables. Odine mustered a smile and followed her with the same measured gait.

"Hello, everyone!" Misty made an entrance from the sunroom. She stopped on the top step. The attendees spun around and gawked at her. No wonder. She had strapped fairy wings on her back and was holding a wand in her right hand. "I'm here to grant wishes! As I make my way among you, whisper your deepest desire in my ear."

"Not on a bet!" Odine shouted.

"Me either," Phoebe said.

Misty traipsed down the final steps to join everyone. Some tried to hug her, but the wings made that awkward. Seconds later, Odine removed the wings, and Misty merrily tagged her with the wand before setting it on one of the party tables.

After everyone had a chance to fetch a drink at the bar and the women had huddled into smaller groups, Joss *ping*ed a xylophone with a mallet. She'd alerted me that she was bringing one of her mother's prized possessions that she'd found in the storage unit. Apparently, her mom had collected rare instruments for decades.

"Ladies," Joss announced, "it's time for the games."

The group echoed the word *games* with a question mark and peered at Misty.

"Yes, my wonderful sisters, this is a full-throated fairy party!" Misty cried. "Exactly what Odine hoped for. Happy birthday, my dear friend." She applauded.

"Happy birthday!" the ladies exclaimed.

Odine grinned. Nova sidled to her and bumped her with a hip. Odine wanted none of her friendliness and edged away.

"After the games," Misty said, "we'll dine on wondrous fairy food, and then each of us will make a fairy garden."

Three of the women whooped with glee.

"Back to the games." Joss *plunk*ed the xylophone. "You can choose to play or opt out, but if you join in, I promise you'll have a good time." She proceeded to explain how to play wuzzles. Four of the sorority sisters and Odine raised hands, wanting to participate.

By the time the obstacle course game was underway, eight had joined the fun. Joss's explanation of the fairy wish station had won them over.

When Joss introduced the pass-the-treasure game, everyone was on board.

"Here's how it works," she said. "Stand in a circle. We'll play some music to entertain you as you pass the treasure from one to the next. Each person who holds the treasure must unwrap a layer, close her eyes, and make a wish. When the treasure is revealed, that player will get her wish. We'll then repeat the action, giving a treasure to someone new to start the rotation."

A woman in a slinky blue dress blew a raspberry. "You can't grant all our wishes. I'm wishing for the man of my dreams."

"You'll be surprised," Joss said like a carnival barker. "You'll have a lifetime to find out."

"Aha, there's the catch," the woman said.

Laughter ensued. Many of the women elbowed one another or rolled their eyes, knowing they were being played.

"In the meantime," Joss continued, "you get to keep the treasure you reveal to remind you of your wish."

The women formed a circle. Joss directed me to hand the first treasure to Misty. Meaghan switched on *Song from a Secret Garden* via her cell phone and broadcasted it through a Bose speaker. After a few minutes of passing and unwrapping, the first treasure was revealed: a certificate for the winner's choice of jewelry from Fantasy Awaits. Misty had insisted on coming up with the prizes. I'd suggested less opulent ones, but she had remained resolute.

A half hour later, each of the players had received a treasure—a shopping spree at Open Your Imagination, another at Say Cheese, a pottery lesson at Seize the Clay, dinner for two at Saison, and more. Yes, we had rigged how many openings each treasure would require, so we could pick the starting person, assured that each participant would receive something.

"Lunch is served," I said.

The ladies filed along the buffet, commenting positively about the choices the Hideaway Café had prepared. Two seemed intent on taking as many of the avocado-and-bacon appetizers as they could fit on a plate. Phoebe and Perri jumped the line and took four desserts each. Misty cozied up and chided them. Friendly exchanges ensued.

Nova was lingering by the makeshift bar, waiting while the handsome bartender poured her another glass of wine. I'd noticed she wasn't mingling with the others. Was it because Odine had berated her, or was it because she hadn't been in the same sorority and, therefore, didn't feel like she was one of the gang?

To my surprise, Odine approached her. "Nova, slow down, sugar. You don't need to keep up with B and B." Two of the sorority sisters' names started with Bs. I couldn't remember which two. "They have hollow legs," she added.

"I'm not drinking too much," Nova slurred.

"Okay, you're not, but you don't want to put on weight, do you?"

"I skipped the desserts."

"Alcohol has a lot of carbs."

Nova sneered. "Are you calling me fat, Odine?" She grabbed her glass from the bartender. Wine sloshed over the rim. She mopped it with her fingertips and shook the moisture into the air—not at Odine, which made me breathe a tad easier.

"No, of course I'm not."

"Are you implying I won't get a husband if I'm F-A-T?" She was the farthest thing from that.

"If so," Nova continued, "then we're both in the same boat, my friend." She raised her glass sarcastically. "No husbands forever. Cheers!"

"Nova . . ." Odine warned.

"Face it, O. Hubby Baby is not coming back. No hike will burn off enough calories to work that magic."

"How dare you," Odine said.

"I dare. Tit for tat." Nova stomped toward the sunroom.

"Nova," Misty said as she exited the sunroom with a tray of cookies. "Did you hear how much everyone loves your trinkets?"

"Trinkets?" Nova's eyes blazed with outrage. "They're not trinkets. They're art." She stumbled up the steps and into the sunroom.

Misty started after her, but Odine grabbed her elbow. "Let her be."

Misty's forehead creased. "What just went down, Odine? What did you say to her?"

"Me?"

I went after Nova and found her in the kitchen, eating an appetizer over the sink. Her gaze was fixed on the partygoers outside. "Nova? Are you okay?"

"Yeah," she snarled. "Hunky-dory."

Cedric blazed into the kitchen, Fiona trailing him. He orbited Nova's head while sprinkling a glittery white concoction.

In seconds, the potion vanished. Or had it? Fiona zipped to the floor and whisked her hand along the tile. She sniffed her fingertips. To date, I hadn't seen her use a white potion.

Surprisingly pacified, Nova breathed deeply in and out. Until, without warning, she slammed her glass on the drainboard and whirled on me. "Stop!"

I splayed my hands. "Stop what?"

"Stop poking your nose in where it doesn't belong or

I'll . . . I'll . . ." Without finishing the statement, she bustled out of the kitchen, down the hall, and out of the house.

I shuddered. Or she'd what?

"What was that concoction?" Fiona demanded of Cedric. "It didn't work."

Cedric sputtered. "It . . . it was supposed to make her open to reason."

I thought of a piece of cross-stitched art my mother had hung in my father's office with a quote by George Bernard Shaw: *The reasonable man adapts himself to the world; the unreasonable one persists in trying to adapt the world to himself. Therefore, all progress depends on the unreasonable man.*

Needless to say, Nova had been less than reasonable. Granted, I'd been the one to mention her alibi to the police, but if she wasn't guilty of murder, what did it matter? Why tell me to butt out now? Did she blame me for the argument between her and Odine?

Cedric studied his palms. "I'll have to ask Merryweather what went wrong."

"You don't know?" Fiona squawked.

"My incantation should have worked. I didn't change the words an ounce," he said with stilted primness. "I've utilized it before."

"Perhaps Nova was an unwilling subject," I said. "No matter what you tried, you would not have been able to sway her."

Shaking his head, he returned to the backyard. I saw a sparkle of green disappear into the cypress.

Fiona flew to my shoulder. "This can't be good."

Meaghan forged into the kitchen, her apron splattered with strawberry cream. "What's going on? The weather has grown chilly, and Odine is sniping at some of the women."

I peered down the hallway. Nova had fled but had left the front door open. "Nova and Odine had an argument." I told her how Nova had mentioned Odine's long-lost husband to me at Fantasy Awaits, and how she'd taunted her about him today.

"Why did you go to Odine's shop?" Meaghan asked.

"Cedric suggested I speak to Odine about what you over-heard her housekeeper say. About Misty's money being tight." My mouth went dry. I grabbed a tumbler from a cabinet, poured myself a glass of water, and took a sip.

Meaghan's forehead creased. "Um, who's Cedric?"

"Cedric Winterbottom is an older fairy residing in Misty's cypress."

Meaghan scratched her head. "Exactly how big is the fairy community in Carmel?"

"I haven't a clue. Long story short, Odine swore that Misty was not in debt. She said Misty has always been magnanimous with her funds. She said the contentious conversation between Misty and Farrah about the role in the movie was merely because Misty wants to act. She's ready to be footloose and fancy—"

"Have you seen Nova?" Misty peeked around the archway.

I pointed. "She hurried out. I think she and Odine had a tiff." I did not add that Nova had warned me to keep my distance.

"Dear me." Misty stepped into the room, face flushed. "She can be prickly."

"I could go after her," I said.

"No, that's all right."

"Maybe it's time to start the fairy garden instruction."

"No, wait." Misty studied her fingernails before raising her chin and meeting my gaze. "I heard you and Meaghan talking about me and Farrah." She sounded breathy, tense. "I admit that I was upset with her about a role in a movie. Farrah is . . . *was* an enigma. At times, she could be so warm, and at other times, so imperious. All I'd wanted was an introduction to the director. The role was perfect for me."

"How did you learn about it?" Meaghan asked.

"I'd read about it on an actors' casting site."

I cocked my head. "Misty, didn't you know the director, um, intimately?"

She blinked.

"You and Berto Bagnoli dated during college," I said.

"Twenty years ago," she conceded.

"And because you suggested he meet Farrah, he gave her a role in a movie that launched her career."

"He knew talent when he saw it."

"Yet you didn't feel comfortable asking him for a role for yourself?"

"It's complicated. We . . . the breakup wasn't pretty. He . . . hey!" Misty said sharply, her eyes widening. "You don't believe I killed Farrah because I was angry with her for not helping me, do you? As in, I would *kill* for a part? Heavens, Courtney. How cliché."

The way she said it, it did sound implausible.

"Misty," Meaghan said, "your housekeeper overheard you telling Farrah you needed the job because money was tight."

I added quickly, "Odine denies you have any money issues."

Misty frowned. "You were talking to Odine about me? You had no right."

"Your fairy said—" I balked. I felt my cheeks warm.

"I have a fairy?" She swiveled her head left and right. "You're joshing me."

"No, you do have a fairy. He's been watching over you since you were a girl."

"He? I have a *he* fairy?"

"His name is Cedric."

"Why do I have a *he* fairy?" Her face pinched with bewilderment.

"I don't know why. All I know—"

"Why can you see him, and I can't?" she asked.

"I don't know that, either. You used to. As a girl. Perhaps you aren't open to the possibility now."

Her chest rose and fell. She placed two hands over her heart as if to keep it in check. "A fairy," she muttered.

Since she wasn't questioning my veracity, I continued. "Misty, he was concerned that someone has been stealing things from the house, but when I was waiting for you in the study, I saw receipts on your desk. You've sold off pieces of art. I was concerned. Cedric suggested I talk to Odine, so I did. She swears you're not in debt. She said her husband, your former business manager, would have known and told her." That last point gave me pause. "Do you have a new business manager, seeing as Odine's husband left on his sailing trip?"

Misty hesitated. "No. Having a business degree, I thought I knew enough to manage my own affairs, but . . ." She laced her fingers together. "I might as well tell you the truth. A friend urged me to invest in something that I shouldn't have. Everything, other than this house, is gone."

I gasped. "What did you invest in?"

"A restaurant. A chic, highly exclusive restaurant."

Meaghan said, "That can be a money pit."

"Tell me about it."

"This friend was knowledgeable?" I asked.

"He used to own a very famous restaurant in San Francisco, and it went belly up, but he swore it was his partner's fault. He owned the rights to the name and, with me as his new partner, he wanted to open the restaurant here, for tourists and locals. With my connections, he said, it would be a huge success. I poured money into it. For equipment and rent and fine wine and down payments on employee contracts. My friend wanted the best chef in the world, of course. Everything had a price tag." She faltered. "How I wanted the Carmel socialites to see what a success I could be without my father's help, but when we couldn't get the property or the parking permit, and when we couldn't get the approval of the town council—" She hiccupped. "Suddenly, the money was gone."

"Oh, no!" Meaghan shared a look with me.

"The escrow account I was putting all the money into was empty. And my friend—he who shall forever remain the scourge of the earth—skipped the country. I've been meeting my lawyer these past few days to—" She sucked back a sob. "There's no recourse. I have nothing in writing."

Nothing? Holy heck. My father had drummed into me the value of a contract.

Misty wrapped her arms around herself. "Yes, money is tight. I revealed the truth to Farrah, and she promised to keep my secret. As for the role we argued about—I asked for her help getting an introduction because she owed me."

"Because she'd promised you another role in a Berto Bagnoli film a year ago and reneged."

"How do you know about that?"

"It doesn't matter."

Misty flapped a hand. "I told her that after this financial fiasco I would need personal validation, hence the desire to act. Do you know what she did? She made fun of me. She said I was too old to start. Plus I didn't have the *look.* I hated her at that moment, but would I kill for the role? Courtney, get real."

"Your alibi is weak," I argued.

"I didn't lie. I was here making the flowers for the party." Her eyes widened. "Hey, I can prove it. The windows were open." She shot an arm to the right. "I overheard my neighbors arguing about getting a divorce."

Honestly? Misty was trying to fashion the same kind of alibi that Austin had used, but with a twist? In my heart of hearts, I knew it wouldn't pan out.

"You don't believe me . . . You . . . Hold on." Misty grabbed her cell phone off the kitchen counter and stabbed in a number. "Arista? It's Misty. Next door." She cupped her hand over the phone. "I reached her answering machine." She removed her hand. "Listen, Arista, I need you to verify something for me. Please call me. My friend Courtney Kelly needs to hear it from you." She added her cell phone number and stabbed *End*. "Courtney, I'm not lying. Promise."

Chapter 22

I must follow in their train
Down the crooked fairy lane
Where the coney-rabbits long ago have gone,
And where silverly they sing
In a moving moonlit ring.
—J.R.R. Tolkien, "Goblin Feet"

After each guest had made a fairy garden and the party had wound down, Misty left to have coffee with Odine and the others. Then Joss, Meaghan, Yvanna, and I got to work. We spent the better part of two hours disassembling everything. Around six, Brady's guys came to pick up the tables, Joss left to deliver the tablecloths to the dry cleaner, Meaghan went to Flair to check in with her partner, Yvanna went home to make dinner for her family, and I returned to the shop to pick up Pixie.

The place wasn't in bad shape after the tea, considering. Yoly and Twyla had done a great job cleaning up. Yoly had left numerous sticky notes about how the tea had gone, and how wonderfully the poet had performed, and how much she hoped I would invite Twyla to return and play duets with Meaghan at one of the teas. I tacked the messages to the message board beyond the register.

When I arrived home, I was bleary-eyed with fatigue and nearly tripped over a bouquet of flowers and greenery that was wrapped in burlap and tied with ribbon. I set the cat down and picked up the bouquet off the porch to search for a note, but there wasn't one. Had Brady left it?

"Drop it!" Fiona screeched. "Now!"

Startled, I released the bouquet. It fell by my feet. "What's wrong?"

"Didn't you see the poison ivy mixed in with the greenery?"

In the dim light, I'd missed it. I whirled around, looking for a person who'd left the toxic bouquet. Watching me. Waiting for me to suffer. Was it Nova, sending a second warning to keep my nose out of her business? Was it Misty, upset to have revealed her secret to me and Meaghan?

Trembling, I lifted the bouquet by the stems that stuck out from the bottom of the burlap, tossed it in the garbage can at the side of the house, and bolted inside. I locked the door and checked all the windows, and then went to the laundry room beyond the kitchen, removed my blouse and trousers, and tossed them directly into the washing machine. Next, I scrubbed my hands and forearms for five solid minutes. I'd had a bout of poison ivy when I was eight that, to this day, gave me nightmares. I'd gone hiking with friends, all of us in shorts. None of us had known what poison ivy looked like. An hour later, our legs itched with a vile rash. My mother had nearly bathed me in calamine lotion. Later she'd fed me a delicious tea she'd made with herbs from her garden. Whatever she'd used had helped with the pain.

"Call the police," Fiona said.

"No."

Fingerprints wouldn't show up on burlap, and Summers, given his opinion that I should butt out of his investigation, would try to persuade me that an anonymous admirer who was clueless as to the harmfulness of poison ivy—not a killer with malicious intent—had delivered the bouquet. Some kid who had taken a fairy garden class, he'd say, had developed a crush on me.

"Call Brady," she suggested.

"No."

"Do it. He offered to stay when that guy appeared out of nowhere."

That guy. Austin. Had he put the flowers on the porch, ticked off that I'd told him to tell his secret to the police?

Exhausted and aware that I was shivering with fear, I gave in. I phoned Brady and explained the situation. He arrived within minutes.

"I feel like a fool," I said.

"You don't look like one." He pecked my cheek. "How about I sleep on the couch?"

As much as I wanted to take our relationship to the next level, tonight was not the night.

"Thank you. Yes. That would be appreciated. By the way, your food was a huge hit at the party, and your staff was superb."

He beamed at the compliment. "Good to hear. We aim to please."

I gave him a sheet, blanket, and pillow, made certain the night-lights were working so he wouldn't bump into anything should he need to get up in the dark, kissed his cheek in thanks, and slipped into my bedroom. Minutes later, I crawled into bed. Pixie, as restless as I was, turned ten times on the comforter before settling beside my feet.

Fiona nestled on the pillow beside mine and whispered, "Brady is nice." Leaving it at that, she hummed a sweet ditty until I drifted off.

On Sunday morning, Brady insisted on whipping up a light breakfast of orange juice, sourdough English muffins, cream cheese, and jam. Fear, he said, needed feeding. We sat at the table in the kitchen nook, not saying much. He was probably wondering, as much as I was, what my next move would be.

Before he left for work, he kissed me on the cheek and caressed my back. "Be smart."

"Always."

To bolster my resolve, I threw on a pastel Ruth Bader Ginsburg T-shirt with the quote: *Women belong in all places where decisions are being made.* With a spring in my gait, I drove Pixie to the shop. I'd stowed the unused fairy garden items in the Mini Cooper and had to put them back on the racks. Fiona played with Pixie in the backseat.

The moment I entered the shop, I felt the need for sunshine. I strode to the patio to start my chores. I rotated a number of figurines and other items on the shelves and pinched off dead leaves from the fairy gardens, then I returned to the showroom and opened the top half of the Dutch door to let fresh air waft in. Pixie padded alongside me, the nares of her nose twitching with joy. Fiona rode on Pixie's back, her fingers holding onto the bell of the cat's collar. She looked elated, as if imagining herself on a fairy horse. On occasion, she'd been able to ride other fairies' graceful horses. How she wanted to have one of her own, but that privilege would have to wait until she had earned her third set of adult wings.

"What shall we do next?" I asked my companions.

Fiona said, "Sleep."

"Ha! That's not on my agenda today."

"Perhaps"—Joss breezed into the shop—"we should think about a Valentine's Day display. We only have a few days left until V Day."

"Great idea." I caught sight of her T-shirt and snorted. "Did you have that personally made?"

"Yep." She swiped the air as she recited what was written on the front. "'Roses are red. I'm barely awake. This poem is a dud. Give me a break.' You like?"

Fiona soared into the air, laughing so hard she had to hold her ribs. "That is the worst poem ever!"

"Don't judge."

"I like Shakespeare's sonnets," she chirped.

"Which you recite often," Joss snarked.

"Because you made me memorize them." Fiona held up a finger. "Sonnet one hundred and thirty. 'My mistress' eyes are nothing like the sun'—"

"Don't. Not that one." Joss put her fingers in her ears. "La, la, la."

The poem, Joss's least favorite, was the antithesis of a love poem until the last two lines.

Giggling, Fiona sailed out to the patio. Pixie followed her.

"What else do we need to do today?" Joss moved to the sales counter.

"Put the unused party items back on the racks. That's it. No lessons. No sales."

"Easy peasy."

While we organized things, I told her about the bouquet with poison ivy and calling Brady for protection. "I felt like such a wimp."

"Boss, a warning is a warning. You have to take it seriously. Especially after Austin Pinter took you by surprise."

"You're right."

"Are you positive that you don't want to inform the police?"

"I'd rather not suffer Summers's slings and arrows."

Midmorning, a lean brunette woman with gaunt cheeks entered the shop and made a beeline for me. "Courtney Kelly?"

"That's me."

The woman placed a hand on her chest. "I'm Arista Kenton, Misty Dawn's neighbor."

"Misty telephoned you."

"Yes, I've been meaning to come in earlier. I'd like to arrange a fairy garden party for my daughter. She's ten and adores anything with fairies, elves, and the like."

"No, I mean, Misty telephoned you about verifying . . ." I stopped. "She was hoping you could confirm . . ." I paused again. How could I broach the subject? "Last Friday night, Misty was home making some decorations for her party, and she said she heard . . ." I gulped. There was no easy way to pry this story out of a woman I'd only just met.

Fiona cruised into the showroom and whooshed around Arista's head once. She hovered in front of Arista, opened her arms wide, and craned her head backward. I didn't want to ask what she was doing, but it seemed to have serious intent.

Arista moved closer. "Last Friday my husband and I had a tiff. Did Misty hear us? Oh my." Her soulful eyes grew sad. "Why do people worry that love might have passed them by right before Valentine's Day? I mean, I have a wonderful marriage, or so I thought until my husband told me he wasn't happy. He said I don't make enough time for him."

I glanced at Fiona, who was still midair, arms crossed, looking smug. Whatever she'd done had given Arista the freedom to open up to a stranger. It wasn't truth telling as much as baring her soul.

"I don't know how I can make more time," Arista went on. "I have a dental practice that requires me to be on site eight hours a day. On top of that, our daughter has soccer practice and games on the weekends. She loves it. I won't deny her that joy. Where am I supposed to carve out more time for him? He works out of the house. He makes his own hours. Does he want me to give up everything for him? And what about our daughter? Is she supposed to suspend her activities, as well?"

I didn't know what to say.

Arista shook her head. "We argued like the two of us were drunk. We weren't. We just couldn't keep it bottled up any longer. Our daughter was at a girlfriend's house for a sleepover, so we went at it, tooth and nail, at the top of our lungs. Misty must have heard us. Everyone in the neighborhood probably did."

I let out the breath I'd been holding. Misty was innocent. Her alibi held up.

"Oh heavens!" Arista shuddered. "Did I . . ." She blinked like she was waking from a dream. "Did I just reveal . . . to you? About my . . . *our* marriage problem?"

I smiled warmly and put a hand on her arm. "You obviously needed to air some grievances, and this was the perfect opportunity to do so. My lips are sealed."

Fiona, content with whatever she'd induced, flew to the patio and disappeared into the ficus.

I said, "Arista, let's go outside and have some tea and discuss the fairy garden party you want for your daughter. Maybe we could get your husband involved in the planning, so he feels included. And might I suggest couples' therapy? I know a psychologist in town who might be perfect for the two of you. She'll work around your schedule."

"Bless you."

An hour later, when Arista left, I contacted Misty to tell her the good news. She was so relieved. Then Joss ordered me to take a break. She said I looked frazzled. Laughing, she admitted that she was *mothering* me, but someone had to do it.

I pointed to my T-shirt. "Heed the RBG slogan. I am woman, hear me roar."

She smirked. "Go roar in the office."

She was right. I retreated to the office, settled into my

chair, and stirred the Zen garden for a couple of minutes. When I put down the rake, I spied a mesh pouch holding the extra shawl pins Nova had made for Misty's guests. I dialed her cell phone to see if I could return them as a ruse to suss out whether she was the one who'd left the bouquet for me. She answered on the first ring, which gave me pause. If she'd left the flowers, wouldn't she have let the call go to voicemail?

"Hi, Nova. I'm sorry about how we ended things last night."

"Me, too," she said softly.

I told her about the pins and asked if I could bring them to her. She said she was at Percolate having coffee with Odine. *Making nice*, I hoped. She inquired whether I would bring the pins to her there. I agreed.

Even though the sun was out, the weather was crisp, so I shrugged into my denim jacket and walked to the café. The aroma of fresh-brewed coffee wafted to me as I entered the place. A short line stood in front of the glass display case. Tulip-shaped pendant lights illuminated the wares. On the whitewashed brick wall hung a huge chalkboard with the day's specials. A number of free-floating shelves behind the counter held plants, loaves of bread, tins of tea, and gift boxes. The in-house coffee and tea cups were turquoise, to go with the turquoise café tables and chairs. I ordered a to-go latte and two egg bites. It wasn't like I was starving after eating breakfast, but Percolate made the best egg bites I'd ever tasted, using whole eggs, Gruyere cheese, and minced green onion. I would reheat them in the microwave for lunch.

After receiving my order in the café's signature white-and-turquoise bag, I weaved through the tables to the rear of the room. Nova was sitting with Odine on the leatherette banquet at a table large enough for four. Nova, in funereal black, looked like she'd been crying. Had Odine lashed out at her again? Nova was dabbing her face with the puff from a compact. Odine, in a mauve sweater dress, looked rested and confident.

"Good morning," I said. "Hope you had fun at the party."

Odine smiled. "It was divine, and I feel great. Not a day older than yesterday."

"Is everything okay?" I asked Nova.

She glanced at Odine, who answered for her. "Nova has been begging me to take more of her work on consignment. Sadly, I already have dozens of pieces that haven't sold." She gestured to me. "Sit. Join us."

I slid into a chair opposite the banquette and set my coffee and to-go bag on the table.

"I want her to put my designs on her website, too," Nova said, "and maybe share some posts on social media. Odine and Fantasy Awaits have a great presence and a terrific following, but—" She sniffed. Had Odine belittled her? "But she thinks it would be better if I tried to beef up my own presence. My website . . . well, let's just say it needs work, but I can't afford to pay a professional to bring it up to snuff."

"It's not simply your website, sugar," Odine said. "You need to do more with all the social media platforms. It's free marketing."

"Like when can I do that? In my spare time?" Nova's eyes sparked with frustration.

Apparently, the two of them had a seesaw-style relationship. Up one minute, down the next.

Odine patted Nova's arm. "Perhaps your money would be better spent with a therapist than on . . ." She stopped. What had she intended to say? Than on PR? Than on liquor? "You've lost your confidence. You need to reclaim the power of your inner sorceress." She was referring to Nova's tattoo, I surmised. "Of course, it doesn't help that your mother is demanding that you give up your designing dream and work for your father."

"What does your father do?" I asked.

"He sells stationery."

Odine rolled her eyes. "Boring."

"Nathan would've told me to—" Nova bit her lip and didn't continue.

"Nathan would've told you to dig deep and find your fighting spirit," Odine said.

"Who's Nathan?" I widened my eyes, playing dumb.

"The love of my life, but he's gone." Tears pooled in Nova's eyes. A tiny moan escaped her lips. "Swell, here I go again." She jumped to her feet and hurried toward the ladies' room.

"Poor thing," Odine said. "She's been on edge ever since Farrah came to town. That woman did such a head number on her."

"Head number?"

"Panning her stuff. Making Nova question her talent."

"That is a shame." I sipped my latte and noticed an exotic purse on the seat beside Odine. "Ooh. That is gorgeous." I pointed. "Is it an embroidered peacock?"

"It is."

"Where did you find it?"

"Mumbai."

An airline ticket was jutting from the outer pocket. "I see you're traveling soon. Where to?"

Nova returned and slipped into the booth. "Sorry I broke down. What did I miss?"

I said, "I was asking Odine about her upcoming trip."

"She's traveling to India," Nova answered for her. "To buy new items for the store."

I popped the lid off my latte. "Isn't your husband supposed to be sailing in the Indian Ocean about now, Odine? Will you meet up with him?"

"No." Her eyes narrowed. "Did you bring the items you wanted to return to Nova?"

I laughed. "I nearly forgot." I pulled the mesh pouch from my tote and slid it across the table. "You know, Odine, these shawl pins are gorgeous. You should display them in your shop. They'd make a lovely accessory to the shawls and kimonos you carry."

"Would you, O?" Nova pleaded.

Odine's gaze softened. "Of course."

Nova placed her hand on Odine's. "I'll bring you some of my mother's prized Sterling Silver tea roses as a thank you. They are the prettiest lavender color."

I said, "Nova, that reminds me: I received a bouquet with no note on my porch last night. Did you happen to drop it by?"

She sniffed. "If you'll recall, we didn't part on happy terms yesterday afternoon."

"Yes, but I thought perhaps you brought it as an apology."

"No. Besides, I don't know where you live."

Odine said, "Maybe Misty brought it by as a thank you."

Bummed that I hadn't worked out who had left the bouquet, I returned to the shop grumbling. And I wasn't the only one grumbling, I discovered. Fiona was sitting on top of the register, tapping her feet against the front, waiting for me.

"You went alone," she griped. "Why didn't you whistle to me?"

"I forgot."

"Did you figure out if Nova delivered the bouquet?"

"She said she didn't. Odine was there. She suggested that Misty might have left it, but she wouldn't have. I didn't say there was poison ivy in it."

"Was Odine still being mean to Nova?" Fiona asked.

"No. In fact, she offered to take more of Nova's jewelry on consignment."

"What does consignment mean?" Fiona asked.

I explained.

She drummed her fingers on her knee. "I don't trust Nova."

"Why not?"

"She wears black or white; white or black."

"She wore a black-and-white ensemble to the fairy garden party," I teased.

"Exactly. She wears no color. For an artist, she stays in the shadows. Why?" She poked a finger at me. "What does that say about her?"

Chapter 23

I have gone out and seen the lands of Faery,
And have found sorrow and peace and beauty there.
—Fiona Macleod, "Dreams Within Dreams"

The telephone jangled. My father was calling.

I answered. "Hey, Dad. What's up?"

"I bought way too much Chinese food. Would you like to invite me to dinner?"

I chuckled. "I don't think I've ever said no to Chinese food. Come over at six thirty. I've got wine."

When I arrived home, I breathed easier. My father was sitting on the rocking chair. There were no poison flowers on the porch. No Austin Pinter skulking around the corner. No lurker standing across the street, spying on me from afar. I laughed at myself. Who had been watching way too many noir movies of late?

"Hello, Daughter."

"Hello, Father," I replied in a teasing voice. I set Pixie on the ground and opened the front door. She sprinted inside.

Fiona, who had been loath to leave my side ever since we'd found the bouquet, alit on my father's shoulder. He didn't have a clue. He picked up the to-go bag by his feet and rose to a stand. Tittering, Fiona flitted into the house.

Handing the bag to me, my father grinned smugly, like he knew a secret that I wasn't privy to.

"What's going on?" I accepted the bag and guided him into the kitchen. "Why are you grinning like the Cheshire Cat? Did Brady call you?"

"Why would he have?" His gaze grew dark. "Did something happen?"

"No," I said quickly. "It's nothing."

"*Nothing* doesn't mean nothing."

I sighed. Why couldn't I keep my big trap shut?

"Spill, or I call Brady," my father ordered. "Now." Once a cop, always a cop. He pulled his cell phone from his jacket pocket.

"Fine." I set the food on the counter, fetched a bottle of chardonnay from the wine refrigerator, uncorked it, and poured two glasses. "Follow me to the yard, and I'll tell you everything." I plucked a scarf from the hook by the rear door, slung it around my neck for warmth, and buttoned my denim jacket.

The glow of fairy lights seemed to lessen the dark aura emanating from my father. He sat at the wicker table and leaned forward on his elbows, his wineglass pinned between both hands. "I'm waiting."

I filled him in.

"Sweetheart, you should have phoned Dylan."

"Dad." I swirled my wine in the glass. "Burlap. No fingerprints. What could the police have done?"

"Put a detail on you."

"As if they have cops to spare." I sipped my wine but barely tasted it.

"I'm calling Gus."

"No. Don't."

He ignored me and stabbed a number into his cell phone. "Hey, man. Yeah, it's me." Gus was a security guy for my father's landscaping firm, usually hired to guard projects that required a lot of onsite equipment. "I'm at Courtney's. Uh-huh. Yep. Again." My father chuckled. "Thanks. I owe you one." He ended the call. "He's on his way."

"Da-a-ad, c'mon."

"He knows the kind of trouble you can get into."

"I'm not a damsel in distress."

"I would never think of you that way," my father said, "but someone did leave you a threatening bouquet, and Austin Pinter is not in custody as far as I know."

"He shouldn't be. He didn't kill Farrah. He was in love with her."

"From what I hear, she wasn't all that loveable."

I tilted my head. "Who have you been talking to?"

"I have my sources." He leaned back in his chair and sipped his wine. "Nice night. I hope you like shrimp with lobster sauce."

I glowered at him. "You know I do." And so did Brady, which meant they had talked. That was why my father had smiled smugly, in on the joke that was not really a joke. "I'm starved. You?"

"I could eat."

"Should I reserve some for Gus?"

"He'll have eaten."

We moved inside. Dad removed the white containers from the takeout bag and placed them on the table in the kitchen nook. I arranged place mats, plates, and large serving spoons. Pixie meowed, making me realize I'd forgotten her.

"I'm on it, kitty." I tickled her chin and emptied a can of tuna into a bowl for her. Then I discreetly placed a dish with milk and honey, one of Fiona's favorite foods, on the sill above the kitchen sink.

Pouring more wine into our glasses, I said, "Dad, what did you decide to get Wanda for Valentine's Day?"

"I haven't. Yet."

"Tick-tock."

"Don't remind me."

"The two of you are getting along nicely." I sat at the table and filled my plate with white rice and shrimp in lobster sauce.

Dad shifted in his chair. "We're good friends."

"Friends?" I lifted my wineglass and glanced at him over the rim.

"We've agreed to take this slowly."

"So you haven't, you know, kissed?" I couldn't believe I was having this conversation with my father.

"None of your beeswax, as you used to say when you were a teenager."

He laughed. I liked the sound. He was much easier going now that he and Wanda were dating. When my mother died, his heart broke. Twenty years had been a long time to be emotionally shut down.

Using chopsticks, he nabbed a bite of shrimp. "It's your birthday tomorrow. Any plans?" He popped the shrimp into his mouth.

With all the hoopla, I'd completely forgotten about that. I wasn't much of a birthday person. I certainly wouldn't throw myself a fairy garden party. "I think Meaghan is taking me to lunch."

"Sounds nice."

We ate in silence.

When he finished his dinner, he set his chopsticks on the rim of the plate. "I hear we'll be working together in the spring."

"Yes. Violet Vickers wants some fairy gardens placed discriminately on the property. Will you have a problem with that?"

"You and I will chat once I get an idea of the scope of the project and whether she has a color scheme or theme she wants me to follow."

"I made her one garden already. In a big, blue pot, like the ones I made for the Beauty of Art Spectacular."

He folded his napkin, set it on the table, and leaned back in his chair. "Just promise me no dragons or trolls. Only make pretty gardens. Those are the ones people seem to like the most."

Heart be still. My father had paid attention to which gardens my customers liked?

I found my voice and said, "I promise."

Leaving the house the next morning with Pixie and Fiona, I greeted Gus, who was tucked into the rocking chair, a Mylar blanket wrapped around him for warmth. When he'd folded the blanket, I handed him a disposable to-go cup of coffee and a warm blueberry muffin from a batch I'd made and frozen a week ago. He thanked me and added that he hoped I'd had a restful sleep. In truth, I had.

Next, I went to Percolate. I was craving a double espresso. Waiting in line, I noticed Detective Summers paying for his drink.

On his way out, he passed me and said, "Have a good day."

"You, too."

Monday mornings were typically slow at the shop. Weekend warriors went back to work. Tourists drove home. Whatever sales we did make were usually with repeat customers. So today Joss and I decided a sale was in order. We often put on *flash sales,* never on the same day of any successive week, to entice new customers. The sale could last all day or simply run during the morning or the afternoon.

Two figurines for the price of one were the most popular sales. Customers texted their friends. Passersby, noting the limited hours on the sidewalk sign in front of the shop, didn't dally; they came right in.

Around eleven a.m., Glinda sauntered in with her niece, a grin on her face. "You and I must have gotten the universal dress memo." She wagged a finger between us. We were both wearing light-blue sweaters over jeans. Georgie had on a plaid uniform. "Georgie saw your sales sign on the way to school and texted me. Johnny on the spot, I swooped over there, fibbed to the front office that she had a dental appointment, and voilà. We're here. How many figurines can we buy?"

"Up to a dozen," I said.

"A dozen!" Georgie whooped. Her blond hair bounced. "I've been wanting to create a garden party with all my friends. Do you still have those strands of lights and that wide-mouthed pot?"

"We do." I supplied Georgie with a white basket and guided her and her aunt to the shelves on the patio that held environmental pieces. "These lights will be perfect for your garden." I lifted a silver strand about six inches long and fitted with miniature, colored lightbulbs. "Also, check out the signs that say *This way to the party!*"

Georgie started picking up items. "Ooh, this is so cute. And I love this one. And this one."

I motioned Glinda to follow me to the fountain. The burble of water would mute our voices. "Do you think it's a good idea to fib to the school?"

"*Pfft!*" She swatted the air. "Parents do it all the time. Georgie is a straight *A* student and way too serious for words. She's always hitting the books. Sometimes she'll even skip dinner with the family and eat a sandwich at her desk while doing algebra or Spanish. Sneaking out of school for a day to play hooky with me will loosen her up."

I'd bet Georgie was avoiding the family so she could chat online with friends but kept mum. If a fairy garden foray would bring her joy, who was I to argue?

"Guess what?" Glinda pulled a pair of airplane tickets from her purse and shook them near my face. "In a few weeks, my talented niece is competing in the International Open of Southern California, and Sis has to work, so I will be Georgie's chaperone. I can't wait. San Diego, here we come."

"You'll close the shop?" I asked. Glinda didn't have a partner at Glitz.

"Why not? March is a slow month for me." She gripped my elbow. "I could even slip into Mexico and see if I can find some great steals. That way I can write it off as a business trip."

"You know all the angles."

"It's my crafty pirate heritage." Glinda laughed. She often claimed her ancestors had been pirates that had terrorized the California coast. I didn't buy it, but she was keen on spreading the rumor.

"Aunt Glinda!" Georgie squealed. "Come see this!"

"Duty calls." Glinda mouthed *Thank you* and blew me a kiss before striding to her niece. She looped an arm around the girl's back and snuggled her. "Show me everything."

Meaghan whistled softly to catch my attention as she crossed the threshold to the patio. "Hello, birthday girl." She drew a finger up and down in front of my outfit and frowned. "Did you forget about our lunch?"

"No."

"You're wearing that?"

"What's wrong with it?"

She did a twirl in her lacy, flouncy A-line frock. "I thought we'd dress up. You are, after all, entering a new decade."

"Oof, don't remind me. Thirty-one and counting."

"C'mon, I'm older than you. It's no big deal. But you must dress up. Tell Joss you have to go home and change."

I narrowed my gaze. "You're not throwing some kind of surprise party, are you?"

"*Moi?* No! But Brady will be there, and you want to look your best." She assessed my outfit one more time. "Trust me, this is not it."

I swatted her arm. "Fine. After I ring up Georgie's purchases, I'll go home and change."

"Into that pretty blue dress with the butterflies."

I rolled my eyes. Now she was my stylist?

An hour later, Meaghan and I strolled into Hideaway Café. She had reserved a table on the patio.

I moved through the archway first and was surprised to see Dylan Summers and Renee Rodriguez waiting to be seated. Summers was wearing his standard get-up; Renee, a chic raincoat cinched at the waist. It wasn't raining. Had she thrown it on to cover her casual work clothes?

Summers was scribbling something in his case-notes notebook. He caught sight of me and grinned. "Are you following me?"

"I should ask you the same thing," I countered.

"Except I was here first, so technically . . ." He brandished his pen.

"It's her birthday," Meaghan chimed.

"Happy birthday," Renee said.

"Thanks." I felt my cheeks warm.

Fiona, who'd joined us, said, "Look, there's Merryweather Rose of Song."

A large group of women were sitting at a table on the far

side of the patio. Among them, Lissa Reade, the well-dressed, seventy-something librarian; Brady's mother, Eudora; Violet Vickers; Tish Waterman and her daughter. A stack of books sat in the center of the table. All the women were studying menus. Their waitress was pouring champagne into flutes. Merryweather was circling the table, beaming with pride.

"What do you think the ladies are celebrating?" Meaghan bumped her shoulder to mine.

"Maybe Eudora found her manuscript."

"Not yet," Summers cut in. He removed a rubber band from his wrist and started to wrap it around his notebook but lost hold. Both fell to the patio.

I retrieved them for him.

He snatched the notebook away from me. "Uh-uh. No peeking. Mine."

I offered him the rubber band. "Do you honestly think I could read your chicken scratch?"

Renee bit back a laugh. "She's plucky, Dylan."

"Tell me about it," he groused.

"It's a birthday girl's right," Renee added.

"Every day is not her birthday," he retorted.

Meaghan elbowed me. "*Psst.* Look behind us."

Austin Pinter had joined the line of diners waiting to be seated. He was wearing a pin-striped suit and had a leather, laptop-sized satchel slung crosswise over his jacket.

I spun back to Summers. "Hey, did Austin Pinter come to the precinct and tell you where he really was on the night Farrah Lawson was killed?"

Summers grew somber. "Look—"

"I know, I know," I said. "This is where you ask me to back off. Again."

"And this is where you tell me you'll try, but you won't be capable of doing so."

I stifled a smile. "Did he?"

"No. Was he supposed to?"

"Yes. He showed up at my place. He was angry that I'd sicced you on him."

"He showed up at—" Summers huffed. "And you didn't call us?"

After I explained what went down, I said, "Brady happened to be in the neighborhood and made his presence known. Mr. Pinter left quietly. Between you and me, I think he was afraid of what I could do with a shovel."

I heard Brady's voice and pivoted. He had waylaid Austin, his demeanor ominous. "You have a lot of nerve."

Austin threw up both hands, as if surrendering. "I won't be any trouble."

"You don't have a reservation."

"I made one. I know I did."

"Wait here."

Brady moved to the front of the line, greeted Summers and Renee, and took them to a table, saying to Meaghan and me, "Be right back." He winked at me and whispered, "I like the dress."

Meaghan knuckled my arm. "Told ya."

I felt warm breath on my neck and swiveled my head. Austin was behind me, peeking over my shoulder.

"What do you want?" I sniped.

"I'm looking for my date." He tried to sidle past me.

I threw out an arm to block him. "Look, I don't know what you're up to, but you're not going anywhere until Brady returns. Why didn't you talk to the police?"

"I . . ." He continued to scan the patio's guests. "I meant to."

Fiona leaped onto Austin's shoulder, rubbed her hands together rapidly, and flicked her fingers toward his ear. He reached up and scratched the lobe.

Fiona cupped her hands and chanted to him, "*By dee prood macaw.*"

I understood the translation: *May God make peace upon you.*
Instantly, Austin calmed. *Peace: calm.* It made sense. The flicking of Fiona's fingers must have primed his hearing to some
degree.

"Grill him," Fiona said.

Doing my best not to laugh at her policelike command, I
said, "Austin, you don't really have a date for lunch, do you?"

He shook his head.

"You argued with Farrah on Friday night about stealing
something, didn't you?"

He nodded.

"What did you steal?"

"Eudora Cash's latest manuscript."

"Wrong. It didn't go missing until Tuesday."

"I was casing out her place Friday night. Making a dry
run, as they say in the movies."

Meaghan coughed sarcastically.

Austin sighed. "I had to see what she was working on.
Had to. I was desperate for inspiration. She's known for the
way she diligently outlines and structures her stories. I believed if I could study her draft, I could learn something that
might inspire me. My editor wants my next book, like, yesterday, and I'm drawing a blank."

I said, "You didn't want to admit what you were doing
Friday night—"

"Because it would have exposed my real crime."

"You mean you followed through? You did steal it?"

Meaghan gasped.

Austin nodded, his face pinched with pain. "But I regret
what I've done. It's been making me sick to my stomach.
Today, when I was at the library doing research, I heard Eudora and Lissa making plans for their lunch, so I followed
them. They're forming a new book club, and I thought that
while they were discussing which books they'd consider, I

could slip the manuscript into Eudora's purse"—he patted his satchel—"and no one would be the wiser. She carries a very large tote."

Merryweather Rose of Song zoomed to Fiona and gripped her arm. "What's going on? What have you done?"

"Nothing," she squeaked. "I didn't. I'm positive I used the right incantation."

Merryweather pointed a finger at Austin. "He confessed to a crime."

Boy, she has good ears, I thought.

"It's not my fault!" Fiona cried. "He must have felt the need to." Tears pooled in her eyes. "Believe me, I just calmed him. That's all. Promise."

Merryweather huffed and whizzed to her table. Fiona flew to my shoulder and buried her face in my neck.

I felt someone approaching. Thinking it was Brady ready to seat us, I spun around. It was Summers.

"What's going on over here?" he demanded.

Austin paled and extended his arms, ready to be arrested. "I stole Eudora Cash's manuscript, sir. I came here to return it."

"Clandestinely," Meaghan said.

I threw her a *zip it* look. The guy was penitent. I hoped the police would cut him a break.

"I truly admire her," Austin went on, his voice filled with shame. "She is my idol. I thought I could learn something. I didn't mean to . . ." He hung his head.

"He was casing out Eudora's place on Friday night, Detective," I said. "Which gives him an alibi for the night of Farrah Lawson's murder."

Lissa Reade and Eudora appeared behind Summers.

"Detective, is there some problem?" Eudora straightened the lapel of her soft green linen suit and smoothed a stray hair of her French twist. "I heard my name uttered."

No way could she have heard her name all the way across the patio. A fairy, yes. A human, no. Merryweather must have looped Lissa in, and Lissa informed Eudora.

"Ma'am." Summers explained the situation.

"Austin"—Eudora reached out to him and took his hands in hers—"from one famous author to another, I understand your pain. I've felt like the Sahara at times, and truth be told, about ten years ago, when I was ready to give it all up, knowing I was a fraud and would never be able to write another book, I reached out to Fannie Atwood for guidance."

"Fannie Atwood," Austin whispered with reverence. "The *Duchess of Ambrose* series."

"Exactly." Eudora beamed, the dimple in her cheek deepening. "I remember our sessions fondly. She was gracious and kind, and she filled me with inspiration. So now, because you came here with the best intentions—"

"Sneaky intentions," Fiona carped.

"I won't press charges," Eudora stated. "And if you're open to it, young man, I will mentor you."

Austin gulped, hard, and then he wept.

Lissa clapped her hands demurely. "Eudora, you are positively the best woman in the world."

Brady returned to the group and said, "What did I miss?"

Chapter 24

Hundreds of them, all together,—
Flashing flocks of flying fairies,—
Crowding through the summer weather,
Seeking where the coolest air is.
—Philip Bourke Marston, "Flower Fairies"

My birthday lunch was everything I'd hoped it would be—Meaghan and me talking about life and about how far we'd come and what we hoped for the future, Brady showing up with a miniature decadent chocolate cake with a candle in it, and everyone on the patio singing to me. I didn't typically appreciate being in the limelight, but after the confrontation with Austin Pinter, I'd appreciated the festive atmosphere. As a cherry on top, Twyla left her book club group and slipped over to me to share that Lissa Reade had helped her resolve her gossip mill problem on social media. I was so happy for her.

Upon entering Open Your Imagination with Fiona, I extended a finger. "Are you okay?" She alit on it. I could feel her shivering.

"No. I didn't mean to. It wasn't my intent." She worried her hands.

"Calm down. Why don't you visit Merryweather and see if there is a way to make amends, although I don't think you did anything wrong." Like her, I believed that Austin had wanted to confess and, by her chanting to him, he'd found the courage to do so. Would the queen fairy agree with me, a mere mortal?

"I need to rest," she moaned, and disappeared into the ficus on the patio.

I started after her but stopped when Hattie Hopewell swooped into the showroom followed by The Happy Diggers, all wearing floral T-shirts over jeans or leggings.

"We're here," Hattie crooned.

Joss nicked my elbow. "Did you know they were coming? They aren't on the calendar."

"I was aware she wanted a group lesson, but no, I didn't have a clue it would be today." I smiled. "Don't worry. This afternoon's schedule is clear."

"This way, ladies," Hattie said, toting a well-used leather makeup case. "Courtney, dear, I'm sorry I didn't contact you. This was spur of the moment. Zinnia wanted us to each choose an item from our attics or garages that we could use for containers. It had to have a special meaning for each of us."

Zinnia Walker, a trim sixty-five-year-old with a silver pixie cut, was wealthy beyond belief and with that wealth came knowledge. According to her, she was an influencer and had her finger on the pulse of Carmel's richest families. In her twenties, she had tried her hand at numerous careers, but in her thirties, after bearing two children, she'd admitted to herself that she liked playing golf, fine-tuning her garden, and attending book clubs. Her husband could do the heavy lifting.

"Look at the array." Hattie hoisted the makeup case. "This belonged to my grandmother who was a riveter in the war."

The other containers the women had brought included a

metal pail, miniature wagon, picnic basket, and shallow drawer from a dresser.

"My, my," I said. "We might need to order more soil."

Hattie laughed. "They aren't that big, but if we need some, I'll call the local nursery. The owner owes me a favor." She glanced over her shoulder. "Let's go, girls. To the work-station on the patio."

Like an army, they tramped single-file through the show-room and out the French doors.

None of the Diggers had brought their dogs with them. I was sorry they hadn't. Hattie owned the sweetest brindle Scottie. Pixie loved playing with it.

"Good luck," Joss said. "I'm not certain we have enough figurines after this morning's sale."

"Don't we have some boxes of them in storage?"

"You're right." She tapped her temple. "Brain dead."

"How're you holding up with your mom?" I put a hand on her shoulder. Her eyes were tired and her skin lackluster.

She wriggled free. "I'm good. Strong. No pity parties for this gal." She thumbed her chest. "Got it?"

"Got it."

"I'll come help you when the showroom clears of these last two customers."

I strolled to the patio, checking on the handful of men and women customers who were sitting at tables, considering their selections. None needed my help.

"Courtney. *Psst.*" Hattie stopped me beside the shelves of figurines. She was holding two in her left hand. "Where did you find these wonderful old lady fairies?" She wiggled the craggy-faced one in a wrinkled blue dress. "This one will rep-resent my grandmother. She adored the color blue."

"I commissioned them."

For months I'd been toying with the idea that because

most fairy figurines were young and beautiful, there ought to be older ones. After watching a couple of YouTube videos of artists working with polymer clay—one in particular who had created characters from *The Lion King* and installed them into a simple jungle-themed fairy garden—I'd invited Renee to lunch and talked to her about making older fairies that I could sell at the shop. Some of my more mature clientele, like Hattie, were snapping them up. Renee, who was eager to see a fairy, agreed instantly. She hoped the artistry would open her eyes.

"I love them, and I'll want more in the future." Hattie moseyed to the table and set her selections on top. "Now tell us all you know about Farrah Lawson's murder, seeing as it hasn't been resolved."

"Hattie . . ."

She tittered. "C'mon. You have your finger on the pulse."

"No I don't."

"Of course you do. After all, you are your father's daughter. He was a savvy policeman." She arranged her figurines as I'd taught her, facing each other as if in conversation. "I must say that you were stalwart in making certain Twyla Waterman was no longer a person of interest. Finding the witness. Getting her statement."

I thought of Leanne Cox, so vulnerable and pathetic. I hoped Christopher would be able to find her help.

"Who else do you suspect?" Hattie held up the older fairy in the red polka dot dress. "You've been right in the past. Is Misty Dawn on the list? She invited Farrah Lawson to Carmel."

"Misty wouldn't harm a flea." Zinnia slipped her oversized diamond necklace beneath the collar of her wildly floral T-shirt, then pushed the swing, shaped like a leaf, that she'd chosen for her garden. Upon the swing sat a beautiful pink fairy reading a book.

"What do you know, Zinnia?" carped the oldest Digger, who was ninety-two. She never tired and never pulled punches.

"Misty is simply too kind," Zinnia cooed. "Who else, Courtney?"

Joss brought buckets of dirt to the table. "Yeah, who else, boss?"

Clearly, the group wouldn't let up until I'd answered their questions, so I proceeded. "Nova Pasha, a jewelry designer, has a strong motive and her alibi is weak. She claims she was stargazing."

"I know Nova," Zinnia said. "Lovely woman. I've bought two of her bracelets. She creates eccentric designs, but I like them."

"You like anything eccentric," said the Digger with ocean-blue eyes, who was filling her picnic basket with dirt. "Including your husband."

Zinnia pulled a face. "He's not eccentric. He's unconventional."

Her accuser chuckled.

I continued. "Nova said she drove down the coast and stopped in a turnout to gaze for hours, and no one else used the same turnout."

"That's possible," the Digger with waist-length hair said. "I've gone stargazing and never been bothered."

"Nova wasn't there," Hattie said. "She wasn't stargazing."

"Are you positive?" Joss looked from me to Hattie.

"Absolutely."

I handed Hattie a plastic liner and a cordless glue gun. "Line your makeup case with this before you add dirt."

By now Hattie was an old hand at fairy garden making and handling a glue gun. Following my instructions, she continued, "I know because I saw her outside the Livingstons' house. She looked like a lost soul, slumped in her VW, tears streaming down her face."

"That's so sad," Zinnia said.

"Nova was in love with Nathan Livingston," I said. "Do you know how he died?"

"He's not dead." Hattie waved the glue gun in the air, nearly missing Zinnia's head.

"Watch it!" her friend said.

"Oops. Sorry, Zinnia."

"He's not?" I cocked my head. Why had Nova led everyone to believe that?

"Heavens no. Nathan works with otters at the aquarium. He's a sweet young man, although he's probably not so young." Hattie tapped her chin. "He must be forty now. I know his parents. His father owned one of the nightclubs where I performed." Years ago, she had entertained for a living, but being on the road for months on end had finally taken its toll, and she'd given it up so she could retire near her sisters.

"Do you know how long Nova was parked there, Hattie?" I asked.

"I haven't a clue. I was driving by with Cliff—he lives around the corner—and we saw the light on in the car. We slowed because we were worried someone might need road assistance."

"That was nice of you," said the ninety-two-year-old.

"What time was that?" I tamped down the soil in the oldest Digger's project. I wanted her plants to thrive, and pockets of air weren't good in soil.

"Around eight thirty," Hattie said. "We'd had the loveliest dinner at that bistro on Dolores Street. Nova was stabbing numbers on her cell phone, if that matters. Cliff could see its illumination."

"Had her car broken down?" Zinnia inquired.

"Doubtful. When she spotted us slowing, she slinked down in her seat."

The ponytailed Digger said, "Maybe she was staking out the place."

I gawked at her. Was that the case? Was Nathan *dead* to Nova because he'd cheated on her?

"Do you suspect anyone else?" Hattie asked.

Briefly, I recapped my thoughts about Odine, her absent husband, and Farrah's disgruntled boyfriends, while wondering whether Summers was following other possible leads. Zinnia reiterated that she loved Odine. The eldest Digger thought the husband sounded like a likely prospect. Hattie suggested there might be someone else the police weren't considering.

Fortunately, the conversation waned, and they turned their attention back to their projects. For a half hour, I advised them about the plants that might work best with their particular gardens and how often to water them. When they left, pleased with their creations, I rushed to the office, antsy to satisfy a hunch.

Joss called to me. I didn't respond.

Fiona, having recovered from her distress, followed me. "Courtney, slow down. You're walking very fast. Joss needs you. Didn't you hear her?"

I rounded the desk and woke up the computer.

Joss barged into the office. "What's going on? You look frantic."

"Nova Pasha lied about her alibi. Why? Why not tell me or the police that she'd parked outside Nathan's house?"

"Nathan who?" Joss asked.

"Nathan Livingston, a guy who works at the aquarium. Nova was and still might be in love with him." I moved the cursor to the search bar at the top of the browser. "She was seen parked in front of his house. If she was stalking him, she might not want the police—or Nathan—to know. And yet, even if that was the case, her whereabouts would continue to be iffy. Hattie couldn't confirm how long she was stationed there. Nova could have killed Farrah and then driven to Nathan's to establish an alibi."

"But she didn't say she was there," Joss interjected. "She claimed she was stargazing."

"Because she was embarrassed," Fiona murmured.

I opened the social media page I'd looked at the other day and typed in Nova's name. Deciding to follow the same routine as I had before, I scrolled through her photos until I landed on Nathan's picture, the one where Nova said he was gone forever. Misty and Odine had commented. Farrah's comment had been deleted since I'd viewed it. Had Nova blocked her or reported abuse?

"Visit Nathan's social media page," Joss suggested, rounding the desk and standing behind me, peering over my shoulder.

I typed *Nathan Livingston* into the search bar and hit Enter. Up popped a selection of corresponding names. Beneath one, it said *Works at aquarium,* and the picture looked like Nova's guy. I selected that profile. Without needing to be his friend, I was able to view all his photos. I found a picture of Nova, beaming as she displayed three bracelets on her arm. Nathan's post read: *@NovaPasha. What a talent.*

Beneath were two comments. The first, from Misty saying how right he was. The second, written by Farrah, took my breath away. *@NovaPasha he's too good for you. You're a hack. He should leave you. @NathanLivingston when you learn her secret, you'll end it.*

"Lordy," Joss said.

Fiona landed on my wrist and thrust her arm toward the screen. "Why did Farrah do that?"

I shook my head. "Nova must have done something to upset her."

Joss said, "Even so, Farrah's warning to Nathan about Nova is spiteful and wicked."

I glanced over my shoulder. "And it gives Nova an even better motive for murder."

Chapter 25

Good luck befriend thee, Son; for at thy birth
The faery ladies danced upon the hearth.
—John Milton, "Good Luck Befriend Thee"

"Call the police," Joss said.

"And tell them what?" I grabbed my purse, car keys, and Nova's business card, the one I'd taken at dinner the other night. "We have nothing more than hearsay."

"Hattie saw her."

"At Nathan's. Not at Farrah's rental house." I strode into the showroom, which was devoid of customers.

"She could be the killer," Joss said. "I'm coming with you." She hurried after me, flipped over the *Closed for a short while* sign, and locked up the shop.

"I'm coming, too!" Fiona cried, adding that, if necessary, she could use a spell to knock Nova out.

I didn't believe her for a second, and if she could, would the fairy queen approve? That didn't seem like a spell a good fairy should use, not even a righteous fairy trying to help her human discover the truth. But I didn't quibble with either of them. We piled into my Mini Cooper.

While driving, I phoned Nova. She answered, and I inquired whether I could stop by to purchase a shawl pin for Wanda. The ruse worked. She invited me over.

"At Meaghan's the other night you said you lived on Santa Rita. What's the street number?" I asked.

After she gave it to me, I ended the call and drove quickly.

Nova's parents' home was a black-and-white, shingle-style house with a basic evergreen garden. No bells and whistles. I parked on the street, and then Joss and I climbed the staircase on the side of the garage to the upstairs unit. Fiona settled on my shoulder as I knocked on the door.

"Who is it?" Nova's words slurred together.

Uh-oh. Had she been drinking in the middle of the day? Perhaps Odine was right to be concerned about her.

"It's Courtney Kelly, Nova. We just spoke."

"Is your fairy with you?" She snickered, then snorted.

"As a matter of fact, she is."

Nova whipped the door open, a Ragdoll cat tucked under one arm and a glass of white wine in her other hand. She motioned for us to enter. "Welcome to my palace."

I stepped inside. Joss followed and closed the door.

"Pretty cat," I said.

"His name is Scooter." She set him on the floor. "If I don't hold him when I open the door, he likes to run out. Hence the name." She snickered.

The apartment was a long room with the living area at one end and a kitchenette at the other. The cat scurried to the kitchenette and leaped onto the counter near a sunny window.

Nova smoothed the collar of her black jumper. She was barefoot, no makeup, no jewelry. "I don't see your fairy."

You'd probably need a clear head to stand a chance, I mused.

"She's here," I said. "Right over your left shoulder."

Fiona fluttered near Nova and then zoomed away to meet the cat.

"Hmmph," Nova muttered.

Standing against two of the walls were narrow tables, each holding a selection of jewelry tools. I'd made necklaces and earrings in high school with a girlfriend whose father had been a master jeweler. I recognized many of the tools: wire workers, a soldering kit, pliers, six or seven different hammers, a rotary tool with attachments, needle files, and more. A pair of white folding chairs faced each table. Photographs of fields of flowers and hiking trails hung evenly on the walls. An old Panasonic television stood on a cart close to the kitchen. A black-striped wingback chair faced the TV. Pegboards affixed on either side of the television held numerous pieces of her jewelry. A single bed covered with a black-and-white comforter separated the work room from the kitchenette.

Nova cocked a hip. "Courtney, you said you want to see the shawl pins."

"Not yet. May we sit?" I gestured to the chairs.

"Please do. Want wine?"

"No thanks."

Nova set her wineglass on a design table and pulled two folding chairs closer to the armchair. She sagged into the armchair. "Sit."

I perched on the edge of my chair. Joss did the same.

"Nova," I began, "I was scrolling through social media photos, and I saw some things that I found interesting."

"Social media," she snarled. "What a crock. One site blocked me from being able to advertise. I don't know what I did wrong, so I wrote them, but the stupid behemoth responded with idiotic bot answers."

"Yes, the internet is hard to navigate. Anyway"—I propped my forearms on my thighs and leaned forward in an effort to earn her trust—"I was thinking about your relation-ship with Farrah Lawson—"

"Why would you want to do that? She's—" Nova grew quiet.

"Farrah dissed your work online, but she also dissed your relationship with Nathan Livingston."

The mention of his name made Nova sit taller.

"You posted on your site that he was dead."

"No, I didn't. I wrote that he was gone. Big difference."

Big difference is right, I mused.

"Farrah shouldn't have dissed you," Joss said, getting me back on track.

"Darn tootin'," Nova snapped.

"I searched photos on his profile," I went on, "and I saw a photo of you displaying three bracelets on your arm."

"Yeah, I remember that one. He admired all the bracelets I made."

"In the post for that photo, Nathan wrote that you were quite talented. Misty left a comment. She agreed."

"Yeah, so? What's your point?"

"There was another response. By Farrah." I paused for ef-fect. "She wasn't kind to you."

Nova shrugged a shoulder.

"She labeled you a hack and told Nathan to leave you. She warned that when he learned your secret . . ." I spread my hands. "What secret?"

Nova worked her tongue inside her cheek.

Was it her drinking? I wondered. Or was there something else? Something more dire?

"I lost my brother," Nova revealed, no silver fairy dust forcing her to calm or red dust to make her focus. "To drugs. He was twenty-seven. He couldn't get his career on track. When he overdosed, I lost myself. To alcohol."

"I'm sorry. Nathan didn't know?"

"No. I'm pretty good at hiding it. I want to stop. I try to. Farrah . . . She never understood. She had willpower. She . . ." Nova folded her arms, turning inward like a pill bug, and in a tiny voice said, "She hated me, ever since college. She fell in love with a makeup artist, but he had a crush on me."

Farrah had been holding a grudge since college? Yipes.

"We never hooked up or anything," Nova went on, "but he didn't fall for her, so she blamed me and had it in for me ever since."

"Did Nathan break up with you after her post?"

"No, he—" Her voice cracked.

"He ghosted you," Joss said.

"Yes!"

"It happened to me." Joss pressed a hand to her chest. "I feel your pain."

I said, "You wrote a post saying that the love of your life was gone. I'd interpreted that to mean he was dead. Imagine my surprise when I found out earlier that he's very much alive, and you were seen parked outside his house Friday night."

Nova glared at me.

"You hated Farrah for making him leave you, but you could never act on that hate because she was traipsing all over the globe making movies. When you realized she'd accepted the invitation for Odine's birthday party, you set your plan in place. You found a poison—I'm not certain which one—and either got her to drink it, or you injected her with it, and then you drove to Nathan's house to establish an alibi, except you couldn't admit you were there because you were stalking him."

"No!" She sprang out of the chair, teetering slightly. "I didn't kill her."

I rose. "The timing would have worked out."

"I was stargazing."

Joss scrambled to her feet and flanked me. "You hung outside his place for a while."

I said, "A couple of people saw you. Were you working up the courage to tell him that you killed her for breaking up your relationship?"

"Aren't you listening?" Nova smacked her thigh with her palm. "I didn't kill her. I . . . I was here."

"You said you were stargazing."

"That's a lie. I was here. At home." Her voice cracked. "I was drunk dialing Nathan. I . . ." Tears spilled down her cheeks. "Each time he answered, I hung up, and then when it got dark, I drove there and dialed him over and over."

Hattie's words came whistling to me. She'd said Cliff had seen Nova stabbing numbers on her cell phone. Was Nova telling the truth about calling Nathan? Phone records would prove that and establish the time.

Fiona flew to Nova's shoulder and hummed a lullaby she would often sing to me. So much for knocking her out with a spell. She was calming Nova because she believed her.

Nova said, "I . . . I was embarrassed to admit it to anyone."

"Told you," Fiona gloated.

"I phoned Odine to get her to talk me out of walking up to his door," Nova continued. "She didn't answer, but reaching out to her helped me. I stayed put. In the car. Until almost ten. By then I'd sobered up, and I came home. If you canvass the area, someone must have seen me there. At the time of the murder."

"Nathan never looked out at the street?" I asked.

She hung her head. "Not once."

I flashed on Odine and Nova arguing at Misty's house. "Saturday, at the fairy garden party, you and Odine fought. Were you trying to convince her to say she answered your call? Did she refuse?"

"No. She accused me of telling you about her husband and Farrah. I lied and told her I hadn't. That seemed to appease her." Nova chewed on her fingernail. "She's leaving."

"To Mumbai," I said. "I saw the ticket."

"No, leaving Carmel. For good. She'll go to India first, in case she might run into her rat of a husband, but failing that, she's going home to Texas. She's a yellow rose lover through and through."

"That's it!" Joss cried out of the blue. "Courtney, look at the photos on the walls." She pointed. "Flowers."

Nova looked confused.

"The letter *A* stands for aconite," Joss explained.

Aconite. Of course. I must have overlooked it in my search when I'd landed on the less common acrolein and arsenic. "Aconite comes from wolfsbane, also known as monkshood," I said.

Wolfsbane belongs to the genus Ranunculaceae, native to the Northern Hemisphere. The flowers are distinguishable because of their helmet shape.

"It's very poisonous," Joss added.

No kidding. It was one of the queens of poisons.

"I learned about it during a bird-watching hike with Danny," Joss went on. "The flowers are very pretty, but he warned me about many of them. The purple variety is the most familiar."

Flowers.

I took in the posters on the walls as the mystery started to fall into place. Odine hadn't begged Misty to make sure Farrah would attend the birthday party. She had *implored* her. To exact revenge for seducing her husband and ruining their marriage. How angry she must have been at Farrah.

Pulling my cell phone from my pocket, I opened the social media site where I'd viewed Nova's photographs. Nova drinking wine with Misty. Nova getting tattoos with Odine. Nova hiking and gathering flowers with a bunch of friends.

I selected one of the hiking photographs and spotted Misty, Odine, and Nova. In another, just Odine and Nova.

Joss peeked over my shoulder. "That spot. Right there. That's where Danny and I went bird-watching. It's Lace Lichen Trail."

Odine had slipped purple flowers into the band that was holding her streaked hair in a soft ponytail. How she adored the color purple, everyone said. I visualized the framed photographs of purple flowers hanging on the walls at Fantasy Awaits.

And then I remembered the boxed photographs of honeysuckle in the shop. Honeysuckle, as Fiona had reminded me, was the symbol not only for faith and loyalty but also for lost love.

"Odine—" I hesitated.

"Odine what?" Joss raised an eyebrow.

"Odine has the strongest motive. She said she didn't blame Farrah for her husband's abandonment, but she did."

I flashed on Misty joking about how she and Odine had started out in college with the overblown notion of becoming doctors, but they'd switched gears. Even so, they had probably taken requisite chemistry classes. The topic of poisons might have cropped up. Had Odine studied which flowers were poisonous?

Hold on, Courtney. According to Summers, Odine had a verifiable alibi, thanks to a deli clerk's testimony. Or did she? When Glinda was talking about her niece's study habits at the shop earlier, she'd said that Georgie liked to take food to her room rather than eat with the family so she could do homework, but I'd reflected that she did so in order to hang out with friends online without being monitored. Eating alone provided all sorts of freedom. Did the deli guy deliver Odine's meal to the shop and see her there, or had Odine picked up the sandwich at the deli and mentioned her phony alibi of doing the books, and then contacted Farrah to meet up after Farrah broke away from Austin?

In order to safeguard her alibi, she would have needed to do the deed quickly. Get in and get out. How had she pulled it off?

Chapter 26

How to tell if a fairy is nearby: large patches of four-leaf clover.
—Anonymous

I apologized to Nova for suspecting her and urged her to seek treatment for her *secret*. AA, I told her, had helped a friend of mine a year ago. Maybe when she was clean and sober, she could reach out to Nathan and explain everything that had gone down.

In the meantime, I agreed with Joss. I would call the police. Driving away, I phoned the precinct. Summers and Reddick weren't in. They were handling a nasty car crash on Highway 1. I gave the clerk a message that I was pretty certain Odine Oates had killed Farrah Lawson, and she planned to leave town. If she would tell the detective and officer to meet me at Fantasy Awaits, I'd explain everything.

"I'm going there now," I added. "I'll delay her."

"No, don't!" the clerk ordered. "Stand—"

I ended the call. I would not *stand down*.

Drawing near to the shop, I realized there weren't any

parking spots on the street. I circled the block once, only to find that all the spots were taken. So much for Monday being a light day for tourism.

I double-parked alongside a Mercedes. "She's in the shop," I whispered to Joss, as if Odine could hear me. "She's packing boxes and turning off lights. I'll go inside. You park at the North Lot at Sunset Center and come right back."

"Got it. I'll return in two minutes, tops."

I paused. "What'll I say?"

"What you said to Nova. You need a gift for your father's girlfriend."

I slid out of the car.

Fiona shot out behind me and flapped her wings double time. "I'm your wingman, get it?"

The joke helped loosen the tension in my shoulders.

Joss skirted the car and slipped into the driver's seat. "Two minutes," she repeated.

I pushed the door open, my heart pounding inside my rib cage, and forced myself to sound cheery. "Hello, Odine!" Acting casual, I touched the kimonos. The quality of the silk was top-of-the-line.

"Hi, Courtney," Odine said.

"Getting ready to go on your trip?"

"Sure am."

"Who will run the place while you're gone?"

"No one. This month is slow for business," she said, same as Glinda had.

It wasn't a slow time for us, but then our customers were always in a creative mood, no matter the season. "A little birdie said you're packing up for good and moving home to Texas."

"Who told you that?"

"Um, Misty," I lied.

Odine must have been organizing since early morning.

Items from the rightmost counter rested on top of the glass, including the wave-art sculptures, Tiffany bowls, and crystal vases. A handful of items, ready to go into boxes, were wrapped in burlap—exactly like the material that had held the toxic bouquet I'd found on my porch. My breath snagged in my lungs.

"These are pretty." I selected a royal blue kimono with silver trim and folded it over my arm. "I'd like to buy one."

"Of course."

"And maybe one or two more things. My dad needs something to give his girlfriend."

"Browse for a bit, but I have to leave soon to catch my plane."

"Have you looked for a buyer for this place? There must be a bunch."

She didn't respond.

I ambled to the centermost counter and paused. Trays of charms and necklaces sat atop the glass. In addition, items that had once been near or behind the sales register were amassed on the center counter: the Zen garden, postcards, some of the honeysuckle photographs. I lifted one of the eighteen-inch-long gold necklaces featuring a two-inch round gold-and-red dragon charm. "I love this."

"You said Misty told you I was leaving." Odine glanced at me sideways.

"Mm–hm."

"That's odd. I only informed Nova."

"Nova must have told Misty."

Odine moved to the leftmost glass case and started removing the copper Chinese dragon statues, Samurai swords, and blade-folding pocketknives. "Why are you really here, Courtney?"

"Like I said, I'd like to purchase this kimono. I owe myself a present. It's my birthday today."

"Happy birthday." Her voice was flat.

"Plus I'll get this necklace. Maybe I should get my dad something, too. Perhaps one of those beautiful folding blades." I glanced over my shoulder, wondering what was taking Joss so long. And what about Summers or Reddick? Had they received the alert?

Odine opened and closed one of the blades with a *snap*. "You're positive you want one of these? They're sharp."

Nervous laughter burbled out of me. "It would defeat the purpose if it were dull."

Fiona fluttered beside me. "Breathe."

Odine leveled her gaze at me. "You couldn't help yourself, could you?"

"About buying the knife. I do—"

"Cut the crap. I'm talking about you rooting around. Looking for answers. Yes, you were in charge of the fairy party, but you couldn't keep work and life separate, could you?" Her tone had a bite. "You insinuated yourself into our lives. Even after Austin warned you, and after you received the bouquet on the porch, you pressed on." She set the foldable knife aside and lifted a twelve-inch-long knife. "How about a wakizashi for your father?"

The long narrow blade glinted in the overhead lights. She pinged the blade with her fingernail. I flinched and took a small step toward the exit.

"The other day, when you came into the shop and started asking questions about Misty, I was able to divert you. But when you sought out Nova today, you overstepped." Odine noticed my shock. "Yes, she phoned me the moment you left her place. She said you were off your rocker, believing that I"—she tapped her chest—"might have had something to do with Farrah's death."

Dang it. I should have realized that an inebriated Nova

wouldn't have been able to contain herself. After all, she had drunk-dialed her boyfriend.

Odine flipped the knife expertly in her hand, grabbing it by the hilt. "Did I ever tell you that I studied with fight masters on my journeys to the Orient? I've always been interested in the art of the fight, having been the fight coordinator for our theater group at college. We put on two Shakespearean productions each year. My favorite was the lesser-known *Henry VI, Part 1*."

Fiona whispered, "The theme of that play was about how personal squabbles and petty jealousies tore apart the English political system." She raised a fist. "'Fight to the last gasp!'"

How appropriate, I thought, given the current situation. The aftermath from Farrah's affair with Odine's husband had devastated Odine and made her crazy with jealousy.

Taking the offensive, I said, "You hated Farrah. You killed her because *she* had *insinuated* herself into *your* world." I made a snakelike motion of my hand. "She snared your husband's heart and made it impossible for him to ever return to you."

Odine switched the knife to her other hand. "Yes, I hated her. She had everything. That body. Those looks. A honeyed voice. A way with men that I would never possess. I cherished my husband with all my soul, and she ate him up and spat him out."

"When did you come up with the idea to murder her? Don't tell me. Let me guess. When you were out hiking? You saw the wolfsbane or monkhood"—I pointed to a poster by the dragon-themed display case—"which is extremely common on the hiking trails around here, and thought to yourself, *Aha*. I'll bet you learned in chemistry class, back when you were contemplating becoming a doctor, that you could create a solution of aconite from wolfsbane. Or perhaps you learned about the poison during a chat with a librarian, or you read it—"

"Online."

"You made a solution," I continued, "and then implored Misty to include Farrah at your party—she believed you'd forgiven her—and you sweetly arranged to have her stay at your Airbnb. You were the perfect, magnanimous friend. You set a date that night to catch up and went to the house to wait."

She didn't answer.

"Did you put the solution in a cocktail?"

Her eyes narrowed.

"No. Getting her to drink the whole thing would require too much time and leave too much evidence. You probably injected it with a hypodermic needle. But in order to do that, you would have needed to subdue Farrah first. Otherwise, there would have been a struggle. She was bigger and stronger than you. The police didn't mention a struggle."

Odine switched the wakizashi to her dominant hand.

"I'd bet your old chemistry days were useful in this regard, too. All you needed to do was combine bleach and acetone and add ice cubes to make—"

"Chloroform," she finished, giving herself away.

"Chloroform doesn't have much of a scent. It's sweet smelling. If you knocked her out with that, the police could have missed the scent, due to the cosmos Misty had purchased for everyone earlier."

Odine smirked.

"Using a syringe," I continued, "you injected her with the poison. Between the toes, to make it harder for the coroner to find it."

She pursed her lips, not denying my theory.

"You know what your downfall was?"

"You," she hissed.

"Me, yes, because I'm observant. You shouldn't have published so many photographs of purple flowers on social media and hung posters of them here. If not for the plethora of purple flowers and all the posts on social media of you and Nova hiking, I might not have guessed you were the killer. So tell me how it went down."

Odine glanced between the door and me. "Farrah would do almost anything for Misty—"

"Other than help her get a role in a movie," I said.

Odine snarled. "She was selfish. And egotistical. She believed everyone worshipped the ground she walked on. Even me. When I invited her to stay in the Airbnb, she was thrilled, truly believing that I'd put the past behind us. When I asked to meet her at the house for drinks and a chat, she was eager to talk about old times. Our theater days. Our conquests."

"But you didn't chat."

"Not for one second. She slipped inside, and before she had the chance to close the door, I covered her mouth with the cloth soaked in chloroform. I kicked the door shut and helped her to the floor. When she was succumbing to the drug, I told her I'd lied about being her friend. I admitted that I despised her. She mumbled something, so I removed the cloth to let her have her say. She had the gall to claim it was my husband's fault. She swore that he gave her a phony name. But I knew she'd seen pictures of him on my social media. I had dozens of photos of the two of us together. The two of us . . . *in love*. She pleaded with me. I told her it was too late. I covered her mouth again. When she quieted, I injected her with the poison." Odine's lips stretched tight. "She suffered for quite a while."

"She didn't die instantly?"

"No. That confused me. Perhaps my solution was too weak. I wasn't the best chemistry student. It took six whole minutes before she expired. Then, as you theorized, I came here and waved to passersby as I ate my dinner and did the books."

Man, you are cold.

Odine motioned with the knife toward the register. "Move."

"Right," I said cheerily, taking another backward step toward the exit. "I need to pay for these."

"Don't be cute, Courtney. It doesn't suit you. Move. To the stockroom." She aimed the knife at my throat.

"Eeps!" Fiona squawked. "Courtney, how can I help?"

I didn't have a clue. The knife was menacing, and my lungs were tighter than kite string in a stiff wind. I took another small step toward the exit.

"Actually, stop moving," Odine revised. "Stand still. Right there."

So much for my clandestine efforts to make a run for it. "I've informed the police."

"Everyone says that." With her gaze locked on mine, Odine edged to the door and locked it. Mission accomplished, she returned to me. "Move! Into the stockroom."

"My associate Joss drove me here. She's parking. She'll be—"

"Move!"

"Why are you giving up all of this?" I asked, eager to keep her talking. I swung my head left and right. "You've put your heart and soul into this place."

"Because it reminds me of *him*. He . . . We . . ." She shook free of whatever memory was haunting her. "Nova wants to buy it."

"She doesn't have that kind of money."

"She pleaded with her parents for a loan. They agreed."

I hadn't seen that turn of events. Did Nova realize Odine was a killer? Did she care?

"What about all the property you own?" I asked.

"I'll get a Realtor to handle the sales."

"The police will find you."

"In less than two hours, I'll be long gone under an assumed name."

Wow, she had preplanned. "Does Misty know you killed Farrah?"

"No, she's an innocent. She loves everyone. That's her weakness."

"She'll be devastated when she learns the truth."

Odine stepped closer. "Enough chitchat."

"If you kill me with that, there will be blood."

She blinked, as if she hadn't thought of that. "I have more of the poison. In the back. Let's go."

I recalled a rodeo-themed fairy garden I'd created for a client featuring a clown diverting a bull with a red flag and sparkly beads. I wondered if I could use the items I was holding to divert Odine. Swiftly, I wadded the kimono around my left hand and forearm, and with my right, swung the dragon necklace like a lasso toward the knife. It missed. Odine growled and lunged at me. I blocked the attack with the kimono. The knife grazed the silk but didn't penetrate it. Phew.

Fiona disappeared from my peripheral vision. Where was she going?

I tried again with the necklace. This time it connected. It didn't loop around the blade, but the blade wobbled in Odine's hand. On the third attempt, I slung the chain higher. The loop snared the tip. I yanked downward, throwing Odine off balance.

At the same time, Fiona came into view. She held her hands, palms up, in front of Odine's face and blew hard. Sand from the Zen garden pelted Odine's eyes and cheeks.

"Ow!" she squealed. "What the—" She dropped the wakizashi to rid her eyes of the sand.

Clutching the kimono to my chest, I charged Odine and shoved. She crashed into the sales counter and slumped to the floor. She reached for the knife, but I dove for it and got to it first.

"Don't move!" I shot to my feet and took two steps backward.

Someone pounded on the front door.

"It's Joss!" Fiona cried. "She's waving her arms. And Detective Summers is with her. He doesn't look happy."

I dared to peek over my shoulder. Summers's gaze was, indeed, smoldering. I didn't care. I backed up to the door, as Odine had moments ago, and unlocked it.

Summer barged in. "Miss Kelly, I can't believe you!"

Joss trailed him. "Danged parking lot was filled. I had to go all the way to the one by the precinct."

Summers removed the wakizashi from my hand and eyeballed Odine, daring her to move. Tears streamed down her cheeks, but she remained in place. "Explain, Miss Kelly. From the beginning."

Chapter 27

Flower fairies—have you found them,
When the summer's dusk is falling,
With the glow-worms watching round them;
Have you heard them softly calling?
—Philip Bourke Marston, "Flower Fairies"

Needless to say, Summers let me have an earful. I told him that I'd thought things through, that I'd expected backup within two minutes in the form of Joss, and that I hadn't believed Odine would attack me in full daylight, adding that time had been of the essence because of her travel plans. Given what Odine had said during our exchange, I suggested he examine her passport and ticket. He did and discovered that the passport was, indeed, issued to an alias, and her plane ticket to Mumbai bore that fake name. She hadn't lied to me. She'd planned to flee the country and disappear. Bye-bye, Carmel and Texas and the magnificent US of A.

"Just so you know," Summers said, when he finished grilling me, "if everything pans out, Miss Oates will be going to jail for a long time."

"Good."

"And for your information, she would not have met up

with her husband in India. He's in Australia right now. He has moved there permanently. His sailing days are over."

So the detective had followed that lead. Good.

Summers let me off with a warning and cautioned me to be wiser in the future. I promised I would be. It was an easy promise to make. I mean, honestly, how many more friends would be suspected of murder, and how many more bodies might I stumble across?

I went to Open Your Imagination and made myself a strong cup of Earl Grey tea. Fiona swirled around my head, worrying her hands, blaming herself for not sensing the truth sooner. Joss weighed in, too, but I put her mind at ease. I'd known she would arrive in time.

"Courtney," my father said, rushing through the show-room. "What in the heck were you thinking?"

I gestured to the customers who'd flooded into the shop after we'd reopened. "Office," I said, and led the way.

Fiona settled on top of the computer monitor and stared at my father in the same way I was glaring at him. Without interrupting, we listened to his lecture.

Dylan had called him. He—Dad—was furious with me. For being rash. For taking such a risk.

When he completed his rant, I said, "Did Detective Summers tell you that I called the police, and I was using the buddy system?" In high school, my father had advised me to always go to places in twos.

"Buddy system," he groused.

I held up a hand. "Joss was on her way, and Fiona—"

"Your fairy?" he bellowed. "Don't—"

"No, *you don't*, Dad. She was with me, and she caused quite a stir." I rose to my feet, feeling the spirit of my mother surging within me. "Look, we can argue about this until the daylilies forget to bloom, but we'll never see eye to eye. I did what I had to, and I'm glad I was able to bring justice for Farrah Lawson." Even if she had turned out to be a spiteful woman.

Seeing the concern in his gaze, I moved to him and threw my arms around him.

After a long moment, he pushed me away and said, "A kimono and a necklace? That's what you used as weapons?"

"Yep. I once made a fairy garden—" I began, and stopped. He didn't need to hear what had inspired me. "I'll take more self-defense classes. Will that make you feel better?"

"Yes, it will." He kissed my forehead. "I love you, Daughter."

"I love you, Father."

He gave me a squeeze and left.

An hour before closing, Joss and I tweaked the displays in the showroom.

Near the wind chimes, she said, "I'm sorry," for the twelfth time. "The parking—"

"Can be a bear. How could we have known every Tom, Dick, and Susan would be shopping on this of all days? Chalk it up to the good weather." I sighed. "And let's face it, I made the stupid decision to move toward the register and not stay close to an exit until someone arrived. Fiona saved the day."

Fiona alit on my shoulder. "*Ta.*"

"*Ta,* yourself. The sand trick was brilliant!"

"It came to me when I remembered Georgie and her friends were arguing about boys, and the girl with braces dusted them with sand."

"Like I said, brilliant."

"Ooh, ooh, look!" She raised her wings. "My third set is growing."

I grinned. "They've doubled in size for sure."

Ecstatic, she twirled into the air and shot out to the patio to show Pixie.

Yvanna entered the shop and crossed the showroom to me. "You'll never guess what happened an hour ago. Twyla came into Sweet Treats."

"To buy her favorite cookies?" I asked, not certain why that would be a big deal.

"To ask for a job. Working at the spa isn't her calling. Baking is. She was nervous to ask, but she felt the urge to try. And my boss said yes."

I'd bet Tish's nurturing fairy, Zephyr, had given Twyla the courage.

"Tish is over the moon," Yvanna added. "All she wants is for her daughter to feel good about herself."

I clasped Yvanna's hands. "That's wonderful."

"And don't worry. She'll still have time to help you for teas. She's going to work Monday to Thursday. Gotta go. I wanted to share the news."

Misty and Nova passed Yvanna as she exited the shop.

"Oh, dear," Misty hurried in front of Nova to greet me at the sales counter. "Courtney, we had no idea about Odine. None."

"None," Nova echoed.

"How are you?" Misty clasped my arm. "What a mess. Farrah. Odine. It's all my fault."

"No, it's my fault," Nova mewled. "I was the one who alerted Odine. I was so blind."

I said, "It's okay. It's over. Farrah's murder is solved."

Nova licked her lips. "I know you said I should wait to contact Nathan until after I got into AA, but I couldn't wait. He wants to see me. And Misty . . ." She looked at her friend.

"I'm going to introduce her to a really supportive AA sponsor," Misty said, "so she can get a jump on things."

"That's great," I said. "Nova, Odine told me you wanted to buy Fantasy Awaits. Is that true? She said your parents are giving you a loan."

Nova gazed at Misty. "They won't have to. Misty has some friends who want to invest."

"She'll do it right," Misty said, with a wink. "She'll have a good business plan and a business manager who will give her solid advice."

"Oh . . . Oh!" Nova poked Misty's arm. "Tell Courtney your plan."

"You tell her."

"Violet Vickers called her," Nova said, eager to share. "She was worried about all the items Misty was selling, so Misty told her the truth about the restaurant going belly up, and Violet offered to guide Misty through the next phase of financial recovery. It turns out Violet's husband had tried to start a restaurant, too, and when she realized he was going to run through their savings, Violet stepped in. She even knows how to entrap someone who has fled the country with escrow funds."

"That's wonderful news," I said.

Misty nodded. "Violet said she'd felt inspired to help someone ever since her fairy garden arrived at her house. She said she wants to pay the positive vibes forward."

I smiled, wondering which fairy had had a hand in that inspiration.

At closing time, Merryweather Rose of Song flew into the shop. "Fiona!" she crooned.

Fiona swooped in from the patio. Pixie scampered behind her and pulled to a stop. She sat on her rump, her gaze locked on the mature fairy.

Joss strode to Pixie and picked her up. She, too, seemed entranced by Merryweather.

I elbowed Joss. "Can you see her?"

She nodded, her eyes growing moist.

"Fiona, dear," Merryweather said, "I have consulted the queen fairy about your . . . concerns."

Fiona's concerns about having used the incantation improperly? Uh-oh. What was the verdict?

"She deemed that nothing has been your fault. You did not willfully disobey any of the rules she has set for you, and, therefore, you may continue to learn more spells and use potions as long as they are for the good. And as long as I am the one who teaches you, or I am the one who approves a new mentor for you."

Fiona clasped Merryweather in a hug. "Thank you, thank you!" She released her and spiraled into the air.

"Now, listen up." Merryweather primped her wings. "There is one more stipulation that she will allow."

Fiona met her at eye level, wings fluttering. She threw her shoulders back like a disciplined soldier. "Yes?"

"You may start to socialize with Zephyr, but only Zephyr. Also, Zephyr may teach you how to nurture."

"Whee!" Fiona did a somersault.

Brady called me around five o'clock to check in. He'd heard about the dustup with Odine. "Are you okay?"

"I'm as right as rain."

"You'd tell me otherwise?"

I hesitated. Would I? Yes, I trusted him more than I could possibly say. "Definitely."

"Glad to hear it," he said, his voice warm and caring. "Are we on for tomorrow? You promised to take me to see a portal."

"You bet." I needed a day off in the worst way. "I'll take you where it should be."

"Should be? You mean they aren't constant?"

I laughed. "Oh, you have a lot to learn about the fairy world."

At closing time, I gathered Pixie, and with Fiona flying beside me, walked home, breathing in the evening air, feeling every cell in my body relaxing. A murderer was behind bars, and Carmel was once again safe.

I took the long route. I wasn't very hungry, and I wanted to view the fairy doors again. All of them. I needed to create a mental sketch of who the artist or artists might be. The sudden appearance of so many was eating at me. Who and why?

Plotting my route so I wouldn't be wandering back and forth, I decided to see the door that was farthest from my place first. I strolled past Misty's house and peered at the teensy door with its bistro table and bouquet of daisies on the chair. The crafter had a romantic streak. I put that idea in my hopper and moved on to the coast redwood on Ocean Avenue. I inspected the light-green door with dark-green branches weaving across it. Something seemed familiar about it, as if I'd seen it when I was a child, but I couldn't put my finger on it. Next up was the *Lord of the Rings* hobbit-style cottage entry. I remembered the book being required reading during high school. The fairy door was a good semblance.

I roamed the streets looking at others and paused by the storybook house with the red door. At the base of its huge tree was the blue fairy door. I hadn't inspected it before now because Fiona had done so and had reported back. I bent to examine it and a shiver ran through me. Pixie wriggled in my arms.

"Sorry, kitty."

"Are you okay?" Fiona asked. "Did you find a note?"

"No, I think the air grew chilly." I peered up at her. "You were right. The door does look like the one on our cottage." I shivered again and said, "Let's go home. I'm really cold."

"We should see the door Holly mentioned," she suggested.

"Okay, it's on the way."

We turned toward the beach and cut right on Monte Verde. The house with three gables was on our left. I bent to study the fairy door made of Popsicle sticks and paused. The door was ajar, and a slip of paper was peeking out.

"There's a note," I whispered.

"Read it."

"It's for a fairy."

"Then pull it out and I'll read it." She thumped her chest.

Gingerly, I withdrew the paper and held it up to her. It wasn't any larger than the slip of paper found in a fortune cookie.

She scanned it.

"What does it say?" I asked breathlessly.

"I love apple pie." She frowned. "What does it mean?"

I rose to my feet and peered at the note, and suddenly, everything became clear. Brady loved apple pie, as did I. That was probably the first food we had ever shared at his father's diner. He also adored Popsicles. The red kind. As for the blue fairy door in front of the storybook house, it did represent my door; he knew I loved the architecture of Carmel, in particular the Comstock houses. The *Lord of the Rings* fairy door was a no-brainer. In school my girlfriends and I had waxed rhapsodic about Frodo and his quest, much to the dismay of many who came into contact with us at the time, Brady included. The bistro setup with daisies on the chair in front of Misty's house? Brady knew I adored daisies.

Walking home, I couldn't erase the smile on my face. Brady desperately wanted to see a fairy. Did he hope that by making these doors and having each pertain to one of our memories, his vision would be unlocked?

As I turned down Carmelo, I figured out why one of the fairy doors had been surrounded with butterflies. Brady's grandfather had collected butterflies, like Joss's father did. Brady had loved showing them to me. And the green door with vines? That represented Brady's childhood house. We'd shot hoops in his driveway.

"Brady," I said aloud.

"What about him?" Fiona asked.

"He's doing this."

"Are you sure?"

"Positive." I explained why.

"Well, then," she said, "you should talk to him about it. There he is."

I stared in the direction she was pointing, and sure enough, a person in a hooded jacket and jeans was hunkered down by the gatepost of my cottage. A backpack I recognized lay at his feet.

"Ahem, what do you think you're doing, young man?" I demanded, in my best high school principal voice.

Brady startled and scrambled to his feet. When he realized I was the complainant, he tamped down a smile. "Caught me."

"I knew it was you."

"You did?"

"I just figured it out." I recapped my discoveries. "You want to see a fairy. That's why you're doing this."

"Wrong. I wanted to give you a mystery to solve that didn't involve life-threatening moments."

"Ha!"

Pixie stirred in my arms. She wanted Brady. I offered her to him. He took hold and nuzzled her nose.

"One door has me puzzled," I said. "The blue, red, and yellow one. I can't put a memory to that."

"Really?" He smirked. "I thought that would be the easiest. Think cyan, magenta, yellow, and—"

"Black. The four colors for processing photos." I palm-slapped my forehead. "Clever. What about today's fairy door?" I pointed to the one that was in progress.

"It's a tribute to us."

"Us?" I bent to study it and rose to face him. "A boy and girl fairy sitting on a bench. Sweet."

"With their whole lives ahead of them." He handed the cat back to me and took me in his arms. "What do you say? Do you want to get serious?"

"Yes."

He kissed me tenderly and whispered, "I can't wait until our adventure tomorrow morning, but right now, I have to get back to work."

"Six a.m. sharp," I told him.

"Will do."

Entering the cabin, Fiona sang, "Courtney lo-oves Brady." I murmured, "Yes, she does."

Epilogue

The next morning, I bought two Americanos and maple bars at Percolate and went home to wait for Brady to pick me up. He'd texted me close to midnight and had insisted on driving, teasing that if I drove, I might go in circles so he wouldn't know how to return to the portal on his own. When I told him we were heading to Garland Ranch Waterfall Trail, he gawped. He'd been there many times. He'd never noticed any portals.

In the winter, the trail was wet and lush. We had to be cautious on the bridges and steps. About an hour into our walk, stopping numerous times to take photos, I told Brady to veer left. The portal was off the beaten track, if it was still there.

Drawing near, I threw my hand across his chest. "Hold up," I whispered.

A herd of fairies had convened in a tree. The glow from

their energy was incredible. I spotted Fiona and Merryweather among them and inhaled sharply. Was it a class of some kind?

"What?" Brady peered in the direction I was looking. "I don't see anything but trees and branches."

My heart went out to him. He couldn't see any of them?

"There's a herd of fairies up ahead," I said.

"A herd? They're called a herd?"

"Or a *frollick*."

"A—"

"Frollick. F-R-O-L-L-I-C-K. *Shh.*" I put a finger to his lips. "Do you see it? The portal?" A convergence of branches had created a circle. "Look for the round shape reflected in the leaves of the trees. Do you see it now?"

He squinted. "Sort of."

Fiona whizzed to me and said, *"Shh."*

"What's going on?" I asked in the softest voice I could muster.

"The queen fairy is coming."

"You're kidding."

"No. *Shh.*"

Suddenly sunlight streamed into the valley. The portal lit up like an orb. Slowly it started to open, as if peeling back layer after layer. The fairies gasped collectively.

And then a fairy emerged. Not just any fairy. A gorgeous yellow fairy with golden gossamer wings. She was floating on what appeared to be a cloud lined with silver. She stretched her arms in welcome, and my heart jolted when I recognized her.

She was Aurora, as pretty as the sunrise.

RECIPES

From Courtney:

   I love sweets that are easy to make, but I have to warn the hostess that this is one sticky cake when serving it up. Have plenty of wet towels on hand for your fingertips. Also, the apricot preserves could be any other yellow-ish kind of preserves or even orange marmalade. I wouldn't use a red preserve because that would definitely change the color of the cake itself. Enjoy.

Apricot Preserves Tea Cake

(Yield: 1 loaf)

1½ cups flour
1½ teaspoons baking powder
Dash of salt
10 tablespoons unsalted butter, chilled and cut into small
   pieces
½ cup plus 2 tablespoons granulated sugar
4 tablespoons apricot preserves
2 eggs, lightly beaten
5 tablespoons milk
3 tablespoons apricot preserves for glaze
Powdered sugar, for dusting

   Preheat oven to 350 degrees F. Grease a 9 x 5 loaf pan or line with parchment paper.
   In a food processor, mix the flour, baking powder, salt, and butter until the mixture is like small peas; about 10 pulses.

Add the sugar and pulse again. Add the preserves, eggs, and milk. Pulse about 5–6 times. The mixture will be soft and sticky.

Pour the batter into the loaf pan and bake for 40–45 minutes, or until a toothpick comes out clean.

Cool in the pan at least 20 minutes. Turn out and let cool longer. When ready, warm the preserves in the microwave for a couple of seconds so they're easy to spread, and spread on top of the tea cake. Dust with powdered sugar.

Note to the baker: this is a sticky cake, and you will need to clean your fingers often when eating or serving.

Apricot Preserves Tea Cake—Gluten-Free Version

(Yield: 1 loaf)

1½ cups gluten-free flour
1½ teaspoons baking powder
1 tablespoon whey powder
¼ teaspoon xanthan gum
Dash of salt
10 tablespoons unsalted butter, chilled and cut into small pieces
½ cup plus 2 tablespoons granulated sugar
4 tablespoons apricot preserves
2 eggs, lightly beaten
5 tablespoons milk
3 tablespoons apricot preserves for glaze
Powdered sugar, for dusting

Preheat oven to 350 degrees F. Grease a 9 x 5 loaf pan or line with parchment paper.

In a food processor, mix the gluten-free flour, baking powder, whey powder, xanthan gum, salt, and butter until the mixture is like small peas; about 10 pulses. Add the sugar and pulse again. Add the preserves, eggs, and milk. Pulse about 5–6 times. The mixture will be soft and sticky.

Pour the batter into the loaf pan and bake for 40–45 minutes, or until a toothpick comes out clean.

Cool in the pan at least 20 minutes. Turn out and let cool longer. When ready, warm the preserves in the microwave for a couple of seconds so they're easy to spread, and spread on top of the tea cake. Dust with powdered sugar.

Note: This gluten-free cake needs to be eaten quickly; it will get a little firm in a day or so. If you need to store it, here's a trick: a quick zap in the microwave on medium-high will soften up a slice. I'm not certain why this happens with gluten-free baked goods, but it seems to be a fast and proven rule.

From Meaghan:

Courtney will tell you that I am a fanatic about brownies. Given my surname, Brownie, I've been making brownies all my life. When I tasted a brownie cookie, known as a Brookie, I knew I had to have the recipe. Except the bakery where I'd bought it wouldn't share. Even so, I knew I could master it. Being the kind-hearted soul that I am, I did share with my friend Yvanna. She says these are new favorites with her customers at Sweet Treats. Cool the brookie completely before cutting.

Brookie

(Yield: 20–24)

For the cookie layer:
½ cup butter, softened
½ cup light brown sugar
¼ cup granulated sugar
½ teaspoon vanilla extract
1 egg
1¼ cups all-purpose flour
½ teaspoon salt
½ teaspoon baking soda
1 cup semisweet chocolate chips

For the brownie layer:
1 cup granulated sugar
½ cup butter, melted
1 teaspoon vanilla extract
2 large eggs
⅓ cup cocoa powder
½ cup all-purpose flour

¼ teaspoon baking powder
⅛ teaspoon salt
½ cup semisweet chocolate chips, if desired

Preheat oven to 350 degrees F. Grease a 9 x 13 baking dish.

To make the cookie layer:

In a large bowl, beat softened butter, light brown sugar, granulated sugar, vanilla extract, and egg.

Whisk flour, salt, and baking soda together in a small bowl. Gradually add flour mixture to butter mixture and stir until combined. Stir chocolate chips into the dough. Spread mixture evenly into the bottom of the 9 x 13 dish.

To make the brownie layer:

In a large bowl, stir sugar, melted butter, and vanilla. Add in eggs and beat well. Mix in cocoa powder and mix well. Add flour, baking powder, and salt to the cocoa mixture. Mix well. If desired, stir in the extra chocolate chips. Pour brownie mixture over cookie dough and spread to cover completely.

Bake the brookie in the preheated oven for 20–25 minutes, until a toothpick comes out clean. Cool completely, at least 30 minutes, before cutting into bars.

Brookie—Gluten-Free Version

(Yield: 20–24)

For the cookie layer:
½ cup butter, softened
½ cup light brown sugar
¼ cup granulated sugar
½ teaspoon vanilla extract
1 egg
1¼ cup gluten-free flour★
¾ tablespoon whey powder
¼ teaspoon xanthan gum
½ teaspoon salt
½ teaspoon baking soda
1 cup semisweet chocolate chips

For the brownie layer:
1 cup granulated sugar
½ cup butter, melted
1 teaspoon vanilla extract
2 large eggs
⅓ cup cocoa powder
½ cup gluten-free flour★
½ tablespoon whey powder
¼ teaspoon xanthan gum
½ teaspoon baking powder
⅛ teaspoon salt
½ cup semisweet chocolate chips, if desired

Preheat oven to 350 degrees F. Grease a 9 x 13 baking dish.

★*Yvanna taught me that a mixture of sweet rice flour and tapioca flour makes a really good gluten-free flour base.*

To make the cookie layer:

In a large bowl, beat softened butter, light brown sugar, granulated sugar, vanilla extract, and egg.

Whisk gluten-free flour, whey powder, xanthan gum, salt, and baking soda together in a small bowl. Gradually add gluten-free flour mixture to butter mixture and stir until combined. Stir chocolate chips into the dough. Spread mixture evenly into the bottom of the 9 x 13 dish.

To make the brownie layer:

In a large bowl, stir sugar, melted butter, and vanilla. Add in eggs and beat well. Mix in cocoa powder and mix well. Add gluten-free flour, whey powder, xanthan gum, baking powder, and salt to the cocoa mixture. Mix well. If desired, stir in the extra chocolate chips. Pour brownie mixture over cookie dough and spread to cover completely.

Bake the gluten-free brookie in the preheated oven for 20–25 minutes, until a toothpick comes out clean. Cool completely, at least 30 minutes, before cutting into bars.

From Yvanna:

All tea parties should include chocolate crinkles as a dessert. They are so easy to make, and the fudgy texture is always a winner. You can make them large or small; it all depends on the size of the ball you roll. Yes, there is a lot of sugar in this recipe, but you don't eat sweets hoping to avoid sugar, do you? My abuela always said, "Sugar, in moderation, warms the soul." She was the most soulful person I have ever known.

Chocolate Crinkles

(Yield: 4 dozen)

8 ounces melted butter
4 squares unsweetened chocolate, melted
1½ cups granulated sugar
1½ cups brown sugar
4 eggs
2 teaspoons vanilla
2 cups flour
1 cup cocoa powder
2 teaspoons baking powder
½ teaspoon salt
½ cup extra granulated sugar, for rolling
½ cup powdered sugar

Heat oven to 350 degrees F. Line a cookie sheet with parchment paper.

In a large bowl, mix butter, chocolate, granulated sugar, and brown sugar. Blend in the eggs and vanilla.

In a separate bowl, mix flour, cocoa powder, baking powder, and salt. Add flour mixture to the sugar mixture and stir well.

Roll dough into walnut-sized balls, about 1 tablespoon. You might need to moisten your fingers.

Pour extra granulated sugar into a pie tin. Pour powdered sugar into a separate pie tin. Coat each ball with granulated sugar and then with powdered sugar. Place balls about 2 inches apart on the parchment paper. Bake 10–12 minutes. These will look slightly gooey in the "cracks" when removed from the oven. That's fine. Do not overbake.

Chocolate Crinkles—Gluten-Free Version

(Yield: 4 dozen)

8 ounces melted butter
4 squares unsweetened chocolate, melted
1½ cups granulated sugar
1½ cups brown sugar
4 eggs
2 teaspoons vanilla
2 cups gluten-free flour
1 cup cocoa powder
2 teaspoons baking powder
1 tablespoon whey powder
½ teaspoon xanthan gum
½ teaspoon salt
½ cup extra granulated sugar, for rolling
½ cup powdered sugar

Heat oven to 350 degrees F. Line a cookie sheet with parchment paper.

In a large bowl, mix butter, chocolate, granulated sugar, and brown sugar. Blend in the eggs and vanilla.

In a separate bowl, mix gluten-free flour, cocoa powder, baking powder, whey powder, xanthan gum, and salt. Add flour mixture to the sugar mixture and stir well.

Roll dough into walnut-sized balls, about 1 tablespoon. You might need to moisten your fingers.

Pour extra granulated sugar into a pie tin. Pour powdered sugar into a separate pie tin. Coat each ball with granulated sugar and then with powdered sugar. Place balls about 2 inches apart on the parchment paper. Bake 10–12 minutes. These will look slightly gooey in the "cracks" when removed from the oven. That's fine. Do not overbake.

From Courtney:

My grandmother Nana made delicious sugar cookies. Whenever I was sad, she'd whip up a batch or pull one from the freezer from a previous batch. But she didn't use a recipe, so over the years, I tweaked and tweaked, trying to figure out what she'd added to the cookies that made them so special. When Fiona came into my life, she said the cookies were missing the flavor of almonds. And she was right. So I've named them Fairy Cookies, in honor of her delicious insight.

Fairy Cookies

(Yield: 30–32 cookies)

½ cup butter, softened
½ cup granulated sugar
½ cup sifted powdered sugar
½ teaspoon baking soda
¾ teaspoon cream of tartar
¼ teaspoon salt
½ cup canola oil
1 egg
1 teaspoon almond extract
2¼ cups flour
Colored sugar sprinkles for decorating

Preheat oven to 350 degrees F.

In a large bowl mix butter, granulated sugar, powdered sugar, baking soda, cream of tartar, and salt. Beat until combined.

Add in oil, egg, and almond extract.

Add flour and beat well. Cover and chill for 30 minutes.

Roll dough into walnut-sized balls. Place on ungreased cooking sheet. Flatten to about ¼-inch thick. Sprinkle with colored sugar. These will spread.

Bake for 10–12 minutes or until edges are lightly browned. Let cool on a wire rack.

Fairy Cookies—Gluten-Free Version

(Yield: 30–32 cookies)

½ cup butter, softened
½ cup granulated sugar
½ cup sifted powdered sugar
½ teaspoon baking soda
¾ teaspoon cream of tartar
¼ teaspoon salt
½ cup canola oil
1 egg
1 teaspoon almond extract
2¼ cups gluten-free flour
¼ teaspoon xanthan gum
1 tablespoon whey powder
Colored sugar sprinkles for decorating

Preheat oven to 350 degrees F.

In a large bowl mix butter, granulated sugar, powdered sugar, baking soda, cream of tartar, and salt. Beat until combined.

Add in oil, egg, and almond extract.

In a separate bowl, mix gluten-free flour, xanthan gum, and whey powder. Add to the sugar mixture. Cover and chill for 30 minutes.

Roll dough into walnut-sized balls. Place on an ungreased cookie sheet. Flatten to about ¼-inch thick. Sprinkle with colored sugar. These will spread.

Bake for 10–12 minutes or until edges are lightly browned. Let cool on a wire rack.

From Yvanna:

At Sweet Treats, we like to offer options to our customers. We have many that come in specifically for our gluten-free items, which we make in a safe environment without cross-contamination. These scones are delicious either way. The lemon zest is so important to the flavor. Make sure the lemons are very fresh. An older lemon does not provide the same amount of flavor or zest. The gluten-free version will become tougher in a day. The best way to bring them back to life, as I've taught Courtney, is to put them in the microwave and zap for about 12–15 seconds on medium-high. The moisture appears like magic.

Raspberry Lemon Scones

(Yield: 8)

For the scones:
8 tablespoons unsalted butter, cut into small cubes and frozen
    for 10 minutes
⅓ cup granulated sugar
Zest of 2 medium fresh lemons
2 cups all-purpose flour
1½ teaspoons baking powder
½ teaspoon salt
½ cup plus 2 tablespoons sour cream
1 large egg
1 teaspoon pure vanilla extract
⅔ cup fresh raspberries

For the glaze:
3 tablespoons unsalted butter, melted
1 cup powdered sugar
2 tablespoons freshly squeezed lemon juice

Preheat oven to 400 degrees F. Line a baking sheet with parchment paper.

Cut butter into small cubes and freeze for 10 minutes.

In a food processor, combine the sugar and lemon zest. Add in the flour, baking powder, and salt, and pulse 4–5 times.

Add the frozen butter into the flour mixture. Pulse 4–5 times until combined and it looks like cornmeal.

In a small bowl, whisk the sour cream, egg, and vanilla until smooth.

Add the sour cream mixture into the flour mixture and pulse a few times, until a dough starts to form.

Transfer the mixture to a large bowl and gently fold in the raspberries. This will be a firm dough, and the raspberries may break up a little. That's okay.

Mold the dough into a ball. Turn onto parchment paper that has been lightly floured and pat into a 7-inch circle about ¾-inch thick. If you make it too thin, the scones will be a little firmer and not as fluffy. Use a wet knife to cut the round into 8 triangles.

Place the scones on the prepared baking sheet. Bake until golden, about 15–17 minutes. Cool for 20 minutes and prepare the glaze.

In a medium bowl, prepare the glaze by mixing together the melted butter, powdered sugar, and lemon juice. Mix until smooth. Drizzle the glaze onto your scones. If the mixture is too thin, add more powdered sugar. If it is too firm, add a tablespoon of water.

Raspberry Lemon Scones—Gluten-Free Version

(Yield: 8)

For the scones:
8 tablespoons unsalted butter, cut into small cubes and frozen
    for 10 minutes
⅓ cup granulated sugar
Zest of 2 medium fresh lemons
2 cups gluten-free flour★
1 tablespoon whey powder
½ teaspoon xanthan gum
1½ teaspoons baking powder
½ teaspoon salt
½ cup plus 2 tablespoons sour cream
1 large egg
1 teaspoon pure vanilla extract
⅔ cup fresh raspberries

For the glaze:
3 tablespoons unsalted butter, melted
1 cup powdered sugar
2 tablespoons freshly squeezed lemon juice

Preheat oven to 400 degrees F. Line a baking sheet with parchment paper.

Cut butter into small cubes and freeze for 10 minutes.

In a food processor, combine the sugar and lemon zest. Add in the gluten-free flour, whey powder, xanthan gum, baking powder, and salt, and pulse 4–5 times.

★*I like a mixture of sweet rice flour and tapioca starch for my gluten-free flour base.*

Add the frozen butter into the gluten-free flour mixture. Pulse 4–5 times until combined and it looks like cornmeal.

In a small bowl, whisk the sour cream, egg, and vanilla until smooth.

Add the sour cream mixture into the gluten-free flour mixture and pulse a few times, until a dough starts to form.

Transfer the mixture to a large bowl and gently fold in the raspberries. This will be a firm dough, and the raspberries may break up a little. That's okay.

Mold the dough into a ball. Turn onto parchment paper that has been lightly floured with gluten-free flour and pat into a 7-inch circle about ¾-inch thick. If you make it too thin, the scones will be a little firmer and not as fluffy. Use a wet knife to cut the round into 8 triangles.

Place the scones on the prepared baking sheet. Bake until golden, about 15–17 minutes. Cool for 20 minutes and prepare the glaze.

In a medium bowl, prepare the glaze by mixing together the melted butter, powdered sugar, and lemon juice. Mix until smooth. Drizzle the glaze onto your scones. If the mixture is too thin, add more powdered sugar. If it is too firm, add a tablespoon of water.

From Brady:

    I happen to love appetizers, so I offer a lot of choices at Hideaway Café. I was pleased to come up with a nice selection for the fairy garden party. For this recipe, the portion is really meant to be a meal: a slice of toast and half an avocado. For appetizers, you'll want to cut the portion in fourths. Also, when mashing a lot of avocados at once, you might want to use a potato masher. A fork just won't do the job. Have fun.

Avocado Toast with Bacon

(Yield: 1 portion)

For each portion:
1 slice of bread—use a thick-sliced, whole-grain bread (may
    use a hearty gluten-free bread)
1–2 strips of crisp bacon, crumbled
½ ripe avocado
Dash of salt
Toppings—see below

    Toast the bread until golden and firm. In a toaster, you might need to toast and re-toast. In the oven, at 350 degrees F, toast for about 6–8 minutes.

    In a sauté pan, slowly cook the bacon. Slowly is key. After 4 minutes, flip the bacon, and cook until desired crispness, about another 4 minutes for crispy and 5 minutes for extra-crispy. Remove from the pan and drain on paper towels. When cool, crumble.

    Meanwhile, remove the avocado from its shell using a

spoon and put into a bowl. Mash the avocado until smooth. Add a dash of salt and mix in.

Spread the avocado on toast. Top with crumbled bacon.

Add a topping like green onion salsa, ranch dressing, shredded cheese, etc.

Green Salsa Topping

(Yield: 4 portions)

½ cup parsley leaves, chopped
¼ cup fresh basil, torn or chopped
2 tablespoons chopped green onions
2 teaspoons drained and rinsed brined capers
1 teaspoon grated lemon rind
½ teaspoon anchovy paste
¼ teaspoon Dijon mustard
¼ teaspoon garlic powder, if desired
2 tablespoons extra-virgin olive oil
1 tablespoon water
⅛ teaspoon ground pepper

In a food processor, pulse the parsley, basil, green onions, capers, lemon rind, anchovy paste, mustard, and garlic powder, if desired. Add the olive oil, water, and pepper. If there is some left over, store in an airtight container.

From Brady:

Appetizers should be savory. This particular appetizer is super easy to make and may be made with regular flour and Panko or gluten-free flour and gluten-free Panko. The Buffalo sauce is what matters. Now, I could make my own at the restaurant, but if I did that for every recipe, I'd be cooking twenty-four hours a day. I happen to really enjoy Frank's Buffalo sauce, but you choose the one you enjoy. I will always make the ranch dressing from scratch. Dill is key!

Cauliflower Poppers

1 large cauliflower
½ cup flour★
½ cup Panko★
2 teaspoons sea salt
¼ teaspoon garlic powder, if desired
2 eggs
¼ cup milk
4 tablespoons olive oil
½ cup Buffalo sauce★ (I use Frank's, which is gluten-free)

Preheat oven to 450 degrees F. Line a baking sheet with parchment paper and brush with some of the olive oil.

Cut the cauliflower into medium-size florets and set aside.

In a large freezer bag, combine the flour, Panko, salt, and garlic powder, if desired.

In a large bowl, whisk together the eggs and milk to combine.

★*If you'd like to make this gluten-free, swap the flour and Panko with ½ cup gluten-free flour and ½ cup gluten-free Panko.*

Toss the cauliflower florets in the egg mixture and then add them to the bag with the flour-Panko mixture. Seal the bag and shake to coat all the florets with the mixture.

Place the florets on the prepared baking sheet and brush with the remaining olive oil. Bake the cauliflower for about 20 minutes.

Remove from the oven and toss with Buffalo sauce. Return the florets to the baking sheet and bake for an additional 5–10 minutes or until poppers are crispy.

Serve with ranch dressing.

Ranch Dressing

(Yield: 1½ cups)

½ cup mayonnaise
½ cup sour cream
½ cup milk
1 teaspoon dried dill weed
½ teaspoon dried parsley
½ teaspoon dried chives
½ teaspoon garlic powder, if desired
¼ teaspoon sea salt
⅛ teaspoon finely ground pepper
1–3 teaspoons freshly squeezed lemon juice, to taste

In a small bowl, whisk together the mayonnaise, sour cream, and milk until smooth. Add the dill, parsley, chives, garlic powder (if desired), salt, and pepper. Whisk to combine. Add the lemon and whisk again.

Store in an airtight container in the refrigerator until ready to use.

Read on for a special preview of the next enchanting
Fairy Garden mystery from Daryl Wood Gerber . . .

A Flicker of a Doubt

Forthcoming from Kensington Publishing Corp. in Spring 2023

Chapter 1

Slam! Slam-slam-slam! Slam!

My insides did a jig. I dashed down the hall to the back of Open Your Imagination, dusting my hands off on my denim overalls while wondering what in the world was going on. Fiona, the teensy righteous fairy that appeared to me the day I opened my fairy garden shop, fluttered to my shoulder. Her limbs and gossamer wings were trembling.

"What's happening, Courtney?" she managed to squeak out. She hated loud noises. Hated surprises. I didn't like them, either.

Pixie, my ragdoll cat, trailed us. She mewed.

"Don't worry, you two," I said. "I'm sure it's nothing."

I drew to a halt outside the storage room. The door opened and slammed.

When it opened again, I pressed a hand against it. "Hey! Stop! Meaghan, c'mon."

The door opened wide, and Meaghan Brownie gawked at me. Her face was red, her eyes were ablaze with fury, and her curly hair was writhing like wild snakes.

"What the heck has you so angry?" I asked. I'd sent her to fetch a box of gemstones. I had plenty, so coming up empty wasn't what was upsetting her.

"Nicolas!" She huffed. "He texted me. And . . . And . . ." She waggled her cell phone. "Oo-oh!"

Nicolas was her ex-boyfriend, a temperamental artist. A few months back, she'd asked him to move out while her mother had needed comforting. He'd never returned.

"Oo-oh," she repeated, before grabbing one of the Tupperware boxes filled with gemstones and skirting past me. She stalked toward the main showroom.

Pixie and I followed. Fiona flew above my pal, sprinkling her with a calming silver dust. Fairies couldn't change behavior, but they could offer potions that might help the human solve problems. In this case, to find peace.

"He's so . . . so . . ."

Meaghan was not using her inside voice, but I wasn't worried about her upsetting our customers. It was early. Nobody was in the shop yet. Not even Joss Timberlake, my right-hand helper. She'd asked for the morning off, so I'd invited Meaghan to help me prepare some items. Why did I need help? Because yesterday Violet Vickers, a wealthy widow who donated to numerous worthy causes, had ordered an additional dozen fairy gardens to be used as centerpieces for the theater foundation tea she was serving on Mother's Day. Why *additional*? Because she'd already commissioned me to make a dozen very large, elaborate fairy gardens to be installed when Kelly Landscaping, my father's company, completed the total redo of her backyard.

It was May first. I wasn't hyperventilating. Yet. But I also wasn't sleeping much.

"Let's go to the patio," I said. "I'll bring some tea."

"I don't want tea," Meaghan groused as she breezed out the French doors to the patio, the folds of her white lace skirt wafting behind her.

The shop's telephone jangled. I glanced at it and decided not to answer. Whoever was calling would call back. Meaghan, my best friend who I'd met a little over ten years ago when we were sophomores in college, needed me more. I followed her, glancing at Fiona and wondering why the calming potion wasn't working. Fiona, intuiting my question, shook her head.

"Isn't it a beautiful morning, Meaghan?" I took the box from her and set it on the teaching table in the learning-the-craft area at the far end of the patio. "Gorgeous, in fact."

The fountain was burbling. Sunshine was streaming through the tempered-glass, pyramid-shaped roof. The leaves of the ficus trees were clean and shiny. I'd already wiped down the wrought-iron tables and chairs and organized all the verdigris baker's racks of fairy figurines. Plus I'd removed dead leaves from the various decorative fairy gardens. Presentation mattered to me and to my customers.

Meaghan muttered, "Ugh."

"Start at the beginning," I said. "Nicolas texted you."

"Yes." She plopped onto a bench and rested her elbows on the table.

"What did he write?" I asked.

"He wants me back."

I opened the box of colorful gemstones and ran my hands through them: hematite, labradorite, amethyst, obsidian, and more.

"But I don't want him back," Meaghan said.

Fiona landed on the rim of the box. Her eyes widened. "Are they for the fairy doors, Courtney?"

"Mm-hm."

"They're pretty."

Not only was I making the gardens for Violet, but I had three fairy garden door classes scheduled for the week. Fairy doors were miniature doors, usually set at the base of a tree, behind which might be a small space where people left notes or wishes for fairies. They could also be installed into a fairy garden pot.

"I mean, I used to," Meaghan went on. "But I don't anymore. We have nothing in common." Idly, she drew circles on the tabletop with her fingertip. "I did the right thing, don't you think? I did, didn't I?"

Over the course of our friendship, I'd kept my mouth shut. Nicolas and Meaghan had never made sense. She was outgoing and personable; he was quiet, to the point of being morose. Granted, he was a talented artist, and she, as a premier art gallery owner, appreciated his gift, but that was not enough to sustain a healthy relationship. Not in my book, anyway.

"Did he text anything else?" I asked, not answering her question.

"No . . . Yes. That he loved me." She flopped forward on her arms dramatically.

Pixie pounced onto the bench and nudged Meaghan's hip with her nose.

Meaghan sat up, drew the cat into her lap, and petted her. "You should have seen Ziggy the last time Nicolas contacted me." Ziggy Foxx, an eccentric gay man in his forties, was Meaghan's business partner at Flair Gallery.

Cypress and Ivy Courtyard, where Open Your Imagination was located, boasted a high-end jewelry store, collectibles shop, pet-grooming enterprise, my favorite bakery Sweet Treats, and Flair, Meaghan's gallery.

"Ziggy was finalizing a sale of one of Hunter Hock's items, and when he heard me say Nicolas's name, he nearly threw Hunter's art across the room. Hunter was there at the time."

Hunter Hock, an in-demand artist in his thirties, was known for small pieces of art. Not as tiny as paintings on almonds or bottle caps or even the insides of lockets. More like three-inch-square petite canvases. Many featured a landscape of Carmel-by-the-Sea, my hometown and one of the most incredible places on earth.

"Oh, man, if Hunter could have leaped through the phone receiver"—Meaghan snorted out a laugh—"he would have strangled Nicolas. You know how he likes to protect me."

Every man who'd ever met Meaghan had wanted to protect her. Not that she needed it. She was a force to be reckoned with. But there was something about her femininity that brought out the he-man in men. Me? Most men wanted to be my friend. Period. I was the girl-next-door type. Short blond hair, athletic figure. Meaghan towered above me and had curves.

I said, "I'd bet Hunter also didn't like seeing Ziggy lose his temper."

"Yeah. Destroy a piece of his art? Oh, the insanity!" Her laugh turned into giggles. Fits of giggles. And then tears.

I hurried to her and threw my arm around her. "Hey, c'mon. Deep breaths. You're beyond Nicolas. You have Ziggy."

She arched her eyebrow.

"Okay, you have Hunter," I joked.

She sobered. "I don't have Hunter. He's a friend."

I twirled a finger. "I've seen the way he looks at you."

"Like this?" She made a googly-eyed face.

"That's the spirit!" Fiona spiraled to the roof, did a loop the loop, and returned to Meaghan's shoulder. "No more crying. What's done is done." She caressed my friend's hair.

"Thank you, Fiona." Not everyone could see fairies, and

Meaghan had struggled at first, but now, she was quite in tune with them.

"We move onward and upward," Fiona added. My intrepid fairy knew what she was talking about. She'd messed up in fairy school, so the queen fairy had booted her from the fairy realm and subjected her to probation. But she was making the most of it. By helping humans solve problems, she would earn her way back into the queen fairy's good graces—the queen fairy who, until a few months ago, I hadn't realized was Aurora, the first fairy I'd ever seen; the fairy who had disappeared from my memory when my mother died.

"When you're done with your pity party, Meaghan," I said, "help me sort these stones before we open up."

"And then I need to go to Flair."

I turned on soothing instrumental music that piped through speakers on the patio, and we worked in companionable silence for an hour, organizing and preparing.

When she was ready to leave, she gave me a hug. "Thank you for talking me down from the ledge."

"No thanks required. Nicolas wants you, but you don't want him. All you have to say is no."

"No." Meaghan shook her head from side to side. "No, no, no."

"See?" I grinned. "That isn't too hard."

"Until he comes near me and my knees turn to jelly."

"You won't turn to jelly. You'll be strong. Stalwart. You've been seeing the therapist. She's given you mantras. Repeat those. Over and over."

Fiona said, "And if those don't work, squeeze your eyes shut"—she demonstrated—"and picture what you want out of life." She popped her eyes open. "What do you want?"

"A man who thinks I'm wonderful," Meaghan replied. "A man who doesn't tear me down. A man who truly loves me for me."

I hugged her. "That's my girl."

She bounded to her feet. "Want me to unlatch the Dutch door on my way out?"

I glanced at my watch. It was time to open. "I'll do it."

I followed her through the showroom. In addition to fairy garden items, we sold a variety of specialty pieces, including tea sets, gardening tools, books about fairies, and wind chimes; fairies enjoyed tinkling sounds. I weaved between display tables to the entrance and swung open the door. I stepped outside and drew in a deep, cleansing breath. "Remember, Meaghan, I'm here if you need me."

She jogged up the stairs of the split-level courtyard. "Don't forget I brought you double-chocolate caramel brownies," she yelled as she disappeared from view.

Given her last name, she'd been a brownie maker ever since she'd learned how to bake. I was lucky enough to reap the rewards.

I turned to go back inside.

"Courtney!" a woman called. Violet Vickers exited the silver Rolls Royce coupe she'd parked on the street.

Inwardly, I moaned. I adored Violet, but what did she need now? I didn't have more hours in the day.

"I'm so glad you're here." She triggered the car alarm, and then strode across the sidewalk toward me while smoothing the shawl collar of her lavender jacquard suit. "I tried phoning, but you didn't pick up."

"Hi, Violet. C'mon in." I motioned to the shop. "What's up?" I asked, closing the door behind us. "I'm getting ready to put the fairy garden centerpieces together this morning. Your big pots are done and ready for delivery." I made the larger-sized pots in my backyard using items in my greenhouse.

"Lovely," she said, as she was wont to do. "Has your father seen the big ones?"

My father, a pragmatist in every sense of the word, didn't

believe in fairies. Opening my fairy garden shop had been a bone of contention between us. But at least he was coming around to acknowledging that I and others did see them. And he'd accepted that Violet expected twelve custom-made pots in her garden. No ifs, ands, or buts. Somehow he would make them work with his design.

"Not yet," I said, "but he has approved of the plant selections and color of the pottery."

"Excellent. And the themes of each?"

"Love, love, love," I chimed.

Though she was pushing seventy, Violet applauded like a jubilant schoolgirl. She'd wanted the fairy gardens to reflect love in all its glory. Fiona, who was turning out to be quite the reader, had advised me from the get-go to focus on the greatest love stories of all time: *Romeo and Juliet*, *Wuthering Heights*, *Dr. Zhivago*, *Casablanca*. Creating Rick's Café with its Moroccan decor for the *Casablanca*-themed garden had been a challenge.

Violet tapped her chin. "Now then, the reason I needed to see you—"

Tires screeched outside. A door slammed.

Fiona flew to my shoulder. "What now?" she asked, quivering with newfound fear.

The Dutch door flew open, and Nicolas Buley charged in, his dark hair askew, apparent shaving mishaps checked by tissue, and his paint-splattered shirt untucked from his jeans. "Where is she?"

Visit us online at
KensingtonBooks.com
to read more from your favorite authors,
see books by series, view reading
group guides, and more!